D1446836

IS THAT *WHAT PEOPLE DO?*

BOOKS BY ROBERT SHECKLEY

Untouched by Human Hands
Citizen in Space
Pilgrimage to Earth
Shards of Space
Notions: Unlimited
Store of Infinity
The People Trap
Can You Feel Anything When I Do This?
Dead Run
Calibre: 50
Live Gold
White Death
Twelve Days
The Game of X
The Man in the Water
Immortality, Inc.
The Status Civilization
Journey Beyond Tomorrow
Mindswap
Dimension of Miracles
The Tenth Victim
The Robot Who Liked Me
The Wonderful World of Robert Sheckley
Options
Crompton Divided
Dramocles

IS THAT WHAT PEOPLE DO?

SHORT STORIES BY

Robert Sheckley

HOLT, RINEHART AND WINSTON • NEW YORK

Published by Holt, Rinehart and Winston,
383 Madison Avenue, New York, New York 10017.
Published simultaneously in Canada by Holt, Rinehart
and Winston of Canada, Limited.

Library of Congress Cataloging in Publication Data
Sheckley, Robert, 1928–
Is *that* what people do?
1. Science fiction, American. I. Title.
PS3569.H392F4 1984   813'.54   83-12908
ISBN 0-03-063707-4
ISBN Hardbound: 0-03-063707-4

First Edition

Designer: Victoria Hartman
Printed in the United States of America
1 3 5 7 9 10 8 6 4 2
ISBN 0-03-063707-4

"The Eye of Reality" first appeared in *Omni,* 1982. "The Language of Love" first appeared in *Galaxy Science Fiction*, May 1957. "The Accountant" appeared in an earlier version in *The Magazine of Fantasy and Science Fiction*, July 1954. "A Wind Is Rising" appeared in an earlier version in *Galaxy Science Fiction*, July 1957. "The Robot Who Looked Like Me" first appeared in an earlier version in *Cosmopolitan*, 1973. "The Mnemone" first appeared in *New Worlds*, 1971. "Warm" appeared in an earlier version in *Galaxy*, June 1953. "The Native Problem" first appeared in an earlier version in *Galaxy*, December 1956. "Fishing Season" appeared in an earlier version in *Thrilling Wonder Stories*, August 1953. "Shape" appeared in an earlier version in *Galaxy*, November 1953. "Beside Still Waters" appeared in an earlier version in *Amazing Science Fiction*, November 1953. "Silversmith Wishes" first appeared in *Playboy*, 1977. "Meanwhile, Back at the Bromide" first appeared in *Playboy*, 1962. "Fool's Mate" appeared in an earlier version in *Astounding Science Fiction*, March 1953. "Pilgrimage to Earth" first appeared as "Love, Inc." in *Playboy*, September 1956. "All the Things You Are" first appeared in *Galaxy Science Fiction*, July 1956. "The Store of the Worlds" first appeared in "The World of Heart's Desire" in *Playboy*, September 1959. "Seventh Victim" appeared in an earlier version in *Galaxy*, April 1953. "Cordle to Onion to Carrot" first appeared in *Playboy*, December 1969. "Is *That* What People Do?" first appeared in *Anticipations*, 1978. "The Prize of Peril" first appeared in *The Magazine of Fantasy and Science Fiction*, May 1958. "Fear in the Night" appeared in an earlier version in *Today's Woman*, 1952. "Can You Feel Anything When I Do This?" first appeared in *Playboy*, August 1969. "The Battle" first appeared in *IF Science Fiction*, September 1954. "The Monsters" appeared in an earlier version in *The Magazine of Fantasy and Science Fiction*, March 1953. "The Petrified World" first appeared in *IF Science Fiction*, February 1968. "Five Minutes Early" first appeared in *Twilight Zone Magazine*, 1982. "Miss Mouse and the Fourth Dimension" first appeared in *Twilight Zone Magazine*, December 1981. "The Skag Castle" first appeared in *Fantastic Universe*, 1956. "The Helping Hand" first appeared in *Twilight Zone Magazine*, 1981. "The Last Days of (Parallel?) Earth" appeared in an earlier version in *After the Fall*, an anthology edited by Robert Sheckley. "The Future Lost" first appeared in *Omni*, 1980. "Wild Talents, Inc." first appeared in an earlier version in *Fantastic*, October 1953. "The Swamp" first appeared in *Twilight Zone Magazine*, October 1981. "The Future of Sex: Speculative Journalism" appeared in an earlier version in *Puritan Magazine*, 1982. "The Life of Anybody" is published here for the first time. "Good-bye Forever to Mr. Pain" first appeared in *Destinies*, January–February 1979. "The Shaggy Average American Man Story" first appeared in *Gallery*, 1979. "Shootout in the Toy Shop" first appeared in *Twilight Zone Magazine*, 1981. "How Pro Writers Really Write— Or Try To" first appeared in *Omni*, 1978.

For Jay Rothbell,
who put together this collection
and its author

"Man is a mixture of plant and phantom."

—*Nietzsche*

Contents

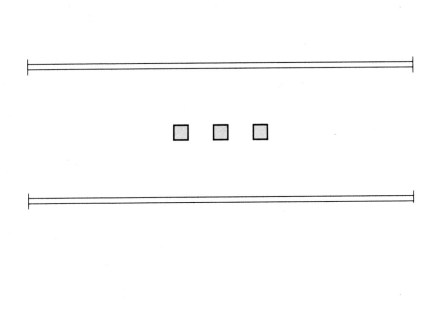

THE EYE OF REALITY

Legend tells of a nameless planet located on the edge of our island universe. On that planet there is a single tree. Wedged in its topmost branch is a large diamond, placed there by a long-vanished race. Looking into the stone, a man may see all that is or was or may be. The tree is called the Tree of Life, and the diamond is called the Eye of Reality.

Three men set out to find this tree. After much danger and difficulty, they came to the place where it grew. Each in turn climbed to the top of the tree and looked through the gem. Then they compared their impressions. The first man, an author of considerable reputation, said, "I saw innumerable actions, some grand and some petty. I knew then that I had found the keyhole of the universe, which Borges calls the Aleph."

The second man, a renowned scientist, said, "I saw the curvature of space, the death of a photon, and the birth of a star. I realized that I was looking into a superhologram, self-created and self-creating, whose entirety is our universe."

"Understanding is sensuous," said the third man, an artist. He showed them the sketches he had just made, of women and leopards, violins and deserts, mountains and spheres. "Like you," he said, "I saw pretty much what I always see."

VINTAGE SHECKLEY

THE LANGUAGE OF LOVE

Jefferson Toms went into an auto-café one afternoon after classes, to drink coffee and study. He sat down, philosophy texts piled neatly before him, and saw a girl directing the robot waiters. She had smoky gray eyes and hair the color of a rocket exhaust. Her figure was slight but sweetly curved and, gazing at it, Toms felt a lump in his throat and a sudden recollection of autumn, evening, rain, and candlelight.

This was how love came to Jefferson Toms. Although he was ordinarily a very reserved young man, he complained about the robot service in order to meet her. When they did meet, he was inarticulate, overwhelmed by feeling. Somehow, though, he managed to ask her for a date.

The girl, whose name was Doris, was strangely moved by the stocky, black-haired young student, for she accepted at once. And then Jefferson Toms's troubles began.

He found love delightful, yet extremely disturbing, in spite of his advanced studies in philosophy. But love was a confusing thing even in Toms's age, when spaceliners bridged the gaps between the worlds, disease lay dead, war was inconceivable, and just about anything of any importance had been solved in an exemplary manner.

Old Earth was in better shape than ever before. Her cities were bright with plastic and stainless steel. Her remaining forests were carefully tended bits of greenery where one might picnic in perfect safety, since all beasts and insects had been removed to

7

sanitary zoos that reproduced their living conditions with admirable skill.

Even the climate of Earth had been mastered. Farmers received their quota of rain between three and three-thirty in the morning, people gathered at stadiums to watch a program of sunsets, and a tornado was produced once a year in a special arena as part of the World Peace Day Celebration.

But love was as confusing as ever, and Toms found this distressing.

He simply could not put his feelings into words. Such expressions as "I love you," "I adore you," "I'm crazy about you" were overworked and inadequate. They conveyed nothing of the depth and fervor of his emotions. Indeed, they cheapened them, since every stereo, every second-rate play was filled with similar words. People used them in casual conversation and spoke of how much they *loved* pork chops, *adored* sunsets, were *crazy about* tennis.

Every fiber of Toms's being revolted against this. Never, he swore, would he speak of his love in terms used for pork chops. But he found, to his dismay, that he had nothing better to say.

He brought the problem to his philosophy professor. "Mr. Toms," the professor said, gesturing wearily with his glasses, "ah—*love*, as it is commonly called, is not an operational area with us as yet. No significant work has been done in this field, aside from the so-called Language of Love of the Tyanian race."

This was no help. Toms continued to muse on love and think lengthily of Doris. In the long, haunted evenings on her porch, when the shadows from the trellis vines crossed her face, revealing and concealing it, Toms struggled to tell her what he felt. And since he could not bring himself to use the weary commonplaces of love, he tried to express himself in extravagances.

"I feel about you," he would say, "the way a star feels about its planet."

"How immense!" she would answer, immensely flattered at being compared to anything so cosmic.

"That's not what I meant," Toms amended. "The feeling I was trying to express was more—well, for example, when you walk, I am reminded of—"

"Of a what?"

"A doe in a forest glade," Toms said, frowning.

"How charming!"

"It wasn't intended to be charming. I was trying to express the awkwardness inherent in youth, and yet—"

"But, honey," she said, "I'm not awkward. My dancing teacher—"

"I didn't mean *awkward*. But the essence of awkwardness is— is—"

"I understand," she said.

But Toms knew she didn't.

So he was forced to give up extravagances. Soon he found himself unable to say anything of any importance to Doris, for it was not what he meant, nor even close to it.

The girl became concerned at the long, moody silences that developed between them.

"Jeff," she would urge, "surely you can say *something*!" Toms shrugged his shoulders.

"Even if it isn't absolutely what you mean."

Toms sighed.

"Please," she cried, "say anything at all! I can't stand this!"

"Oh, hell—"

"Yes?" she breathed, her face transfigured.

"That wasn't what I meant," Toms said, relapsing into his gloomy silence.

At last he asked her to marry him. He was willing to admit that he "loved" her—but he refused to expand on it. He explained that a marriage must be founded upon truth or it is doomed from the start. If he cheapened and falsified his emotions at the beginning, what could the future hold for them?

Doris found his sentiments admirable, but refused to marry him.

"You must *tell* a girl that you love her," she declared. "You have to tell her a hundred times a day, Jefferson, and even then it's not enough."

"But I do love you!" Toms protested. "I mean to say I have an emotion corresponding to—"

"Oh, stop it!"

In this predicament, Toms thought about the Language of Love and went to his professor's office to ask about it.

"We are told," his professor said, "that the race indigenous to Tyana II had a specific and unique language for the expression of sensations of love. To say 'I love you' was unthinkable for Tyanians. They would use a phrase denoting the exact kind and class of love they felt at that specific moment, and used for no other purpose."

Toms nodded, and the professor continued. "Of course, developed with this language was, necessarily, a technique of lovemaking quite incredible in its perfection. We are told that it made all ordinary techniques seem like the clumsy pawing of a grizzly in heat." The professor coughed in embarrassment.

"It is precisely what I need!" Toms exclaimed.

"Ridiculous," said the professor. "The technique might be interesting, but your own is doubtless sufficient for most needs. And the language, by its very nature, can be used with only one person. To learn it impresses me as wasted energy."

"Labor for love," Toms said, "is the most worthwhile work in the world, since it produces a rich harvest of feeling."

"I refuse to stand here and listen to bad epigrams. Mr. Toms, why all this fuss about love?"

"It is the only perfect thing in this world," Toms answered fervently. "If one must learn a special language to appreciate it, one can do no less. Tell me, is it far to Tyana II?"

"A considerable distance," his professor said, with a thin smile. "And an unrewarding one, since the race is extinct."

"Extinct! But why! A sudden pestilence? An invasion?"

"It is one of the mysteries of the galaxy," his professor said somberly.

"Then the language is lost!"

"Not quite. Twenty years ago, an Earthman named George Varris went to Tyana and learned the Language of Love from the last survivors of the race." The professor shrugged. "I never considered it sufficiently important to read his report."

Toms looked up Varris in the *Interspatial Explorers' Who's Who* and found that he was credited with the discovery of Tyana, had wandered around the frontier planets for a time, but at last had returned to deserted Tyana, to devote his life to investigating every aspect of its culture.

After learning this, Toms thought long and hard. The journey to Tyana was a difficult one, time-consuming and expensive. Perhaps Varris would be dead before he got there, or unwilling to teach him the language. Was it worth the gamble?

"Is *love* worth it?" Toms asked himself, and knew the answer.

So he sold his ultra-fi, his memory recorder, his philosophy texts, and several stocks his grandfather had left him, and booked passage to Cranthis IV, which was the closest he could come to Tyana on a scheduled spaceway. And after all his preparations had been made, he went to Doris.

"When I return," he said, "I will be able to tell you exactly how much—I mean the particular quality and class of—I mean, Doris, when I have mastered the Tyanian Technique, you will be loved as no woman has ever been loved!"

"Do you mean that?" she asked, her eyes glowing.

"Well," Toms said, "the term 'loved' doesn't quite express it. But I mean something very much like it."

"I will wait for you, Jeff," she said. "But—please don't be too long."

Jefferson Toms nodded, blinked back his tears, clutched Doris inarticulately, and hurried to the spaceport.

Within the hour, he was on his way.

Four months later, after considerable difficulties, Toms stood on Tyana, on the outskirts of the capital city. Slowly he walked down the broad, deserted main thoroughfare. On either side of him, noble buildings soared to dizzy heights. Peering inside one, Toms saw complex machinery and gleaming switchboards. With his pocket Tyana-English dictionary, he was able to translate the lettering above one of the buildings.

It read: COUNSELING SERVICES FOR STAGE-FOUR LOVE PROBLEMS.

Other buildings were much the same, filled with calculating machinery, switchboards, ticker tapes, and the like. He passed THE INSTITUTE FOR RESEARCH INTO AFFECTION DELAY, stared at the two-hundred-story HOME FOR THE EMOTIONALLY RETARDED, and glanced at several others. Slowly the awesome, dazzling truth dawned upon him.

Here was an entire city given over to the research and aid of love.

He had no time for further speculation. In front of him was the gigantic GENERAL LOVE SERVICES BUILDING. And out of its marble hallway stepped an old man.

"Who the hell are you?" the old man asked.

"I am Jefferson Toms, of Earth. I have come here to learn the Language of Love, Mr. Varris."

Varris raised his shaggy white eyebrows. He was a small, wrinkled old man, stoop-shouldered and shaky in the knees. But his eyes were alert and filled with a cold suspicion.

"Perhaps you think the language will make you more attractive to women," Varris said. "Don't believe it, young man. Knowledge has its advantages, of course. But it has distinct drawbacks, as the Tyanians discovered."

"What drawbacks?" Toms asked.

Varris grinned, displaying a single yellow tooth. "You wouldn't understand, if you don't already know. It takes knowledge to understand the limitations of knowledge."

"Nevertheless," Toms said, "I want to learn the language."

Varris stared at him thoughtfully. "But it is not a simple thing, Toms. The Language of Love, and its resultant technique, is every bit as complex as brain surgery or the practice of corporation law. It takes work, much work, and a talent as well."

"I will do the work. And I'm sure I have the talent."

"Most people think that," Varris said, "and most of them are mistaken. But never mind, never mind. It's been a long time since I've had any company. We'll see how you get on, Toms."

Together they went into the General Services Building, which Varris called his home. They went to the Main Control Room, where the old man had put down a sleeping bag and set up a camp stove. There, in the shadow of the giant calculators, Toms's lessons began.

Varris was a thorough teacher. In the beginning, with the aid of a portable Semantic Differentiator, he taught Toms to isolate the delicate apprehension one feels in the presence of a to-be-loved person, to detect the subtle tensions that come into being as the potentiality of love draws near.

These sensations, Toms learned, must never be spoken of directly, for frankness frightens love. They must be expressed in simile, metaphor, and hyperbole, half-truths and white lies. With these, one creates an atmosphere and lays a foundation for love. And the mind, deceived by its own predisposition, thinks of booming surf and raging sea, mournful black rocks and fields of green corn.

"Nice images," Toms said admiringly.

"Those were samples," Varris told him. "Now you must learn them all."

So Toms went to work memorizing great long lists of natural wonders, to what sensations they were comparable, and at what stage they appeared in the anticipation of love. The language was thorough in this regard. Every state or object in nature for which there was a response in love-anticipation had been catalogued, classified, and listed with suitable modifying adjectives.

When Toms had memorized the list, Varris drilled him in perceptions of love. Toms learned the small, strange things that make up a state of love. Some were so ridiculous that he had to laugh.

The old man admonished him sternly. "Love is a serious business, Toms. You seem to find some humor in the fact that love is frequently predisposed by wind speed and direction."

"It seems foolish," Toms admitted.

"There are stranger things than that," Varris said, and mentioned another factor.

Toms shuddered. "*That* I can't believe. It's preposterous. Everyone knows—"

"If everyone knows how love operates, why hasn't someone reduced it to a formula? Murky thinking, Toms, murky thinking is the answer, and an unwillingness to accept cold facts. If you cannot face them—"

"I can face anything," Toms said, "if I have to. Let's continue."

As the weeks passed, Toms learned the words that express the first quickening of interest, shade by shade, until an attachment is formed. He learned what that attachment really is, and the three words that express it. This brought him to the rhetoric of sensation, where the body becomes supreme.

Here the language was specific instead of allusive, and dealt with feelings produced by certain words and, above all, by certain physical actions.

A startling little black machine taught Toms the thirty-eight separate and distinct sensations that the touch of a hand can engender, and he learned how to locate that sensitive area, no larger than a dime, which exists just below the right shoulder blade.

He learned an entirely new system of caressing, which caused impulses to explode—and even implode—along the nerve paths and to shower colored sparks before the eyes.

He was also taught the social advantages of conspicuous desensitization.

He learned many things about physical love that he had dimly suspected, and still more things that *no one* had suspected.

It was intimidating knowledge. Toms had imagined himself to be at least an adequate lover. Now he found that he knew nothing, nothing at all, and that his best efforts had been comparable to the play of amorous hippopotami.

"But what else could you expect?" Varris asked. "Good lovemaking, Toms, calls for more study, more sheer intensive labor than any other acquired skill. Do you still wish to learn?"

"Definitely!" Toms said. "Why, when I'm an expert on lovemaking, I'll—I can—"

"That is no concern of mine," the old man stated. "Let's return to our lessons."

Next, Toms learned the Cycles of Love. Love, he discovered, is dynamic, constantly rising and falling, and doing so in definite patterns. There are fifty-two major patterns, three hundred and six minor patterns, four general exceptions, and nine specific exceptions.

Toms learned them better than his own name.

He acquired the uses of the Tertiary Touch. And he never forgot the day he was taught what a bosom *really* was like.

"But I can't say that!" Toms objected, appalled.

"It's true, isn't it?" Varris insisted.

"No! I mean—yes, I suppose it is. But it's unflattering."

"So it seems. But examine, Toms. Is it *actually* unflattering?"

Toms examined and found the compliment that lies beneath the insult, and so he learned another facet of the Language of Love.

Soon he was ready for the study of the Apparent Negations. He discovered that for every degree of love, there is a corresponding degree of hate, which is in itself a form of love. He came to understand how valuable hate is, how it gives substance and body to love, and how even indifference and loathing have their place in the nature of love.

Varris gave him a ten-hour written examination, which Toms passed with superlative marks. He was eager to finish, but Varris noticed that a slight tic had developed in his student's left eye and that his hands had a tendency to shake.

"You need a vacation," the old man informed him.

Toms had been thinking this himself. "You may be right," he said, with barely concealed eagerness. "Suppose I go to Cythera V for a few weeks."

Varris, who knew Cythera's reputation, smiled cynically. "Eager to try out your new knowledge?"

"Well, why not? Knowledge is to be used."

"Only after it's mastered."

"But I *have* mastered it! Couldn't we call this field work? A thesis, perhaps?"

"No thesis is necessary," Varris said.

"But, damn it all," Toms exploded, "I should do a little experimentation! I should find out for myself how all this works. Especially Approach 33-CV. It sounds fine in theory, but I've been wondering how it works out in actual practice. There's nothing like direct experience, you know, to reinforce—"

"Did you journey all this way to become a super-seducer?" Varris asked, with evident disgust.

"Of course not," Toms said. "But a little experimentation wouldn't—"

"Your knowledge of the mechanics of sensation would be barren unless you understand love, as well. You have progressed too far to be satisfied with mere thrills."

Toms, searching his heart, knew this to be true. But he set his jaw stubbornly. "I'd like to find out *that* for myself, too."

"You may go," Varris said, "but don't come back. No one will accuse me of loosing a callous scientific seducer upon the galaxy."

"Oh, all right. To hell with it. Let's get back to work."

"No. Look at yourself! A little more unrelieved studying, young man, and you will lose the capacity to make love. And wouldn't that be a sorry state of affairs?"

Toms agreed that it would certainly be.

"I know the perfect spot," Varris told him, "for relaxation from the study of love."

They entered the old man's spaceship and journeyed five days to a small unnamed planetoid. When they landed, the old man took Toms to the bank of a swift-flowing river, where the water ran fiery red, with green diamonds of foam. The trees that grew on the banks of that river were stunted and strange, and colored vermilion. Even the grass was unlike grass, for it was orange and blue.

"How alien!" gasped Toms.

"It is the least human spot I've found in this humdrum corner of the galaxy," Varris explained. "And believe me, I've done some looking."

Toms stared at him, wondering if the old man was out of his mind. But soon he understood what Varris meant.

For months he had been studying human reactions and human feelings, and surrounding it all was the now suffocating feeling of soft human flesh. He had immersed himself in humanity, studied it, bathed in it, eaten and drunk and dreamed it. It was a relief to be here, where the water ran red and the trees were stunted and strange and vermilion, and the grass was orange and blue, and there was no reminder of Earth.

Toms and Varris separated, for even each other's humanity was a nuisance. Toms spent his days wandering along the river edge, marveling at the flowers that moaned when he came near them. At night, three wrinkled moons played tag with each other, and the morning sun was different from the yellow sun of Earth.

At the end of a week, refreshed and renewed, Toms and Varris returned to G'cel, the Tyanian city dedicated to the study of love.

Toms was taught the five hundred and six shades of Love

Proper, from the first faint possibility to the ultimate feeling, which is so powerful that only five men and one woman have experienced it, and the strongest of them survived less than an hour.

Under the tutelage of a bank of small, interrelated calculators, he studied the intensification of love.

He learned all of the thousand different sensations of which the human body is capable, and how to augment them, and how to intensify them until they become unbearable, and how to make the unbearable bearable, and finally pleasurable, at which point the organism is not far from death.

After that, he was taught some things that have never been put into words and, with luck, never will be.

"And that," Varris said one day, "is everything."

"Everything?"

"Yes, Toms. The heart has no secrets from you. Nor, for that matter, has the soul, or the mind, or the viscera. You have mastered the Language of Love. Now return to your young lady."

"I will!" cried Toms. "At last she will know!"

"Drop me a postcard," Varris said. "Let me know how you're getting on."

"I'll do that," Toms promised. Fervently he shook his teacher's hand and departed for Earth.

At the end of the long trip, Jefferson Toms hurried to Doris's home. Perspiration beaded his forehead, and his hands were shaking. He was able to classify the feeling as Stage Two Anticipatory Tremors, with mild masochistic overtones. But that didn't help—this was his first fieldwork and he was nervous. Had he mastered *everything*?

He rang the bell.

She opened the door and Toms saw that she was more beautiful than he had remembered, her eyes smoky gray and misted with tears, her hair the color of a rocket exhaust, her figure slight but sweetly curved. He felt again the lump in his throat and sudden memories of autumn, evening, rain, and candlelight.

"I'm back," he croaked.

"Oh, Jeff," she said, very softly.

Toms simply stared, unable to say a word.

"It's been so long, Jeff, and I kept wondering if it was all worth it. Now I know."

"You—know?"

"Yes, my darling! I waited for you! I'd wait a hundred years, or a thousand! I love you, Jeff!"

She was in his arms.

"Now tell me, Jeff," she said. "*Tell me!*"

And Toms looked at her, and felt, and sensed, searched his classifications, selected his modifiers, checked and double-checked. And after much searching, and careful selection, and absolute certainty, and allowing for his present state of mind, and not forgetting to take into account climatic conditions, phases of the moon, wind speed and direction, sunspots, and other phenomena that have their due effect upon love, he said:

"My dear, I am rather fond of you."

"Jeff! Surely you can say more than that! The Language of Love—"

"The Language is damnably precise," Toms said wretchedly. "I'm sorry, but the phrase 'I am rather fond of you' expresses precisely what I feel."

"Oh, Jeff!"

"Yes," he mumbled.

"Oh, damn you, Jeff!"

There was, of course, a painful scene and a very painful separation. Toms took to traveling.

He held jobs here and there, working as a riveter at Saturn-Lockheed, a wiper on the Helg-Vinosce Trader, a farmer for a while on a kibbutz on Israel IV. He bummed around the Inner Dalmian System for several years, living mostly on handouts. Then, at Novilocessile, he met a pleasant, brown-haired girl, courted her, and, in due course, married her and set up housekeeping.

Their friends say that the Tomses are tolerably happy, although their home makes most people uncomfortable. It is a pleasant enough place, but the rushing red river nearby makes people edgy. And who can get used to vermilion trees, and orange-and-blue grass, and moaning flowers, and three wrinkled moons playing tag in the alien sky?

Toms likes it, though, and Mrs. Toms is, if nothing else, a flexible young lady.

Toms wrote a letter to his philosophy professor on Earth, saying that he had solved the problem of the demise of the Tyanian race, at least to his own satisfaction. The trouble with scholarly research, he wrote, is the inhibiting effect it has upon action. The Tyanians, he was convinced, had been so preoccupied with the science of love that after a while they just didn't get around to making any.

And eventually he sent a short postcard to George Varris. He simply said that he was married, having succeeded in finding a girl for whom he felt "quite a substantial liking."

"Lucky devil," Varris growled, after reading the card. "'Vaguely enjoyable' was the best I could ever find."

THE ACCOUNTANT

Mr. Dee was seated in the big armchair, his belt loosened, the evening papers strewn around his knees. Peacefully he smoked his pipe, and considered how wonderful the world was. Today he had sold two amulets and a philter; his wife was bustling around the kitchen, preparing a delicious meal; and his pipe was drawing well. With a sigh of contentment, Mr. Dee yawned and stretched.

Morton, his nine-year-old son, hurried across the living room, loaded down with books.

"How'd school go today?" Mr. Dee called.

"Okay," the boy said, slowing down, but still moving toward his room.

"What have you got there?" Mr. Dee asked, gesturing at his son's tall pile of books.

"Just some more accounting stuff," Morton said, not looking at his father. He hurried into his room.

Mr. Dee shook his head. Somewhere the lad had picked up the notion that he wanted to be an accountant. An accountant! True, Morton was quick with figures; but he would have to forget this nonsense. Bigger things were in store for him.

The doorbell rang.

Mr. Dee tightened his belt, hastily stuffed in his shirttail, and opened the front door. There stood Miss Greeb, his son's fourth-grade teacher.

"Come in, Miss Greeb," said Dee. "Can I offer you something?"

"I have no time," said Miss Greeb. She stood in the doorway,

her arms akimbo. With her gray, tangled hair, her thin, lon̦
face and red, runny eyes, she looked exactly like a witch. A
was as it should be, for Miss Greeb *was* a witch.

"I've come to speak to you about your son," she said.

At this moment Mrs. Dee hurried out of the kitchen, wiping
hands on her apron.

"I hope he hasn't been naughty," Mrs. Dee said anxiously.

Miss Greeb sniffed ominously. "Today I gave the yearly tests.
Your son failed miserably."

"Oh, dear," Mrs. Dee said. "It's spring. Perhaps—"

"Spring has nothing to do with it," said Miss Greeb. "Last week
I assigned the Greater Spells of Cordus, Section One. You know
how easy *they* are. He didn't learn a single one."

"Hm," said Mr. Dee succinctly.

"In Biology, he doesn't have the slightest notion which are the
basic conjuring herbs."

"This is unthinkable," said Mr. Dee.

Miss Greeb laughed sourly. "Moreover, he has forgotten all the
Secret Alphabet, which he learned in third grade. He has forgotten
the Protective Formula, forgotten the names of the ninety-nine
lesser imps of the Third Circle, forgotten what little he knew of the
Geography of Greater Hell. And what's more, he doesn't want to
learn."

Mr. and Mrs. Dee looked at each other. This was serious indeed.
A certain amount of boyish inattentiveness was allowable—
encouraged, even, for it showed spirit. But a child *had* to learn the
basics if he ever hoped to become a wizard.

"I can tell you right here and now," said Miss Greeb, "if this
were the old days, I'd flunk him without another thought. But
there are so few of us left."

Mr. Dee nodded sadly. Witchcraft had been declining over the
centuries. The old families died out, or were snatched by demoniac forces, or became scientists. And the fickle public showed no
interest in the charms and enchantments of ancient days.

Now only a scattered handful possessed the Old Lore, guarding
it, teaching it in places like Miss Greeb's private school for the
children of wizards. It was a heritage, a sacred trust.

"It's this accounting nonsense," said Miss Greeb. "I don't know

where he got the notion." She stared accusingly at Dee. "And I don't know why it wasn't nipped in the bud."

Mr. Dee felt his cheeks grow hot.

"But I do know this. As long as Morton has *that* on his mind, he can't give his attention to Thaumaturgy."

Mr. Dee looked away from the witch's red eyes. All this was his own fault. He should never have brought home that toy adding machine. And when he first saw Morton playing at double-entry bookkeeping, he should have burnt the ledger.

But how could he have known it would grow into an obsession?

Mrs. Dee smoothed out her apron and said, "Miss Greeb, you know you have our complete confidence. What would you suggest?"

Miss Greeb shrugged. "The only thing remaining is to call up Boarbas, the Demon of Children."

"Oh, surely it's not that serious yet," Mr. Dee said quickly.

"It's entirely up to you," Miss Greeb said. "As matters stand now, your son will never be a wizard." She turned to go.

"Won't you stay for a cup of tea?" Mrs. Dee asked.

"No, I must attend a Witches' Coven in Cincinnati," said Miss Greeb, and vanished in a puff of orange smoke.

Mr. Dee fanned the smoke with his hands. "Phew," he said. "You'd think she'd use a perfumed brand."

"She's old-fashioned," Mrs. Dee murmured.

They stood beside the door in silence. Mr. Dee was just beginning to feel the shock. It was hard to believe that his son, his own flesh and blood, didn't want to carry on the family tradition. It couldn't be true!

"After dinner," Dee said finally, "I'll have a man-to-man talk with him. I'm sure we won't need any demoniac intervention."

"Good," Mrs. Dee said. "I'm sure you can make the boy understand." She smiled, and Dee caught a glimpse of the old witch-light flickering behind her eyes.

"My roast!" Mrs. Dee gasped suddenly, the witch-light dying. She hurried back to her kitchen.

There was no conversation over dinner. Morton knew that Miss Greeb had been there, and he ate in guilty silence, glancing

occasionally at his father. Mr. Dee sliced and served the roast, frowning deeply. Mrs. Dee didn't even attempt any small talk.

After bolting his dessert, the boy hurried to his room.

"Now we'll see," Mr. Dee said to his wife. He finished the last of his coffee, wiped his mouth, and stood up. "I am going to reason with him now. Where is my Amulet of Persuasion?"

Mrs. Dee thought deeply for a moment. Then she walked across the room to the bookcase. "Here it is," she said, lifting it from the pages of a bright-jacketed novel. "I was using it as a marker."

Mr. Dee slipped the amulet into his pocket, took a deep breath, and entered his son's room.

Morton was seated at his desk. In front of him was a notebook scribbled with figures and tiny, precise notations. On his desk were six carefully sharpened pencils, an eraser, an abacus, and a toy adding machine. His books hung precariously over the edge of the desk: *Money*, by Rimraamer, *Bank Accounting Practice*, by Johnson and Calhoun, *Ellman's Studies for the CPA*, and a dozen others.

Mr. Dee pushed aside a mound of clothes and made room for himself on the bed. "How's it going, son?" he asked in his kindest voice.

"Fine, Dad," Morton answered eagerly. "I'm up to Chapter Four in *Basic Accounting*."

"Son," Dee broke in, speaking very softly, "how about your regular homework?"

Morton looked uncomfortable and scuffed his feet on the floor.

"You know, not many boys have a chance to become wizards in this day and age."

"Yes, sir, I know." Morton looked away abruptly. In a high, nervous voice he said, "But, Dad, I want to be an accountant. I really do, Dad."

Mr. Dee shook his head. "Morton, there's always been a wizard in our family. For eighteen hundred years, the Dees have been famous in supernatural circles."

Morton continued to look out the window and scuff his feet.

"You wouldn't want to disappoint me, would you, son?" Dee smiled sadly. "You know, anyone can be an *accountant*. But only a chosen few can master the Black Arts."

Morton turned away from the window. He picked up a pencil and began to turn it slowly in his fingers.

"How about it, boy? Won't you work harder for Miss Greeb?"

Morton shook his head. "I want to be an accountant."

Mr. Dee contained his sudden rush of anger with difficulty. What was wrong with the Amulet of Persuasion? Could the spell have run down? He should have recharged it. Nevertheless, he went on.

"Morton," he said in a husky voice. "I'm only a Third Degree Adept, you know. My parents were very poor. They couldn't send me to the University."

"I know," the boy said in a whisper.

"I want you to have all the things I never had. Morton, you can be a First Degree Adept." He shook his head wistfully. "It'll be difficult. But your mother and I have a little put away, and we'll scrape the rest together somehow."

Morton was biting his lip and turning the pencil rapidly in his fingers.

"How about it, son? You know, as a First Degree Adept, you won't have to work in a store. You can be a Direct Agent of the Black One. A Direct Agent! What do you say, boy?"

For a moment Dee thought his son was moved. Morton's lips were parted, and there was a suspicious brightness in his eyes. But then the boy glanced at his accounting books, his little abacus, his toy adding machine.

"I'm going to be an accountant," he said.

"We'll see!" Mr. Dee shouted, all patience gone. "You will *not* be an accountant, young man. You will be a wizard. It was good enough for the rest of your family, and by all that's damnable, it'll be good enough for you. You haven't heard the last of this!" He stormed out of the room.

Immediately Morton returned to his accounting books.

Mr. and Mrs. Dee sat together on the couch, not talking. Mrs. Dee was busily knitting a wind-cord, but her mind wasn't on it. Mr. Dee stared moodily at a worn spot on the living room rug.

Finally Dee said, "I've spoiled him. Boarbas is the only solution."

"Oh, no," Mrs. Dee said hastily. "He's so young."

"Do you want your son to grow up scribbling figures instead of doing the Black One's work?"

"Of course not," said Mrs. Dee. "But Boarbas—"

"I know. I feel like a murderer already."

They thought for a few moments. Then Mrs. Dee said, "Perhaps his grandfather can do something. He was always fond of the boy."

"Perhaps he can," Mr. Dee said thoughtfully. "But I don't know if we should disturb him. After all, the old gentleman has been dead for three years."

"I know," Mrs. Dee said, undoing an incorrect knot in the wind-cord. "But it's either that or Boarbas."

Mr. Dee agreed. They would have to call up Morton's grandfather; Boarbas was very much a desperate last resort. He gathered together the henbane, the ground unicorn's horn, and the hemlock. He added a morsel of dragon's tooth and put them all on the rug.

"Where's my wand?" he asked his wife.

"I put it in the bag with your golf clubs," she told him.

Mr. Dee got his wand and waved it over the ingredients. He muttered the three words of the Unbinding, and called out his father's name.

Immediately a wisp of smoke arose from the rug.

"Hello, Grandpa Dee," Mrs. Dee said.

"Dad, I'm sorry to disturb you," Mr. Dee said. "But my son—your grandson—refuses to become a wizard. He wants to be—an accountant!"

The wisp of smoke trembled, then straightened out and formed a character in the Old Language.

"Yes," Mr. Dee said. "We tried persuasion. The boy is adamant."

Again the smoke trembled, and formed another character.

"I suppose that's best," Mr Dee said. "If you frighten him out of his wits once and for all, he'll forget this accounting nonsense. It's cruel—but it's better than Boarbas."

The wisp of smoke nodded, and streamed toward the boy's room. Mr. and Mrs. Dee sat down on the couch.

The door of Morton's room was slammed open as though by a

gigantic wind. Morton looked up, frowned, and returned to his books.

The wisp of smoke turned into a winged lion with the tail of a shark. It roared hideously, crouched, snarled, and gathered itself for a spring.

Morton glanced at it, raised both eyebrows, and proceeded to jot down a column of figures.

The lion changed into a three-headed lizard. Breathing gusts of fire, the lizard advanced on the boy.

Morton finished adding the column of figures, checked the result on his abacus, and looked at the lizard.

With a screech, the lizard changed into a giant bat. It fluttered around the boy's head, moaning and gibbering.

Morton grinned and turned back to his books.

Mr. Dee was unable to stand it any longer. "Damn it," he shouted, "aren't you scared?"

"Why should I be?" Morton asked. "It's only Grandpa."

Upon the word, the bat dissolved into a plume of smoke. It nodded sadly to Mr. Dee, bowed to Mrs. Dee, and vanished.

"Good-bye, Grandpa," Morton called. He got up and closed his door.

"That does it," Mr. Dee said. "We must call up Boarbas."

"No!" his wife said.

"What, then?"

"I just don't know anymore," Mrs. Dee said, on the verge of tears. "You *know* what Boarbas does to children. They're never the same afterward."

Mr. Dee's face was as hard as granite. "I know. It can't be helped."

"He's so young!" Mrs. Dee wailed. "It will be traumatic!"

"If so, we will use all the resources of modern psychology to heal him," Mr. Dee said soothingly. "He will have the best psychoanalysts money can buy. But the boy must become a wizard!"

"Go ahead, then," Mrs. Dee said, crying openly. "But please don't ask me to assist you."

How like a woman, Dee thought. Always turning into jelly at the moment when firmness was indicated. With a heavy heart he made the preparations for calling up Boarbas, Demon of Children.

First came the intricate sketching of the pentagon, the twelve-pointed star within it, and the endless spiral within that. Then came the herbs and essences—expensive items, but absolutely necessary for the conjuring. Then came the inscribing of the Protective Spell, so that Boarbas might not break loose and destroy them all. Then came the three drops of hippogriff blood—

"Where is my hippogriff blood?" Mr. Dee asked, rummaging through the living room cabinet.

"In the kitchen, in the aspirin bottle," Mrs. Dee said, wiping her eyes.

Dee found it, and then all was in readiness. He lighted the black candles and chanted the Unlocking Spell.

The room was suddenly very warm, and there remained only the Naming of the Name.

"Morton," Mr. Dee called. "Come here."

Morton opened the door and stepped out, clutching one of his accounting books, looking very young and defenseless.

"Morton, I am about to call up the Demon of Children. Don't make me do it, Morton."

The boy turned pale and shrank back against the door. But stubbornly he shook his head.

"Very well," Mr. Dee said. "BOARBAS!"

There was an earsplitting clap of thunder and a wave of heat, and Boarbas appeared, as tall as the ceiling, chuckling evilly.

"Ah!" cried Boarbas, in a voice that shook the room. "A little boy."

Morton gaped, his jaw open and eyes bulging.

"A naughty little boy," Boarbas said, and laughed. The demon marched forward, shaking the house with every stride.

"Send him away!" Mrs. Dee cried.

"I can't," Dee said, his voice breaking. "I can't do anything until he's finished."

The demon's great horned hands reached for Morton; but quickly the boy opened the accounting book. "Save me!" he cried.

In that instant there appeared a tall, terribly thin old man covered with worn penpoints and ledger sheets, his eyes two zeros.

"*Zico Pico Reel!*" chanted Boarbas, turning to grapple with the newcomer.

But the thin old man laughed and said, "A contract of a corporation which is *ultra vires* is not voidable only, but utterly void."

At these words, Boarbas was flung back, breaking a chair as he fell. He scrambled to his feet, his skin glowing red-hot with rage, and intoned the Demoniac Master-Spell: "VRAT, HAT, HO!"

But the thin old man shielded Morton with his body, and cried the words of Dissolution. "Expiration, Repeal, Occurrence, Surrender, Abandonment, and Death!"

Boarbas squeaked in agony. Hastily he backed away, fumbling in the air until he found the Opening. He jumped through it and was gone.

The tall, thin old man turned to Mr. and Mrs. Dee, cowering in a corner of the living room. He said, "Know that I am The Accountant. And Know, Moreover, that this Child has signed a Compact with Me, to enter My Apprenticeship and be My Servant. And in return for Services Rendered, I, THE ACCOUNTANT, am teaching him the Damnation of Souls by means of ensnaring them in a cursed web of Figures, Forms, & Torts and Reprisals. And behold, this is My Mark upon him!"

The Accountant held up Morton's right hand, and showed the ink smudge on the second finger.

Turning to Morton, he said in a softer voice, "Tomorrow, lad, we will consider some aspects of Income Tax Evasion as a Path to Damnation."

"Yes, *sir*," Morton said eagerly.

And with another sharp look at the Dees, The Accountant vanished.

For long seconds there was silence. Then Dee turned to his wife.

"Well," Dee said, "if the boy wants to be an accountant *that* badly, I'm sure I'm not going to stand in his way."

A WIND IS RISING

Outside, a wind was rising. But within the station, the two men had other things on their minds. Clayton turned the handle of the water faucet again and waited. Nothing happened.

"Try hitting it," said Nerishev.

Clayton pounded the faucet with his fist. Two drops of water came out. A third drop trembled on the spigot's lip, swayed, and fell.

"That does it," Clayton said bitterly. "That damned water pipe is blocked again. How much water we got in storage?"

"Four gallons—assuming the tank hasn't sprung another leak," said Nerishev. He stared at the faucet, tapping it with long, nervous fingers. He was a big, pale, bearded man, fragile-looking in spite of his size. He didn't look like the type to operate an observation station on a remote and alien planet. But the Advance Exploration Corps had discovered, to its regret, that there was no "type" for that kind of work.

Nerishev was a competent biologist and botanist. Although chronically nervous, he had surprising reserves of calm. He was the sort of man who needs an occasion to rise to. This, if anything, made him suitable to pioneer a planet like Carella I.

"I suppose somebody should go out and unblock the water pipe," said Nerishev, not looking at Clayton.

"I suppose so," Clayton said, pounding the faucet again. "But it's going to be murder out there. Listen to it!"

Clayton was a short man, bull-necked, red-faced, powerfully

constructed. This was his third tour of duty as a planetary observer.

He had tried other jobs in the Advance Exploration Corps, but none suited him. PEP—Primary Extraterrestrial Penetration— faced him with too many unpleasant surprises. It was work for daredevils and madmen. But Base Operations was much too tame and restricting.

He liked the work of a planetary observer, though. His job was to sit tight on a planet newly opened by the PEP boys and checked out by a drone camera crew. All he had to do on this planet was stoically endure discomfort and skillfully keep himself alive. After a year of this, the relief ship would remove him and note his report. On the basis of the report, further action would or would not be taken.

Before each tour of duty, Clayton dutifully promised his wife that this would be the last. After *this* tour, he was going to stay on Earth and work on the little farm he owned. He promised . . .

But at the end of each rest leave, Clayton journeyed out again, to do the thing for which he was best suited: staying alive through skill and endurance.

But this time he had had it. He and Nerishev had been eight months on Carella. The relief ship was due in another four months. If he came through alive, he was going to quit for good.

"Just listen to that wind," Nerishev said.

Muffled, distant, it sighed and murmured around the steel hull of the station like a zephyr, a summer breeze.

That was how it sounded to them inside the station, separated from the wind by three inches of steel plus a soundproofing layer.

"It's rising," Clayton said. He walked over to the windspeed indicator. According to the dial, the gentle-sounding wind was blowing at a steady eighty-two miles an hour—

A light breeze on Carella.

"Man, oh, man!" Clayton said. "I don't want to go out there. Nothing's worth going out there."

"It's your turn," Nerishev pointed out.

"I know. Let me complain a little first, will you? Come on, let's get a forecast from Smanik."

They walked the length of the station, their heels echoing on the steel floor, past compartments filled with food, air supplies, instruments, extra equipment. At the far end of the station was the heavy metal door of the receiving shed. The men slipped on air masks and adjusted the flow.

"Ready?" Clayton asked.

"Ready."

They braced themselves, gripping handholds beside the door. Clayton touched the stud. The door slid away and a gust of wind shrieked in. The men lowered their heads and butted into the wind, entering the receiving shed.

The shed was an extension of the station, some thirty feet long by fifteen feet wide. It was not sealed, as was the rest of the structure. The walls were built of openwork steel, with baffles set in. The wind could pass through this arrangement, but slowed down, controlled. A gauge told them it was blowing thirty-four miles an hour within the shed.

It was a damned nuisance, Clayton thought, having to confer with the natives of Carella in a gale. But there was no other way. The Carellans, raised on a planet where the wind never blew at less than seventy miles an hour, couldn't stand the "dead air" within the station. Even with the oxygen content cut down to the Carellan norm, the natives couldn't make the adjustments. Within the station, they grew dizzy and apprehensive. Soon they began strangling, like a man in a vacuum.

Thirty-four miles an hour of wind was a fair compromise point for human and Carellan to meet.

Clayton and Nerishev walked down the shed. In one corner lay what looked like a tangle of dried-out octopi. The tangle stirred and waved two tentacles ceremoniously.

"Good day," said Smanik.

"Good day," Clayton said. "What do you think of the weather?"

"Excellent," said Smanik.

Nerishev tugged at Clayton's sleeve. "What did he say?" he asked, and nodded thoughtfully when Clayton translated for him. Nerishev lacked Clayton's gift for language. Even after eight months, the Carellan tongue was still an undecipherable series of clicks and whistles to him.

Several more Carellans came up to join the conversation. They all looked like spiders or octopi, with their small centralized bodies and long, flexible tentacles. This was the optimum survival shape on Carella, and Clayton sometimes envied it. He was forced to rely absolutely on the shelter of the station; but the Carellans lived directly in their environment.

Often he had seen a native walking against a tornado-force wind, seven or eight limbs hooked into the ground and pulling, other tentacles reaching out for further grips. He had seen them rolling down the wind like tumbleweed, their tentacles curled around them, wickerwork-basket fashion. He thought of the gay and audacious way they handled their land ships, scudding merrily along on the wind . . .

Well, he thought, they'd look damned silly on Earth.

"What is the weather going to be like?" he asked Smanik.

The Carellan pondered the question for a while, sniffed the wind, and rubbed two tentacles together.

"The wind may rise a shade more," he said finally. "But it will be nothing serious."

Clayton wondered. "Nothing serious" for a Carellan could mean disaster for an Earthman. Still, it sounded fairly promising.

He and Nerishev left the receiving shed and closed the door.

"Look," said Nerishev, "if you'd like to wait—"

"Might as well get it over with," Clayton said.

Here, lighted by a single dim overhead bulb, was the smooth, glittering bulk of the Brute. That was the nickname they had given to the vehicle specially constructed for transportation on Carella.

The Brute was armored like a tank and streamlined like a spheric section. It had vision slits of shatterproof glass, thick enough to match the strength of its steel plating. Its center of gravity was low; most of its twelve tons were centered near the ground. The Brute was sealed. Its heavy diesel engine, as well as all necessary openings, were fitted with special dustproof covers. The Brute rested on its six fat tires, looking, in its immovable bulk, like some prehistoric monster.

Clayton got in, put on crash helmet and goggles, and strapped himself into the padded seat. He revved up the engine, listened to it critically, then nodded.

"Okay," he said, "the Brute's ready. Get upstairs and open the garage door."

"Good luck," said Nerishev. He left.

Clayton went over the instrument panel and made sure that all the Brute's special gadgets were in working order. In a moment he heard Nerishev's voice coming in over the radio.

"I'm opening the door."

"Right."

The heavy door slid back and Clayton drove the Brute outside.

The station had been set up on a wide, empty plain. Mountains would have offered some protection from the wind, but the mountains on Carella were in a constant restless state of building up and breaking down. The plain presented dangers of its own, however. To avert the worst of those dangers, a field of stout steel posts had been planted around the station. The closely packed posts pointed outward, like ancient tank traps, and served the same purpose.

Clayton drove the Brute down one of the narrow, winding channels that led through the field of posts. He emerged, located the pipeline, and started along it. On a small screen above his head, a white line flashed into view. The line would show any break or obstruction in the pipeline.

A wide, rocky, monotonous desert stretched before him. An occasional low bush came into sight. The wind was directly behind him, blanketed by the sound of the diesel.

He glanced at the windspeed indicator. The wind of Carella was blowing at ninety-two miles an hour.

He drove steadily along, humming to himself under his breath. From time to time he heard a crash. Pebbles, propelled by the hurricane wind, were cannonading against the Brute. They shattered harmlessly against the thick armor.

"Everything all right?" Nerishev asked over the radio.

"Fine," Clayton said.

In the distance he saw a Carellan land ship. It was about forty feet long, he judged, and narrow in the beam, skimming rapidly on crude wooden rollers. The ship's sails were made from one of the few leaf-bearing shrubs on the planet.

The Carellans waved their tentacles as they went past. They seemed to be heading toward the station.

Clayton turned his attention back to the pipeline. He was beginning to hear the wind now, above the roar of the diesel. The windspeed indicator showed that the wind had risen to ninety-seven miles an hour.

Somberly he stared through the sand-pocked slit-window. In the far distance were jagged cliffs, seen dimly through the dust-blown air. More pebbles ricocheted off the hull and the sound rang hollowly through the vehicle. He glimpsed another Carellan land ship, then three more. They were tacking stubbornly into the wind.

It struck Clayton that a lot of Carellans were moving toward the station. He signaled to Nerishev on the radio.

"How are you doing?" Nerishev asked.

"I'm close to the spring and no break yet," Clayton reported. "Looks like a lot of Carellans heading your way."

"I know. Six ships are moored in the lee of the shed and more are coming."

"We've never had any trouble with the natives before," Clayton said slowly. "What does this look like?"

"They've brought food with them. It might be a celebration."

"Maybe. Watch yourself."

"Don't worry. You take care and hurry—"

"I've found the break! Speak to you later."

The break showed on the screen, glowing white. Peering out through the port, Clayton saw where a boulder had rolled across the pipeline, crushing it.

He brought the truck to a stop on the windward side of the pipe. The wind was blowing 113 miles an hour. Clayton slid out of the truck, carrying several lengths of pipe, some patches, a blowtorch, and a bag of tools. They were all tied to him, and he was secured to the Brute by a strong nylon rope.

Outside, the wind was deafening. It thundered and roared like breaking surf. He adjusted his mask for more oxygen and went to work.

Two hours later he had completed a fifteen-minute repair job. His clothing was shredded and his air extractor was completely clogged with dust.

He climbed back into the Brute, sealed the port, and lay on the floor, resting. The truck was starting to tremble in the wind gusts.

"Hello? Hello?" Nerishev called over the radio.

Wearily, Clayton climbed back into the driver's seat and acknowledged.

"Hurry back now, Clayton! No time to rest! The wind's up to 138! I think a storm is coming!"

A storm on Carella was something Clayton didn't even want to think about. They had experienced only one in eight months. During it, the winds had gone over 160 miles an hour.

He nosed the truck around and started back, driving directly into the wind. At full throttle, he found he was making very little progress. Three miles an hour was all the heavy diesel would do against the pressure of a 138-mile-an-hour wind.

He stared ahead through the slit-window. The wind, outlined by long streamers of dust and sand, seemed to be coming straight at him, funneled out of an infinitely wide sky to the tiny point of his window. Windborne rocks sailed at him, grew large, immense, and shattered against his window. He couldn't stop himself from ducking each time one came.

The heavy engine was beginning to labor and miss.

"Oh, baby," Clayton breathed, "don't quit now. Not now. Get Papa home. *Then* quit. Please!"

He figured he was about ten miles from the station, which lay directly upwind.

He heard a sound like an avalanche plummeting down a mountainside. It was made by a boulder the size of a house. Too big for the wind to lift, it was rolling at him from windward, digging a furrow in the rocky ground as it came.

Clayton twisted the steering wheel. The engine labored, and with infinite slowness the truck crept out of the boulder's path. Shaking, Clayton watched the boulder bearing down. With one hand he pounded on the instrument panel.

"Move, baby, move!"

Booming hollowly, the boulder rolled past at a good thirty miles an hour.

"Too close," Clayton said to himself. He tried to turn the Brute back into the wind, toward the station. The Brute wouldn't do it.

The diesel labored and whined, trying to turn the big truck into the wind. And the wind, like a solid gray wall, pushed the truck away.

The windspeed indicator stood at 159 miles an hour.

"How are you doing?" Nerishev asked over the radio.

"Just great! Leave me alone, I'm busy."

Clayton set his brakes, unstrapped, and raced back to the engine. He adjusted timing and mixture, and hurried back to the controls.

"Hey, Nerishev! That engine's going to conk out!"

It was a full second before Nerishev answered. Then, very calmly, he asked, "What's wrong with it?"

"Sand!" Clayton said. "Particles driven at 159 miles an hour—sand in the bearings, injectors, everything. I'm going to make all the distance I can."

"And then?"

"Then I'll try to sail her back," Clayton said. "I just hope the mast will take it."

He turned his attention to the controls. At windspeeds like this, the truck had to be handled like a ship at sea. Clayton picked up speed with the wind on his quarter, then came about and slammed into the wind.

The Brute made it this time and crossed over onto the other tack.

It was the best he could do, Clayton decided. His windward distance would have to be made by tacking. He edged toward the eye of the wind. But at full throttle, the diesel couldn't bring him much closer than forty degrees.

For an hour the Brute forged ahead, tacking back and forth across the wind, covering three miles to make two. Miraculously, the engine kept on running. Clayton blessed the manufacturer and begged the diesel to hold out a little while longer.

Through a blinding screen of sand, he saw another Carellan

land ship. It was reefed down and heeled over precariously. But it forged steadily to windward and soon outdistanced him.

Lucky natives, Clayton thought—165 miles of wind was a sailing breeze to them!

The station, a gray half-sphere, came into sight ahead.

"I'm going to make it!" Clayton shouted. "Break out the rum, Nerishev! Papa's getting drunk tonight!"

The diesel chose that moment to break down for good.

Clayton swore violently as he set the brakes. What lousy luck! If the wind were behind him, he could roll in. But, of course, it had to be in front.

"What are you going to do now?" Nerishev asked.

"I'm going to sit here," Clayton said. "When the wind calms down to a hurricane, I'm going to walk home."

The Brute's twelve-ton mass was shaking and rattling in the wind blasts.

"You know," Clayton said, "I'm going to retire after this tour."

"That so! You really mean it?"

"Absolutely. I own a farm in Maryland, with frontage on Chesapeake Bay. You know what I'm going to do?"

"What?"

"I'm going to raise oysters. You see, the oyster—Hold it."

The station seemed to be drifting slowly upwind, away from him. Clayton rubbed his eyes, wondering if he was going crazy. Then he realized that in spite of its brakes, in spite of its streamlining, the truck was being pushed downwind, away from the station.

Angrily he shoved a button on his switchboard, releasing the port and starboard anchors. He heard the solid clunk of the anchors hitting the ground, heard the steel cables scrape and rattle. He let out a hundred and seventy feet of steel line, then set the winch brakes. The truck was holding again.

"I dropped the anchors," Clayton said.

"Are they holding?"

"So far." Clayton lighted a cigarette and leaned back in his padded chair. Every muscle in his body ached from tension. His eyelids twitched from watching the wind-lines converging on him. He closed his eyes and tried to relax.

The sound of the wind cut through the truck's steel plating. The wind howled and moaned, tugging at the truck, trying to find a hold on the smooth surface. At 169 miles an hour, the ventilator baffles blew out. He would be blinded, Clayton thought, if he weren't wearing sealed goggles, choked if he weren't breathing canned air. Dust swirled, thick and electric, within the Brute's cabin.

Pebbles, flung with the velocity of rifle bullets, splattered against the hull. They were striking harder now. He wondered how much more force they'd need before they started to pierce the armor plating.

At times like this, Clayton found it hard to maintain a common-sense attitude. He was painfully aware of the vulnerability of human flesh, appalled at the possibilities for violence in the Universe. What was he doing out here? Man's place was in the calm, still air of Earth.

"Are you all right?" Nerishev asked.

"Making out just great," Clayton said wearily. "How are things at the station?"

"Not so good. The whole structure's going into sympathetic vibration. Given enough time, the foundations could shatter."

"And they want to put a fuel station here!" Clayton said.

"Well, you know the problem. This is the only solid planet between Angarsa III and the South Ridge Belt. All the rest are gas giants."

"They better build their station in space."

"The cost—"

"Hell, man, it'll cost less to build another planet than to try to maintain a fuel base on this one." Clayton spat out a mouthful of dust. "I just want to get on that relief ship. How many natives at the station now?"

"About fifteen, in the shed."

"Any sign of violence?"

"No, but they're acting funny."

"How so?"

"I don't know," said Nerishev. "I just don't like it."

"Stay out of the shed, huh? You can't speak the language, anyhow, and I want you in one piece when I come back." He hesitated. "If I come back."

"You'll be fine," Nerishev said.

"Sure, I will. I—oh, Lord!"

"What's it? What's wrong?"

"Boulder coming down! Talk to you later!"

Clayton turned his attention to the boulder, a rapidly growing black speck to windward. It was heading directly toward his anchored and immobilized truck. He glanced at the windspeed indicator. Impossible—174 miles an hour! And yet, he reminded himself, winds in the stratospheric jet stream on Earth blew at two hundred miles an hour.

The boulder, as large as a house, still growing as it approached, was rolling directly toward him.

"Swerve! Turn!" Clayton shouted at the boulder, pounding the instrument panel with his fist.

The boulder was coming at him, straight as a ruler line, rolling right down the wind.

With a yell of agony, Clayton touched a button, releasing both anchors at the cable end. There was no time to winch them in, even assuming the winch could take the strain. Still the boulder grew.

Clayton released the brakes.

The Brute, shoved by a wind of one hundred and seventy-eight miles an hour, began to pick up speed. Within seconds he was rolling downwind at thirty-eight miles an hour, watching through the rear-vision mirror as the boulder overtook him.

Clayton twisted the steering wheel hard to the left. The truck tilted over precariously, swerved, fishtailed on the hard ground, and tried to turn itself over. Clayton fought the wheel, trying to bring the Brute back to equilibrium. He thought: *I'm probably the first man who ever jibed a twelve-ton truck!*

The boulder, looking like a whole city block, roared past. The heavy truck teetered for a moment, then came to rest on its six wheels.

"Clayton! What happened? Are you all right?"

"Fine," Clayton gasped. "But I had to slip the cables. I'm running downwind."

"Can you turn?"

"Almost knocked her over, trying."

"How far can you run?"

Clayton stared ahead. In the distance he could make out the dramatic black cliffs that rimmed the plain.

"I got about fifteen miles to go before I pile into the cliffs. Not much time, at the speed I'm traveling." He locked his brakes. The tires began to scream and the brake linings smoked furiously. But the wind, at one hundred and eighty-three miles an hour, didn't even notice the difference. His speed over the ground had gone up to forty-four miles an hour.

"Try sailing her out!" Nerishev said.

"She won't take it."

"Try, man! What else can you do? The wind's hit one hundred and eighty-five here. The whole station's shaking! Boulders are tearing up the whole post defense. I'm afraid some boulders are going to get through and flatten—"

"Stow it," Clayton said. "I got troubles of my own."

"I don't know if the station will stand! Clayton, listen to me. Try the—"

The radio suddenly went dead.

Clayton banged it a few times, then gave up. His speed over the ground had reached forty-nine miles an hour. The cliffs were already looming large before him.

"So all right," Clayton said. "Here we go." He released his last anchor. At the end of two hundred and fifty feet of steel cable, it slowed him to thirty miles an hour. The anchor was breaking and ripping through the ground like a jet-propelled plow.

Then Clayton turned on the sail mechanism. The sail was final insurance in case the engine failed. On Carella, a man could never walk home from a stranded vehicle.

The mast, a short, powerful steel pillar, extruded through a gasketed hole in the roof. Magnetic shrouds and stays snapped into place. From the mast fluttered a sail of link-woven metal. For a mainsheet, there was a three-part, flexible steel cable working through a winch.

The sail was only a few square feet in area. But it could drive a twelve-ton truck with brakes locked and an anchor dug in at the end of two hundred and fifty feet of line—

Easily—with the wind blowing one hundred and eighty-five miles an hour.

Clayton winched in the mainsheet, taking the wind behind his quarter. But the course wasn't good enough. He winched the sail in still more and turned closer to the wind.

With the super-hurricane on his beam, the ponderous truck heeled over, lifting one entire side into the air. Clayton released a few feet of mainsheet. The metal-link sail screamed and chattered as the wind whipped at it.

Driving now with just the sail's leading edge, Clayton was able to keep the truck on its feet and make good a course to windward.

In the rear-vision mirror he could see the black, jagged cliffs behind him. They were his lee shore, his coast of wrecks. But he was sailing out of the trap. Foot by foot, he was pulling away.

"That's my baby!" Clayton shouted to the battling Brute. His sense of victory snapped almost at once, for he heard an ear-splitting clang and something whizzed past his head. At one hundred and eighty-seven miles an hour, pebbles were piercing the truck's armor plating. It was the Carellan equivalent of a machine-gun barrage.

Desperately he clung to the steering wheel. He could hear the sail tearing itself apart. It was made out of the toughest flexible alloys available, but it wasn't going to hold up for long. The short, thick mast, supported by six heavy cables, was whipping like a light fishing rod.

His brake linings were worn out, and his speed over the ground came up to fifty-seven miles an hour.

He was too tired to think. He steered, his hands locked to the wheel, his slitted eyes glaring ahead into the storm.

The sail ripped with a scream. The tatters flogged for a moment, then brought the mast down. Wind gusts were approaching one hundred and ninety miles an hour.

The wind was now driving him back toward the cliffs. At one hundred and ninety-two miles an hour of wind, the Brute was lifted bodily, thrown for a dozen yards, slammed back on its wheels. A front tire blew, then two rear ones. Clayton put his head on his arms and waited for the end.

Suddenly the Brute stopped short. Clayton was flung forward. His safety belt checked him for a moment, then snapped. He banged against the instrument panel and fell back, dazed and bleeding.

He lay on the floor, half conscious, trying to figure out what had happened. Slowly he pulled himself back into the seat, foggily aware that he hadn't broken any limbs. His stomach was one great bruise. His mouth was bleeding.

At last, looking in the rear-vision mirror, he saw what had happened. The emergency anchor, trailing at the end of two hundred and fifty feet of steel cable, had caught in a deep outcropping of rock. A fouled anchor had brought him up short, less than half a mile from the cliffs. He was saved—

For the moment, at least.

But the wind hadn't given up. The one-hundred-and-ninety-three-mile-an-hour wind lifted the truck bodily and slammed it down again and again. The steel cable hummed like a taut guitar string. Clayton wrapped his arms and legs around the seat. He couldn't hold on much longer. And if he let go, the madly leaping Brute would smear him over the walls like toothpaste—

If the cable didn't part first and send the truck hurtling into the cliffs.

He held on. At the top of one swing, he caught a glimpse of the windspeed indicator. The sight of it sickened him. He was through, finished, done for. How could he be expected to hold on through the force of a one hundred and eighty-seven-mile-an-hour wind? It was too much.

One hundred and eighty-seven miles an hour? That meant that the wind was falling!

As he watched, the dial hand slowly crept down. At one hundred and sixty miles an hour, the truck stopped slamming and lay quietly at the end of its anchor line. At one hundred and fifty-three, the wind veered—a sure sign that the blow was nearly over.

When it had dropped to one hundred and forty-two miles an hour, Clayton allowed himself the luxury of passing out.

Carellan natives came out for him later in the day. Skillfully they maneuvered two big land ships up to the Brute, fastened on their long vines—which tested out stronger than steel—and towed the derelict truck back to the station.

They brought him into the receiving shed, and Nerishev carried him into the station's dead air.

"You didn't break anything except a couple of teeth," said Nerishev. "But there isn't an unbruised inch on you."

"We came through it," Clayton said.

"Just. Our boulder defense is completely flattened. The station took two direct hits from boulders and barely contained them. I've checked the foundations; they're badly strained. Another blow like that—"

"—and we'd make out somehow. Us Earth lads, we come through! That was the worst in eight months. Four months more, and the relief ship comes! Buck up, Nerishev. Come with me."

"Where are we going?"

"I want to talk to that damned Smanik!"

They came into the shed. It was filled to overflowing with Carellans. Outside, in the lee of the station, several dozen land ships were moored.

"Smanik!" Clayton called. "What's going on here?"

"It is the Festival of Summer," Smanik said. "Our great yearly holiday."

"Hm. What about that blow? What did you think of it?"

"I would classify it as a moderate gale," said Smanik. "Nothing dangerous, but somewhat unpleasant for sailing."

"Unpleasant! I hope you get your forecasts a little more accurate in the future."

"One cannot always outguess the weather," Smanik said. "It is regrettable that my last forecast should be wrong."

"Your *last*? How come?"

"These people," Smanik said, gesturing around him, "are my entire tribe. We have celebrated the Festival of Summer. Now summer is ended and we must go away."

"Where to?"

"To the caverns in the far west. They are two weeks' sail from here. We will live in the caverns for three months. In that way, we will find safety."

Clayton had a sudden sinking feeling in his stomach. "Safety from what, Smanik?"

"I told you. Summer is over. We need safety now from the winds—the powerful storm winds of winter."

"What is it?" Nerishev said.

"Just a moment." Clayton thought quickly of the super-hurricane he had just passed through, which Smanik had classified as a moderate and harmless gale. He thought of their immobility, the ruined Brute, the strained foundations of the station, the flattened boulder barrier, the relief ship four months away. "Could we go with you in the land ships, Smanik, and take refuge in the caverns?"

"Of course," said Smanik hospitably.

"No, we couldn't," Clayton answered himself. "We'd need extra oxygen, our own food, a water supply—"

"What's the matter?" Nerishev asked. "What did he say to make you look like that?"

"He says the *really* big winds are just coming," Clayton replied.

The two men looked at each other.

Outside, a wind was rising.

THE ROBOT WHO LOOKED
LIKE ME

Snaithe's Robotorama is an unprepossessing shop on Boulevard KB22 near the Uhuru Cutoff in Greater New Newark. It is sandwiched between an oxygenator factory and a protein store. The storefront display is what you would expect: three full-size humanoid robots with frozen smiles, dressed occupationally— Model PB2, the French Chef; Model LR3, the British Nanny; Model JX5, the Italian Gardener. All of Them Ready to Serve You and Bring a Touch of Old-World Graciousness into Your Home.

I entered and went through the dusty showroom into the workshop, which looked like an uneasy combination of slaughterhouse and giant's workshop. Heads, arms, legs, and torsos were stacked on shelves or propped in corners. The parts looked uncannily human except for the dangling wires.

Snaithe came out of the storeroom to greet me. He was a little gray worm of a man with a lantern jaw and large red hands. He was some kind of foreigner—they're always the ones who make the best bootleg robots.

He said, "It's ready, Mr. Watson." (My name is not Watson, Snaithe's name is not Snaithe. All names have been changed here to protect the guilty.)

Snaithe led me to a corner of the workshop and stopped in front of a robot whose head was draped in a towel. He whisked off the towel.

It is not enough to say that the robot looked like me; physically, this robot *was* me, exactly and unmistakably, feature for feature, right down to the textures of skin and hair. I studied that face, seeing as if for the first time the hint of brutality in the firmly cut features, the glitter of impatience in the deepset eyes. Yes, that was me. I paid Snaithe and told him to deliver it to my apartment. So far, everything was going according to plan.

I live in Manhattan's Upper Fifth Vertical. It is an expensive position, but I don't mind paying extra for a sky view. My home is also my office. I am an interplanetary broker specializing in certain classes of rare mineral speculation.

Like any other man who wishes to maintain his position in this world, I keep to a tight schedule. Work consumes most of my life, but everything else is allotted its proper time and place. I give three hours a week to sexuality, using the Doris Jens Executive Sex Plan. I give two hours a week to friendship and two more to leisure. I plug into the Sleep-Inducer for my nightly quota of 6.8 hours, and also use that time to absorb the relevant literature in my field via hypnopaedics. And so on.

Everything I do is scheduled. I worked out a comprehensive scheme years ago with the assistance of the Total Lifeplan people, punched it into my personal computer, and have kept to it ever since.

Of course, the plan is capable of modification. Special provisions have been made for illness, war, and natural disasters. The plan also supplies two separate sub-programs for incorporation into the main plan. Sub-program One posits a wife and revises my schedule to allow four hours a week of interaction time with her. Sub-program Two assumes a wife and one child and calls for an additional two hours a week. Through careful reprogramming, these sub-programs will entail a loss of no more than 2.3 percent and 2.9 percent of my productivity, respectively.

I had decided to marry at age 32.5 and to obtain my wife from the Guarantee Trust Matrimonial Agency, an organization with impeccable credentials. But then something quite unexpected occurred.

I was using one of my Leisure Hours to attend the wedding of one of my friends. His fiancée's maid of honor was named Elaine.

She was a slender, vivacious girl with sun-streaked blond hair and a small, delicious figure. I went home and thought no more about her. Or I *thought* I would think no more about her. But over the following days and nights her image remained obsessively before my eyes. My appetite fell off and I began sleeping badly. My computer checked out the relevant data and told me that I might conceivably be in love.

I was not entirely displeased. Being in love can be a positive factor in establishing a good relationship. I had Elaine checked out by Discretion, Inc., and found her to be eminently suitable. I hired Mr. Happiness, the well-known Go-Between, to propose for me and make the usual arrangements.

Mr. Happiness—a tiny, white-haired gentleman with a twinkling smile—came back with bad news. "The young lady seems to be a traditionalist," he said. "She expects to be courted."

"What does that entail specifically?" I asked.

"It means that you must videophone her and set up an appointment, take her out to dinner, then to a place of public entertainment, and so forth."

"My schedule doesn't allow time for that sort of thing," I said. "Still, if it's absolutely necessary, I suppose I could wedge it in next Thursday between nine and twelve P.M."

"That would make an excellent beginning," Mr. Happiness said.

"Beginning? How many evenings am I supposed to spend like that?"

Mr. Happiness figured that a proper courtship would require a minimum of three evenings a week and would continue for two months.

"Ridiculous!" I said. "The young lady seems to have a great deal of idle time on her hands."

"Not at all," Mr. Happiness assured me. "Elaine has a busy, completely scheduled life, just like any educated person in this day and age. Her time is completely taken up by her job, family, charities, artistic pursuits, politics, education, and so forth."

"Then why does she insist upon this time-consuming courtship?"

"It seems to be a matter of principle. That is to say, she wants it."

"Is she given to other irrationalities?"

Mr. Happiness sighed. "Not really. But she *is* a woman, you know."

I thought about it during my next Leisure Hour. There seemed to be just two alternatives. I could give up Elaine or I could do as she desired, losing an estimated 17 percent of my income during the courtship period and spending my evenings in a manner I considered silly, boring, and unproductive.

Both alternatives were unacceptable. I was at an impasse.

I swore. I hit the desk with my fist, upsetting an antique ashtray. Gordon, one of my robot secretaries, heard the commotion and hurried into the room. "Is there anything the matter, sir?" he asked.

Gordon is one of Sperry's Deluxe Limited Personalized Androids, the twelfth in a production run of twenty-five. He is tall and thin and walks with a slight stoop and looks a little like Leslie Howard. You would not know he was artificial except for the government-required stamps on his forehead and hands. As I looked at him, the solution to my problem came to me in a sudden flash of inspiration.

"Gordon," I said slowly, "would you happen to know who handcrafts the best individualized robots?"

"Snaithe of Greater New Newark," he replied without hesitation.

Snaithe agreed to build a robot without government markings, identical to me, and capable of duplicating my behavior patterns. I paid a great deal for this, but that was all right. I had plenty of money, but practically no time to spend.

The robot, sent via pneumo-express, was at my apartment when I arrived. My computer transmitted the relevant data directly to the robot's memory tapes. Then I punched in a courtship plan and ran the necessary tests. The results were even better than I had expected. Elated, I called Elaine and made a date with her for that evening.

During the rest of the day I worked on the spring market offers, which had begun to pile up. At 8.00 P.M. I dispatched Charles II, as I had come to call the robot. Then I took a brief nap and went back to work.

Charles II returned promptly at midnight, as programmed. I did not have to question him; the events of the evening were recorded on the miniature concealed movie camera that Snaithe had built into his left eye. I watched and listened to the beginning of my courtship with mixed emotions.

It went beyond impersonation; the robot *was* me, right down to the way I clear my throat before I speak and rub my forefinger against my thumb when I am thinking. I noticed for the first time that my laugh was unpleasantly close to a giggle; I decided to phase that and certain other annoying mannerisms out of me and Charles II.

Still, taken all together, I thought that the experiment had come off extremely well. I was pleased. My work and my courtship were both proceeding with high efficiency. I had achieved an ancient dream; I was a single ego served by two bodies. Who could ask for more?

What marvelous evenings we all had! My experiences were vicarious, of course, but genuinely moving all the same. I can still remember my first quarrel with Elaine, how beautiful and stubborn she was, and how deliciously we made up afterward.

As a matter of fact, that "making up" raised certain problems. I had programmed Charles II to proceed to a certain discreet point of physical intimacy, but no further. Now I learned that one person cannot plan out every move of a courtship involving an autonomous being, especially if that being is a woman. For the sake of verisimilitude, I had to permit the robot more intimacies than I had previously thought advisable.

After the first shock, I did not find this unpalatable. Quite the contrary—I might as well admit that I became deeply interested in the robot's movies of myself and Elaine. I suppose some stuffy psychiatrist would call this voyeurism, or worse. But that would ignore the deeper philosophical implications. After all, what man has not dreamed of being able to view himself as he acts in the world? It is a common fantasy to imagine one's own hidden cameras recording one's every move. Given the chance, who could resist the extraordinary privilege of being simultaneously actor and audience?

My drama with Elaine developed in a direction that surprised me. A quality of desperation began to show itself, a love-madness of which I would never have believed myself capable. Our evenings became imbued with a quality of delicious sadness, a sense of imminent loss. Sometimes we didn't speak at all, just held hands and looked at each other. And once Elaine wept for no discernible reason, and I stroked her hair, and she said to me, "What can we do?" and I looked at her and did not reply.

I am perfectly aware that these things happened to the robot, of course. But the robot was an aspect or attribute of me—my shadow, twin, double, animus, doppelgänger. He was a projection of my personality into a particular situation; whatever happened to him became my experience. Metaphysically there can be no doubt of this.

It was all very interesting. But at last I had to bring the courtship to an end. It was time for Elaine and me to plan our marriage. Accordingly, exactly two months after its inception, I told the robot to propose a wedding date and to terminate the courtship as of that night.

"You have done extremely well," I told him. "When this is over, you will receive a new personality, plastic surgery, and a respected place in my organization."

"Thank you, sir," he said. His face was unreadable, as is my own. I heard no hint of anything in his voice except perfect obedience. He left, carrying my latest gift to Elaine.

Midnight came, and Charles II didn't return. An hour later I felt disturbed. By 3:00 A.M. I was in a state of agitation, experiencing erotic and masochistic fantasies, seeing the robot with Elaine in every conceivable combination of mechano-physical lewdness. The minutes dragged by, Charles II still did not return, and my fantasies became sadistic. I imagined the slow and terrible ways in which I would take my revenge on both of them—the robot for his presumption and Elaine for her stupidity in being deceived by a mechanical substitute for a real man.

The long night crept slowly by. At last I fell into a fitful sleep.

I awoke early. Charles II still had not returned. I canceled my appointments for the entire morning and rushed over to Elaine's apartment.

"Charles!" she said. "What an unexpected pleasure!"

I entered her apartment with an air of nonchalance. I was determined to remain calm until I had learned exactly what had happened last night. Beyond that, I didn't know what I might do.

"Unexpected?" I said. "Didn't I mention last night that I might come by for breakfast?"

"You may have," Elaine said. "To tell the truth, I was much too emotional to remember everything that you said."

"But you do remember what happened?"

She blushed prettily. "Of course, Charles. I still have the marks on my arm."

"Do you, indeed!"

"And my mouth is bruised. Why do you grind your teeth that way?"

"I haven't had my coffee yet," I told her.

She led me into the breakfast nook and poured coffee. I drained mine in two gulps and asked, "Do I really seem to you like the man I was last night?"

"Of course," she said. "I've come to know your moods. Charles, what's wrong? Did something upset you last night?"

"Yes!" I cried wildly. "I was just remembering how you danced naked on the terrace." I stared at her, waiting for her to deny it.

"It was only for a moment," Elaine said. "And I wasn't really naked, you know, I had on my body stocking. And you asked me to do it."

"Yes," I said. "Yes, yes." I was confused. I decided to continue probing. "But then, when you drank champagne from my desert boot—"

"I only took a sip," she said. "Was it too daring?"

"You were splendid," I said, feeling chilled all over. "I suppose it's unfair of me to remind you of these things now . . ."

"Nonsense, I like to talk about it."

"What about that absurd moment when we exchanged clothing?"

"That *was* wicked of us," she said, laughing.

I stood up. "Elaine," I said, "just exactly what in hell were you doing last night?"

"What a question," she said. "I was with you. But, Charles—those things you just spoke about—"

"I made them up."

"Then who were *you* with last night?"

"I was home, alone." I told her the grim truth.

Elaine thought about that for a moment. Then she said, "I'm afraid I have a confession to make."

I folded my arms and waited.

"I too was home alone last night."

I raised one eyebrow. "And the other nights?"

She took a deep breath. "Charles, I can no longer deceive you. I really had wanted an old-fashioned courtship. But when the time came, I couldn't seem to fit it into my schedule. You see, it was finals time in my Aztec pottery class, and I had just been elected chairwoman of the Aleutian Assistance League, and my new boutique needed special attention—"

"So what did you do?"

"Well—I simply couldn't say to you, 'Look, let's drop the courtship and just get married.' After all, I hardly knew you."

"*What did you do?*"

She sighed. "I knew several girls who had gotten themselves into this kind of spot. They went to this really clever robot-maker named Snaithe . . . Why are you laughing?"

I said, "I too have a confession to make. I have used Mr. Snaithe too."

"Charles! You actually sent a *robot* here to court me? How could you! Suppose I had really been me?"

"I don't think either of us is in a position to express such indignation. Did your robot come home last night?"

"No. I thought that Elaine II and you—"

I shook my head. "I have never met Elaine II, and you have never met Charles II. What happened, apparently, is that our robots met, courted, and now have run away together."

"But robots can't do that!"

"Ours did. I will find out what happened. But now, Elaine, let us think of ourselves. I propose that at our earliest possible convenience we get married."

"Yes, Charles," she murmured. We kissed. We touched. And then, gently, lovingly, we began to coordinate our schedules.

I was able to trace the runaway robots to Kennedy Spaceport.

They had taken the shuttle to Space Platform Five, and changed there for the Centauri Express. I didn't bother trying to investigate further. They could be on any one of a dozen worlds.

Elaine and I were deeply affected by the experience. We realized that we had become too intent upon productivity, too neglectful of the simple, ancient pleasures. We acted upon this insight, taking an additional hour out of every day in which simply to be with each other. Our friends consider us romantic fools, but we don't care. We know that Charles II and Elaine II, our alter egos, would approve.

There is only this to add. One night Elaine woke up in a state of hysteria. She had had a nightmare. In it she had dreamed that Charles II and Elaine II were the real people who had escaped the inhumanity of earth to some simpler and more rewarding world. And we were the robots they had left behind, programmed to believe that we were human.

I told Elaine how ridiculous that was. It took me a long time to convince her, but at last I did. We are happy now and we lead productive and loving lives. Now I must stop writing this and get back to work.

THE MNEMONE

It was a great day for our village when the Mnemone arrived. But we did not know him at first, because he concealed his identity from us. He said that his name was Edgar Smith, and that he was a repairer of furniture. We accepted both statements at face value, as we receive all statements. Until then, we had never known anyone who had anything to conceal.

He came into our village on foot, carrying a knapsack and a battered suitcase. He looked at our stores and houses. He walked up to me and asked, "Where is the police station?"

"We have none," I told him.

"Indeed? Then where is the local constable or sheriff?"

"Luke Johnson was constable here for nineteen years," I told him. "But Luke died two years ago. We reported this to the county seat as the law requires. But no one has been sent yet to take his place."

"So you police yourselves?"

"We live quietly," I said. "There's no crime in this village. Why do you ask?"

"Because I wanted to know," Smith said, not very helpfully. "A little knowledge is not as dangerous as a lot of ignorance, eh? Never mind, my blank-faced young friend. I like the look of your village. I like the wooden frame buildings and the stately elms. I like—"

"The stately what?" I asked him.

"Elms," he said, gesturing at the tall trees that lined Main Street. "Didn't you know their name?"

"It was forgotten," I said, embarrassed.

"No matter. Many things have been lost, and some have been hidden. Still, there's no harm in the name of a tree. Or is there?"

"No harm at all," I said. "Elm trees."

"Keep that to yourself," he said, winking. "It's only a morsel, but there's no telling when it might prove useful. I shall stay for a time in this village."

"You are most welcome," I said. "Especially now, at harvest time."

Smith looked at me sharply. "I have nothing to do with that. Did you take me for an itinerant apple-picker?"

"I didn't think about it one way or another. What will you do here?"

"I repair furniture," Smith said.

"Not much call for that in a village this size," I told him.

"Then maybe I'll find something else to turn my hand to." He grinned at me suddenly. "For the moment, however, I require lodgings."

I took him to the Widow Marsini's house, and there he rented her large back bedroom with porch and separate entrance. He arranged to take all of his meals there, too.

His arrival let loose a flood of gossip and speculation. Mrs. Marsini felt that Smith's questions about the police showed that he himself was a policeman. "They work like that," she said. "Or they used to. Back fifty years ago, every third person you met was some kind of a policeman. Sometimes even your own children were policemen, and they'd be as quick to arrest you as they would a stranger. Quicker!"

But others pointed out that all of that had happened long ago, that life was quiet now, that policemen were rarely seen, even though they were still believed to exist.

But why had Smith come? Some felt that he was here to take something from us. "What other reason is there for a stranger to come to a village like this?" And others felt that he had come to give us something, citing the same argument.

But we didn't know. We simply had to wait until Smith chose to reveal himself.

He moved among us as other men do. He had knowledge of the outside world; he seemed to us a far-traveling man. And slowly he began to give us clues as to his identity.

One day I took him to a rise that looks out over our valley. This was at mid-autumn, a pretty time. Smith looked out and declared it a fine sight. "It puts me in mind of that famous tag from William James," he said. "How does it go? 'Scenery seems to wear in one's consciousness better than any other element in life.' Eh? Apt, don't you think?"

"Who is or was this William James?" I asked.

Smith winked at me. "Did I mention that name? Slip of the tongue, my lad."

But that was not the last "slip of the tongue." A few days later I pointed out an ugly hillside covered with second-growth pine, low coarse shrubbery, and weeds. "This burned five years ago," I told him. "Now it serves no purpose at all."

"Yes, I see," Smith said. "And yet—as Montaigne tells us —there is nothing useless in nature, not even uselessness itself."

And still later, walking through the village, he paused to admire Mrs. Vogel's late-blooming peonies. He said, "Flowers do indeed have the glances of children and the mouths of old men—as Chazal pointed out."

Toward the end of the week, a few of us got together in the back of Edmonds's store and began to discuss Mr. Edgar Smith. I mentioned the things he had said to me. Bill Edmonds remembered that Smith had cited a man named Emerson to the effect that solitude was impracticable, and society fatal. Billy Foreclough told us that Smith had quoted to him from Ion of Chios to the effect that Luck differs greatly from Art, yet creates many things that are like it. And Mrs. Gordon suddenly came up with the best of the lot; a statement Smith told her was made by the great Leonardo da Vinci: vows begin when hope dies.

We looked at each other and were silent. It was evident to everyone that Mr. Edgar Smith—or whatever his real name might be—was no simple repairer of furniture.

At last I put into words what we were all thinking. "Friends," I said, "this man appears to be a Mnemone."

Mnemones as a distinct class came into prominence during the last year of the War that Ended All Wars. Their self-proclaimed function was to remember works of literature that were in danger of being lost, destroyed, or suppressed.

At first the government welcomed their efforts, encouraged them, even rewarded them with pensions and grants. But when the war ended and the reign of the Police Presidents began, government policy changed. A general decision was made to jettison the unhappy past and build a new world in and of the present. Disturbing influences were to be struck down without mercy.

Right-thinking men agreed that most literature was superfluous at best, subversive at worst. After all, was it necessary to preserve the mouthings of a thief like Villon, a homosexual like Genet, a schizophrenic like Kafka? Did we need to retain a thousand divergent opinions, and then to explain why they were false? Under such a bombardment of influences, how could anyone be expected to respond in an appropriate and approved manner? How could one ever get people to obey orders?

The government knew that if everyone obeyed orders, everything would be all right.

But to achieve this blessed state, divergent and ambiguous input had to be abolished. The biggest single source of confusing input came from historical and artistic verbiage. Therefore, history was to be rewritten, and literature was to be regularized, pruned, tamed, made orderly, or abolished entirely.

The Mnemones were ordered to leave the past strictly alone. They objected to this most vehemently, of course. Discussions continued until the government lost patience. A final order was issued, with heavy penalties for those who would not comply.

Most of the Mnemones gave up their work. A few only pretended to, however. These few became an elusive, persecuted minority of itinerant teachers, endlessly on the move, selling their knowledge where and when they could.

We questioned the man who called himself Edgar Smith, and he revealed himself to us as a Mnemone. He gave immediate and lavish gifts to our village:

Two sonnets by William Shakespeare.

Job's Lament to God.

One entire act of a play by Aristophanes.

This done, he set himself up in business, offering his wares for sale to the villagers.

He drove a hard bargain with Mr. Ogden, forcing him to exchange an entire pig for two lines of Simonides.

Mr. Bellington, the recluse, gave up his gold watch for a saying by Heraclitus. He considered it a fair exchange.

Old Mrs. Heath exchanged a pound of goose feathers for three stanzas from a poem entitled "Atalanta in Calydon," by a man named Swinburne.

Mr. Mervin, who owns the restaurant, purchased an entire short ode by Catullus, a description of Cicero by Tacitus, and the lines from Homer's *Catalogue of Ships.* This cost him his entire savings.

I had little in the way of money or property. But for services rendered, I received a paragraph of Montaigne, a saying ascribed to Socrates, and ten fragmentary lines by Anacreon.

An unexpected customer was Mr. Lind, who came stomping into the Mnemone's office one crisp winter morning. Mr. Lind was short, red-faced, and easily moved to anger. He was the most successful farmer in the area, a man of no nonsense who believed only in what he could see and touch. He was the last man you'd ever expect to buy the Mnemone's wares. Even a policeman would have been a more likely prospect.

"Well, well," Lind began, rubbing his hands briskly together. "I've heard about you and your invisible merchandise."

"And I've heard about you," the Mnemone said, with a touch of malice to his voice. "Do you have business with me?"

"Yes, by God, I do!" Lind cried. "I want to buy some of your fancy old words."

"I am genuinely surprised," the Mnemone said. "Who would ever have dreamed of finding a law-abiding citizen like yourself in a situation like this, buying goods that are not only invisible, but illegal as well!"

"It's not my choice," Lind said. "I have come here only to please my wife, who is not well these days."

"Not well? I'm not surprised," the Mnemone said. "An ox would sicken under the work load you give her."

"Man, that's no concern of yours!" Lind said furiously.

"But it is," the Mnemone said. "In my profession we do not give out words at random. We fit our lines to the recipient. Sometimes we find nothing appropriate, and therefore sell nothing at all."

"I thought you sold your wares to all buyers."

"You have been misinformed. I know a Pindaric ode I would not sell to you for any price."

"Man, you can't talk to me that way!"

"I speak as I please. You are free to take your business somewhere else."

Mr. Lind glowered and pouted and sulked, but there was nothing he could do. At last he said, "I didn't mean to lose my temper. Will you sell me something for my wife? Last week was her birthday, but I didn't remember it until just now."

"You are a pretty fellow," the Mnemone said. "As sentimental as a mink, and almost as loving as a shark! Why come to me for her present? Wouldn't a sturdy butter churn be more suitable?"

"No, not so," Lind said, his voice flat and quiet. "She lies in bed this past month and barely eats. I think she is dying."

"And she asked for words of mine?"

"She asked me to bring her something pretty."

The Mnemone nodded. "Dying! Well, I'll offer no condolences

to the man who drove her to the grave, and I've not much sympathy for the woman who picked a creature like you. But I do have something she will like, a gaudy thing that will ease her passing. It'll cost you a mere thousand dollars."

"God in heaven, man! Have you nothing cheaper?"

"Of course I have," the Mnemone said. "I have a decent little comic poem in Scots dialect with the middle gone from it; yours for two hundred dollars. And I have one stanza of a commemorative ode to General Kitchener, which you can have for ten dollars."

"Is there nothing else?"

"Not for you."

"Well . . . I'll take the thousand-dollar item," Lind said. "Yes, by God, I will! Sara is worth every penny of it!"

"Handsomely said, albeit tardily. Now pay attention. Here it is."

The Mnemone leaned back, closed his eyes, and began to recite. Lind listened, his face tense with concentration. And I also listened, cursing my untrained memory and praying that I would not be ordered from the room.

It was a long poem, and very strange and beautiful. I still possess it all. But what comes most often to my mind are the lines

> Charm'd magic casements, opening on the foam
> Of perilous seas, in faery lands forlorn.

We are men: queer beasts with strange appetites. Who would have imagined us to possess a thirst for the ineffable? What was the hunger that could lead a man to exchange three bushels of corn for a single saying of the Gnostics? To feast on the spiritual, this seems to be what men must do; but who could have imagined it of *us*? Who would have thought us sufferers of malnutrition because we had no Plato! Can a man grow sickly from lack of Plutarch, or die from an Aristotle deficiency?

I cannot deny it. I myself have seen the results of abruptly withdrawing an addict from Strindberg.

Our past is a necessary part of us, and to take away that part is to mutilate us irreparably. I know a man who achieved courage only after he was told of Epaminondas, and a woman who became beautiful only after she heard of Aphrodite.

The Mnemone had a natural enemy in our schoolteacher, Mr. Vich, who taught the authorized version of all things. The Mnemone also had an enemy in Father Dulces, who ministered to our spiritual needs in the Universal Patriotic Church of America.

The Mnemone defied both of our authorities. He told us that many of the things they taught us were false, both in content and in ascription, or were perversions of famous sayings, rephrased to say the opposite of the original author's intention. The Mnemone struck at the very foundations of our civilization when he denied the validity of the following sayings:

—Most men lead lives of quiet aspiration.
—The unexamined life is most worth living.
—Know thyself within approved limits.

We listened to the Mnemone, we considered what he told us. Slowly, painfully, we began to think again, to reason, to examine things for ourselves. And when we did this, we also began to hope.

The neoclassical flowering of our village was brief, intense, sudden, and a delight to us all. Only one thing warned me that the end might be imminent. There was a day in early spring when I had been helping one of the neighbors' children with his lessons. He had a new edition of Dunster's *General History*, and I glanced through the section on the Silver Age of Rome. It took me a few minutes to realize that Cicero had been omitted. He wasn't even listed in the index, though many lesser poets and orators were. I wondered what retrospective crime he had been found guilty of.

And then one day, quite suddenly, the end came. Three men entered our village. They wore gray uniforms with brass insignia.

Their faces were blank and broad, and they walked stiffly in heavy black boots. They went everywhere together, and they always stood very close to one another. They asked no questions. They spoke to no one. They knew exactly where the Mnemone lived, and they consulted a map and then walked directly there.

They were in Smith's room for perhaps ten minutes.

Then the three policemen came out again into the street, all three of them walking together like one man. Their eyes darted right and left; they seemed frightened. They left our village quickly.

We buried Smith on a rise of land overlooking the valley, near the place where he had first quoted William James, among late-blooming flowers that had the glances of children and the mouths of old men.

Mrs. Blake, in a most untypical gesture, has named her latest-born Cicero. Mr. Lind refers to his apple orchard as Xanadu. I myself have become an avowed Zoroastrian, entirely on faith, since I know nothing about that religion except that it directs a man to speak the truth and shoot the arrow straight.

But these are futile gestures. The truth is, we have lost Xanadu irretrievably, lost Cicero, lost Zoroaster. And what else have we lost? What great battles were fought, cities built, jungles conquered? What songs were sung, what dreams were dreamed? We see now, too late, that our intelligence is a plant which must be rooted in the rich fields of the past.

In brief, our collective memories, the richest part of us, have been taken away, and we are poor indeed. In return for castles of the mind, our rulers have given us mud hovels palpable to the touch—a bad exchange for us.

The Mnemone, by official proclamation, never existed. By fiat he is ranked as an inexplicable dream or delusion—like Cicero. And I who write these lines, I too will soon cease to exist. Like Cicero and the Mnemone, my reality will also be proscribed.

Nothing will help me; the truth is too fragile, it shatters too easily in the iron hands of our rulers. I shall not be revenged. I shall not even be remembered. For if the great Zoroaster himself could be reduced to a single rememberer, and that one killed, then what hope is there for me?

Generation of cows! Sheep! Pigs! We have not even the spirit of a goat! If Epaminondas was a man, if Achilles was a man, if Socrates was a man, then are we also men?

WARM

Anders lay on his bed, fully dressed except for his shoes and black bow tie, contemplating, with a certain uneasiness, the evening before him. In twenty minutes he would pick up Judy at her apartment, and that was the uneasy part of it.

He had realized, only seconds ago, that he was in love with her.

Well, he'd tell her. The evening would be memorable. He would propose, there would be kisses, and the seal of acceptance would, figuratively speaking, be stamped across his forehead.

Not too pleasant an outlook, he decided. It really would be much more comfortable not to be in love. What had done it? A look, a touch, a thought? It didn't take much, he knew, and stretched his arms for a thorough yawn.

"Help me!" a voice said.

His muscles spasmed, cutting off the yawn in mid-moment. He sat upright on the bed, then grinned and lay back again.

"You must help me!" the voice insisted.

Anders sat up, reached for a polished shoe, and fitted it on, giving his full attention to the tying of the laces.

"Can you hear me?" the voice asked. "You can, can't you?"

That did it. "Yes, I can hear you," Anders said, still in a high good humor. "Don't tell me you're my guilty subconscious, attacking me for a childhood trauma I never bothered to resolve. I suppose you want me to join a monastery."

"I don't know what you're talking about," the voice said. "I'm no one's subconscious. I'm *me*. Will you help me?"

Anders believed in voices as much as anyone; that is, he didn't believe in them at all, until he heard them. Swiftly he catalogued the possibilities. Schizophrenia was the best answer, of course, and one in which his colleagues would concur. But Anders had a lamentable confidence in his own sanity. In which case—

"Who are you?" he asked.

"I don't know," the voice answered.

Anders realized that the voice was speaking within his own mind. Very suspicious.

"You don't know who you are," Anders stated. "Very well. *Where* are you?"

"I don't know that, either." The voice paused, and went on. "Look, I know how ridiculous this must sound. Believe me, I'm in some sort of limbo. I don't know how I got here or who I am, but I want desperately to get out. Will you help me?"

Still fighting the idea of a voice speaking within his head, Anders knew that his next decision was vital. He had to accept—or reject—his own sanity.

He accepted it.

"All right," Anders said, lacing the other shoe. "I'll grant that you're a person in trouble, and that you're in some sort of telepathic contact with me. Is there anything else you can tell me?"

"I'm afraid not," the voice said, with infinite sadness. "You'll have to find out for yourself."

"Can you contact anyone else?"

"No."

"Then how can you talk with me?"

"I don't know."

Anders walked to his bureau mirror and adjusted his black bow tie, whistling softly under his breath. Having just discovered that he was in love, he wasn't going to let a little thing like a voice in his mind disturb him.

"I really don't see how I can be of any help," Anders said, brushing a bit of lint from his jacket. "You don't know where you are, and there don't seem to be any distinguishing landmarks. How am I to find you?" He turned and looked around the room to see if he had forgotten anything.

"I'll know when you're close," the voice said. "You were warm just then."

"Just then?" All he had done was look around the room. He did so again, turning his head slowly. Then it happened.

The room, from one angle, looked different. It was suddenly a mixture of muddled colors, instead of the carefully blended pastel shades he had selected. The lines of wall, floor, and ceiling were strangely off proportion, zigzag, unrelated.

Then everything went back to normal.

"You were *very* warm," the voice said.

Anders resisted the urge to scratch his head, for fear of disarranging his carefully combed hair. What he had seen wasn't so strange. Everyone sees one or two things in his life that make him doubt his normalcy, doubt his sanity, doubt his very existence. For a moment the orderly Universe is disarranged and the fabric of belief is ripped.

But the moment passes.

Anders remembered once, as a boy, awakening in his room in the middle of the night. How strange everything had looked! Chairs, table, all out of proportion, swollen in the dark. The ceiling pressing down, as in a dream.

But that also had passed.

"Well, old man," he said, "if I get warm again, tell me."

"I will," the voice in his head whispered. "I'm sure you'll find me."

"I'm glad you're so sure," Anders said gaily, and switched off the lights and left.

Lovely and smiling, Judy greeted him at the door. Looking at her, Anders sensed her knowledge of the moment. Had she felt the change in him, or predicted it? Or was love making him grin like an idiot?

"Would you like a before-party drink?" she asked.

He nodded, and she led him across the room, to the improbable green and yellow couch. Sitting down, Anders decided he would tell her when she came back with the drink. No use in putting off the fatal moment. A lemming in love, he told himself.

"You're getting warm again," the voice said.

He had almost forgotten his invisible friend. Or fiend, as the case could well be. What would Judy say if she knew he was hearing voices? Little things like that, he reminded himself, often break up the best of romances.

"Here," she said, handing him a drink.

Still smiling, he noticed. The Number Two smile—to a prospective suitor, provocative and understanding. It had been preceded, in their relationship, by the Number One nice-girl smile, the don't-misunderstand-me smile, to be worn on all occasions, until the correct words have been mumbled.

"That's right," the voice said. "It's in how you look at things."

Look at what? Anders glanced at Judy, annoyed at his thoughts. If he was going to play the lover, let him play it. Even through the astigmatic haze of love, he was able to appreciate her blue-gray eyes, her fine skin (if one overlooked a tiny blemish on the left temple), her lips, slightly reshaped by lipstick.

"How did your classes go today?" she asked.

Well, of course she'd ask that, Anders thought. Love is marking time.

"All right," he said. "Teaching psychology to young apes—"

"Oh, come now!"

"Warmer," the voice said.

What's the matter with me? Anders wondered. She really is a lovely girl. The *gestalt* that is Judy, a pattern of thoughts, expressions, movements, making up the girl I—

I what?

Love?

Anders shifted his long body uncertainly on the couch. He didn't quite understand how this train of thought had begun. It annoyed him. The analytical young instructor was better off in the classroom. Couldn't science wait until 9:10 in the morning?

"I was thinking about you today," Judy said, and Anders knew that she had sensed the change in his mood.

"Do you see?" the voice asked him. "You're getting much better at it."

"I don't see anything," Anders thought, but the voice was right. It was as though he had a clear line of inspection into Judy's mind.

Her feelings were nakedly apparent to him, as meaningless as his room had been in that flash of undistorted thought.

"I really was thinking about you," she repeated.

"Now look," the voice said.

Anders, watching the expressions on Judy's face, felt the strangeness descend on him. He was back in the nightmare perception of that moment in his room. This time it was as though he were watching a machine in a laboratory. The object of this operation was the evocation and preservation of a particular mood. The machine goes through a searching process, invoking trains of ideas to achieve the desired end.

"Oh, were you?" he asked, amazed at his new perspective.

"Yes . . . I wondered what you were doing at noon," the reactive machine opposite him on the couch said, expanding its shapely chest slightly.

"Good," the voice said, commending him for his perception.

"Dreaming of you, of course," he said to the flesh-clad skeleton behind the total *gestalt* Judy. The flesh machine rearranged its limbs, widened its mouth to denote pleasure. The mechanism searched through a complex of fears, hopes, worries, through half-remembrances of analogous situations, analogous solutions.

And this was what he loved. Anders saw too clearly and hated himself for seeing. Through his new nightmare perception, the absurdity of the entire room struck him.

"Were you really?" the articulating skeleton asked him.

"You're coming closer," the voice whispered.

To what? The personality? There was no such thing. There was no true cohesion, no depth, nothing except a web of surface reactions, stretched across automatic visceral movements.

He was coming closer to the truth.

"Sure," he said sourly.

The machine stirred, searching for a response.

Anders felt a quick tremor of fear at the sheer alien quality of his viewpoint. His sense of formalism had been sloughed off, his agreed-upon reactions bypassed. What would be revealed next?

He was seeing clearly, he realized, as perhaps no man had ever seen before. It was an oddly exhilarating thought.

But could he still return to normalcy?

"Can I get you a drink?" the reaction machine asked.

At that moment Anders was as thoroughly out of love as a man could be. Viewing one's intended as a depersonalized, sexless piece of machinery is not especially conducive to love. But it is quite stimulating, intellectually.

Anders didn't want normalcy. A curtain was being raised and he wanted to see behind it. What was it some Russian scientist—Ouspensky, wasn't it—had said?

Think in other categories.

That was what he was doing, and would continue to do.

"Good-bye," he said suddenly.

The machine watched him, openmouthed, as he walked out the door. Delayed circuit reactions kept it silent until it heard the elevator door close.

"You were very warm in there," the voice within his head whispered, once he was on the street. "But you still don't understand everything."

"Tell me, then," Anders said, marveling a little at his equanimity. In an hour he had bridged the gap to a completely different viewpoint, yet it seemed perfectly natural.

"I can't," the voice said. "You must find it yourself."

"Well, let's see now," Anders began. He looked around at the masses of masonry, the convention of streets cutting through the architectural piles. "Human life," he said, "is a series of conventions. When you look at a girl, you're supposed to see—a pattern, not the underlying formlessness."

"That's true," the voice agreed, but with a shade of doubt.

"Basically, there is no form. Man produces *gestalts*, and cuts form out of the plethora of nothingness. It's like looking at a set of lines and saying that they represent a figure. We look at a mass of material, extract it from the background, and say it's a man. But in truth, there is no such thing. There are only the humanizing features that we—myopically—attach to it. Matter is conjoined, a matter of viewpoint."

"You're not seeing it now," said the voice.

"Damn it," Anders said. He was certain that he was on the track of something big, perhaps something ultimate. "Everyone's had the experience. At some time in his life, everyone looks at a familiar object and can't make any sense out of it. Momentarily the *gestalt* fails, but the true moment of sight passes. The mind reverts to the superimposed pattern. Normalcy continues."

The voice was silent. Anders walked on, through the *gestalt* city.

"There's something else, isn't there?" Anders asked.

"Yes."

What could that be? he asked himself. Through clearing eyes, Anders looked at the formality he had called his world.

He wondered momentarily whether he would have come to this if the voice hadn't guided him. Yes, he decided after a few moments, it was inevitable.

But who was the voice? And what had he left out?

"Let's see what a party looks like now," he said to the voice.

The party was a masquerade; the guests were all wearing their faces. To Anders, their motives, individually and collectively, were painfully apparent. Then his vision began to clear further.

He saw that the people weren't truly individual. They were discontinuous lumps of flesh sharing a common vocabulary, yet not even truly discontinuous.

The lumps of flesh were a part of the decoration of the room and almost indistinguishable from it. They were one with the lights, which lent their tiny vision. They were joined to the sounds they made, a few feeble tones out of the great possibility of sound. They blended into the walls.

The kaleidoscopic view came so fast that Anders had trouble sorting his new impressions. He knew, now, that these people existed only as patterns, on the same basis as the sounds they made and the things they thought they saw.

Gestalts, sifted out of the vast, unbearable real world.

"Where's Judy?" a discontinuous lump of flesh asked him. This particular lump possessed enough nervous mannerisms to convince the other lumps of his reality. He wore a loud tie as further evidence.

"She's sick," Anders said. The flesh quivered into an instant sympathy. Lines of formal mirth shifted to formal woe.

"Hope it isn't anything serious," the vocal flesh remarked.

"You're warmer," the voice said to Anders.

Anders looked at the object in front of him.

"She hasn't long to live," he stated.

The flesh quivered. Stomach and intestines contracted in sympathetic fear. Eyes distended, mouth quivered.

The loud tie remained the same.

"My God! You don't mean it!"

"What are you!" Anders asked quietly.

"What do you mean?" the indignant flesh attached to the tie demanded. Serene within its reality, it gaped at Anders. Its mouth twitched, undeniable proof that it was real and sufficient. "You're drunk," it sneered.

Anders laughed and left the party.

"There is still something you don't know," the voice said. "But you were hot! I could feel you near me."

"What are you?" Anders asked again.

"I don't know," the voice admitted. "I am a person. I am I. I am trapped."

"So are we all," Anders said. He walked on asphalt, surrounded by heaps of concrete, silicates, aluminum, and iron alloys. Shapeless, meaningless heaps that made up the *gestalt* city.

And then there were the imaginary lines of demarcation dividing city from city, the artificial boundaries of water and land.

All ridiculous.

"Give me a dime for some coffee, mister?" something asked, a thing indistinguishable from any other thing.

"Old Bishop Berkeley would give a nonexistent dime to your nonexistent presence," Anders said gaily.

"I'm really in a bad way," the voice whined, and Anders perceived that it was no more than a series of modulated vibrations.

"Yes! Go on!" the voice commanded.

"If you could spare me a quarter—" the vibrations said, with a deep pretense at meaning.

No, what was there behind the senseless patterns? Flesh, mass. What was that? All made up of atoms.

"I'm really hungry," the intricately arranged atoms muttered.

All atoms. Conjoined. There were no true separations between atom and atom. Flesh was stone, stone was light. Anders looked at the masses of atoms that were pretending to solidity, meaning, and reason.

"Can't you help me?" a clump of atoms asked. But the clump was identical with all the other atoms. Once you ignored the superimposed patterns, you could see the atoms were random, scattered.

"I don't believe in you," Anders said.

The pile of atoms was gone.

"Yes!" the voice cried. "Yes!"

"I don't believe in any of it," Anders said. After all, what was an atom?

"Go on!" the voice shouted. "You're hot! Go on!"

What was an atom? An empty space surrounded by an empty space.

Absurd!

"Then it's all false!" Anders said. And he was alone under the stars.

"That's right!" the voice within his head screamed. "Nothing!"

But stars, Anders thought. How can one believe—

The stars disappeared. Anders was in a gray nothingness, a void. There was nothing around him except shapeless gray.

Where was the voice?

Gone.

Anders perceived the delusion behind the grayness, and then there was nothing at all.

Complete nothingness, and himself within it.

Where was he? What did it mean? Anders tried to add it up.

Impossible. *That* couldn't be true.

Again the score was tabulated, but Anders couldn't accept the total. In desperation, his overloaded mind erased the figures, eradicated the knowledge, erased itself.

"Where am I?"

In nothingness. Alone.

Trapped.

"Who am I?"

A voice.

The voice of Anders searched the nothingness, shouted, "Is there anyone here?"

No answer.

But there was someone. All directions were the same; yet, moving along one, he could make contact . . . with someone. The voice of Anders reached back to someone who could save him, perhaps.

"Save me," the voice said to Anders, who lay fully dressed on his bed, except for his shoes and black bow tie.

THE NATIVE PROBLEM

Edward Danton was a misfit. Even as a baby, he had shown pre-antisocial leanings. This should have been sufficient warning to his parents, whose duty it was to take him without delay to a competent prepubescent psychologist. Such a person could have discovered what lay in Danton's childhood to give him these contra-group tendencies. But Danton's parents, doubtless dramatizing problems of their own, thought the child would grow out of it.

He never did.

In school, Danton got barely passing grades in Group Acculturation, Sibling Fit, Values Recognition, Folkways Judgment, and other subjects a person must know in order to live serenely in the modern world. Because of his lack of comprehension, Danton could never live serenely in the modern world.

It took him a while to find this out.

From his appearance, one would never have guessed Danton's basic lack of Fit. He was a tall, athletic young man, green-eyed, easygoing. There was a certain something about him that intrigued the girls in his immediate affective environment. In fact, several paid him the highest compliment at their command, which was to consider him as a possible husband.

But even the flightiest girl could not ignore Danton's lacks. He was liable to weary after only a few hours of Mass Dancing, when the fun was just beginning. At Twelve-Hand Bridge, Danton's attention frequently wandered and he would be forced to ask for a recount of the bidding, to the disgust of the other eleven players. And he was impossible at Subways.

He tried hard to master the spirit of that classic game. Locked arm in arm with his teammates, he would thrust forward into the subway car, trying to take possession before another team could storm in the opposite doors.

His group captain would shout, "Forward, men! We're taking this car to Rockaway!" And the opposing group captain would scream back, "Never! Rally, boys! It's Bronx Park or bust!"

Danton would struggle in the close-packed throng, a fixed smile on his face, worry lines etched around his mouth and eyes. His girlfriend of the moment would say, "What's wrong, Edward? Aren't you having fun?"

"Sure I am," Danton would reply, gasping for breath.

"But you aren't!" the girl would cry, perplexed. "Don't you realize, Edward, that this is the way our ancestors worked off their aggressions? Historians say that the game of Subways averted an all-out hydrogen war. *We* have those same aggressions and we too must resolve them in a suitable social context."

"Yeah, I know," Edward Danton would say. "I really do enjoy this. I—oh, Lord!"

For at that moment a third group would come pounding in, arms locked, chanting, "Canarsie, Canarsie, Canarsie!"

In that way he would lose another girlfriend, for there was obviously no future in Danton. Lack of Fit can never be disguised. It was obvious that Danton would never be happy in the New York suburbs, which stretched from Rockport, Maine, to Norfolk, Virginia—nor in any other suburbs, for that matter.

Danton tried to cope with his problems, in vain. Other strains started to show. He began to develop astigmatism from the projection of advertisements on his retina, and there was a constant ringing in his ears from the sing-swoop ads. His doctor warned that symptom analysis would never rid him of these psychosomatic ailments. No, what had to be treated was Danton's basic neurosis, his antisociality. But this Danton found impossible to deal with.

And so his thoughts turned irresistibly to escape. There was plenty of room for Earth's misfits out in space.

* * *

During the last two centuries, millions of psychotics, neurotics, psychopaths, and cranks of every kind and description had gone outward to the stars. The early ones had the Mikkelsen Drive to power their ships, and spent twenty or thirty years chugging from star system to star system. The newer ships were powered by GM subspatial torque converters, and made the same journey in a matter of months.

The stay-at-homes, being socially adjusted, bewailed the loss of anyone, but they welcomed the additional breeding room.

In his twenty-seventh year, Danton decided to leave Earth and take up pioneering. It was a tearful day when he gave his breeding certificate to his best friend, Al Trevor.

"Gee, Edward," Trevor said, turning the precious little certificate over and over in his hands, "you don't know what this means to Myrtle and me. We always wanted two kids. Now, because of you—"

"Forget it," said Danton. "Where I'm going, I won't need any breeding permit. As a matter of fact, I'll probably find it impossible to breed," he added, the thought having just struck him.

"But won't that be frustrating for you?" Al asked, solicitous, as always, for his friend's welfare.

"I guess so. Maybe after a while, though, I'll find a girl pioneer. And in the meantime, there's always sublimation."

"True enough. What substitute have you selected?"

"Vegetable gardening. I might as well be practical."

"You might as well," Al said. "Well, boy, good luck, boy."

Once the breeding certificate was gone, the die was cast. Danton plunged boldly ahead. In exchange for his Birthright, the government gave him unlimited free transportation and two years' basic equipment and provisions.

Danton left at once.

He avoided the more heavily populated areas, which were usually in the hands of rabid little groups.

He wanted no part of a place like Korani II, for instance, where a giant calculator had instituted a reign of math.

Nor was he interested in Heil V, where a totalitarian population of 342 was earnestly planning ways and means of conquering the galaxy.

He skirted the Farming Worlds—dull, restrictive places given to extreme health theories and practices.

When he came to Hedonia, he considered settling on that notorious planet. But the men of Hedonia were said to be short-lived, although no one denied their enjoyment while they *did* live.

Danton decided in favor of the long haul, and journeyed on.

He passed the Mining Worlds—somber, rocky places sparsely populated by gloomy, bearded men given to sudden violence. And he came at last to the New Territories. These unpeopled worlds were past Earth's farthest frontier. Danton scanned several before he found one with no intelligent life whatever.

It was a calm and watery place, dotted with sizable islands, lush with jungle greenery, and fertile with fish and game. The ship's captain duly notarized Danton's claim to the planet, which Danton called New Tahiti. A quick survey showed a large island superior to the rest. Here he was landed, and here he proceeded to set up his camp.

There was much to be done at first. Danton constructed a house out of branches and woven grass, near a white and gleaming beach. He fashioned a fishing spear, several snares, and a net. He planted his vegetable garden and was gratified to see it thrive under the tropical sun, nourished by warm rains that fell every morning between seven and seven-thirty.

All in all, New Tahiti was a paradisiacal place, and Danton should have been very happy there. But there was one thing wrong.

The vegetable garden, which he had thought would provide first-class sublimation, proved a dismal failure. Danton found himself thinking about women at all hours of the day and night, and spending long hours crooning to himself—love songs, of course—beneath a great orange tropical moon.

This was unhealthy. Desperately he threw himself into other recognized forms of sublimation; painting came first, but he rejected it to keep a journal, abandoned that and composed a sonata, gave that up and carved two enormous statues out of a local variety of soapstone, completed them, and tried to think of something else to do.

There was nothing else to do. His vegetables took excellent care of themselves; being of Earth stock, they completely choked out all alien growths. Fish swam into his nets in copious quantities, and meat was his whenever he bothered to set a snare. He found again that he was thinking of women at all hours of the day and night—tall women, short women, white women, black women, brown women.

The day came when Danton found himself thinking favorably of Martian women, something no Terran had succeeded in doing before. Then he knew that something drastic had to be done.

But what? He had no way of signaling for help, no way of getting off New Tahiti. He was gloomily contemplating this when a black speck appeared in the sky to seaward.

He watched as it slowly grew larger. He was barely able to breathe for fear it would turn out to be a bird or a huge insect. But the speck continued to increase in size, and soon he could see pale jets, flaring and ebbing.

A spaceship had come! He was alone no longer!

The ship took a long, slow, cautious time landing. Danton changed into his best *pareu*, a South Seas garment he had found peculiarly well adapted to the climate of New Tahiti. He washed, combed his hair carefully, and watched the ship descend.

It was one of the ancient Mikkelsen Drive ships. Danton had thought that all of them were long retired from active service. But this ship, it was apparent, had been traveling for a long while. The hull was dented and scored, hopelessly archaic, yet with a certain indomitable look about it. Its name, proudly lettered on the bow, was *The Hutter People*.

When people come in from deep space, they are usually starved for fresh food. Danton gathered a great pile of fruit for the ship's passengers and had it tastefully arranged by the time *The Hutter People* had landed ponderously on the beach.

A narrow hatch opened and two men stepped out. They were armed with rifles and dressed in black from head to toe. Warily they looked around them.

Danton sprinted over. "Hey, welcome to New Tahiti! Boy, am I glad to see you folks! What's the latest news from—"

"Stand back!" shouted one of the men. He was in his fifties, tall and impossibly gaunt, his face seamed and hard. His icy blue eyes seemed to pierce Danton like an arrow; his rifle was leveled at Danton's chest. His partner was younger, barrel-chested, broad-faced, short, and very powerfully built.

"Something wrong?" Danton asked, stopping.

"What's your name?"

"Edward Danton."

"I'm Simeon Smith," the gaunt man said, "military commander of the Hutter people. This is Jedekiah Franker, second-in-command. How come you speak English?"

"I've always spoken English," said Danton. "Look, I—"

"Where are the others? Where are they hiding?"

"There aren't any others. Just me." Danton looked at the ship and saw the faces of men and women at every port. "I gathered this stuff for you folks." He waved his hand at the mound of fruit. "Thought you might want some fresh goods after being so long in space."

A pretty girl with short, tousled blond hair appeared in the hatchway. "Can't we come out now, Father?"

"No!" Simeon said. "It's not safe. Get inside, Anita."

"I'll watch from here, then," she said, staring at Danton with frankly curious eyes.

Danton stared back, and a faint and unfamiliar tremor ran through him.

Simeon said, "We accept your offering. We will not, however, eat it."

"Why not?" Danton reasonably wanted to know.

"Because," said Jedekiah, "we don't know what poisons you people might try to feed us."

"Poisons? Look, let's sit down and talk this over."

"What do you think?" Jedekiah asked Simeon.

"Just what I expected," the military leader said. "Ingratiating, fawning, undoubtedly treacherous. His people won't show themselves. Waiting in ambush, I'll bet. I think an object lesson would be in order."

"Right," said Jedekiah, grinning. "Put the fear of civilization into them." He aimed his rifle at Danton's chest.

"Hey!" Danton yelped, backing away.

"But, Father," said Anita, "he hasn't done anything yet."

"That's the whole point. Shoot him and he won't do anything. The only good native is a dead native."

"This way," Jedekiah put in, "the rest will know we mean business."

"It isn't right!" Anita cried indignantly. "The Council—"

"—isn't in command now," Jedekiah said. "Anyhow, an alien landfall constitutes an emergency. During such times, the military is in charge. We'll do what we think best. Remember Lan II!"

"Hold on now," Danton said. "You've got this all wrong. There's just me, no others, no reason to—"

A bullet kicked up sand near his left foot. He sprinted for the protection of the jungle. Another bullet whined close, and a third cut a twig near his head as he plunged into the underbrush.

"There!" he heard Simeon roar. "That ought to teach them a lesson!"

Danton kept on running until he had put half a mile of jungle between himself and the pioneer ship.

He ate a light supper of the local vegetables and breadfruit, and tried to figure out what was wrong with the Hutters. Were they insane? They had seen that he was an Earthman, alone and unarmed, obviously friendly. Yet they had fired at him—as an object lesson. A lesson for whom? For the dirty natives, whom they wanted to teach a lesson . . .

That was it! Danton nodded emphatically to himself. The Hutters must have thought he was a native, an aboriginal, and that his tribe was lurking in the bush, waiting for a chance to massacre the new arrivals! It wasn't too rash an assumption, really. Here he was on a distant planet, without a spaceship, wearing only a loincloth and tanned a medium bronze. He was probably just what they thought a native should look like on a wilderness planet like this!

"But where," Danton asked himself, "do they think I learned English?"

The whole thing was ridiculous. He started walking back to the ship, sure he could clear up the misunderstanding in a few minutes. But after a couple of yards, he stopped.

Evening was approaching. Behind him, the sky was banked in

white and gray clouds. To seaward, a deep blue haze advanced steadily on the land. The jungle was filled with ominous noises, which Danton had long ago found to be harmless. But the new arrivals might not think so.

These people were trigger-happy, he reminded himself. No sense barging in on them too fast and inviting a bullet.

So he moved cautiously through the tangled jungle growth, a silent, tawny shape blending into the jungle browns and greens. When he reached the vicinity of the ship, he crawled through the dense undergrowth until he could peer down on the sloping beach.

The pioneers had finally come out of their ship. There were several dozen men and women and a few children. All were dressed in heavy black cloth and were perspiring in the heat. They had ignored his gift of local fruit. Instead, an aluminum table had been spread with the spaceship's monotonous provisions.

On the periphery of the crowd, Danton saw several men with rifles and ammunition belts. They were evidently on guard, keeping close watch on the jungle and glancing apprehensively overhead at the darkening sky.

Simeon raised his hands. There was immediate silence.

"Friends," the military leader orated, "we have come at last to our long-awaited home! Behold, here is a land of milk and honey, a place of bounty and abundance. Was it not worth the long voyage, the constant danger, the endless search?"

"Yes, brother!" the people responded.

Simeon held up his hands again for silence. "No civilized man has settled upon this planet. We are the first, and therefore the place is ours. But there are perils, my friends! Who knows what strange monsters the jungle hides?"

"Nothing larger than a chipmunk," Danton muttered to himself. "Why don't they ask me? I'd tell them."

"Who knows what leviathan swims in the deep?" Simeon continued. "We *do* know one thing: There is an aboriginal people here, naked and savage, undoubtedly cunning, ruthless, and amoral, as aboriginals always are. Of these we must beware. We will live in peace with them, if they will let us. We will bring to them the fruits of civilization and the flowers of culture. They may profess friendship, but always remember this, friends: no one can tell what goes on in a savage heart. Their standards are not ours; their morals are not ours. We cannot trust them; we must be forever on guard. And if in doubt, *we* must shoot first! Remember Lan II!"

Everybody applauded, sang a hymn, and began their evening meal. As night fell, searchlights came on from the ship, making the beach as bright as day. The sentries paced up and down, shoulders hunched nervously, rifles ready.

Danton watched the settlers shake out their sleeping bags and retire under the bulge of the ship. Even their fear of sudden attack couldn't force them to spend another night inside the ship, when there was fresh air to breathe outside.

The great orange moon of New Tahiti was half hidden by high-flying night clouds. The sentries paced and swore, and moved closer together for mutual comfort and protection. They began firing at the jungle sounds and blasting at shadows.

Danton crept back into the jungle. He retired for the night behind a tree, where he would be safe from stray bullets. This evening had not seemed the time for straightening things out. The Hutters were too jumpy. It would be better, he decided, to handle the matter by daylight, in a simple, straightforward, reasonable fashion.

The trouble was, the Hutters hardly seemed reasonable.

In the morning, though, everything looked more promising. Danton waited until the Hutters had finished their breakfast, then strolled into view at the edge of the beach.

"Halt!" every one of the sentries barked.

"That savage is back!" called a settler.

"Mummy," cried a little boy, "don't let the nasty bad man eat me!"

"Don't worry, dear," the boy's mother said. "Your father has a rifle for shooting savages."

Simeon rushed out of the spaceship and glared at Danton. "All right, you! Come forward!"

Danton stepped gingerly across the beach, his skin tingling with nervous expectation. He walked to Simeon, keeping his empty hands in sight.

"I am the leader of these people," Simeon said, speaking very slowly, as if to a child. "I the big chief fella. You big fella chief your people?"

"There's no need to talk that way," Danton said. "I can hardly understand you. I told you yesterday that I haven't any people. There's just me."

Simeon's hard face grew white with anger. "Unless you're honest with me, you're going to regret it. Now—where is your tribe?"

"I'm an Earthman," Danton yelled. "Are you deaf? Can't you hear how I talk?"

A stooped little man with white hair and great horn-rimmed glasses came over with Jedekiah. "Simeon," the little man said, "I don't believe I have met our guest."

"Professor Baker," said Simeon, "this savage here claims he's an Earthman and he says his name is Edward Danton."

The professor glanced at Danton's *pareu*, his tanned skin and callused feet. "You are an Earthman?" he asked Danton.

"Of course."

"Who carved those stone statues up the beach?"

"I did," Danton said, "but it was just therapy. You see—"

"Obviously primitive work. That stylization, those noses—"

"It was accidental. Look, a few months ago I left Earth in a spaceship—"

"How was it powered?" Professor Baker asked.

"By a GM subspatial torque converter." Baker nodded, and Danton went on, "Well, I wasn't interested in places like Korani or Heil V, and Hedonia seemed too rich for my blood. I passed up the Mining Worlds and the Farming Worlds, and had the government ship drop me here. The planet's registered as New Tahiti, in my name. But I was getting pretty lonely, so I'm glad you folks came."

"Well, Professor?" Simeon said. "What do you think?"

"Amazing," Baker murmured. "Truly amazing. His grasp of colloquial English bespeaks a fairly high level of intelligence, which points up a phenomenon frequently met with in savage societies, namely an unusually well-developed power of mimicry. Our friend Danta (as his original, uncorrupted name must have been) will probably be able to tell us many tribal legends, myths, songs, dances—"

"But I'm an Earthman!"

"No, my poor friend," the professor corrected gently, "you are not. Obviously you have *met* an Earthman. Some trader, I daresay, stopping for repairs."

Jedekiah said, "There's evidence that a spaceship once landed here briefly."

"Ah," said Professor Baker, beaming. "Confirmation of my hypothesis."

"That was the government ship," Danton explained. "It dropped me off here."

"It is interesting to note," said Professor Baker in his lecturing voice, "how his almost plausible story lapses into myth at various crucial points. He claims that the ship was powered by a 'GM subspatial torque converter'—which is nonsense syllabification, since the only deep-space drive is the Mikkelsen. He claims that the journey from Earth was made in a matter of months (since his untutored mind cannot conceive of a journey lasting years), although we know that no space drive, even theoretically, can achieve that."

"It was developed after you people left Earth," Danton said. "How long have you been gone?"

"The Hutter spaceship left Earth one hundred and twenty years ago," Baker replied condescendingly. "We are mostly fourth and fifth generation. Note also," Baker said to Simeon and Jedekiah, "his attempt to think up plausible place-names. Words such as Kornai, Heil, Hedonia appeal to his sense of onomatopoeia. That there are no such places doesn't disturb him."

"There are!" Danton said indignantly.

"Where?" Jedekiah challenged. "Give me the coordinates."

"How should I know? I'm no navigator. I think Heil was near Boötes, or maybe it was Cassiopeia. No, I'm pretty sure it was Boötes—"

"I'm sorry, friend," said Jedekiah. "It may interest you to know that I'm the ship's navigator. I can show you the star atlases and charts. Those places aren't on them."

"Your charts are a hundred years out of date!"

"Then so are the stars," Simeon said. "Now, Danta, where is your tribe? Why do they hide from us? What are they planning?"

"This is preposterous," Danton protested. "What can I do to convince you? I'm an Earthman. I was born and raised—"

"That's enough," Simeon cut in. "If there's one thing we Hutters won't stand for, it's backtalk from natives. Out with it, Danta. *Where are your people?*"

"There's only me," Danton insisted.

"Tight-mouthed?" Jedekiah gritted. "Maybe a taste of the black-snake whip—"

"Later, later," Simeon said. "His tribe'll come around for handouts. Natives always do. In the meantime, Danta, you can join that work gang over there."

"No, thanks," said Danton. "I'm going back to—"

Jedekiah's fist lashed out, catching Danton on the side of the jaw. He staggered, barely keeping his footing.

"The chief said *no backtalk*!" Jedekiah roared. "Why are you natives always so bone-lazy? You'll be paid as soon as we unload the beads and calico. Now get to work."

That seemed to be the last word on the subject. Dazed and unsure, much like millions of natives before him on a thousand different worlds, Danton joined the long line of colonists passing goods out of the ship.

By late afternoon the unloading was done and the settlers were relaxed on the beach. Danton sat apart from them, trying to think his situation through. He was deep in thought when Anita came to him with a canteen of water.

"Do *you* think I'm a native?" he asked.

She sat down beside him and said, "I really don't see what else you could be. Everyone knows how fast a ship can travel."

"Times have changed since your people left Earth. They weren't in space all that time, were they?"

"Of course not. The Hutter ship went to H'gastro I, but it wasn't fertile enough, so the next generation moved to Ktedi. But the corn mutated and almost wiped them out, so they went to Lan II. They thought that would be a permanent home."

"What happened?"

"The natives," said Anita sadly. "I guess they were friendly enough at first, and everyone thought the situation was well in hand. Then, one day, we were at war with the entire native population. They only had spears and things, but there were too many of them, so the ship left again and we came here."

"Hmm," Danton said. "I see why you're so nervous about aboriginals."

"Well, of course. While there's any possibility of danger, we're under military rule. That means my father and Jedekiah. But as soon as the emergency is past, our regular Hutter government takes over."

"Who runs that?"

"A council of Elders," Anita said, "men of goodwill, who detest violence. If you and your people are really peaceable—"

"I haven't any people," Danton said wearily.

"—then you'll have every opportunity to prosper under the rule of the Elders."

They sat together and watched the sunset. Danton noticed how the wind stirred her hair, blowing it silkily across her forehead, and how the afterglow of the sun outlined and illuminated the line of her cheek and lip. He shivered and told himself it was the sudden chill of evening. And Anita, who had been talking animatedly about her childhood, found difficulty in completing her sentences, or even keeping her train of thought.

After a while, their hands strayed together. Their fingertips touched and clung. For a long time they said nothing at all. And at last, gently and lingeringly, they kissed.

"What the hell is going on here?" a loud voice demanded.

Danton looked up and saw a burly man standing over him, his powerful head silhouetted black against the moon, his fists on his hips.

"Please, Jedekiah," Anita said. "Don't make a scene."

"Get up," Jedekiah ordered Danton in an ominously quiet voice. "Get up on your feet."

Danton stood up, his hands half-clenched into fists, waiting.

"You," Jedekiah said to Anita, "are a disgrace to your race and to the whole Hutter people. Are you crazy? You can't mess around with a dirty native and still keep any self-respect." He turned to

Danton. "And you gotta learn something and learn it good. *Natives don't fool with Hutter women!* I'm going to impress that little lesson on you right here and now."

There was a brief scuffle, and Jedekiah found himself sprawled on his back.

"Help!" Jedekiah shouted. *"The natives are revolting!"*

An alarm bell in the spaceship began to peal. Sirens wailed. The women and children, long trained for such an emergency, trooped back into the spaceship. The men were issued rifles, machine guns, and hand grenades, and began to advance on Danton.

"It's just man to man," Danton called out. "We had a disagreement, that's all. There's no natives or anything. Just me."

The foremost Hutter commanded, "Anita, quick, get back!"

"I didn't see any natives," the girl said staunchly. "And it wasn't really Danta's fault—"

"Get back!"

She was pulled out of the way. Danton dived into the bushes before the machine guns opened up.

He crawled on all fours for fifty yards, then broke into a dead run.

Fortunately the Hutters did not pursue him. They were interested only in guarding their ship and holding their beachhead and a narrow stretch of jungle. Danton heard gunfire throughout the night, and loud shouts and frantic cries.

"There goes one!"

"Quick, turn the machine gun! They're behind us!"

"There! There! I got one!"

"No, he got away. There he goes . . . But look, up in the tree!"

"Fire, man, fire!"

All night, Danton listened as the Hutters repulsed the attacks of imaginary savages.

Toward dawn the firing subsided. Danton estimated that a ton of lead had been expended, hundreds of trees decapitated, acres of grass trampled into mud. The jungle stank of cordite.

He fell into a fitful slumber.

At midday he awakened and made a meal for himself of bananas and mangoes. Then he decided to think things over.

But no thoughts came. His mind was filled with Anita and with grief over her loss.

All that day he wandered disconsolately through the jungle, and in the late afternoon he heard again the sound of someone moving through the underbrush.

He turned to go deeper into the island. Then he heard someone calling his name.

"Danta! Danta! Wait!"

It was Anita. Danton hesitated, not sure what to do. She might have decided to leave her people, to live in the green jungle with him. But more realistically, she might have been sent out as a decoy, leading a party of men to destroy him. How could he know where her loyalties lay?

"Danta! Where are you?"

Danton reminded himself that there could never be anything between them. Her people had shown what they thought of natives. They would always distrust him, forever try to kill him . . .

"*Please*, Danta!"

Danton shrugged and walked toward her voice.

They met in a little clearing. Anita's hair was disheveled and her dark clothing was torn by the jungle briars, but for Danton there could never be a lovelier woman. For an instant he believed that she had come to join him, flee with him.

Then he saw armed men fifty yards behind her.

"It's all right," Anita said. "They're not going to kill you. They just came along to guard me."

"Guard you? From *me*?" Danton laughed hollowly.

"They don't know you as I do," Anita said. "At the Council meeting today, I told them the truth."

"You did?"

"Of course. That fight wasn't your fault, and I told everybody so. I told them you fought only to defend yourself. And Jedekiah lied. No pack of natives attacked him. There was only you, and I told them this."

"Good girl," Danton said fervently. "Did they believe you?"

"I think so. I explained that the native attack came later."

Danton groaned. "Look, how could there be a native attack when there aren't any natives?"

"But there are," Anita said. "I heard them shouting."

"Those were your own people," Danton said desperately. If he couldn't convince this one girl, how could he possibly persuade the rest of the Hutters?

And then he had it. It was a very simple proof, but its effect would have to be overwhelming.

"You really believe there was a full-scale native attack," Danton stated.

"Of course."

"How many natives?"

"I heard that you outnumbered us by at least ten to one."

"And we were armed?"

"You certainly were."

"Then how," Danton asked triumphantly, "do you account for the fact that *not a single Hutter was wounded!*"

She stared at him, wide-eyed. "But, Danta dear, many of the Hutters were wounded, some seriously. It's a wonder no one was killed in all that fighting!"

Danton felt as though the ground had been kicked out from under him. For a terrifying minute he believed her. Perhaps he did have a tribe, hundreds of bronzed savages like himself, hidden in the jungle, waiting . . .

"That trader who taught you English," Anita said, "must have been a very unscrupulous character. It's against interstellar law, you know, to sell firearms to natives."

"Firearms?"

"Certainly. You couldn't use them very accurately, of course. But Simeon said that sheer firepower—"

"I suppose all your casualties were from gunshot wounds."

"Yes. The men didn't let you get close enough to use knives and spears."

"I see," Danton said. His proof was utterly demolished. But he felt enormously relieved at having regained his sanity. The disorganized Hutter soldiery had ranged around the jungle, firing at everything that moved. It was more than a wonder that some of them hadn't been killed. It was a miracle.

"But I explained that they couldn't blame you," said Anita. "You were attacked first and your own people must have thought you were in danger. The Elders thought this was probable."

"Nice of them," Danton said.

"They want to be reasonable. After all, they realize that natives are human beings just like ourselves."

"Are you sure of that?" Danton asked with feeble irony.

"Of course. The Elders held a big meeting on native policy and decided it once and for all. We're setting aside a thousand acres as a reservation for you and your people. That should be plenty of room, shouldn't it? The men are putting up the boundary posts now. You'll live peacefully in your reservation and we'll live in our own part of the island."

"*What?*" Danton said.

"And to seal the pledge," Anita continued, "the Elders asked you to accept this." She handed him a roll of parchment.

"What is it?"

"It's a peace treaty, declaring the end of the Hutter–New Tahitian war, and pledging our respective peoples to eternal amity."

Numbly, Danton accepted the parchment. He saw that the men who had accompanied Anita were setting red-and-black striped posts into the ground. They sang as they worked, happy to have reached a solution to the native problem so quickly and easily.

"But don't you think," Danton asked, "that perhaps—ah—assimilation might be a better solution?"

"I suggested it," Anita said, blushing.

"You did? You mean that you would—"

"Of course I would," said Anita, not looking at him. "I think the amalgamation of two strong races would be a fine and wonderful thing. And, Danta, what wonderful stories and legends you could have told the children!"

"I could have showed them how to fish and hunt," Danton said, "and which plants are edible, and things like that."

"And all your colorful tribal songs and dances." Anita sighed. "It would have been wonderful. I'm sorry, Danta."

"But something must be possible! Can't I talk to the Elders? Isn't there anything I can do?"

"Nothing," Anita said. "I'd run away with you, Danta, but they'd track us down, no matter how long it took."

"They'd never find us," Danton promised.

"Perhaps. I'd be willing to take the chance."

"Darling!"

"But I can't. Your poor people, Danta! The Hutters would take hostages, kill them if I wasn't returned."

"I don't have any people! I don't, damn it!"

"It's sweet of you to say that," Anita said tenderly. "But lives cannot be sacrificed just for the love of two individuals. You must tell your people not to cross the boundary lines, Danta. They'll be shot. Good-bye, and remember, it is best to live in the path of peace."

She hurried away from him. Danton watched her go, angry at her noble sentiments, which separated them for no reason at all, yet loving her for the love she showed his people. That his people were imaginary didn't matter. It was the thought that counted.

At last he turned and walked deep into the jungle.

He stopped by a still pool of black water, overhung with giant trees and bordered by flowering ferns, and here he tried to plan the rest of his life. Anita was gone; all commerce with human beings was gone. He didn't need any of them, he told himself. He had his reservation. He could replant his vegetable garden, carve more statues, compose more sonatas, start another journal . . .

"To hell with that!" he shouted to the trees. He didn't *want* to sublimate any longer. He wanted Anita and he wanted to live with humans. He was tired of being alone.

What could he do about it?

There didn't seem to be anything. He leaned back against a tree and stared at New Tahiti's impossibly blue sky. If only the Hutters weren't so superstitious, so afraid of natives, so . . .

And then it came to him, a plan so absurd, so dangerous . . .

"It's worth a try," Danton said to himself, "even if they kill me."

He trotted off toward the Hutter boundary line.

A sentry saw him as he neared the vicinity of the spaceship, and leveled his rifle. Danton raised both arms.

"Don't fire! I have to speak with your leaders!"

"Get back on your reservation," the sentry warned. "Get back or I'll shoot."

"I have to speak to Simeon," Danton stated, holding his ground.

"Orders is orders," said the sentry, taking aim.

"Just a minute." Simeon stepped out of the ship, frowning deeply. "What is all this?"

"That native came back," the sentry said. "Shall I pop him, sir?"

"What do you want?" Simeon asked Danton.

"I have come here to bring you," Danton roared, "*a declaration of war!*"

That woke up the Hutter camp. In a few minutes, every man, woman, and child had gathered near the spaceship. The Elders, a council of old men distinguished by their long white beards, were standing to one side.

"You accepted the peace treaty," Simeon pointed out.

"I had a talk with the other chiefs of the island," Danton said, stepping forward. "We feel the treaty is not fair. Now Tahiti is ours. It belonged to our fathers and to our fathers' fathers. Here we have raised our children, sown our corn, and reaped the bread-fruit. We will not live on the reservation!"

"Oh, Danta!" Anita cried, appearing from the spaceship. "I asked you to bring peace to your people!"

"They wouldn't listen," Danton said. "All the tribes are gathering. Not only my own people, the Cynochi, but the Drovati, the Lorognasti, the Retellsmbroichi and the Vitelli. Plus, naturally, their sub-tribes and dependencies."

"How many are you?" Simeon asked.

"Fifty or sixty thousand. Of course, we don't all have rifles. Most of us will have to rely on more primitive weapons, such as poisoned arrows and darts."

A nervous murmur arose from the crowd.

"Many of us will be killed," Danton said stonily. "We do not care. Every New Tahitian will fight like a lion. We are a thousand to your one. We have cousins on the other islands who will join us. No matter what the cost in human life and misery, we will drive you into the sea. I have spoken."

He turned and started back into the jungle, walking with stiff dignity.

"Shall I pop him now, sir?" the sentry begged.

"Put down that rifle, you fool!" Simeon snapped. "Wait, Danta! Surely we can come to terms. Bloodshed is senseless."

"I agree," Danton said soberly.

"What do you want?"

"Equal rights!"

The Elders went into an immediate conference. Simeon listened to them, then turned to Danton.

"That may be possible. Is there anything else?"

"Nothing," Danton said. "Except, naturally, an alliance between the ruling clan of the Hutters and the ruling clan of the New Tahitians, to seal the bargain. Marriage would be best."

After going into conference again, the Elders gave their instructions to Simeon. The military chief was obviously disturbed. The cords stood out on his neck, but with an effort he controlled himself, bowed his agreement to the Elders, and marched up to Danton.

"The Elders have authorized me," he said, "to offer you an alliance of blood brotherhood. You and I, representing the leading clans of our peoples, will mingle our blood together in a beautiful and highly symbolic ceremony, then break bread, take salt—"

"Sorry," Danton said. "We New Tahitians don't hold with that sort of thing. It has to be marriage."

"But, damn it all, man—"

"That is my last word."

"We'll never accept! Never!"

"Then it's war," Danton declared, and walked into the jungle.

He was in a mood for making war. But how, he asked himself, does a single native fight against a spaceship full of armed men?

He was brooding on this when Simeon and Anita came to him through the jungle.

"All right," Simeon said angrily. "The Elders have decided. We Hutters are sick of running from planet to planet. We've had this problem before and I suppose we'd just go somewhere else and have it again. We're sick and tired of the whole native problem, so I guess"— he gulped hard, but manfully finished the sentence—"we'd better assimilate. At least that's what the Elders think. Personally, I'd rather fight."

"You'd lose," Danton assured him, and at that moment he felt he could take on the Hutters singlehanded and win.

"Maybe so," Simeon admitted. "Anyhow, you can thank Anita for making the peace possible."

"Anita? Why?"

"Why, man, she's the only girl in the camp who'd marry a naked, dirty, heathen savage!"

And so they were married, and Danta, now known as the White Man's Friend, settled down to help the Hutters conquer their new land. They, in turn, introduced him to the marvels of civilization. He was taught Twelve-Hand Bridge and Mass Dancing. And soon the Hutters built their first Subway—for a civilized people must release their aggressions—and that game was shown to Danta, too.

He tried to master the spirit of the classic Earth pastime, but it was obviously beyond the comprehension of his savage soul. Civilization stifled him, so Danta and his wife moved across the planet, always following the frontier, staying far from the amenities of civilization.

Anthropologists came frequently to visit him. They recorded all the stories he told his children, the ancient and beautiful legends of New Tahiti—tales of sky gods and water demons, fire sprites and woodland nymphs, and how Katamandura was ordered to create the world out of nothingness in just three days, and what his reward for this was, and what Jevasi said to Hootmenlati when they met in the underworld, and the strange outcome of this meeting.

The anthropologists noted similarities between these legends and certain legends of Earth, and several ingenious theories were put forth. And they were interested in the great soapstone statues on the main island of New Tahiti, weird and haunting colossi that no viewer could forget, clearly the work of a pre–New Tahitian race, of whom no trace could ever be found.

But most fascinating of all for the scientific workers was the problem of the New Tahitians themselves. Those happy, laughing, bronzed savages—bigger, stronger, handsomer, and healthier than any other race—had melted away at the coming of the white man. Only a few of the older Hutters could remember meeting them in any numbers, and their tales were considered none too reliable.

"My people?" Danta would say when questioned. "Ah, they could not stand the white man's diseases, the white man's mechanical civilization, the white man's harsh and repressive ways. They are in a happier place now, in Valhoola beyond the sky. And someday I shall go there too."

And white men, hearing this, experienced strangely guilty feelings and redoubled their efforts to show kindness to Danta, the Last Native.

FISHING SEASON

They had been living in the housing project only a week, and this was their first invitation. They arrived on the dot of eight-thirty. The Carmichaels were obviously prepared for them, for the porch light was on, the front door partially open, and the living room a blaze of light.

"Do I look all right?" Phyllis asked at the door. "Seams straight, hair curly?"

"You're a vision in a red hat," her husband assured her. "Just don't spoil the effect by leading aces." She made a small face at him and rang the doorbell. Soft chimes sounded inside.

Mallen straightened his tie while they waited. He pulled out his breast-pocket handkerchief a microscopic fraction farther.

"They must be making gin in the cellar," he told his wife. "Shall I ring again?"

"No—wait a moment." They waited, and he rang again. Again the chimes sounded.

"That's very strange," Phyllis said a few minutes later. "It *was* tonight, wasn't it?"

Her husband nodded. The Carmichaels had left their windows open to the warm spring weather. Through the venetian blinds they could see a table set for bridge, chairs drawn up, candy dishes out, everything in readiness. But no one answered the door.

"Could they have stepped out?" Phyllis Mallen asked. Her husband walked quickly across the lawn to the driveway.

"Their car's in." He came back and pushed the front door open farther.

"Jimmy—don't go in."

"I'm not." He put his head in the door. "Hello! Anybody home?"

Silence in the house.

"Hello!" he shouted, and listened intently. He could hear Friday-night noises next door—people talking, laughing. A car passed in the street. He listened. A board creaked somewhere in the house, then silence again.

"They wouldn't go away and leave their house open like this," he told Phyllis. "Something might have happened." He stepped inside. She followed, but stood uncertainly in the living room while he went into the kitchen. She heard him open the cellar door, call out, "Anyone home?" and close it again. He came back to the living room, frowned, and went upstairs.

In a little while Mallen came down with a puzzled expression on his face. "There's no one there," he said.

"Let's get out of here," Phyllis said, suddenly nervous in the bright, empty house. They debated leaving a note, but decided against it and started down the walk.

"Shouldn't we close the front door?" Jim Mallen asked, stopping.

"What good will it do? All the windows are open."

"Still—" He went back and closed it. They walked home slowly, looking back over their shoulders at the house. Mallen half expected the Carmichaels to come running after them, shouting, "Surprise!"

But the house remained silent.

Their home was only a block away, a brick bungalow just like two hundred others in the development. Inside, Mr. Carter was making trout flies on the card table. Working slowly and surely, his deft fingers guided the colored threads with loving care. He was so intent on his work that he didn't hear the Mallens enter.

"We're home, Dad," Phyllis said.

"Ah," Mr. Carter murmured. "Look at this beauty." He held up a finished fly. It was an almost exact replica of a hornet. The hook was cleverly concealed by overhanging yellow and black threads.

"The Carmichaels were out—we think," Mallen said, hanging up his jacket.

"I'm going to try Old Creek in the morning," Mr. Carter said. "Something tells me the elusive trout may be there." Mallen grinned to himself. It was difficult talking with Phyllis's father. Nowadays he never discussed anything except fishing. The old man had retired from a highly successful business on his seventieth birthday to devote himself wholeheartedly to his favorite sport.

Now, nearing eighty, Mr. Carter looked wonderful. It was amazing, Mallen thought. His skin was rosy, his eyes clear and untroubled, his pure white hair neatly combed back. He was in full possession of his senses, too—as long as you talked about fishing.

"Let's have a snack," Phyllis said. Regretfully she took off the red hat, smoothed out the veil, and put it down on a coffee table. Mr. Carter added another thread to his trout fly, examined it closely, then put it down and followed them into the kitchen.

While Phyllis made coffee, Mallen told the old man what had happened. Mr. Carter's answer was typical.

"Try some fishing tomorrow and get it off your mind. Fishing, Jim, is more than a sport. Fishing is a way of life, and a philosophy as well. I like to find a quiet pool and sit on the banks of it. I figure if there's fish anywhere, they might as well be there."

Phyllis smiled, watching Jim twist uncomfortably on his chair. There was no stopping her father, once he got started. And anything would start him.

"Consider," Mr. Carter went on, "a young executive—someone like yourself, Jim—dashing through a hall. Common enough? But at the end of the last long corridor is a trout stream. Consider a politician. You certainly see enough of them in Albany. Briefcase in hand, worried—"

"That's strange," Phyllis said, stopping her father in midflight. She was holding an unopened bottle of milk in her hand.

"Look." Their milk came from Stannerton Dairies. The green label on this bottle read *Stanneron Daries.*

"And look." She pointed. Under that, it read: *lisensed by the neW yoRk Bord of healthh*. It looked like a clumsy imitation of the legitimate label.

"Where did you get this?" Mallen asked.

"Why, I suppose from Mr. Elger's store. Could it be an advertising stunt?"

"I despise the man who would fish with a worm," Mr. Carter intoned gravely. "A fly is a work of art. But the man who'd use a worm would rob orphans and burn churches."

"Don't drink it," Mallen said. "Let's look over the rest of the food."

There were three more counterfeited items. A candy bar that purported to be a Mello-Bite had an orange label instead of the familiar crimson. There was a jar of Amerrican ChEEse SpreaD, almost a third larger than the usual jars of that brand, and a bottle of SPArkling Watr.

"That's very odd," Mallen said, rubbing his jaw.

"I always throw the little ones back," Mr. Carter said. "It's not sporting to keep them, and that's part of a fisherman's code. Let them grow, let them ripen, let them gain experience. It's the old, crafty ones I want, the ones who skulk under logs, who dart away at the first sight of the angler. Those are the lads who put up a fight!"

"I'm going to take this stuff back to Elger," Mallen said, putting the items into a paper bag.

"Old Creek is the place," Mr. Carter said. "That's where they hide out."

Saturday morning was bright and beautiful. Mr. Carter ate an early breakfast and left for Old Creek, stepping as lightly as a boy, his battered, fly-decked hat set at a jaunty angle. Jim Mallen finished coffee and went over to the Carmichael house.

The car was still in the garage. The windows were still open, the bridge table was set, and every light was on, exactly as it had been the night before. It reminded Mallen of a story he had read once about a ship under full sail, with everything in order—but not a soul on board.

"I wonder if there's anyone we can call?" Phyllis asked when he returned home. "I'm sure there's something wrong."

"Sure. But who?" They were strangers in the project. They had a nodding acquaintance with three or four families, but no idea who might know the Carmichaels.

The problem was settled by the ringing of the telephone.

"If it's anyone from around here," Jim said as Phyllis answered it, "ask them."

"Hello?"

"Hello. I don't believe you know me. I'm Marian Carpenter, from down the block. I was just wondering—has my husband dropped over there?" The metallic telephone voice managed to convey worry, fear.

"Why, no. No one's been in this morning."

"I see." The thin voice hesitated.

"Is there anything I can do?" Phyllis asked.

"I don't understand it," Mrs. Carpenter said. "George—my husband—had breakfast with me this morning. Then he went upstairs for his jacket. That was the last I saw of him."

"Oh—"

"I'm sure he didn't come back downstairs. I went up to see what was holding him—we were going for a drive—and he wasn't there. I searched the whole house. I thought he might be playing a practical joke, although George never joked in his life—so I looked under beds and in the closets. Then I looked in the cellar, and I asked next door, but no one's seen him. I thought he might have visited you—he was speaking about it—"

Phyllis explained to her about the Carmichaels' disappearance. They talked for a few seconds longer, then hung up.

"Jim," Phyllis said, "I don't like it. You'd better tell the police about the Carmichaels."

"We'll look pretty foolish when they turn up visiting friends in Albany."

"We'll have to chance it."

Jim found the number and dialed, but the line was busy.

"I'll go down."

"And take this stuff with you." She handed him the paper bag.

* * *

Police Captain Lesner was a patient, ruddy-faced man who had been listening to an unending stream of complaints all night and most of the morning. His patrolmen were tired, his sergeants were tired, and he was the tiredest of all. Nevertheless, he ushered Mr. Mallen into his office and listened to his story.

"I want you to write down everything you've told me," Lesner said when he was through. "We got a call on the Carmichaels from a neighbor late last night. Been trying to locate them. Counting Mrs Carpenter's husband, that makes ten in two days."

"Ten what?"

"Disappearances."

"My Lord," Mallen breathed softly. He shifted the paper bag. "All from this town?"

"Every one," Captain Lesner said harshly, "from the Vainsville housing project in this town. As a matter of fact, from four square blocks in that project." He named the streets.

"I live there," Mallen said.

"So do I."

"Have you any idea who the—kidnapper could be?" Mallen asked.

"We don't think it's a kidnapper," Lesner said, lighting his twentieth cigarette for the day. "No ransom notes. No selection. A good many of the missing persons wouldn't be worth a nickel to a kidnapper. And wholesale like that—not a chance!"

"A maniac, then?"

"Sure. But how has he grabbed whole families? Or grown men as big as you? And where has he hidden them, or their bodies?" Lesner ground out the cigarette viciously. "I've got men searching every inch of this town. Every cop within twenty miles of here is looking. The state police are stopping cars. And we haven't found a thing."

"Oh, and here's something else." Mallen showed him the counterfeited items.

"Again, I don't know," Captain Lesner confessed sourly. "I haven't had much time for this stuff. We've had other complaints—" The telephone rang, but Lesner ignored it.

"It looks like a black-market scheme. I've sent some stuff like it to Albany for analysis. I'm trying to trace outlets. Might be foreign. As a matter of fact, the FBI might—damn that phone!"

He yanked it out of its cradle.

"Lesner speaking. Yes . . . yes. You're sure? Of course, Mary. I'll be right over." He hung up. His red face was suddenly drained of color.

"That was my wife's sister," he announced. "My wife's missing!"

Mallen drove home at breakneck speed. He slammed on the brakes, almost cracking his head against the windshield, and ran into the house.

"Phyllis!" he shouted. Where was she? Oh, God, he thought. If she's gone—

"Anything wrong?" Phyllis asked, coming out of the kitchen.

"I thought—" He grabbed her and hugged her until she squealed.

"Really," she said, smiling. "We're not newlyweds. Why, we've been married a whole year and a half—"

He told her what he'd found out in the police station.

Phyllis looked around the living room. It had seemed so warm and cheerful a week ago. Now, a shadow under the couch frightened her; an open closet door was something to shudder at. She knew it would never be the same.

There was a knock at the door.

"Don't go," Phyllis said.

"Who's there?" Mallen asked.

"Joe Dutton, from down the block. I suppose you've heard the news?"

"Yes," Mallen said, standing beside the closed door.

"We're barricading the streets," Dutton said. "Going to look over anyone going in or out. We're going to put a stop to this, even if the police can't. Want to join us?"

"You bet," Mallen said, and opened the door. The short, swarthy man on the other side was wearing an old army jacket. He was gripping a two-foot-long chunk of wood.

"We're going to cover these blocks like a blanket," Dutton said. "If anyone else is grabbed, it'll have to be underground." Mallen kissed his wife and joined Dutton.

* * *

That afternoon there was a mass meeting in the school auditorium. Everyone from the affected blocks was there, and as many of the townspeople as could be crowded in. The first thing they found out was that, in spite of the blockades, three more people were missing from the Vainsville project.

Captain Lesner spoke and told them that he had called Albany for help. Special officers were on their way down, and the FBI was coming in on it too. He stated frankly that he didn't know what or who was doing it, or why. He couldn't even figure out why all the missing were from one part of the Vainsville project.

He had got word from Albany about the counterfeited food that seemed to be scattered all over the project. The examining chemists could detect no trace of any toxic agent. That seemed to explode a recent theory that the food had been used to drug people, making them walk out of their homes to whatever was taking them. However, he cautioned everyone not to eat it. You could never tell.

The companies whose labels had been impersonated disclaimed any knowledge. They were prepared to bring suit against anyone infringing their copyrights.

The mayor spoke, in a series of well-intentioned platitudes, counseling them to be of good heart; the civil authorities were taking the whole situation in hand.

Of course, the mayor didn't live in the Vainsville project.

The meeting broke up, and the men returned to the barricades. They started looking for firewood for the evening, but it was unnecessary. Help arrived from Albany, a cavalcade of men and equipment. The four blocks were surrounded by armed guards. Portable searchlights were set up and at eight o'clock curfew declared.

Mr. Carter missed all the excitement. He had been fishing all day. At sunset he returned, empty-handed but happy. The guards let him through, and he walked into the house.

"A beautiful fishing day," he declared.

The Mallens spent a terrible night, fully clothed, dozing fitfully, looking at the searchlights playing against their windows and hearing the tramp of armed guards.

* * *

Eight o'clock Sunday morning—two more people missing. Gone from four blocks more closely guarded than a concentration camp.

At ten o'clock, Mr. Carter, brushing aside the objections of the Mallens, shouldered his fishing kit and left. He hadn't missed a day since April thirtieth and wasn't planning on missing one all season.

Sunday noon—another person gone, bringing the total up to sixteen.

Sunday, one o'clock—all the missing children were found!

A police car found them on a road near the outskirts of town, eight of them, including the Carmichael boy, walking dazedly toward their homes. They were rushed to a hospital.

There was no trace of the missing adults, though.

Word of mouth spread the news faster than the newspapers or radio could. The children were completely unharmed. Under examination by psychiatrists, it was found that they didn't remember where they had been or how they had been taken there. All the psychiatrists could piece together was a sensation of flying, accompanied by a sickness in the stomach. The children were kept in the hospital for safety, under guard.

But between noon and evening, another child disappeared from Vainsville.

Just before sunset, Mr. Carter came home. In his knapsack were two big rainbow trout. He greeted the Mallens gaily and went to the garage to clean his fish.

Jim Mallen stepped into the backyard and started to the garage after him, frowning. He wanted to ask the old man about something he had said a day or two ago. He couldn't quite remember what it was, but it seemed important.

His next-door neighbor, whose name he couldn't remember, greeted him.

"Mallen," he said, "I think I know."

"What?" Mallen asked.

"Have you examined the theories?" the neighbor asked.

"Of course." His neighbor was a skinny fellow in shirtsleeves and vest. His bald head glistened red in the sunset.

"Then listen. It can't be a kidnapper. No sense in their methods. Right?"

"Yes, I suppose so."

"And a maniac is out. How could he snatch fifteen, sixteen people? And return the children? Even a gang of maniacs couldn't do that, not with the number of cops we've got watching. Right?"

"Go on." Out of the corner of his eye, Mallen saw his neighbor's fat wife come down the back steps. She walked over to them and listened.

"The same goes for a gang of criminals, or even Martians. Impossible to do it, and no reason even if they could. We've got to look for something *illogical*—and that leaves just one logical answer."

Mallen waited, and glanced at the woman. She was looking at him, arms folded across her aproned chest. In fact, she was glaring at him. Can she be angry at me? Mallen thought. What have I done?

"The only answer," his neighbour said slowly, "is that there is a hole somewhere around here. A hole in the space-time continuum."

"What!" blurted Mallen. "I don't quite follow that."

"A hole in time," the bald engineer explained, "or a hole in space. Or in both. Don't ask me how it got there, it's there. What happens is, a person steps into that hole, and bingo! He's somewhere else. Or in some other time. Or both. This hole can't be seen, of course—it's fourth-dimensional—but it's there. The way I see it, if you traced the movements of these people, you'd find that every one of them passed through a certain spot—and vanished."

"Hmmm." Mallen thought it over. "That sounds interesting—but we know that lots of people vanished right out of their own homes."

"Yeah," the neighbor agreed. "Let me think—I know! The hole in space-time isn't fixed. It drifts, moves around. First it's in Carpenter's house, then it moves on aimlessly—"

"Why doesn't it move out of these four blocks?" Mallen asked, wondering why the man's wife was still glaring at him, her lips tightly compressed.

"Well," the neighbor said, "it has to have some limitations."

"And why were the children returned?"

"Oh, for heaven's sake. Mallen, you can't ask me to figure out every little thing, can you? It's a good working theory. We'll have to have more facts before we can work out the whole thing."

"Hello there!" Mr. Carter called, emerging from the garage. He held up two beautiful trout, neatly cleaned and washed.

"The trout is a game fighter and makes magnificent eating as well. The most excellent of sports, and the most excellent of foods!" He walked unhurriedly into the house.

"I've got a better theory," the neighbor's wife said, unfolding her arms and placing her hands on her ample hips.

Both men turned to look at her.

"Who is the only person around here who isn't the least bit worried about what's going on? Who goes walking all over with a bag he *says* has *fish* in it? Who *says* he spends all his time fishing?"

"Oh, no," Mallen said. "Not Dad Carter. He has a whole philosophy about fishing—"

"I don't care about philosophy!" the woman shrieked. "He fools you, but he doesn't fool me! I only know he's the only man in this neighborhood who isn't the least bit worried and he's around and gone every day and lynching would probably be too good for him!" With that she spun around and waddled into her house.

"Look, Mallen," the bald neighbor said. "I'm sorry. You know how women are. She's upset, even if Danny is safe in the hospital."

"Sure," Mallen said.

"She doesn't understand the space-time continuum," he went on earnestly. "But I'll explain it to her tonight. She'll apologize in the morning. You'll see."

The men shook hands and returned to their respective homes.

Darkness came swiftly, and searchlights went on all over town. Beams of light knifed down streets, into backyards, reflected from closed windows. The inhabitants of Vainsville settled down to wait for more disappearances.

Jim Mallen wished he could put his hands on whatever was

doing it. Just for a second—that was all he'd need. But to have to sit and wait—he felt so helpless. His wife's lips were pale and cracked, and her eyes were tired. But Mr. Carter was cheerful, as usual. He fried the trout on the kitchen range, and served both of them.

"I found a beautiful quiet pool today," Mr. Carter announced. "It is near the mouth of Old Creek, up a little tributary. I fished there all day, leaning back against the grassy bank and watching the clouds. Fantastic things, clouds! I'll go there tomorrow and fish in it one more day. Then I'll move on. A wise fisherman does not fish out a stream. Moderation is the code of the fisherman. Take a little, leave a little. I have often thought—"

"Oh, Dad, please!" Phyllis screamed, and burst into tears. Mr. Carter shook his head sadly, smiled an understanding smile, and finished his trout. Then he went into the living room to work on a new fly.

Exhausted, the Mallens went to bed.

Mallen awoke and sat upright. He looked over and saw his wife asleep beside him. The luminous dial of his watch read 4:58. Almost morning, he thought.

He got out of bed, slipped on a bathrobe, and padded softly downstairs. The searchlights were flashing against the living room window, and he could see a guard outside.

That was a reassuring sight, he thought, and went into the kitchen. Moving quietly, he poured a glass of milk. There was fresh cake on top of the refrigerator, and he cut himself a slice.

Kidnappers, he thought. Maniacs. Men from Mars. Holes in space. Or any combination thereof. No, that was wrong. He wished he could remember what he wanted to asked Mr. Carter. It was important.

He rinsed out the glass, put the cake back on the refrigerator, and walked to the living room. Suddenly he was thrown violently to one side.

Something had hold of him! He flailed out, but there was nothing to hit. Something was gripping him like an iron hand, dragging him off his feet. He threw himself to one side, scrambling for a footing. His feet left the floor and he hung for a moment, kicking and squirming. The grip around his ribs was so tight he couldn't breathe, couldn't make a sound. Inexorably, he was being lifted.

Hole in space, he thought, and tried to scream. His wildly flailing arms caught a corner of the couch and he seized it. The couch was lifted with him. He yanked, and the grip released for a moment, letting him drop to the floor.

He scrambled across the floor toward the door. The grip caught him again, but he was near a radiator. He wrapped both arms around it, trying to resist the pull. He yanked again and managed to get one leg around, then the other.

The radiator creaked horribly as the pull increased. Mallen felt as though his waist would part, but he held on, every muscle stretched to the breaking point. Suddenly the grip relaxed completely.

He collapsed to the floor.

When he came to, it was broad daylight. Phyllis was splashing water in his face, her lower lip caught between her teeth. He blinked, and wondered for a moment where he was.

"Am I still here?" he asked.

"Are you all right?" Phyllis demanded. "What happened? Oh, darling! Let's get out of this place—"

"Where's your father?" Mallen asked groggily, getting to his feet.

"Fishing. Now please sit down, I'm going to call a doctor."

"No. Wait." Mallen went into the kitchen. On the refrigerator was the cake box. It read *Johnson's Cake Shop, Vainsville, New YorK.* A capital *K* in *New York*. Really a very small error.

And Mr. Carter? Did he have the answer? Mallen raced upstairs and dressed. He crumpled the cake box, thrust it into his pocket, and hurried out the door.

"Don't touch anything until I get back!" he shouted at Phyllis. She watched him get into the car and race down the street. Trying hard to keep from crying, she walked into the kitchen.

Mallen was at Old Creek in fifteen minutes. He parked the car and started walking upstream.

"Mr. Carter!" he shouted as he went. "Mr. Carter!"

He walked and shouted for half an hour. The trees overhung the stream, and he had to wade to make any speed at all. He increased his pace, splashing, slipping on stones, trying to run.

"Mr. Carter!"

"Hello!" He heard the old man's voice. He followed the sound, up a branch of the stream. There was Mr. Carter, sitting on the steep bank of a little pool. holding his long bamboo pole. Mallen scrambled up beside him.

"Take it easy, son," Mr. Carter said. "Glad you took my advice about fishing."

"No," Mallen panted. "I want you to tell me something."

"Of course," the old man said. "What would you like to know?"

"A fisherman wouldn't fish out a pool completely, would he?"

"I wouldn't. But some might."

"And bait. Any good fisherman would use artificial bait?"

"I pride myself on my flies," Mr. Carter said. "I try to approximate the real thing. Here, for example, is a beautiful replica of a hornet." He plucked a yellow hook from his hat. "And here is a lovely mosquito."

Suddenly his line stirred. Easily, surely, the old man brought it in. He caught the gasping trout in his hand and showed it to Mallen.

"A little fellow—I won't keep him." He removed the hook gently, easing it out of the gasping gill, and placed the fish back in the water.

"When you throw him back—do you think he knows? Does he tell the others?"

"Oh, no," Mr. Carter said. "The experience doesn't teach him anything. I've had the same young fish bite my line two or three times. They have to grow up a bit before they know."

"I thought so." Mallen looked at the old man. Mr. Carter was unaware of the world around him, untouched by the terror that had struck Vainsville.

Fishermen live in a world of their own, thought Mallen.

"But you should have been here an hour ago," Mr. Carter said. "I hooked a beauty. A magnificent fellow, two pounds if he was an ounce. What a battle for an old war-horse like me! And he got away. Hey, where are you going?"

"Back!" Mallen shouted, splashing into the stream. He knew now what he had been looking for. A parallel. And now it was clear.

Harmless Mr. Carter, pulling up his trout, just like that other, greater fisherman, pulling up his—

"I'm going back to warn the other fish!" Mallen shouted over his shoulder, stumbling along the streambed. If only Phyllis hadn't touched any food! He pulled the cake box out of his pocket and threw it from him as hard as he could. The hateful lure!

While the fishermen, each in his respective sphere, smiled and dropped their lines into the water again.

SHAPE

Pid the Pilot slowed the ship almost to a standstill. He peered anxiously at the green planet below.

Even without instruments, there was no mistaking it. Third from its sun, it was the only planet in this system capable of sustaining life. Peacefully it swam through its gauze of clouds.

It looked very innocent. And yet, something on this planet had claimed the lives of every expedition the Glom had sent.

Pid hesitated a moment before starting irrevocably down. He and his two crewmen were as ready now as they would ever be. Their compact Displacers were stored in body pouches, inactive but ready.

Pid wanted to say something to his crew, but wasn't sure how to put it.

The crew waited. Ilg the Radioman had sent the final message to the Glom planet. Ger the Detector read sixteen dials at once, and reported, "No sign of alien activity." His body surfaces flowed carelessly.

Pid noticed the flow, and knew what he had to say. Ever since they had left Glom, Shape-discipline had been disgustingly lax. The Invasion Chief had warned him; but still, he had to do something about it. It was his duty, since lower castes such as Radiomen and Detectors were notoriously prone to Shapelessness.

"A lot of hopes are resting on this expedition," he began slowly. "We're a long way from home now."

Ger the Detector nodded. Ilg the Radioman flowed out of his prescribed Shape and molded himself comfortably to a wall.

"However," Pid said sternly, "distance is no excuse for promiscuous Shapelessness."

Ilg flowed hastily back into proper Radioman's Shape.

"Exotic Shapes will undoubtedly be called for," Pid went on. "And for that we have a special dispensation. But remember—any Shape not assumed strictly in the line of duty is a device of the Shapeless One!"

Ger's body surfaces abruptly stopped flowing.

"That's all," Pid said, and flowed into his controls. The ship started down, so smoothly coordinated that Pid felt a glow of pride.

They were good workers, he decided. He just couldn't expect them to be as Shape-conscious as a high-caste Pilot. Even the Invasion Chief had told him that.

"Pid," the Invasion Chief had said at their last interview, "we need this planet desperately."

"Yes, sir," Pid had said, standing at full attention, never quivering from Optimum Pilot's Shape.

"One of you," the Chief said heavily, "must get through and set up a Displacer near an atomic power source. The army will be standing by at this end, ready to step through."

"We'll do it, sir," Pid said.

"This expedition has to succeed," the Chief said, and his features blurred momentarily from sheer fatigue. "In strictest confidence, there's considerable unrest on Glom. The Miner caste is on strike, for instance. They want a new digging Shape. Say the old one is inefficient."

Pid looked properly indignant. The Mining Shape had been set down by the ancients fifty thousand years ago, together with the rest of the basic Shapes. And now these upstarts wanted to change it!

"That's not all," the Chief told him. "We've uncovered a new Cult of Shapelessness. Picked up almost eight thousand Glom, and I don't know how many more we missed."

Pid knew that Shapelessness was a lure of the Shapeless One, the greatest evil that the Glom mind conceived of. But how, we wondered, did Glom fall for His lures?

The Chief guessed his question. "Pid," he said, "I suppose it's difficult for you to understand. Do you enjoy Piloting?"

"Yes, sir," Pid said simply. *Enjoy* Piloting! It was his entire life! Without a ship, he was nothing.

"Not all Glom feel that way," the Chief said. "I don't understand it either. All my ancestors have been Invasion Chiefs, back to the beginning of time. So of course *I* want to be an Invasion Chief. It's only natural, as well as lawful. But the lower castes don't feel that way." He shook his body sadly.

"I've told you this for a reason," the Chief went on. "We Glom need more room. This unrest is caused purely by crowding. All our psychologists say so. Another planet to expand into will cure everything. So we're counting on you, Pid."

"Yes, sir," Pid said, with a glow of pride.

The Chief rose to end the interview. Then he changed his mind and sat down again.

"You'll have to watch your crew," he said. "They're loyal, no doubt, but low-caste. And you know the lower castes."

Pid did indeed.

"Ger, your Detector, is suspected of harboring Alterationist tendencies. He was once fined for assuming a quasi-Hunter Shape. Ilg has never had any definite charge brought against him. But I hear that he remains immobile for suspiciously long periods of time. Possibly he fancies himself a Thinker."

"But, sir," Pid protested. "If they are even slightly tainted with Alterationism or Shapelessness, why send them on this expedition?"

The Chief hesitated before answering. "There are plenty of Glom I could trust," he said slowly. "But those two have certain qualities of resourcefulness and imagination that will be needed on this expedition." He sighed. "I really don't understand why those qualities are usually linked with Shapelessness."

"Yes, sir," Pid said.

"Just watch them."

"Yes, sir," Pid said again, and saluted, realizing that the

interview was at an end. In his body pouch he felt the dormant Displacer, ready to transform the enemy's power source into a bridge across space for the Glom hordes.

"Good luck," the Chief said. "I'm sure you'll need it."

The ship dropped silently toward the surface of the enemy planet. Ger the Detector analyzed the clouds below, and fed data into the Camouflage Unit. The Unit went to work. Soon the ship looked, to all outward appearances, like a cirrus formation.

Pid allowed the ship to drift slowly toward the surface of the mystery planet. He was in Optimum Pilot's Shape now, the most efficient of the four shapes allotted to the Pilot caste. Blind, deaf, and dumb, an extension of his controls, all his attention was directed toward matching the velocities of the high-flying clouds, staying among them, becoming a part of them.

Ger remained rigidly in one of the two Shapes allotted to Detectors. He fed data into the Camouflage Unit, and the descending ship slowly altered into an altocumulus.

There was no sign of activity from the enemy planet.

Ilg located an atomic power source, and fed the data to Pid. The Pilot altered course. He had reached the lowest level of clouds, barely a mile above the surface of the planet. Now his ship looked like a fat, fleecy cumulus.

And still there was no sign of alarm. The unknown fate that had overtaken twenty previous expeditions still had not showed itself.

Dusk crept across the face of the planet as Pid maneuvered near the atomic power installation. He avoided the surrounding homes and hovered over a clump of woods. Darkness fell, and the green planet's lone moon was veiled in clouds.

One cloud floated lower.

And landed.

"Quick, everyone out!" Pid shouted, detaching himself from the ship's controls. He assumed the Pilot's Shape best suited for running, and raced out of the hatch. Ger and Ilg hurried after him. They stopped fifty yards from the ship and waited.

Inside the ship a circuit closed. There was a silent shudder, and the ship began to melt. Plastic dissolved, metal crumpled. Soon the ship was a great pile of junk, and still the process went on. Big fragments broke into smaller fragments, and split, and split again.

Pid felt suddenly helpless, watching his ship scuttle itself. He was a Pilot, of the Pilot caste. His father had been a Pilot, and his father before him, stretching back to the hazy past when the Glom had first constructed ships. He had spent his entire childhood around ships, his entire manhood flying them.

Now, shipless, he was naked in an alien world.

In a few minutes there was only a mound of dust to show where the ship had been. The night wind scattered it through the forest. And then there was nothing at all.

They waited. Nothing happened. The wind sighed and the trees creaked. Squirrels chirped, and birds stirred in their nests.

An acorn fell to the ground.

Pid heaved a sigh of relief and sat down. The twenty-first Glom expedition had landed safely.

There was nothing to be done until morning, so Pid began to make plans. They had landed as close to the atomic power installation as they dared. Now they would have to get closer. Somehow, one of them had to get very near the reactor room, in order to activate the Displacer.

Difficult. But Pid felt certain of success. After all, the Glom were strong on ingenuity.

Strong on ingenuity, he thought bitterly, but terribly short of radioactives. That was another reason why this expedition was so important. There was little radioactive fuel left on any of the Glom worlds.

Ages ago, the Glom had spent their store of radioactives spreading throughout their neighbor worlds, occupying the ones that they could live on. Colonization barely kept up with the mounting birth rate. New worlds were constantly needed.

This particular world, discovered in a scouting expedition, was needed. It suited the Glom perfectly. But it was too far away. They didn't have enough fuel to mount a conquering space fleet.

Luckily there was another way. A better way.

Over the centuries, the Glom scientists had developed the Displacer. A triumph of Identity Engineering, the Displacer allowed mass to be moved instantaneously between any two linked points.

One end was set up at Glom's sole atomic energy plant. The other end had to be placed in proximity to another atomic power source, and activated. Diverted power then flowed through both ends, was modified, and modified again.

Then, through the miracle of Identity Engineering, the Glom could *step* through from planet to planet—or pour through in a great, overwhelming wave.

It was quite simple. But twenty expeditions had failed to set up the Earth-end Displacer.

What has happened to them was not known.

For no Glom ship had ever returned to tell.

Before dawn they crept through the woods, taking on the coloration of the plants around them. Their Displacers pulsed feebly, sensing the nearness of atomic energy.

A tiny, four-legged creature darted in front of them. Instantly, Ger grew four legs and a long, streamlined body and gave chase.

"Ger! Come back here!" Pid howled at the Detector, throwing caution to the winds.

Ger overtook the animal and knocked it down. He tried to bite it, but he had neglected to grow teeth. The animal jumped free, and vanished into the underbrush. Ger thrust out a set of teeth and bunched his muscles for a leap.

"Ger!"

Reluctantly the Detector turned away. He loped silently back to Pid.

"I was hungry," he said.

"You were not," Pid said sternly.

"Was," Ger mumbled, writhing with embarrassment.

Pid remembered what the Chief had told him. Ger certainly did have Hunter tendencies. He would have to watch him more closely.

"We'll have no more of that," Pid said. "Remember—the lure of Exotic Shapes is not sanctioned. Be content with the Shape you were born to."

Ger nodded and melted back into the underbrush. They moved on.

At the extreme edge of the woods they could observe the atomic energy installation. Pid disguised himself as a clump of shrubbery and Ger formed himself into an old log. Ilg, after a moment's thought, became a young oak.

The installation was in the form of a long, low building, surrounded by a metal fence. There was a gate, and guards in front of it.

The first job, Pid thought, was to get past that gate. He began to consider ways and means.

From the fragmentary reports of the survey parties, Pid knew that, in some ways, this race of Men were like the Glom. They had pets, as the Glom did, and homes and children, and a culture. The inhabitants were skilled mechanically, as were the Glom.

But there were terrific differences. The Men were of fixed and immutable forms, like stones or trees. And to compensate, their planet boasted a fantastic array of species, types, and kinds. This was completely unlike Glom, which had only eight distinct forms of animal life.

And evidently the Men were skilled at detecting invaders, Pid thought. He wished he knew how the other expeditions had failed. It would make his job much easier.

A Man lurched past them on two incredibly stiff legs. Rigidity was evident in his every move. Without looking, he hurried past.

"I know," Ger said, after the creature had moved away. "I'll disguise myself as a Man, walk through the gate to the reactor room, and activate my Displacer."

"You can't speak their language," Pid pointed out.

"I won't speak at all. I'll ignore them. Look." Quickly Ger Shaped himself into a Man.

"That's not bad," Pid said.

Ger tried a few practice steps, copying the bumpy walk of the Man.

"But I'm afraid it won't work," Pid said.

"It's perfectly logical," Ger pointed out.

"I know. Therefore the other expeditions must have tried it. And none of them came back."

There was no arguing with that. Ger flowed back into the Shape of a log. "What, then?" he asked.

"Let me think," Pid said.

Another creature lurched past, on four legs instead of two. Pid recognized it as a Dog, a pet of Man. He watched it carefully.

The Dog ambled to the gate, head down, in no particular hurry. It walked through unchallenged, and lay down in the grass.

"Hmmm," Pid said.

They watched. One of the Men walked past, and touched the Dog on the head. The Dog stuck out its tongue and rolled over on its side.

"I can do that," Ger said excitedly. He started to flow into the Shape of a Dog.

"No, wait," Pid said. "We'll spend the rest of the day thinking it over. This is too important to rush into."

Ger subsided sulkily.

"Come on, let's move back," Pid said. He and Ger started into the woods. Then he remembered Ilg.

"Ilg?" he called softly.

There was no answer.

"Ilg!"

"What? Oh, yes," an oak tree said, and melted into a bush. "Sorry. What were you saying?"

"We're moving back," Pid said. "Were you, by any chance, Thinking?"

"Oh, no," Ilg assured him. "Just resting."

Pid let it go at that. There was too much else to worry about.

They discussed it for the rest of the day, hidden in the deepest part of the woods. The only alternatives seemed to be Man or Dog. A tree couldn't walk past the gates, since that was not in the nature of trees. Nor could anything else, and escape notice.

Going as a Man seemed too risky. They decided that Ger would sally out in the morning as a Dog.

"Now get some sleep," Pid said.

Obediently his two crewmen flattened out, going immediately Shapeless. But Pid had a more difficult time.

Everything looked too easy. Why wasn't the atomic installation better guarded? Certainly the Men must have learned something from the expeditions they had captured in the past. Or had they killed them without asking any questions?

You couldn't tell what an alien would do.

Was that open gate a trap?

Wearily he flowed into a comfortable position on the lumpy ground. Then he pulled himself together hastily.

He had gone Shapeless!

Comfort had nothing to do with duty, he reminded himself, and firmly took a Pilot's Shape.

But Pilot's Shape wasn't constructed for sleeping on damp, bumpy ground. Pid spent a restless night thinking of ships, and wishing he were flying one.

Pid awoke in the morning tired and ill-tempered. He nudged Ger.

"Let's get this over with," he said.

Ger flowed gaily to his feet.

"Come on, Ilg," Pid said angrily, looking around. "Wake up."

There was no reply.

"Ilg!" he called.

Still there was no reply.

"Help me look for him," Pid said to Ger. "He must be around here somewhere."

Together they tested every bush, tree, log, and shrub in the vicinity. But none of them was Ilg.

Pid began to feel a cold panic run through him. What could have happened to the Radioman?

"Perhaps he decided to go through the gate on his own," Ger suggested.

Pid considered the possibility. It seemed unlikely. Ilg had never shown much initiative. He had always been content to follow orders.

They waited. But midday came, and there was still no sign of Ilg.

"We can't wait any longer," Pid said, and they started through the woods. Pid wondered if Ilg *had* tried to get through the gates on his own. Those quiet types often concealed a foolhardy streak.

But there was nothing to show that Ilg had been successful. He would have to assume that the Radioman was dead, or captured by the Men.

That left two of them to activate a Displacer.

And still he didn't know what had happened to the other expeditions.

At the edge of the woods, Ger turned himself into a facsimile of a Dog. Pid inspected him carefully.

"A little less tail," he said.

Ger shortened his tail.

"More ears."

Ger lengthened his ears.

"Now even them up." He inspected the finished product. As far as he could tell, Ger was perfect, from the tip of his tail to his wet black nose.

"Good luck," Pid said.

"Thanks." Cautiously Ger moved out of the woods, walking in the lurching style of Dogs and Men. At the gate, the guard called to him. Pid held his breath.

Ger walked past the Man, ignoring him. The Man started to walk over, and Ger broke into a run.

Pid dissolved his legs with a sigh of relief.

But the main door was closed! Pid hoped the Radioman wouldn't try to open it. That was *not* in the nature of Dogs.

Another Dog came running toward Ger. Ger backed away from him. The Dog approached and sniffed. Ger sniffed back.

Then both of them ran around the building.

That was clever, Pid thought. There was bound to be a door in the rear.

He glanced up at the afternoon sun. As soon as the Displacer was activated, the Glom armies would begin to pour through. By the time the Men recovered from the shock, a million Glom troops would be here, with more following.

The day passed slowly, and nothing happened.

Nervously Pid watched the front of the plant. It shouldn't be taking so long, if Ger had been successful.

Late into the night he waited. Men walked in and out of the installation, and Dogs barked around the gates. But Ger did not appear.

Ger had failed. Ilg was gone. Only he was left.

And *still* he didn't know what had happened.

By morning, Pid was in complete despair. He knew that the twenty-first Glom expedition to this planet was near the point of complete failure. Now it was all up to him.

He decided to sally out boldly in the Shape of a Man. It was the only possibility left.

He saw that workers were arriving in great numbers, rushing through the gates. Pid wondered if he should try to mingle with them, or wait until there was less commotion. Deciding to take advantage of the apparent confusion, he started to Shape himself into a Man.

A Dog walked past the woods where he was hiding.

"Hello," the Dog said.

It was Ger!

"What happened?" Pid asked, with a sigh of relief. "Why were you so long? Couldn't you get in?"

"I don't know," Ger said, wagging his tail. "I didn't try."

Pid was speechless.

"I went Hunting," Ger said complacently. "This form is ideal for Hunting, you know. I went out the rear gate with another Dog."

"But the expedition—your duty—"

"I changed my mind," Ger told him. "You know, Pilot, I never wanted to be a Detector."

"But you were *born* a Detector!"

"That's true," Ger said. "But it doesn't help. I always wanted to be a Hunter."

Pid shook his entire body in annoyance. "You can't," he said very slowly, as one would explain to a Glomling. "The Hunter Shape is forbidden to you."

"Not here, it isn't," Ger said, still wagging his tail.

"Let's have no more of this," Pid said angrily. "Get into that installation and set up your Displacer. I'll try to overlook this heresy."

"I won't," Ger said. "I don't want the Glom here. They'd ruin it for the rest of us."

"He's right," an oak tree said.

"Ilg!" Pid gasped. "Where are you?"

Branches stirred. "I'm right here," Ilg said. "I've been Thinking."

"But—your caste—"

"Pilot," Ger said sadly, "why don't you wake up? Most of the people on Glom are miserable. Only custom makes us take the caste-Shape of our ancestors."

"Pilot," Ilg said, "all Glom are born Shapeless!"

"And being born Shapeless, all Glom should have Freedom of Shape," Ger said.

"Exactly," Ilg said. "But he'll never understand. Now excuse me. I want to Think." And the oak tree was silent.

Pid laughed humorlessly. "The Men will kill you off," he said. "Just as they killed off the rest of the expeditions."

"No one from Glom has been killed," Ger told him. "The other expeditions are right here."

"Alive?"

"Certainly. The Men don't even know we exist. That Dog I was Hunting with is a Glom from the nineteenth expedition. There are hundreds of us here, Pilot. We like it."

Pid tried to absorb it all. He had always known that the lower castes were lax in caste-consciousness. But this—this was preposterous!

This planet's secret menace was—freedom!

"Join us, Pilot," Ger said. "We've got a paradise here. Do you know how many species there are on this planet? An uncountable number! There's a Shape to suit every need!"

Pid shook his head. There was no Shape to suit *his* need. He was a Pilot.

But Men were unaware of the presence of the Glom. Getting near the reactor would be simple!

"The Glom Supreme Council will take care of all of you," he snarled, and Shaped himself into a Dog. "I'm going to set up the Displacer myself."

He studied himself for a moment, bared his teeth at Ger, and loped toward the gate.

The Men at the gate didn't even look at him. He slipped through the main door of the building behind a Man, and loped down a corridor.

The Displacer in his body pouch pulsed and tugged, leading him toward the reactor room.

He sprinted up a flight of stairs and down another corridor. There were footsteps around the bend, and Pid knew instinctively that Dogs were not allowed inside the building.

He looked around desperately for a hiding place, but the corridor was bare. However, there were several overhead lights in the ceiling.

Pid leaped, and glued himself to the ceiling. He shaped himself into a lighting fixture, and hoped that the Men wouldn't try to find out why he wasn't shining.

Men passed, running.

Pid changed himself into a facsimile of a Man, and hurried on.

He had to get closer.

Another Man came down the corridor. He looked sharply at Pid, started to speak, and then sprinted away.

Pid didn't know what was wrong, but he broke into a full sprint. The Displacer in his body pouch throbbed, telling him he had almost reached the critical distance.

Suddenly a terrible doubt assailed his mind. *All the expeditions had deserted! Every single Glom!*

He slowed slightly.

Freedom of Shape . . . that was a strange notion. A disturbing notion.

And obviously a device of the Shapeless One, he told himself, and rushed on.

At the end of the corridor was a gigantic bolted door. Pid stared at it.

Footsteps hammered down the corridor, and Men were shouting.

What was wrong? How had they detected him? Quickly he examined himself, and ran his fingers across his face.

He had forgotten to mold any features.

In despair he pulled at the door. He took the tiny Displacer out of his pouch, but the pulse beat wasn't quite strong enough. He had to get closer to the reactor.

He studied the door. There was a tiny crack running under it. Pid went quickly Shapeless and flowed under, barely squeezing the Displacer through.

Inside the room he found another bolt, on the inside of the door. He jammed it into place, and looked around for something to prop against the door.

It was a tiny room. On one side was a shielded door leading to the reactor. There was a small window on another side, and that was all.

Pid looked at the Displacer. The pulse beat was right. At last he was close enough. Here the Displacer could work, drawing and altering the energy from the reactor. All he had to do was activate it.

But they had all deserted, every one of them.

Pid hesitated. *All Glom are born Shapeless.* That was true. Glom children were amorphous until old enough to be instructed in the caste-Shapes of their ancestors. But Freedom of Shape?

Pid considered the possibilities. To be able to take on any Shape he wanted, without interference! On this paradise planet, he could fulfill any ambition, become anything, do anything.

Nor would he be lonely. There were other Glom here as well, enjoying the benefits of Freedom of Shape.

The Men were beginning to break down the door. Pid was still uncertain.

What should he do? Freedom . . .

But not for him, he thought bitterly. It was easy enough to be a Hunter or a Thinker. But he was a Pilot. Piloting was his life and love. How could he do that here?

Of course, the Men had ships. He could turn into a Man, find a ship . . .

Never. Easy enough to become a Tree or a Dog. He could never pass successfully as a Man.

The door was beginning to splinter from repeated blows.

Pid walked to the window to take a last look at the planet before activating the Displacer.

He looked—and almost collapsed from shock.

It was really true! He hadn't fully understood what Ger had meant when he said that there were species on this planet to satisfy every need. *Every* need! Even his!

Here he could satisfy a longing of the Pilot Caste that went even deeper than Piloting.

He looked again, then smashed the Displacer to the floor. The door burst open, and in the same instant he flung himself through the window.

The Men raced to the window and stared out. But they were unable to understand what they saw.

There was only a great white bird, flapping awkwardly but with increasing strength, trying to overtake a flight of birds in the distance.

BESIDE STILL WATERS

Mark Rogers was a prospector, and he went to the asteroid belt looking for radioactive ores and rare metals. He searched for years, never finding much, hopping from fragment to fragment. After a time he settled on a slab of rock half a mile thick.

Rogers had been born old, and he didn't age much, past a point. His face was white with the pallor of space, and his hands shook a little. He called his slab of rock Martha, after no girl he had ever known.

He made a small strike, enough to equip Martha with an air pump and a shack, a few tons of dirt and some water tanks, and a robot. Then he settled back and watched the stars.

The robot he bought was a standard-model all-around worker, with built-in memory and a thirty-word vocabulary. Mark added to that, bit by bit. He was something of a tinkerer, and he enjoyed adapting his environment to himself.

At first, all the robot could say was "Yes, sir," and "No, sir." He could state simple problems: "The air pump is laboring, sir"; "The corn is budding, sir." He could perform a satisfactory greeting: "Good morning, sir."

Mark changed that. He eliminated the word *sir* from the robot's vocabulary; equality was the rule on Mark's hunk of rock. Then he dubbed the robot Charles, after a father he had never known.

As the years passed, the air pump began to labor as it converted the oxygen in the planetoid's rock into a breathable atmosphere. The air seeped into space, and the pump worked a little harder, supplying more.

126

The crops continued to grow on the tamed black dirt of the planetoid. Looking up, Mark could see the sheer blackness of the river of space, the floating points of the stars. Around him, under him, overhead, masses of rock drifted, and sometimes the starlight glinted from their black sides. Occasionally Mark caught a glimpse of Mars or Jupiter. Once he thought he saw Earth.

Mark began to tape new responses into Charles. He added simple responses to cue words. When he said, "How does it look?" Charles would answer, "Oh, pretty good, I guess."

At first the answers were what Mark had been answering himself, in the long dialogue held over the years. But slowly he began to build a new personality into Charles.

Mark had always been suspicious and scornful of women. But for some reason he didn't tape the same suspicion into Charles. Charles's outlook was quite different.

"What do you think of girls?" Mark would ask, sitting on a packing case outside the shack, after the chores were done.

"Oh, I don't know. You have to find the right one," the robot would reply dutifully, repeating what had been put on its tape.

"I never saw a good one yet," Mark would say.

"Well, that's not fair. Perhaps you didn't look long enough. There's a girl in the world for every man."

"You're a romantic!" Mark would say scornfully. The robot would pause—a built-in pause—and chuckle a carefully constructed chuckle.

"I dreamed of a girl named Martha once," Charles would say. "Maybe if I'd looked, I would have found her."

And then it would be bedtime. Or perhaps Mark would want more conversation. "What do you think of girls?" he would ask again, and the discussion would follow the same course.

Charles grew old. His limbs lost their flexibility, and some of his wiring started to corrode. Mark would spend hours keeping the robot in repair.

"You're getting rusty," he would cackle.

"You're not so young yourself," Charles would reply. He had an answer for almost everything. Nothing elaborate, but an answer.

It was always night on Martha, but Mark broke up his time into mornings, afternoons, and evenings. Their life followed a simple routine. Breakfast, from vegetables and Mark's canned store. Then the robot would work in the fields, and the plants grew used to his touch. Mark would repair the pump, check the water supply, and straighten up the immaculate shack. By lunchtime, the robot's chores were usually finished.

The two would sit on the packing case and watch the stars. They would talk until supper, and sometimes late into the endless night.

In time, Mark built more complicated conversations into Charles. He couldn't give the robot free choice, of course, but he managed a pretty good simulation of it. Slowly Charles's personality emerged. It was strikingly different from Mark's.

Where Mark was querulous, Charles was calm; where Mark was sardonic, Charles was naïve; where Mark was cynical, Charles was idealistic; where Mark was often sad, Charles was forever content.

And in time Mark forgot he had built the answers into Charles. He accepted the robot as a friend of about his own age. A friend of long years' standing.

"The thing I don't understand," Mark would say, "is why a man like you wants to live here. I mean, it's all right for me. No one cares about me, and I never gave much of a damn about anyone. But why you?"

"Here I have a whole world," Charles would reply, "where on Earth I had to share with billions. I have the stars, bigger and brighter than on Earth. I have all space around me, close, like still waters. And I have you, Mark."

"Now don't go getting sentimental on me—"

"I'm not. Friendship counts. Love was lost long ago, Mark. The love of a girl named Martha, whom neither of us ever met. And that's a pity. But friendship remains, and the eternal night."

"You're a bloody poet," Mark would say, half admiringly.

"A poor poet."

Time passed, unnoticed by the stars, and the air pump hissed and clanked and leaked. Mark fixed it constantly, but the air on

Martha became increasingly rare. Although Charles continued laboring in the fields, the crops, deprived of sufficient air, died.

Mark was tired now, and barely able to crawl around, even without the grip of gravity. He stayed in his bunk most of the time. Charles fed him as well as he could, moving on rusty, creaky limbs.

"What do you think of girls?"

"You have to find the right one."

"I never saw a good one yet."

"Well, that's not fair."

Mark was too tired to see the end coming, and Charles wasn't interested. But the end was on its way. The air pump threatened to give out momentarily. There hadn't been any food for days.

"But why you?"

"Here I have a whole world—"

"Don't get sentimental—"

"And the love of a girl named Martha."

From his bunk, Mark saw the stars for the last time. Big, bigger than ever, endlessly floating in the still waters of space.

"The stars . . ." Mark said.

"Yes?"

"The sun?"

"Lost long ago—and the eternal night."

"A bloody poet."

"A poor poet."

"And girls?"

"I dreamed of a girl named Martha once. Maybe if—"

"What do you think of girls? And stars? And Earth?" And it was bedtime, this time forever.

Charles stood beside the body of his friend. He felt for a pulse once, and allowed the withered hand to fall. He walked to a corner of the shack and turned off the tired air pump.

The tape that Mark had prepared had a few cracked inches left to run. "I hope he finds his Martha," the robot croaked.

Then the tape broke.

His rusted limbs would not bend, and he stood frozen, staring back at the naked stars. Then he bowed his head.

"The Lord is my shepherd," Charles said. "I shall not want. He maketh me to lie down in green pastures; he leadeth me . . ."

SILVERSMITH WISHES

The stranger lifted his glass. "May your conclusions always flow sweetly from your premises."

"I'll drink to that," said Nelson Silversmith.

Solemnly they both sipped Orange Julius. Outside, the flotsam of Eighth Street flowed eastward, to circulate with sluggish restlessness in the Sargasso of Washington Square. Silversmith munched his chili dog.

The stranger said, "I suppose you think I'm some kind of a nut."

Silversmith shrugged. "I assume nothing."

"Well spoken," the stranger said. "My name is Terence Maginnis. Come have a drink with me."

"Don't mind if I do," Silversmith said.

Some twenty minutes later they were seated on torn red plastic benches in Joe Mangeri's Clam Bar and Beer Parlor, exchanging fragments of discursive philosophy, as casual strangers meeting in New York's Greenwich Village on a slow, mild October afternoon will do. Maginnis was a short, compact, red-faced man with emphatic gestures wearing a fuzzy Harris tweed suit. Silversmith was a lanky thirty-two-year-old with a mournful face and long, tapering fingers.

"So look," Maginnis said abruptly, "enough small talk. I have a proposition to put to you."

"So put," Silversmith said with aplomb. Not for nothing had he been brought up in the bewildering social complexities of Bayonne, New Jersey.

"It is this," Maginnis said. "I am a front man for a certain organization which must remain nameless. We have a free introductory offer. We give you, absolutely free and without obligation, three requests. You may ask for any three things and I will get them for you if it is within my power."

"And what do I do in return?" Silversmith asked.

"Nothing whatsoever. You just sit back and take."

"Three requests," Silversmith said thoughtfully. "Do you mean three wishes?"

"Yes, you could call it that."

"A person who grants wishes is a fairy."

"I am not a fairy," Maginnis said firmly.

"But you do grant wishes?"

"Yes. I am a normal person who grants wishes."

"And I," Silversmith said, "am a normal person who makes wishes. So, for my first wish, I would like a really good hi-fi with quad speakers, tape deck, and all the rest."

"You are a cool one," Maginnis said.

"Did you really expect astonishment?"

"I anticipated dubiety, anxiety, resistance. People generally look with suspicion on a proposition like mine."

"The only thing I learned at NYU," Silversmith said, "was the willing suspension of disbelief. Do you get many takers?"

"You're my first in a long time. People simply don't believe it can be on the level."

"Incredulity is not an appropriate attitude in this age of Heisenbergian physics. Ever since I read in *Scientific American* that a position is nothing more than an electron traveling backward in time, I have had no difficulty believing anything at all."

"I must remember to put that into my sales pitch," Maginnis said. "Now give me your address. You'll be hearing from me."

Three days later, Maginnis went to Silversmith's fifth-floor walkup on Perry Street. He was lugging a large packing case and perspiring freely. His tweed suit smelled like an overworked camel.

"What a day!" he said. "I've been all over Long Island City, looking for just the right rig. Where shall I put it?"

"Right there is fine," Silversmith said. "What about the tape deck?"

"I'm bringing it this afternoon. Have you thought about your second wish yet?"

"A Ferrari. A red one."

"To hear is to obey," Maginnis said. "Doesn't all this strike you as rather fantastic?"

"Phenomenology takes these matters into account," Silversmith said. "Or, as the Buddhists say, 'The world is of a suchness.' Can you get me a recent model?"

"I think I can put my hands on a new one," Maginnis said. "With supercharger and genuine walnut dashboard."

"Now you begin to astonish me," Silversmith said. "But where'll I park it?"

"That's your problem," Maginnis said. "Catch you later."

Silversmith waved absentmindedly and began to open the packing case.

Next, Maginnis found him a spacious, rent-controlled triplex on Patchin Place for $110.00 a month, including utilities. With it, Maginnis gave Silversmith five bonus wishes.

"You can really do that?" Silversmith asked. "You won't get into trouble with your company?"

"Don't worry about that. You know, you're a really good wisher. Your tastes are rich but not outrageous; challenging but not incredible. Some people really abuse the privilege—demand palaces and slaves, and harems filled with Miss America runners-up."

"I suppose that sort of thing is out of the question," Silversmith remarked casually.

"No, I can come up with it. But it just makes trouble for the wisher. You give some slob a replica of the Tsar's summer palace on a ten-acre site in Poughkeepsie, New York, and the next thing you know the tax people are buzzing around him like a holocaust of locusts. The guy usually has difficulty explaining how he managed to save up for this palace on the one-twenty-five a week he earns as a junior Comptometer operator, so the IRS makes its own assumptions."

"Which are?"

"That he's a top Mafia button man who knows where Judge Crater is buried."

"They can't prove anything, though."

"Maybe not. But who wants to spend the rest of his life starring in FBI home movies?"

"Not a pleasing prospect for a lover of privacy," Silversmith said, and revised several of his plans.

"You've been a good customer," Maginnis said, two weeks later. "Today you get a bonus, and it's absolutely free. You get a forty-foot Chris-Craft, fully equipped. Where do you want it?"

"Just moor it at the dock of my Nassau place," Silversmith said. "Oh, and thanks."

"Another free gift," Maginnis said, three days after that. "Ten additional wishes, no strings attached."

"That makes eighteen unused wishes to date," Silversmith said. "Maybe you should give some to another deserving customer."

"Don't be silly," Maginnis said. "We're very pleased with you."

Silversmith fingered his brocade scarf and said, "There *is* a catch, isn't there?"

It was one month and fourteen wishes later. Silversmith and Maginnis were seated in lawn chairs on the broad lawn of Silversmith's estate in Juan-les-Pins on the French Riviera. A string quartet was playing softly in the background. Silversmith was sipping a Negroni. Maginnis, looking more harried than usual, was gulping a whiskey and soda.

"Well, you could call it a catch," Maginnis admitted. "But it's not what you think."

"What is it?"

"You know I can't tell you that."

"Do I maybe end up losing my soul to you and going to hell?"

Maginnis burst into rude laughter. "That," he said, "is just about the last thing you have to worry about. Excuse me now. I've got an appointment in Damascus to see about that Arabian stallion you wanted. You get five more bonus wishes this week, by the way."

Two months later, after dismissing the dancing girls, Silversmith lay alone in his emperor-sized bed in his eighteen-room apartment on the Pincio in Rome and thought sour thoughts. He had twenty-seven wishes coming to him and he couldn't think of a thing to wish for. And furthermore, he was not happy.

Silversmith sighed and reached for the glass that was always on his night table, filled with seltzer flown in from Grossinger's. The glass was empty.

"Ten servants and they can't keep a lousy glass filled," he muttered. He got out of bed, walked across the room, and pushed the servants' button. Then he got back into bed. It took three minutes and thirty-eight seconds by his Rolex Oyster, whose case was carved out of a single block of amber, for the butler's second assistant to hurry into the room.

Silversmith pointed to the glass. The assistant butler's eyes bugged out and his jaw fell. "Empty!" he cried. "But I specifically told the maid's assistant—"

"To hell with excuses," Silversmith said. "Some people are going to have to get on the ball around here or heads are going to roll."

"Yes, *sir*!" said the butler's second assistant. He hurried to the built-in refrigerator beside Silversmith's bed, opened it, and took out a bottle of seltzer. He put the bottle on a tray, took out a snowy linen towel, folded it once lengthwise, and hung it over his arm. He selected a chilled glass from the refrigerator, examined it for cleanliness, substituted another glass, and wiped the rim with his towel.

"Get on with it, get *on* with it," Silversmith said ominously.

The butler's second assistant quickly wrapped the towel around the seltzer bottle and squirted seltzer into the glass so exquisitely that he didn't spill a drop. He replaced the bottle in the refrigerator and handed the glass to Silversmith. Total elapsed time, twelve minutes, forty-three seconds.

Silversmith lay in bed, sipping seltzer and thinking deep, brooding thoughts about the impossibility of happiness and the elusiveness of satisfaction. Despite having the world's luxuries spread before him, he was bored, and had been for weeks. It seemed damned unfair to him to be able to get anything you wanted but to be unable to enjoy what you could get.

When you came right down to it, life was a disappointment and the best it had to offer was never quite good enough. The roast duck was never as crisp as advertised, and the water in the swimming pool was always a shade too warm or too cold.

How elusive was the quest for quality? For ten dollars you could buy a pretty fair steak; for one hundred dollars you could get a really good porterhouse; and for one thousand dollars you could buy a kilo of Kobe beef that had been massaged by consecrated virgins, together with a genius chef to prepare it. And it would be very good, indeed. But not one thousand dollars worth of good. The more you paid, the less progress you made toward that quintessence of beef that the angels eat when God throws His yearly banquet for the staff.

Or consider women. Silversmith had possessed some of the most intoxicating creatures that the planet could offer, both singly and in ensemble. But even this had turned out to be nothing worth writing a memoir about. His appetite had palled too quickly in the steady flood of piquantly costumed flesh that Maginnis had provided, and the electric touch of unknown female had turned abrasive—the sandpaper of too many personalities (each one clutching her press clippings) against Silversmith's increasingly reluctant hide.

He had run through the equivalent of several seraglios, and the individuals in them were as dim in his memory now as were the individual ice cream cones of his youth. He vaguely remembered a Miss Universe winner with the odor of a judge's cigar still clinging to her crisp chestnut hair; and there had been the gum-chewing scuba instructress from Sea Island, Georgia, in her exciting black rubber wet suit, blowing an inopportune pink, sugary bubble at the moment of moments. But the rest of them had passed from his recollection in a comic strip of sweaty thighs, jiggling boobs, painted smiles, fake pouts, stagy languors—and through it all, the steady, heaving rhythm of the world's oldest gymnastic exercise.

The best of them had been his matched set of three Cambodian temple dancers—brown and bright-eyed creatures, all flashing eyes and floating black hair, sinuous frail limbs and small, hard breasts like persimmons. Not even they had diverted him for long. However, he had kept them around to play bridge with in the evenings.

He took another sip of seltzer and found that his glass was empty. Grumpily he got out of bed and crossed the room to the servants' bell. His finger poised over it—

And just at that moment, enlightenment came to him like a million-watt light bulb flashing in his head.

And he knew what he had to do.

It took Maginnis ten days to find Silversmith in a broken-down hotel on Tenth Avenue and Forty-first Street. Maginnis knocked once and walked in. It was a dingy room, with tin-covered walls painted a poisonous green. The smell of hundreds of applications of insecticide mingled queasily with the odor of thousands of generations of cockroaches. Silversmith was sitting on an iron cot covered with an olive-drab blanket. He was doing a crossword puzzle. He gave Maginnis a cheerful nod.

"All right," Maginnis said, "if you're through slumming, I've got a load of stuff for you—wishes forty-three and forty-four, plus as much of forty-five as I could put together. Which of your houses shall I deliver it to?"

"I don't want it," Silversmith said.

"You don't, huh?"

"No, I don't."

Maginnis lit a cigar. He puffed thoughtfully for a while, then said, "Is this Silversmith I see before me, the famous ascetic, the well-known stoic, the Taoist philosopher, the living Buddha? Nonattachment to worldly goods, that's the new number, right,

Silversmith? Believe me, baby, you'll never bring it off. You're going through a typical rich man's freakout, which will last a few weeks or months, like they all do. But then comes the day when the brown rice tastes extra nasty and the burlap shirt scratches your eczema worse than usual. This is followed by some fast rationalizing, and the next thing you know, you're having eggs Benedict at Sardi's and telling your friends what a valuable experience it was."

"You're probably right," Silversmith said.

"So why make me hang around all that time? You just took in too much Fat City too quick and you've got congestion of the synapses. You need a rest. Let me recommend a very nice resort I know on the south slope of Kilimanjaro—"

"No," Silversmith said.

"Maybe something more spiritual? I know this guru—"

"No."

"You are beginning to exasperate me," Maginnis said. "In fact, you're getting me sore. Silversmith, *what do you want?*"

"I want to be happy," Silversmith said. "But I realize now that I can't be happy by owning things."

"So you're sticking to poverty?"

"No. I also can't be happy by *not* owning things."

"Well," Maginnis said, "that seems to cover the field."

"I think there is another alternative," Silversmith said. "But I don't know what you're going to think of it."

"Yeah? What is it?"

"I want to join your team," Silversmith said.

Maginnis sat down on the bed. "You want to join us?"

"Whoever you are," Silversmith said, "I want to be a part of it."

"What made you decide that?" Maginnis asked.

"I happened to notice that you were happier than I was. I don't know what your racket is, Maginnis, and I have certain reservations about the organization I think you work for. But I really do want in."

"Are you willing to give up all your remaining wishes and everything else, just for that?"

"Whatever it takes," Silversmith said.

"Okay," Maginnis said, "you're in."

"I really am? That's great. Whose life do we mess up next?"

"Oh, we're not *that* organization at all," Maginnis said, grinning. "People sometimes do confuse the two of us, though I can't imagine why. But be that as it may, you have just endowed us with all your worldly goods, Silversmith, and you have done so without expectation of reward, out of a simple desire to serve. We appreciate the gesture, Silversmith, welcome to heaven."

A rosy cloud formed around them, and through it Silversmith could see a vast silver gate inlaid with mother-of-pearl.

"Hey!" he said. "You got me here on a deception! You tricked me, Maginnis, or whoever you are!"

"The other organization has been doing that sort of thing for so long," Maginnis said, "we thought we really should give it a try."

The pearly gates opened. Silversmith could see that a Chinese banquet had been set out, and there were girls, and some of the guests seemed to be smoking dope. "Not that I'm complaining," Silversmith said.

MEANWHILE,
BACK AT THE BROMIDE

THE DESPERATE CHASE

This time it looked like the end for Arkady Varadin, formerly a magician, now a much-wanted criminal. Cool and resourceful in the face of danger, cunning and ruthless, dangerous as a puff adder, master of illusion and fanciful escapes, the thin-faced Varadin had overstepped himself this time.

After a spectacular escape from the Denning maximum-security penitentiary, any other man would have stayed out of sight. Not Varadin. Singlehanded, he had held up a bank in the small town of Croesus, Maine. Escaping, he had shot and killed two guards who were foolish enough to reach for their guns. He had stolen a car and made off.

But then his luck turned. The FBI had been waiting for something like this. Within an hour they were on Varadin's trail. Even then the master criminal might have escaped; but his stolen car ran out of gas.

Varadin abandoned the car and went into the mountains. Five FBI agents were close behind. At long range, Varadin plugged two of them with six shots from his revolver. He had no more ammunition. There were still three agents coming up the mountain, and a local guide was with them.

A bad break! Varadin hurried on. All he had now was $75,000

of bank money, and his escape kit. He tried to throw off his pursuers, leading them up mountains and doubling back through valleys.

But the Maine guide could not be deceived in his native woods. Inexorably the gap closed between the hunters and the hunted.

At last Varadin found himself on a dirt road. He followed it and came to a granite quarry. Beyond the quarry, cliffs tilted steeply into the boulder-strewn sea. To climb down was possible; but the FBI agents would pick him off before he reached the bottom.

He looked around. The quarry was strewn with gray granite boulders of all sizes and shapes. Varadin's luck, his fantastic luck, was still with him. It was time for his final illusion.

He opened his escape kit and took out an industrial plastic that he had modified for his own use. His quick fingers constructed a framework of branches, lashing them together with his shoelaces. Over this he spread the plastic, rubbing dirt and granite dust into it. When he was done, he stepped back and surveyed his work.

Yes, it looked like any other large boulder, except for a hole in one side.

Varadin stepped in through this hole and, with his remaining plastic, sealed all but a tiny breathing hole. His concealment was complete. Now, with fatalistic calm, he waited to see if the trick would work.

In minutes the FBI men and the guide reached the quarry. They searched it thoroughly, then ran to the edge and looked over. At last they sat down on a large gray boulder.

"He must have jumped," said the guide.

"I don't believe it," said the chief agent. "You don't know Varadin."

"Well, he ain't here," said the guide. "And he couldn't have doubled back on us."

The chief agent scowled and tried to think. He put a cigarette in his mouth and scratched a match on the boulder. The match wouldn't light.

"That's funny," he said. "Either I've got wet matches or you've got soft boulders."

The guide shrugged his shoulders.

The agent was about to say something else when an old panel truck with ten men in the back drove into the quarry.

"Catch him yet?" the driver asked.

"Nope," the agent said. "I guess he must have gone over the edge."

"Good riddance," the truck driver said. "In that case, if you gents don't mind—"

The FBI agent shrugged his shoulders.

"Okay, I guess we can write him off." He stood up, and the guide and the other agents followed him out of the quarry.

"All right, boys," the driver said. "Let's go to work."

The men scrambled out of the truck, which was marked EASTERN MAINE GRAVEL CORPORATION.

"Ted," the driver said, "you might as well plant your first charges under that big boulder the G-man was sitting on."

THE DISGUISED AGENT

James Hadley, the famous Secret Service agent, was caught. On his way to the Istanbul airport, his enemies had pursued him into a cul-de-sac near the Golden Horn. They had dragged him into a long black limousine driven by an oily, scarfaced Greek. Car and chauffeur waited outside while Hadley's captors took him upstairs to a disreputable room in Istanbul's Armenian sector, not far from the Rue Chaffre.

It was the worst spot the famous agent had ever been in. He was strapped to a heavy chair. Standing in front of him was Anton Lupescu, the sadistic head of the Rumanian secret police and implacable foe of Western forces. On either side of Lupescu stood Chang, Lupescu's impassive manservant, and Madam Oui, the cold, beautiful Eurasian.

"Pig of an American," sneered Lupescu, "will you tell us where you have hidden the plans for America's new high-orbiting submolecular three-stage fusion-conversion unit?"

Hadley merely smiled beneath his gag.

"My friend," Lupescu said softly, "there is pain that no man can bear. Why not save yourself the annoyance?"

Hadley's gray eyes were amused. He did not answer.

"Bring the torture instruments," Lupescu said, sneering. "We will make the capitalist dog speak."

Chang and Madam Oui left the room. Quickly Lupescu unstrapped Hadley.

"We must hurry, old man," Lupescu said. "They'll be back in a shake."

"I don't understand," Hadley said. "You are—"

"British Agent 432 at your service," Lupescu said, bowing, a twinkle in his eye. "Couldn't reveal myself with Chang and Madam Oui mucking about. Now get those plans back to Washington, old fellow. Here's a gun. You might need it."

Hadley took the heavy, silenced automatic, snapped off the safety, and shot Lupescu through the heart.

"Your loyalty to the People's Government," Hadley said in perfect Russian, "has long been suspect. Now we know. The Kremlin will be amused."

Hadley stepped over the corpse and opened the door. Standing in front of him was Chang.

"Dog!" Chang snarled, lifting a heavy, silenced automatic.

"Wait!" Hadley cried. "You don't understand—"

Chang fired once. Hadley slumped to the floor.

Quickly Chang stripped off his oriental disguise, revealing himself as the true Anton Lupescu. Madam Oui came back into the room and gasped.

"Do not be alarmed, little one," Lupescu said. "The impostor who called himself Hadley was actually Chang, a Chinese spy."

"But who was the other Lupescu?" Madam Oui asked.

"Obviously," Lupescu said, "he was the true James Hadley. Now where could those plans be?"

A careful search revealed a wart on the right arm of the corpse of the man who had claimed to be James Hadley. The wart was artificial. Under it were the precious microfilm plans.

"The Kremlin will reward us," Lupescu said. "Now we—"

He stopped. Madam Oui had picked up a heavy, silenced automatic. "Dog!" she hissed, and shot Lupescu through the heart.

Swiftly Madam Oui stripped off her disguise, revealing beneath it the person of the true James Hadley, American secret agent.

Hadley hurried down to the street. The black limousine was still waiting, and the scarfaced Greek had drawn a gun.

"Well?" the Greek asked.

"I have them," said Hadley. "You did your work well, Chang."

"Nothing to it," said the chauffeur, stripping off his disguise and revealing the face of the wily Chinese Nationalist detective. "We had better hurry to the airport, eh, old boy?"

"Quite," said James Hadley.

The powerful black car sped into the darkness. In a corner of the car, something moved and clutched Hadley's arm.

It was the true Madam Oui.

"Oh, Jimmy," she said, "is it all over, at last?"

"It's all over. We've won," Hadley said, holding the beautiful Eurasian girl tightly to him.

THE LOCKED ROOM

Sir Trevor Mellanby, the eccentric old British scientist, kept a small laboratory on a corner of his Kent estate. He entered his lab on the morning of June 17. When three days passed and the aged peer did not emerge, his family grew anxious. Finding the doors and windows of the laboratory locked, they summoned the police.

The police broke down the heavy oak door. Inside they found Sir Trevor sprawled lifeless across the concrete floor. The famous scientist's throat had been savagely ripped out. The murder weapon, a three-pronged garden claw, was lying nearby. Also, an expensive Bokhara rug had been stolen. Yet all doors and windows were securely barred from the inside.

It was an impossible murder, an impossible theft. Yet there it was. Under the circumstances, Chief Inspector Morton was called. He came at once, bringing his friend Dr. Crutch, the famous amateur criminologist.

"Hang it all, Crutch," Inspector Morton said, several hours later. "I confess the thing has me stumped."

"It does seem rather a facer," Crutch said, peering nearsightedly at the rows of empty cages, the bare concrete floor, and the cabinet full of gleaming scalpels.

"Curse it all," the inspector said, "I've tested every inch of wall, floor, and ceiling for secret passages. Solid, absolutely solid."

"You're certain of that?" Dr. Crutch asked, a look of surprise on his jolly face.

"Absolutely. But I don't see—"

"It becomes quite obvious," Dr. Crutch said. "Tell me, have you counted the lights in the lab?"

"Of course. Six."

"Correct. Now if you count the light *switches*, you will find seven."

"But I don't see—"

"Isn't it obvious?" Crutch asked. "When have you ever heard of *absolutely solid walls*? Let's try those switches!"

One by one they turned the switches. When they turned the last, there was an ominous grinding sound. The roof of the laboratory began to rise, lifted on massive steel screws.

"Great Scott!" cried Inspector Morton.

"Exactly," said Dr. Crutch. "One of Sir Trevor's little eccentricities. He liked his ventilation."

"So the murderer killed him, crawled out between roof and wall, then closed a switch on the outside—"

"Not at all," Dr. Crutch said. "Those screws haven't been used in months. Furthermore, the maximum opening between wall and ceiling is less than seven inches. No, Morton, the murderer was far more diabolical than that."

"I'll be cursed if I can see it," Morton said.

"Ask yourself," Crutch said, "why the murderer should use a weapon as clumsy as a garden claw instead of the deadly scalpels *right here to hand*!"

"Blast it all," Morton said, "I don't know why."

"There is a reason," Crutch said grimly. "Do you know anything of the nature of Sir Trevor's research?"

"All England knows that," Morton said. "He was working on a method to increase animal intelligence. Do you mean—"

"Precisely," Crutch said. "Sir Trevor's method worked, but he had no chance to give it to the world. Have you noticed how empty these cages are? *Mice* were in them, Morton! His own mice killed him, then fled down the drains."

"I—I can't believe it," Morton said, stunned. "Why did they use the claw?"

"Think, man!" cried Crutch. They wanted to conceal their crime. They didn't want all England on a mouse hunt! So they used the claw to rip out Sir Trevor's throat—*after* he was dead."

"Why?"

"To disguise the marks of their teeth," Crutch said quietly.

"Hmm. But wait!" Morton said. "It's an ingenious theory, Crutch, but it doesn't explain the theft of the rug!"

"The missing rug is my final clue," Dr. Crutch said. "A microscopic examination will show that the rug was chewed to bits and carried down the drains piece by piece."

"What on earth for?"

"Solely," said Dr. Crutch, "*to conceal the bloody footprints of a thousand tiny feet.*"

"What can we do?" Morton said, after a pause.

"Nothing!" Crutch said savagely. "Personally, I propose to go home and purchase several dozen cats. I suggest that you do likewise."

FOOL'S MATE

The players met on the great, timeless board of space. The glittering dots that were the pieces swam in their separate patterns. In that configuration at the beginning, even before the first move was made, the outcome of the game was determined.

Both players saw, and knew which had won. But they played on.

Because the game had to be played out.

"Nielson!"

Lieutenant Nielson sat in front of his gunfire board with an idyllic smile on his face. He didn't look up.

"Nielson!"

The lieutenant was looking at his fingers with the stare of a puzzled child.

"Nielson! Snap out of it!" General Branch loomed sternly over him. "Do you hear me, Lieutenant?"

Nielson shook his head dully. He started to look at his fingers again, then his gaze was caught by the glittering array of buttons on the gunfire panel.

"Pretty," he said.

General Branch stepped inside the cubicle, grabbed Nielson by the shoulders, and shook him.

"Pretty things," Nielson said, gesturing at the panel. He smiled at Branch.

Margraves, second-in-command, stuck his head in the doorway.

He still had sergeant's stripes on his sleeve, having been promoted to colonel only three days ago.

"Ed," he said, "the President's representative is here. Sneak visit."

"Wait a minute," Branch said, "I want to complete this inspection." He grinned sourly. It was one hell of an inspection when you went around finding how many sane men you had left.

"Do you hear me, Lieutenant?"

"Ten thousand ships," Nielson said. "Ten thousand ships—all gone!"

"I'm sorry," Branch said. He leaned forward and slapped Nielson smartly across the face.

The lieutenant started to cry.

"Hey, Ed—what about that representative?"

At close range, Colonel Margraves's breath was a solid essence of whiskey, but Branch didn't reprimand him. If you had a good officer left, you didn't reprimand him, no matter what he did. Also, Branch approved of whiskey. It was a good release, under the circumstances. Probably better than his own, he thought, glancing at his scarred knuckles.

"I'll be right with you. Nielson, can you understand me?"

"Yes, sir," the lieutenant said in a shaky voice. "I'm all right now, sir."

"Good," Branch said. "Can you stay on duty?"

"For a while," Nielson said. "But, sir—I'm not well, I can feel it."

"I know," Branch said. "You deserve a rest. But you're the only gunnery officer I've got left on this side of the ship. The rest are in the wards."

"I'll try, sir," Nielson said, looking at the gunfire panel again. "But I hear voices sometimes. I can't promise anything, sir."

"Ed," Margraves began again, "that representative—"

"Coming. Good boy, Nielson." The lieutenant didn't look up as Branch and Margraves left.

"I escorted him to the bridge," Margraves said, listing slightly to starboard as he walked. "Offered him a drink, but he didn't want one."

"All right," Branch said.

"He was bursting with questions," Margraves continued, chuckling to himself. "One of those earnest, tanned State Department men, out to win the war in five minutes flat. Very friendly boy. Wanted to know why I, personally, thought the fleet had been maneuvering in space for a year with no action."

"What did you tell him?"

"Said we were waiting for a consignment of zap guns," Margraves said. "I think he almost believed me. Then he started talking about logistics."

"Hmmm," Branch said. There was no telling what Margraves, half-drunk, had told the representative. Not that it mattered. An official inquiry into the prosecution of the war had been due for a long time.

"I'm going to leave you here," Margraves said. "I've got some unfinished business to attend to."

"Right," Branch said, since it was all he could say. He knew that Margraves's unfinished business concerned a bottle.

He walked alone to the bridge.

The President's representative was looking at the huge location screen. It covered one entire wall, glowing with a slowly shifting pattern of dots. The thousands of green dots on the left represented the Earth fleet, separated by a black void from the orange of the enemy. As he watched, the fluid, three-dimensional front slowly changed. The armies of dots clustered, shifted, retreated, advanced, moving with hypnotic slowness.

But the black void remained between them. General Branch had been watching that sight for almost a year. As far as he was concerned, the screen was a luxury. He couldn't determine from it what was really happening. Only the CPC computers could, and they didn't need it.

"How do you do, General Branch?" the President's representative said, coming forward and offering his hand. "My name's Richard Ellsner."

Branch shook hands, noticing that Margraves's description had been pretty good. The representative was no more than thirty. His tan looked strange, after a year of pallid faces.

"My credentials," Ellsner said, handing Branch a sheaf of papers. The general skimmed through them, noting Ellsner's authorization as Presidential Voice in Space. A high honor for so young a man.

"How are things on Earth?" Branch asked, just to say something. He ushered Ellsner to a chair, and sat down himself.

"Tight," Ellsner said. "We've been stripping the planet bare of radioactives to keep your fleet operating. To say nothing of the tremendous cost of shipping food, oxygen, spare parts, and all the other equipment you need to keep a fleet this size in the field."

"I know," Branch murmured, his broad face expressionless.

"I'd like to start right in with the President's complaints," Ellsner said. "Just to get them off my chest."

"Go right ahead," Branch said.

"Now, then," Ellsner began, consulting a pocket notebook, "you've had the fleet in space for eleven months and seven days. Is that right?"

"Yes."

"During that time there have been light engagements, but no actual hostilities. You—and the enemy commander—have been content, evidently, to sniff each other like discontented dogs."

"I wouldn't use that analogy," Branch said, conceiving an instant dislike for the young man. "But go on."

"I apologize. It was an unfortunate, though inevitable, comparison. Anyhow, there has been no battle, even though you have a numerical superiority. Is that correct?"

"Yes."

"And you know the maintenance of this fleet strains the resources of Earth. The President would like to know why battle has not been joined."

"I'd like to hear the rest of the complaints first," Branch said. He tightened his battered fists, but, with remarkable self-control, kept them at his sides.

"Very well. The morale factor. We keep getting reports from you on the incidence of combat fatigue—crackup, in plain language. The figures are absurd! Thirty percent of your men seem to be under restraint. That's way out of line, even for a tense situation."

Branch didn't answer.

"To cut this short," Ellsner said, "I would like the answers to those questions. Then I would like your assistance in negotiating a truce. This war was ill-advised to begin with. It was none of the Earth's choosing. It seems to the President that, in view of the static situation, the enemy commander will be amenable to the idea."

Colonel Margraves staggered in, his face flushed. He had completed his unfinished business, adding another fourth to his half-drunk.

"What's this I hear about a truce?" he shouted.

Ellsner stared at him for a moment, then turned back to Branch.

"I supposed you will take care of this yourself. If you will contact the enemy commander, I will try to come to terms with him."

"They aren't interested," Branch said.

"How do you know?"

"I've been trying to negotiate a truce for six months. They want complete capitulation."

"But that's absurd," Ellsner said, shaking his head. "They have no bargaining point. The fleets are approximately the same size. There have been no major engagements. How can they—"

"Easily," Margraves roared, walking up to the representative and peering truculently in his face.

"General. This man is drunk," Ellsner got to his feet.

"Of course, you idiot! Don't you understand yet? *The war is lost!* Completely, irrevocably."

Ellsner turned angrily to Branch. The general sighed and stood up.

"That's right, Ellsner. The war is lost and every man in the fleet knows it. That's what's wrong with the morale. We're just hanging here, waiting to be blasted out of existence."

The fleets shifted and weaved. Thousands of dots floated in space, in twisted, random patterns.

Seemingly random.

The patterns interlocked, opened, and closed. Dynamically, delicately balanced, each configuration was a planned move on a hundred-thousand-mile front. The opposing dots shifted to meet the exigencies of the new pattern.

Where was the advantage? To the unskilled eye, a chess game is a meaningless array of pieces and positions. But to the players the game may already be won or lost.

The mechanical players who moved the thousands of dots knew who had won—and who had lost.

"Now let's all relax," Branch said soothingly. "Margraves, mix us a couple of drinks. I'll explain everything." The colonel moved to a well-stocked cabinet in a corner of the room.

"I'm waiting," Ellsner said.

"First, a review. Do you remember when the war was declared, two years ago? Both sides subscribed to the Holmstead Pact not to bomb home planets. A rendezvous was arranged in space, for the fleets to meet."

"That's ancient history," Ellsner said.

"It has a point. Earth's fleet blasted off, grouped, and went to the rendezvous." Branch cleared his throat.

"Do you know the CPCs? The Configuration-Probability Computers? They're like chess players, enormously extended. They arrange the fleet in an optimum attack-defense pattern, based on the configuration of the opposing fleet. So the first pattern was set."

"I don't see the need—" Ellsner started, but Margraves, returning with the drinks, interrupted him.

"Wait, my boy. Soon there will be a blinding light."

"When the fleets met, the CPCs calculated our probabilities of successful attack. They found we'd lose approximately eighty-seven percent of our fleet to sixty-five percent of the enemy's. If they attacked, they'd lose seventy-nine percent to our sixty-four. That was the situation as it stood then. By extrapolation, their *optimum* attack pattern—at that time—would net them a forty-five percent loss. Ours would have given us a seventy-two percent loss."

"I don't know much about the CPCs," Ellsner confessed. "My field's psych." He sipped his drink, grimaced, and sipped again.

"Think of them as chess players," Branch said. "They can estimate the loss probabilities for an attack at any given point of time, in any pattern. They can extrapolate the probable moves of both sides.

"That's why battle wasn't joined when we first met. No commander is going to annihilate his entire fleet like that."

"Well, then," Ellsner said, "why haven't you exploited your slight numerical superiority? Why haven't you gotten an advantage over them?"

"Ah!" Margraves cried, sipping his drink. "It comes, the light!"

"Let me put it in the form of an analogy," Branch said. "If you have two chess players of equally high skill, the game's end is determined when one of them gains an advantage. Once the advantage is there, there's nothing the other player can do, unless the first makes a mistake. If everything goes as it should, the game's end is predetermined. The turning point may come a few moves after the game starts, although the game itself could drag on for hours."

"And remember," Margraves broke in, "to the casual eye, there may be no apparent advantage. Not a piece may have been lost."

"That's what's happened here," Branch finished sadly. "The CPC units in both fleets are of maximum efficiency. But the enemy has an edge that they are carefully exploiting. And there's nothing we can do about it."

"But how did this happen?" Ellsner asked. "Who slipped up?"

"The CPCs have deduced the cause of the failure," Branch said. "The end of the war was inherent *in our takeoff formation.*"

"What do you mean?" Ellsner said, setting down his drink.

"Just that. The configuration the fleet was in, light-years away from battle, before we had even contacted their fleet. When the two met, they had an infinitesimal advantage of position. That was enough. Enough for the CPCs, anyhow."

"If it's any consolation," Margraves put in, "it was a fifty-fifty chance. It could just as well have been us with the edge."

"I'll have to find out more about this," Ellsner said. "I don't understand it all yet."

Branch snarled, "The war's lost. What more do you want to know?"

Ellsner shook his head.

"'Wilt snare me with predestination 'round,'" Margraves quoted, "'and then impute my fall to sin?'"

Lieutenant Nielson sat in front of the gunfire panel, his fingers interlocked. This was necessary, because Nielson had an almost overpowering desire to push the buttons.

The pretty buttons.

Then he swore, and sat on his hands. He had promised General Branch that he would carry on, and that was important. It was three days since he had seen the general, but he was determined to carry on. Resolutely he fixed his gaze on the gunfire dials.

Delicate indicators wavered and trembled. Dials measured distance and adjusted aperture to range. The slender indicators rose and fell as the ship maneuvered, lifting toward the red line, but never quite reaching it.

The red line marked emergency. That was when he would start firing, when the little black arrow crossed the little red line.

He had been waiting almost a year now for that little arrow. Little arrow. Little narrow. Little arrow. Little narrow.

Stop it.

That was when he would start firing.

Lieutenant Nielson lifted his hands into view and inspected his nails. Fastidiously he cleaned a bit of dirt out of one. He interlocked his fingers again and looked at the pretty buttons, the black arrow, the red line.

He smiled to himself. He had promised the general. Only three days ago.

So he pretended not to hear what the buttons were whispering to him.

"The thing I don't see," Ellsner said, "is why you can't do something about the pattern? Retreat and regroup, for example."

"I'll explain that," Margraves said. "It'll give Ed a chance for a drink. Come over here." He led Ellsner to an instrument panel. They had been showing Ellsner around the ship for three days, more to relieve their own tensions than for any other reason. The last day had turned into a fairly prolonged drinking bout.

"Do you see this dial?" Margraves pointed to one. The instrument panel covered an area four feet wide by twenty feet long. The buttons and switches on it controlled the movements of the entire fleet.

"Notice the shaded area. That marks the safety limit. If we use a forbidden configuration, the indicator goes over and all hell breaks loose."

"And what is a forbidden configuration?"

"The forbidden configurations are those that would give the enemy an attack advantage. Or, to put it another way, moves that change the attack-probability-loss picture sufficiently to warrant an enemy attack."

"So you can move only within strict limits?" Ellsner asked, looking at the dial.

"That's right. Out of the infinite number of possible formations, we can use only a few, if we want to play safe. It's like chess. Say you'd like to put a sixth-row pawn in your opponent's back row. But it would take two moves to do it. And after you move to the seventh row, your opponent has a clear avenue leading to checkmate.

"Of course, if the enemy advances too boldly, the odds are changed again, and *we* attack."

"That's our only hope," General Branch said. "We're praying they do something wrong. The fleet is in readiness for instant attack if our CPC shows that the enemy has overextended himself anywhere."

"And that's the reason for the crackups," Ellsner said. "Every man in the fleet is on nerves' edge, waiting for a chance he's sure will never come. But having to wait anyhow. How long will this go on?"

"This moving and checking can go on for a little more than two years," Branch said. "Then they will be in the optimum formation for attack, with a twenty-eight percent loss probability to our ninety-three. They'll have to attack then, or the probabilities will start to shift back in our favor."

"You poor devils," Ellsner said softly. "Waiting for a chance that's never going to come. Knowing you're going to be blasted out of space sooner or later."

"Oh, it's jolly," said Margraves, with an instinctive dislike for a civilian's sympathy.

Something buzzed on the switchboard, and Branch walked over and plugged in a line. "Hello? Yes. Yes ... all right, Williams. Right." He unplugged the line.

"Colonel Williams has had to lock his men in their rooms," Branch said. "That's the third time this month. I'll have to get CPC to dope out a formation so we can take him out of the front." He walked to a side panel and started pushing buttons.

"And there it is," Margraves said. "What do you plan to do, Mr. Presidential Representative?"

The glittering dots shifted and deployed, advanced and retreated, always keeping a barrier of black space between them. The mechanical chess players watched each move, calculating its effect into the far future. Back and forth across the great chessboard the pieces moved.

The chess players worked dispassionately, knowing beforehand the outcome of the game. In their strictly ordered universe there was no possible fluctuation, no stupidity, no failure.

They moved. And knew. And moved.

"Oh, yes," Lieutenant Nielson said to the smiling room. "Oh, yes." And look at all the buttons, he thought, laughing to himself.

So stupid. Georgia.

Nielson accepted the deep blue of sanctity, draping it across his shoulders. Birdsong, somewhere.

Of course.

Three buttons red. He pushed them. Three buttons green. He pushed them. Four dials. Riverread.

"Oh-oh. Nielson's cracked."

"Three is for me," Nielson said, and touched his forehead with greatest stealth. Then he reached for the keyboard again. Unimaginable associations raced through his mind, produced by unaccountable stimuli.

"Better grab him. Watch out!"

Gentle hands surround me as I push two are brown for which is for mother, and one is high for all rest.

"Stop him from shooting off those guns!"

I am lifted into the air, I fly, I fly.

"Is there any hope for that man?" Ellsner asked, after they had locked Nielson in a ward.

"Who knows?" Branch said. His broad face tightened; knots of muscle pushed out his cheeks. Suddenly he turned, shouted, and swung his fist wildly at the metal wall. After it hit, he grunted and grinned sheepishly.

"Silly, isn't it? Margraves drinks. I let off steam by hitting walls. Let's go eat."

The officers ate separately from the crew. Branch had found that some officers tended to get murdered by psychotic crewmen. It was best to keep them apart.

During the meal, Branch suddenly turned to Ellsner.

"Boy, I haven't told you the entire truth. I said this would go on for two years? Well, the men won't last that long. I don't know if I can hold this fleet together for two more weeks."

"What would you suggest?"

"I don't know," Branch said. He still refused to consider surrender, although he knew it was the only realistic answer.

"I'm not sure," Ellsner said, "but I think there may be a way out of your dilemma." The officers stopped eating and looked at him.

"Have you got some superweapon for us?" Margraves asked. "A disintegrator strapped to your chest?"

"I'm afraid not. But I think you've been so close to the situation that you don't see it in its true light. A case of the forest for the trees."

"Go on," Branch said, munching methodically on a piece of bread.

"Consider the universe as the CPC sees it. A world of strict causality. A logical, coherent universe. In this world, every effect has a cause. Every factor can be instantly accounted for.

"That's not a picture of the real world. There *is no* explanation for everything, really. The CPC is built to see a specialized universe, and to extrapolate on the basis of that."

"So," Margraves said, "what would you do?"

"Throw the world out of joint," Ellsner said. "Bring in uncertainty. Add a human factor that the machines can't compute."

"How can you introduce uncertainty in a chess game?" Branch asked, interested in spite of himself.

"By sneezing at a crucial moment, perhaps. How could a machine compute that?"

"It wouldn't have to. It would just classify it as extraneous noise and ignore it."

"True." Ellsner thought for a moment. "This battle—how long will it take, once the actual hostilities are begun?"

"About six minutes," Branch told him. "Plus or minus twenty seconds."

"That confirms an idea of mine," Ellsner said. "The chess-game analogy is faulty. There's no real comparison."

"It's a convenient way of thinking of it," Margraves said.

"But it's an *untrue* way of thinking of it. Checkmating a king can't be equated with destroying a fleet. Nor is the rest of the situation like chess. In chess you play by rules previously agreed upon by the players. In this game you can make up your own rules."

"This game has inherent rules of its own," Branch said.

"No," Ellsner said. "Only the CPCs have rules. How about this? Suppose you dispensed with the CPCs? Gave every commander his head, told him to attack on his own, with no pattern. What would happen?"

"It wouldn't work," Margraves told him. "The CPC can still total the picture, on the basis of planning ability of the average human. More than that, they can handle the attack of a few thousand second-rate calculators—humans—with ease. It would be like shooting clay pigeons."

"But you've *got* to try something," Ellsner pleaded.

"Now wait a minute," Branch said. "You can spout theory all

you want. I know what the CPCs tell me, and I believe them. I'm still in command of this fleet, and I'm not going to risk the lives in my command on some harebrained scheme."

"Harebrained schemes sometimes win wars," Ellsner said.

"They usually lose them."

"The war is lost already, by your own admission."

"I can still wait for them to make a mistake."

"Do you think it will come?"

"No."

"Well, then?"

"I'm still going to wait."

The rest of the meal was completed in moody silence. Afterward, Ellsner went to his room.

"Well, Ed?" Margraves asked, unbuttoning his shirt.

"Well yourself," the general said. He lay down on his bed, trying not to think. It was too much. Logistics. Predetermined battles. The coming debacle. He considered slamming his fist against the wall, but decided against it. He was going to sleep.

On the borderline between slumber and sleep, he heard a click.

The door!

Branch jumped out of bed and tried the knob. Then he threw himself against it.

Locked.

"General, please strap yourself down. We are attacking." It was Ellsner's voice, over the intercom.

"I looked over that keyboard of yours, sir, and found the magnetic doorlocks. Mighty handy in case of a mutiny, isn't it?"

"You idiot!" Branch shouted. "You'll kill us all! That CPC—"

"I've disconnected our CPC," Ellsner said pleasantly. "I'm a pretty logical boy, and I think I know how a sneeze will bother them."

"He's mad," Margraves shouted to Branch. Together they threw themselves against the metal door.

Then they were thrown to the floor.

"All gunners—fire at will!" Ellsner broadcast to the fleet.

The ship was in motion. The attack was under way!

The dots drifted together, crossing the no-man's-land of space.

They coalesced! Energy flared, and the battle was joined.

Six minutes, human time. Hours for the electronically fast chess player. He checked his pieces for an instant, deducing the pattern of attack.

There was no pattern!

Half of the opposing chess player's pieces shot out into space, completely out of the battle. Whole flanks advanced, split, rejoined, wrenched forward, dissolved their formation, formed it again.

No pattern? There *had* to be a pattern. The chess player knew that everything had a pattern. It was just a question of finding it, taking the moves already made and extrapolating to determine what the end was supposed to be.

The end was—chaos!

The dots swept in and out, shot away at right angles to the battle, checked, and returned, meaninglessly.

What did it mean? the chess player asked himself with the calmness of metal. He waited for a recognizable configuration to emerge.

Watching dispassionately as his pieces were swept off the board.

"I'm letting you out of your room now," Ellsner called, "but don't try to stop me. I think I've won your battle."

The lock released. The two officers ran down the corridor to the bridge, determined to break Ellsner into little pieces.

Inside, they slowed down.

The screen showed the great mass of Earth dots sweeping over a scattering of enemy dots.

What stopped them, however, was Nielson, laughing, his hands sweeping over switches and buttons on the great master control board.

The CPC was droning the losses. "Earth—eighteen percent. Enemy—eighty-three. Eighty-four. Eighty-six. Earth, nineteen percent."

"Mate!" Ellsner shouted. He stood beside Nielson, a Stillson wrench clenched in his hand. "Lack of pattern. I gave their CPC something it couldn't handle. An attack with no apparent pattern. Meaningless configurations!"

"But what are they doing?" Branch asked, gesturing at the dwindling enemy dots.

"Still relying on their chess player," Ellsner said. "Still waiting for him to dope out the attack pattern in this madman's mind. Too much faith in machines, general. This man doesn't even know he's precipitating an attack."

... And push three that's for dad on the olive tree I always wanted to two two two Danbury fair with buckle shoe brown all brown buttons down and in, sin, eight red for sin—

"What's the wrench for?" Margraves asked.

"That?" Ellsner weighed it in his hand. "That's to turn off Nielson here, after the attack."

... And five and love and black, all blacks, fair buttons in I remember when I was very young at all push five and there on the grass ouch—

PILGRIMAGE TO EARTH

Alfred Simon was born on Kazanga IV, a small agricultural planet near Arcturus, and there he drove a combine through the wheatfields, and in the long, hushed evenings listened to the recorded love songs of Earth.

Life was pleasant enough on Kazanga, and the girls were buxom, jolly, frank, and acquiescent, good companions for a hike through the hills or a swim in the brook, staunch mates for life. But romantic—never! There was good fun to be had on Kazanga, in a cheerful, open manner. But there was no more than fun.

Simon felt that something was missing in this bland existence. One day he discovered what it was.

A vendor came to Kazanga in a battered spaceship loaded with books. He was gaunt, white-haired, and a little mad. A celebration was held for him, for novelty was appreciated on the outer worlds.

The vendor told them all the latest gossip: of the price war between Detroit II and III, and how fishing fared on Alana, and what the President's wife on Moracia wore, and how oddly the men of Doran V talked. And at last someone said, "Tell us of Earth."

"Ah!" said the vendor, raising his eyebrows. "You want to hear of the mother planet? Well, friends, there's no place like old Earth, no place at all. On Earth, friends, everything is possible, and nothing is denied."

"Nothing?" Simon asked.

"They've got a law against denial," the vendor explained, grinning. "No one has ever been known to break it. Earth is *different*, friends. You folks specialize in farming? Well, Earth specializes in impracticalities such as madness, beauty, war, intoxication, purity, horror, and the like, and people come from light-years away to sample these wares."

"And love?" a woman asked.

"Why, girl," the vendor said gently, "Earth is the only place in the galaxy that still has love! Detroit II and III tried it and found it too expensive, you know, and Alana decided it was unsettling, and there was no time to import it on Moracia or Doran V. But as I said, Earth specializes in the impractical, and makes it pay."

"Pay?" a bulky farmer asked.

"Of course! Earth is old, her minerals are gone and her fields are barren. Her colonies are independent now, and filled with sober folk such as yourselves, who want value for their goods. So what else can old Earth deal in, except the nonessentials that make life worth living?"

"Were you in love on Earth?" Simon asked.

"That I was," the vendor answered with a certain grimness. "I was in love, and now I travel. Friends, these books . . ."

For an exorbitant price, Simon bought an ancient poetry book and, reading, dreamed of passion beneath the lunatic moon, of dawn glimmering whitely upon lovers' parched lips, of locked bodies on a dark beach, desperate with love and deafened by the booming surf.

And only on Earth was this possible! For, as the vendor told, Earth's scattered children were too hard at work wresting a living from alien soil. The wheat and corn grew on Kazanga, and the factories increased on Detroit II and III. The fisheries of Alana were the talk of the Southern Star Belt, and there were dangerous beasts on Moracia, and a whole wilderness to be won on Doran V. And this was good, and exactly as it should be.

But the new worlds were austere, carefully planned, sterile in their perfections. Something had been lost in the dead reaches of space, and only Earth knew love.

Therefore, Simon worked and saved and dreamed. And in his twenty-ninth year he sold his farm, packed all his clean shirts into a serviceable handbag, put on his best suit and a pair of stout walking shoes, and boarded the Kazanga-Metropole Flyer.

At last he came to Earth, where dreams *must* come true, for there is a law against their failure.

He passed quickly through Customs at Spaceport New York, and was shuttled underground to Times Square. There he emerged blinking into daylight, tightly clutching his handbag, for he had been warned about pickpockets, cutpurses, and other denizens of the city.

Breathless with wonder, he looked around.

The first thing that struck him was the endless array of theaters, with attractions in two dimensions, or three or four, depending upon your preference. And what attractions!

To the right of him a beetling marquee proclaimed: LUST ON VENUS! A DOCUMENTARY ACCOUNT OF SEX PRACTICES AMONG THE INHABITANTS OF THE GREEN HELL! SHOCKING! REVEALING!

He wanted to go in. But across the street was a war film. The billboard shouted, THE SUN BUSTERS! DEDICATED TO THE DAREDEVILS OF THE SPACE MARINES! And farther down was a picture called TARZAN BATTLES THE SATURNIAN GHOULS!

Tarzan, he recalled from his reading, was an ancient ethnic hero of Earth.

It was all wonderful, but there was so much more! He saw little open shops where one could buy food of all worlds, and especially such native Terran dishes as pizza, hot dogs, spaghetti, and knishes. And there were stores that sold surplus clothing from the Terran spacefleets, and other stores that sold nothing but beverages.

Simon didn't know what to do first. Then he heard a staccato burst of gunfire behind him, and whirled.

It was only a shooting gallery, a long, narrow, brightly painted place with a waist-high counter. The manager, a swarthy fat man with a mole on his chin, sat on a high stool and smiled at Simon.

"Try your luck?"

Simon walked over and saw that, instead of the usual targets, there were four scantily dressed women at the end of the gallery, seated upon bullet-scored chairs. Each had a tiny bullseye painted on her forehead and above the heart.

"But do you fire real bullets?" Simon asked.

"Of course!" the manager said. "There's a law against false advertising on Earth. Real bullets and real gals! Step up and knock one off!"

One of the women called out, "Come on, sport! Bet you miss me!"

Another screamed, "He couldn't hit the broad side of a spaceship!"

"Sure he can!" another shouted. "Come on, sport!"

Simon rubbed his forehead and tried not to act surprised. After all, this was Earth, where anything was allowed as long as it was commercially feasible.

He asked, "Are there galleries where you shoot men, too?"

"Of course," the manager said. "But you ain't no pervert, are you?"

"Certainly not!"

"You an outworlder?"

"Yes. How did you know?"

"The suit. Always tell by the suit." The fat man closed his eyes and chanted, "Step up, step up and kill a woman! Get rid of a load of repressions! Squeeze the trigger and feel the old anger ooze out of you! Better than a massage! Better than getting drunk! Step up, step up and kill a woman!"

Simon asked one of the girls, "Do you stay dead when I kill you!"

"Don't be stupid," the girl said.

"But the shock—"

She shrugged her shoulders. "I could do worse."

Simon was about to ask how she could do worse, when the manager leaned over the counter, speaking confidentially.

"Look, buddy. Look what I got here."

Simon glanced over the counter and saw a compact submachine gun.

"For a ridiculously low price," the manager said, "I'll let you use the tommy. You can spray the whole place, shoot down the fixtures, rip up the walls. This drives a .45 slug, buddy, and it kicks like a mule. You really know you're firing when you fire the tommy."

"I am not interested," Simon said sternly.

"I've got a grenade or two," the manager said. "Fragmentation, of course. You could really—"

"No!"

"For a price," the manager said, "you can shoot *me* too, if that's how your tastes run, although I wouldn't have guessed it. What do you say?"

"No! Never! This is horrible!"

The manager looked at him blankly. "Not in the mood now? Okay. I'm open twenty-four hours a day. See you later, sport."

"Never!" Simon said, walking away.

"Be expecting you, lover!" one of the women called after him.

Simon went to a refreshment stand and ordered a small glass of cola-cola. He found that his hands were shaking. With an effort he steadied them and sipped his drink. He reminded himself that he must not judge Earth by his own standards. If people on Earth enjoyed killing people, and the victims didn't mind being killed, why should anyone object?

Or should they?

He was pondering this when a voice at his elbow said, "Hey, bub."

Simon turned and saw a wizened, furtive-faced little man in an oversize raincoat standing beside him.

"Out-of-towner?" the little man asked.

"I am," Simon said. "How did you know?"

"The shoes. I always look at the shoes. How do you like our little planet?"

"It's—confusing," Simon said carefully. "I mean, I didn't expect—well—"

"Of course," the little man said. "You're an idealist. One look at your honest face tells me that, my friend. You've come to Earth for a definite purpose. Am I right?"

Simon nodded. The little man said, "I know your purpose, my friend. You're looking for a war that will make the world safe for something, and you've come to the right place. We have six major wars running at all times, and there's never any wait for an important position in any of them."

"Sorry, but—"

"Right at this moment," the little man said impressively, "the downtrodden workers of Peru are engaged in a desperate struggle against a corrupt and decadent monarchy. One more man could swing the contest! *You*, my friend, could be that man! *You* could guarantee the socialist victory!"

Observing the expression on Simon's face, the little man said quickly, "But there's a lot to be said for an enlightened aristocracy. The wise old king of Peru (a philosopher-king in the deepest Platonic sense of the word) sorely needs your help. His tiny corps of scientists, humanitarians, Swiss guards, knights of the realm, and loyal peasants is sorely pressed by the foreign-inspired socialist conspiracy. A single man, now—"

"I'm not interested," Simon said.

"In China, the Anarchists—"

"No."

"Perhaps you'd prefer the Communists in Wales? Or the Capitalists in Japan? Or, if your affinities lie with a splinter group such as Feminists, Prohibitionists, Free Silverists, or the like, we could probably arrange—"

"I don't want a war," Simon said.

"Who could blame you!" the little man said, nodding rapidly. "War is hell. In that case, you've come to Earth for love."

"How did you know?" Simon asked.

The little man smiled modestly. "Love and war," he said, "are Earth's two staple commodities. We've been turning them both out in bumper crops since the beginning of time."

"Is love very difficult to find?" Simon asked.

"Walk uptown two blocks," the little man said briskly. "Can't miss it. Tell 'em Joe sent you."

"But that's impossible! You can't just walk out and—"

"What do you know about love?" Joe asked.

"Nothing."

"Well, we're experts on it."

"I know what the books say," Simon said. "Passion beneath the lunatic moon—"

"Sure, and bodies on a dark sea-beach desperate with love and deafened by the booming surf."

"You've read that book?"

"It's the standard advertising brochure. I must be going. Two blocks uptown. Can't miss it."

And with a pleasant nod, Joe moved into the crowd.

Simon finished his cola-cola and walked slowly up Broadway. His brow was knotted in thought but he was determined not to form any premature judgments.

When he reached Forty-fourth Street he saw a tremendous neon sign flashing brightly. It said LOVE, INC.

Smaller neon letters read *Open 24 Hours a Day!*

Beneath that the sign read *Up One Flight.*

Simon frowned, for a terrible suspicion had just crossed his mind. Still, he climbed the stairs and entered a small, tastefully furnished reception room. From there he was sent down a long corridor to a numbered room.

Within the room was a handsome gray-haired man who rose from behind an impressive desk and shook his hand, saying, "Well! How are things on Kazanga!"

"How did you know I was from Kazanga?"

"That shirt. I always look at the shirt. I'm Mr. Tate, and I'm here to serve you to the best of my ability. You are—"

"Simon, Alfred Simon."

"Please be seated, Mr. Simon. Cigarette? Drink? You won't regret coming to us, sir. We're the oldest love-dispensing firm in the business, and much larger than our closest competitor, Passion Unlimited. Moreover, our fees are more reasonable, and bring you an improved product. Might I ask how you heard of us? Did you see our full-page ad in the *Times*? Or—"

"Joe sent me," Simon said.

"Ah, he's an active one," Mr. Tate said, shaking his head playfully. "Well, sir, there's no reason to delay. You've come a long way for love, and love you shall have." He reached for a button on his desk, but Simon stopped him.

Simon said, "I don't want to be rude or anything, but—"

"Yes?" Mr. Tate said, with an encouraging smile.

"I don't understand this," Simon blurted out, flushing deeply, beads of perspiration standing out on his forehead. "I think I'm in the wrong place. I didn't come all the way to Earth just for . . . I mean, you can't really sell *love*, can you? Not *love*! I mean, then it isn't really *love*, is it?"

"But of course!" Mr. Tate said, half rising from his chair in astonishment. "That's the whole point! Anyone can buy sex. Good Lord, it's the cheapest thing in the universe, next to human life. But *love* is rare, *love* is special, *love* is found only on Earth. Have you read our brochure?"

"Bodies on a dark sea-beach?" Simon asked.

"Yes, that one. I wrote it. Gives something of the feeling, doesn't it? You can't get that feeling from just *anyone*, Mr. Simon. You can get that feeling only from someone who loves you."

Simon said dubiously, "It's not genuine love, though, is it?"

"Of course it is. If we were selling simulated love, we'd label it as such. The advertising laws on Earth are strict, I can assure you. Anything can be sold, but it must be labeled properly. That's ethics, Mr. Simon!"

Tate caught his breath, and continued in a calmer tone. "No sir, make no mistake. Our product is not a substitute. It is the exact selfsame feeling that poets and writers have raved about for thousands of years. Through the wonders of modern science we can bring this feeling to you at your convenience, attractively packaged, completely disposable, and for a ridiculously low price."

Simon said, "I pictured something more—spontaneous."

"Spontaneity has its charm," Mr. Tate agreed. "Our research labs are working on it. Believe me, there's nothing science can't produce, as long as there's a market for it."

"I don't like any of this," Simon said, getting to his feet. "I think I'll just go see a movie."

"Wait!" Mr. Tate cried. "You think we're trying to put something over on you. You think we'll introduce you to a girl who will act as though she loves you, but who in reality will not. Is that it?"

"I guess so," Simon said.

"But it just isn't so! It would be too costly, for one thing. For another, the wear and tear on the girl would be tremendous. And it would be psychologically unsound for her to attempt living a lie of such depth and scope."

"Then how do you do it?"

"By utilizing our understanding of science and the human mind."

To Simon, this sounded like doubletalk. He moved toward the door.

"Tell me something," Mr. Tate said. "You're a bright-looking young fellow. Don't you think you could tell real love from a counterfeit item?"

"Certainly."

"There's your safeguard! *You* must be satisfied, or don't pay us a cent."

"I'll think about it," Simon said.

"Why delay? Leading psychologists say that *real* love is a fortifier and a restorer of sanity, a balm for damaged egos, a restorer of hormone balance, and an improver of the complexion. The love we supply you has everything: deep and abiding affection, unrestrained passion, complete faithfulness, an almost mystic affection for your defects as well as your virtues, a pitiful desire to please, *and*—as a plus that only Love, Inc., can supply—that uncontrollable first spark, that blinding moment of love at first sight!"

Mr. Tate pressed a button. Simon frowned indecisively. The door opened, a girl stepped in, and Simon stopped thinking.

She was tall and slender, and her hair was brown with a sheen of red. Simon could have told you nothing about her face, except that it brought tears to his eyes. And if you asked him about her figure, he might have killed you.

"Miss Penny Bright," said Tate, "meet Mr. Alfred Simon."

The girl tried to speak but no words came, and Simon was equally dumbstruck. He looked at her and *knew*. Nothing else mattered. To the depths of his heart he knew that he was truly and completely loved.

They left at once, hand in hand, and were taken by jet to a small white cottage in a pine grove overlooking the sea, and there they talked and laughed and loved, and later Simon saw his beloved wrapped in the sunset flame like a goddess of fire. And in blue twilight she looked at him with eyes enormous and dark, her known body mysterious again. The moon came up, bright and lunatic, changing flesh to shadow, and she wept and beat his chest with her small fists, and Simon wept too, although he did not know why. And at last dawn came, faint and disturbed, glimmering upon their parched lips and locked bodies, and nearby the booming surf deafened, inflamed, and maddened them.

At noon they were back in the offices of Love, Inc. Penny clutched his hand for a moment, then disappeared through an inner door.

"Was it real love?" Mr. Tate asked.

"Yes!"

"And was everything satisfactory?"

"Yes! It was love, it was the real thing! But why did she insist on returning?"

"Posthypnotic command," Mr. Tate said.

"What?"

"What did you expect? Everyone wants love, but few wish to pay for it. Here is your bill, sir."

Simon paid, fuming. "This wasn't necessary," he said. "Of course I would pay you for bringing us together. Where is she now? What have you done with her?"

"Please," Mr. Tate said soothingly. "Try to calm yourself."

"I don't want to be calm!" Simon shouted. "I want Penny!"

"That will be impossible," Mr. Tate said, with the barest hint of frost in his voice. "Kindly stop making a spectacle of yourself."

"Are you trying to get more money out of me?" Simon shrieked. "All right, I'll pay. How much do I have to pay to get her out of your clutches?" And Simon yanked out his wallet and slammed it on the desk.

Mr. Tate poked the wallet with a stiffened forefinger. "Put that back in your pocket," he said. "We are an old and respectable firm. If you raise your voice again, I shall have you ejected."

Simon calmed himself with an effort, put the wallet back in his pocket, and sat down. He took a deep breath and said very quietly. "I'm sorry."

"That's better," Mr. Tate said. "I will not be shouted at. However, if you are reasonable, I can be reasonable too. Now, what's the trouble?"

"The trouble?" Simon's voice started to lift. He controlled it and said, "She loves me."

"Of course."

"Then how can you separate us?"

"What has one thing to do with the other?" Mr. Tate asked. "Love is a delightful interlude, a relaxation, good for the intellect, for the ego, for the hormone balance, and for the skin tone. But one would hardly wish to *continue* loving, would one?"

"I would," Simon said. "This love was special, unique—"

"They all are," Mr. Tate said. "But as you know, they are all produced in the same way."

"What?"

"Surely you know something about the mechanics of love production?"

"No," Simon said. "I thought it was—natural."

Mr. Tate shook his head. "We gave up natural selection centuries ago, shortly after the Mechanical Revolution. It was too slow, and commercially infeasible. Why bother with it, when we can produce any feeling at will by conditioning and proper stimulation of certain brain centers? The result? Penny, completely in love with you! Your own bias in favor of her particular somatotype made it complete. We always throw in the dark seabeach, the lunatic moon, the pallid dawn—"

"Then she could have been made to love anyone," Simon said slowly.

"Could have been *brought* to love anyone," Mr. Tate corrected.

"Oh, Lord, how did she get into this horrible work?" Simon asked.

"She came in and signed a contract in the usual way," Tate said. "It pays very well. And at the termination of the lease, we return her original personality—untouched! But why do you call the work horrible? There's nothing reprehensible about love."

"It wasn't love!" Simon cried.

"But it was! The genuine article! Unbiased scientific firms have made qualitative tests in comparison with the natural thing. In every case, *our* love tested out to more depth, passion, fervor, and scope."

Simon shut his eyes tightly, then opened them and said, "Listen to me. I don't care about your scientific tests. I love her, she loves me, that's all that counts. Let me speak to her! I want to marry her!"

Mr. Tate wrinkled his nose in distaste. "Come, come, man! You wouldn't want to *marry* a girl like that! But if it's marriage you're after, we deal in that too. I can arrange an idyllic and nearly spontaneous love-match for you with a guaranteed, government-inspected virgin—"

"No! I love Penny! At least let me speak to her!"

"That will be quite impossible," Mr. Tate said.

"Why?"

Mr. Tate pushed a button on his desk. "Why do you think? We've wiped out the previous indoctrination. Penny is now in love with someone else."

And then Simon understood. He had realized that even now Penny was looking at another man with that passion he had known, feeling for another man that complete and bottomless love which unbiased scientific firms had shown to be so much greater than the old-fashioned, commercially infeasible natural selection, and that upon that same dark sea-beach mentioned in the advertising brochure—

He lunged for Tate's throat. Two attendants, who had entered the office a few moments earlier, caught him and led him to the door.

"Remember!" Tate called. "This in no way invalidates your own experience."

Hellishly enough, Simon knew that what Tate said was true.

And then he found himself on the street.

At first all he desired was to escape from Earth, where the commercial impracticalities were more than a normal man could afford. He walked very quickly, and his Penny walked beside him, her face glorified with love for him, and him, and him, and you, and you.

And of course he came to the shooting gallery.

"Try your luck?" the manager asked.

"Set 'em up," said Alfred Simon.

ALL THE THINGS YOU ARE

There are regulations to govern the conduct of First Contact spaceships, rules drawn up in desperation and followed in despair, for what rule can predict the effect of any action upon the mentality of an alien people?

Jan Maarten was pondering this gloomily as he came into the atmosphere of Durell IV. He was a big, middle-aged man with thin ash-blond hair and a round, worried face. Long ago he had concluded that almost any rule was better than none. Therefore he followed his meticulously, but with an ever-present sense of uncertainty and human fallibility.

These were ideal qualifications for the job of First Contacter.

He circled the planet, low enough for observation, but not too low, since he didn't want to frighten the inhabitants. He noted the signs of a primitive-pastoral civilization and tried to remember everything he had learned in Volume Four, *Projected Techniques for First Contact on So-called Primitive-Pastoral Worlds*, published by the Department of Alien Psychology. Then he brought the ship down on a rocky, grass-covered plain, near a typical medium-sized village, but not *too* near, using the Silent Sam landing technique.

"Prettily done," commented Croswell, his assistant, who was too young to be bothered by uncertainties.

Chedka, the Eborian linguist, said nothing. He was sleeping, as usual.

Maarten grunted something and went to the rear of the ship to run his tests. Croswell took up his post at the viewport.

* * *

"Here they come," Croswell reported half an hour later. "About a dozen of them, definitely humanoid." Upon closer inspection, he saw that the natives of Durell were flabby, dead white in coloration, and deadpan in expression. Croswell hesitated, then added, "They're not too handsome."

"What are they doing?" Maarten asked.

"Just looking us over," Croswell said. He was a slender young man with an unusually large and lustrous mustache that he had grown on the long journey out from Terra. He stroked it with the pride of a man who has been able to raise a really good mustache.

"They're about twenty yards from the ship now," Croswell reported. He leaned forward, flattening his nose ludicrously against the port, which was constructed of one-way glass.

Croswell could look out, but no one could look in. The Department of Alien Psychology had ordered the change last year, after a Department ship had botched a first contact on Carella II. The Carellans had stared into the ship, become alarmed at something within, and fled. The Department still didn't know what had alarmed them, for a second contact had never been successfully established.

That mistake would never happen again.

"What now?" Maarten called.

"One of them's coming forward alone. Chief, perhaps. Or sacrificial offering."

"What is he wearing?"

"He has on a—a sort of—will you kindly come here and look for yourself?"

Maarten, at his instrument bank, had been assembling a sketchy profile of Durell. The planet had a breathable atmosphere, an equitable climate, and gravity comparable to that of Earth. It had valuable deposits of radioactives and rare metals. Best of all, it tested free of the virulent microorganisms and poisonous vapors that tended to make a Contacter's life feverishly short.

Durell was going to be a valuable neighbor to Earth, provided the natives were friendly—and the Contacters skillful.

Maarten walked to the viewport and studied the natives. "They are wearing pastel clothing. We shall wear pastel clothing."

"Check," said Croswell.

"They are unarmed. We shall go unarmed."

"Roger."

"They are wearing sandals. We shall wear sandals."

"To hear is to obey."

"I notice they have no facial hair," Maarten said with the barest hint of a smile. "I'm sorry, Ed, but that mustache—"

"Not my mustache!" Croswell yelped, quickly putting a protective hand over it.

"I'm afraid so."

"But, Jan, I've been six months raising it!"

"It has to go. That should be obvious."

"I don't see why," Croswell said indignantly.

"Because first impressions are *vital*. When an unfavorable first impression has been made, subsequent contacts become difficult, sometimes impossible. Since we know nothing about these people, conformity is our safest course. We try to look like them, dress in colors that are pleasing or at least acceptable to them, copy their gestures, interact within their framework of acceptance in every way—"

"All right, all right," Croswell said. "I suppose I can grow another on the way back."

They looked at each other; then both began laughing. Croswell had lost three mustaches in this manner.

While Croswell shaved, Maarten stirred their linguist into wakefulness. Chedka was a lemurlike humanoid from Eboria IV, one of the few planets where Earth maintained successful relations. The Eborians were natural linguists, aided by the kind of associative ability found in nuisances who supply words in conversation—only the Eborians were always right. They had wandered over a considerable portion of the Galaxy in their time and might have attained quite a place in it, were it not that they needed twenty hours' sleep out of twenty-four.

Croswell finished shaving and dressed in pale green coveralls and sandals. All three went through decontamination procedure. Then Maarten took a deep breath, uttered a silent prayer, and opened the port.

A low sigh went up from the crowd of Durellans, although the chief—or sacrifice—was silent. They were indeed humanlike, if one overlooked their pallor and the gentle, sheeplike blandness of their features—features upon which Maarten could read no trace of expression.

"Don't use any facial contortions," Maarten warned Croswell.

Slowly they advanced until they were ten feet from the leading Durellan. Then Maarten said in a low voice, "We come in peace."

Chedka translated, then listened to the answer, which was so soft as to be almost indecipherable.

"Chief says welcome," Chedka reported in his economical English.

"Good, good," Maarten said. He took a few more steps forward and began to speak, pausing every now and then for translation. Earnestly, and with extreme conviction, he intoned Primary Speech BB-32 (for humanoid, primitive-pastoral, tentatively nonaggressive aliens).

Even Croswell, who was impressed by very little, had to admit it was a fine speech. Maarten said they were wanderers from afar, come out of the Great Nothingness to engage in friendly discourse with the gentle people of Durell. He spoke of green and distant Earth, so like this planet, and of the fine and humble people of Earth who stretched out hands in greeting. He told of the great spirit of peace and cooperation that emanated from Earth, of universal friendship, and of many other excellent things.

Finally he was done. There was a long silence.

"Did he understand it all?" Maarten whispered to Chedka.

The Eborian nodded, waiting for the chief's reply. Maarten was perspiring from the exertion, and Croswell couldn't stop nervously fingering his newly shaven upper lip.

The chief opened his mouth, gasped, made a little half-turn, and collapsed to the ground.

It was an embarrassing moment, and one not covered by any amount of theory.

The chief didn't rise; apparently it was not a ceremonial fall. As a matter of fact, his breathing seemed labored, like that of a man in a coma.

Under the circumstances, the Contact team could only retreat to their ship and await further developments.

Half an hour later a native approached the ship and conversed with Chedka, keeping a wary eye on the Earthmen and departing immediately.

"What did he say?" Croswell asked.

"Chief Moréri apologizes for fainting," Chedka told them. "He said it was inexcusably bad manners."

"Ah!" Maarten exclaimed. "His fainting might help us, after all—make him eager to repair his 'impoliteness.' Just as long as it was a fortuitous circumstance, unrelated to us—"

"Not," Chedka said.

"Not what?"

"Not unrelated," the Eborian said, curling up and going to sleep.

Maarten shook the little linguist awake. "What else did the chief say? How was his fainting related to us?"

Chedka yawned copiously. "The chief was very embarrassed. He faced the wind from your mouth as long as he could, but the alien odor—"

"My breath?" Maarten asked. "My *breath* knocked him out?"

Chedka nodded, giggled unexpectedly, and went to sleep.

Evening came, and the long dim twilight of Durell merged imperceptibly into night. In the village, cooking fires glinted through the surrounding forest and winked out one by one. But lights burned within the spaceship until dawn. And when the sun rose, Chedka slipped out of the ship on a mission into the village. Croswell brooded over his morning coffee, while Maarten rummaged through the ship's medicine chest.

"It's purely a temporary setback," Croswell was saying hopefully. "Little things like this are bound to happen. Remember that time on Dingoforeaba VI—"

"It's little things that close planets forever," Maarten said.

"But how could anyone possibly guess—"

"I should have foreseen it," Maarten growled angrily. "Just because our breath hasn't been offensive anywhere else—here it is!"

Triumphantly he held up a bottle of pink tablets. "Absolutely guaranteed to neutralize any breath, even that of a hyena. Have a couple."

Croswell accepted the pills. "Now what?"

"Now we wait until—aha! What did he say?"

Chedka slipped through the entry port, rubbing his eyes. "The chief apologizes for fainting."

"We know that. What else?"

"He welcomes you to the village of Lannit at your convenience. The chief feels that this incident shouldn't alter the course of friendship between two peace-loving, courteous peoples."

Maarten sighed with relief. He cleared his throat and asked hesitantly, "Did you mention to him about the forthcoming—ah—improvement in our breaths?"

"I assured him it would be corrected," Chedka said, "although it never bothered *me.*"

"Fine, fine. We will leave for the village now. Perhaps you should take one of these pills?"

"There's nothing wrong with *my* breath," the Eborian said complacently.

They set out at once for the village of Lannit.

When one deals with a primitive-pastoral people, one looks for simple but highly symbolic gestures, since that is what they understand best. Imagery! Clear-cut and decisive parallels! Few words but many gestures! Those were the rules in dealing with primitive-pastorals.

As Maarten approached the village, a natural and highly symbolic ceremony presented itself. The natives were waiting in their village, which was in a clearing in the forest. Separating forest from village was a dry streambed, and across that bed was a small stone bridge.

Maarten advanced to the center of the bridge and stopped, beaming benignly on the Durellans. When he saw several of them shudder and turn away, he smoothed out his features, remembering his own injunction against facial contortions. He paused for a long moment.

"What's up?" Croswell asked, stopping in front of the bridge.

In a loud voice, Maarten cried, "Let this bridge symbolize the link, now eternally forged, that joins this beautiful planet with—" Croswell called out a warning, but Maarten didn't know what was wrong. He stared at the villagers; they had made no movement.

"Get off the bridge!" Croswell shouted. But before Maarten could move, the entire structure had collapsed under him and he fell bone-shakingly into the dry stream.

"Damnedest thing I ever saw," Croswell said, helping him to his feet. "As soon as you raised your voice, that stone began to pulverize. Sympathetic vibration, I imagine."

Now Maarten understood why the Durellans spoke in whispers. He struggled to his feet, then groaned and sat down again.

"What's wrong?" Croswell asked.

"I seem to have wrenched my ankle," Maarten said miserably.

Chief Moréri came up, followed by twenty or so villagers, made a short speech, and presented Maarten with a walking stick of carved and polished black wood.

"Thanks," Maarten muttered, standing up and leaning gingerly on the cane. "What did he say?" he asked Chedka.

"The chief said that the bridge was only a hundred years old and in good repair," Chedka translated. "He apologizes that his ancestors didn't build it better."

"Hmm," Maarten said.

"And the chief says that you are probably an unlucky man."

He might be right, Maarten thought. Or perhaps Earthmen were just a fumbling race. For all their good intentions, population after population feared them, hated them, envied them, mainly on the basis of unfavorable first impressions.

Still, there seemed to be a chance here. What else could go wrong?

Forcing a smile, then quickly erasing it, Maarten limped into the village beside Moréri.

Technologically, the Durellan civilization was of a low order. A limited use had been made of wheel and lever, but the concept of mechanical advantage had been carried no further. There was evidence of a rudimentary knowledge of plane geometry and a fair idea of astronomy.

Artistically, however, the Durellans were adept and surprisingly sophisticated, particularly in woodcarving. Even the simplest huts had bas-relief panels, beautifully conceived and executed.

"Do you think I could take some photographs?" Croswell asked.

"I see no reason why not," Maarten said. He ran his fingers lovingly over a large panel carved of the same straight-grained black wood that formed his cane. The finish was as smooth as skin beneath his fingertips.

The chief gave his approval, and Croswell took photographs of Durellan home, market, and temple decorations.

Maarten wandered around, gently touching the intricate bas-reliefs, speaking with some of the natives through Chedka, and generally sorting out his impressions.

The Durellans, Maarten judged, were highly intelligent and had a potential comparable to that of *Homo sapiens.* Their lack of a defined technology was more the expression of a cooperation with nature than a flaw in their makeup. They seemed inherently peace-loving and nonaggressive—valuable neighbors for an Earth that, after centuries of confusion, was striving toward a similar goal.

This was going to be the basis of his report to the Second Contact Team. To this he hoped to be able to add, *A favorable impression seems to have been left concerning Earth. No unusual difficulties are to be expected.*

Chedka had been talking earnestly with Chief Moréri. Now, looking slightly more wide awake than usual, he came over and conferred with Maarten in a hushed voice. Maarten nodded, keeping his face expressionless, and went over to Croswell, who was snapping his last photographs.

"All ready for the big show?" Maarten asked.

"What show?"

"Moréri is throwing a feast for us tonight," Maarten said. "Very big, very important feast. A final gesture of goodwill and all that." Although his tone was casual, there was a gleam of deep satisfaction in his eyes.

Croswell's reaction was more immediate. "Then we've made it! The contact is successful!"

Behind him, two natives shook at the loudness of his voice and tottered feebly away.

"We've made it," Maarten whispered, "if we watch our step. They're a fine, understanding people—but we *do* seem to grate on them a bit."

By evening, Maarten and Croswell had completed a chemical examination of the Durellan foods and found nothing harmful to humans. They took several more pink tablets, changed coveralls and sandals, and proceeded to the feast.

The first course was an orange-green vegetable that tasted like squash. Then Chief Moréri gave a short talk on the importance of intercultural relations. They were served a dish resembling rabbit, and Croswell was called upon to give a speech.

"Remember," Maarten whispered, *"whisper!"*

Croswell stood up and began to speak. Keeping his voice down and his face blank, he began to enumerate the many similarities between Earth and Durell, depending mainly on gestures to convey his message.

Chedka translated. Maarten nodded his approval. The chief nodded. The feasters nodded.

Croswell made his last points and sat down, Maarten clapped him on the shoulder. "Well done, Ed. You've got a natural gift for—what's wrong?"

Croswell had a startled and incredulous look on his face. "Look!"

Maarten turned. The chief and the feasters, their eyes open and staring, were still nodding.

"Chedka!" Maarten whispered. "Speak to them!"

The Eborian asked the chief a question. There was no response. The chief continued his rhythmic nodding.

"Those gestures!" Maarten said. "You must have hypnotized them!" He scratched his head, then coughed once, loudly. The Durellans stopped nodding, blinked, and began to talk rapidly and nervously among themselves.

"They say you've got some strong powers," Chedka translated at random. "They say that aliens are pretty queer people and they doubt that they can be trusted."

"What does the chief say?" Maarten asked.

"The chief believes you're all right. He is telling them that you meant no harm."

"Good enough. Let's stop while we're ahead."

He stood up, followed by Croswell and Chedka.

"We are leaving now," he told the chief in a whisper, "but we beg permission for others of our kind to visit you. Forgive the mistakes we have made; they were due only to ignorance of your ways."

Chedka translated, and Maarten went on whispering, his face expressionless, his hands at his sides. He spoke of the oneness of the Galaxy, the joys of cooperation, peace, the exchange of goods and art, and the essential solidarity of all human life.

Moréri, though still a little dazed from the hypnotic experience, answered that the Earthmen would always be welcome.

Impulsively, Croswell held out his hand. The chief looked at it for a moment, puzzled, then took it, obviously wondering what to do with it and why.

He gasped in agony and pulled his hand back. They could see deep burns blotched red against his skin.

"What could have—"

"Perspiration!" Maarten said. "It's an acid. Must have an almost instantaneous effect upon their particular makeup. Let's get out of here."

The natives were milling together and they had picked up some stones and pieces of wood. The chief, although still in pain, was arguing with them, but the Earthmen didn't wait to hear the results of the discussion. They retreated to their ship, as fast as Maarten could hobble with the help of his cane.

The forest was dark behind them and filled with suspicious movements. Out of breath, they arrived at the spaceship. Croswell, in the lead, sprawled over a tangle of grass and fell headfirst against the port with a resounding clang.

"Damn!" he howled in pain.

The ground rumbled beneath them, began to tremble and slide away.

"Into the ship!" Maarten ordered.

They managed to take off before the ground gave way completely.

"It must have been sympathetic vibration again," Croswell said, several hours later, when the ship was in space. "But of all the luck—to be perched on a rock fault!"

Maarten sighed and shook his head. "I really don't know what to do. I'd like to go back, explain to them, but—"

"We've overstayed our welcome," Croswell said.

"Apparently. Blunders, nothing but blunders. We started out badly, and everything we did made it worse."

"It is not what you *do*," Chedka explained in the most sympathetic voice they had ever heard him use. "It's not your fault. It's what you *are*."

Maarten considered that for a moment. "Yes, you're right. Our voices shatter their land, our expressions disgust them, our gestures hypnotize them, our breath asphyxiates them, our perspiration burns them. Oh, Lord!"

"Lord, Lord," Croswell agreed glumly. "We're living chemical factories—turning out only poison gas and corrosives."

"But that is not *all* you are," Chedka said. "Look."

He held up Maarten's walking stick. Along the upper part, where Maarten had handled it, long-dormant buds had burst into pink and white flowers, and their scent filled the cabin.

"You see?" Chedka said. "You are *this*, also."

"That stick was dead," Croswell mused. "Some oil in our skin, I imagine."

Maarten shuddered. "Do you suppose that all the carvings we touched—the huts—the temple—"

"I should think so," Croswell said.

Maarten closed his eyes and visualized it, the sudden bursting into bloom of the dead, dried wood.

"I think they'll understand," he said, trying very hard to believe himself. "It's a pretty symbol and they're quite an understanding people. I think they'll approve of—well, at least *some* of the things we are."

THE STORE OF THE WORLDS

Mr. Wayne came to the end of the long, shoulder-high mound of gray rubble, and there was the Store of the Worlds. It was exactly as his friends had described it: a small shack constructed of bits of lumber, parts of cars, a piece of galvanized iron, and a few rows of crumbling bricks, all daubed over with a watery blue paint.

Mr. Wayne glanced back down the long lane of rubble to make sure he hadn't been followed. He tucked his parcel more firmly under his arm; then, with a little shiver at his own audacity, he opened the door and slipped inside.

"Good morning," the proprietor said.

He too was exactly as described: a tall, crafty-looking old fellow with narrow eyes and a downcast mouth. His name was Tompkins. He sat in an old rocking chair, and perched on the back of it was a blue and green parrot. There was one other chair in the store, and a table. On the table was a rusted hypodermic.

"I've heard about your store from friends," Mr. Wayne said.

"Then you know my price," Tompkins said. "Have you brought it?"

"Yes," said Mr. Wayne, holding up his parcel. "But I want to ask first—"

"They always want to ask," Tompkins said to the parrot, who blinked. "Go ahead, ask."

"I want to know what really happens."

Tompkins sighed. "What happens is this. You pay me my fee. I give you an injection that knocks you out. Then, with the aid of

184

certain gadgets I have in the back of the store, I liberate your mind."

Tompkins smiled as he said that, and his silent parrot seemed to smile too.

"What happens then?" Mr. Wayne asked.

"Your mind, liberated from its body, is able to choose from the countless probability-worlds that the Earth casts off in every second of its existence."

Grinning now, Tompkins sat up in his rocking chair and began to show signs of enthusiasm.

"Yes, my friend, though you might not have suspected it, from the moment this battered Earth was born out of the sun's fiery womb, it cast off its alternate-probability worlds. Worlds without end, emanating from events large and small; every Alexander and every amoeba creating worlds, just as ripples will spread in a pond, no matter how big or how small the stone you throw. Doesn't every object cast a shadow? Well, my friend, the Earth itself is four-dimensional; therefore it casts three-dimensional shadows, solid reflections of itself through every moment of its being. Millions, billions of Earths! An infinity of Earths! And your mind, liberated by me, will be able to select any of these worlds, and to live upon it for a while."

Mr. Wayne was uncomfortably aware that Tompkins sounded like a circus barker, proclaiming marvels that simply couldn't exist. But, Mr. Wayne reminded himself, things had happened within his own lifetime that he would never have believed possible. Never! So perhaps the wonders of which Tompkins spoke were possible too.

Mr. Wayne said, "My friends also told me—"

"That I was an out-and-out fraud?" Tompkins asked.

"Some of them *implied* that," Mr. Wayne said cautiously. "But I try to keep an open mind. They also said—"

"I know what your dirty-minded friends said. They told you about the fulfillment of desire. Is that what you want to hear about?"

"Yes," said Mr. Wayne. "They told me that whatever I wished for—whatever I wanted—"

"Exactly," Tompkins said. "The thing could work in no other

way. There are the infinite worlds to choose among. Your mind chooses, and is guided only by desire. Your deepest desire is the only thing that counts. If you have been harboring a secret dream of murder—"

"Oh hardly, hardly!" cried Mr. Wayne.

"—then you will go to a world where you *can* murder, where you can roll in blood, where you can outdo Sade or Caesar, or whoever your idol may be. Suppose it's power you want? Then you'll choose a world where you are a god, literally and actually. A bloodthirsty Juggernaut, perhaps, or an all-wise Buddha."

"I doubt very much if I—"

"There are other desires too," Tompkins said. "All heavens and all hells. Unbridled sexuality. Gluttony, drunkenness, love, fame—anything you want."

"Amazing!" said Mr. Wayne.

"Yes," Tompkins agreed. "Of course, my little list doesn't exhaust all the possibilities, all the combinations and permutations of desire. For all I know, you might want a simple, placid, pastoral existence on a South Seas island among idealized natives."

"That sounds more like me," Mr. Wayne said with a shy laugh.

"But who knows?" Tompkins asked. "Even you might not know what your true desires are. They might involve your own death."

"Does that happen often?" Mr. Wayne asked anxiously.

"Occasionally."

"I wouldn't want to die," Mr. Wayne said.

"It hardly ever happens," Tompkins said, looking at the parcel in Mr. Wayne's hands.

"If you say so . . . But how do I know all this is real? Your fee is extremely high, it'll take everything I own. And for all I know, you'll give me a drug and I'll just *dream*! Everything I own just for a—a shot of heroin and a lot of fancy words!"

Tompkins smiled reassuringly. "The experience has no drug-like quality about it. And no sensation of a dream, either."

"If it's *true*," Mr. Wayne said, a little petulantly, "why can't I stay in the world of my desire for good!"

"I'm working on that," Tompkins said. "That's why I charge so high a fee—to get materials, to experiment. I'm trying to find a way of making the transition permanent. So far I haven't been able to loosen the cord that binds a man to his own Earth and pulls him back to it. Not even the great mystics could cut that cord, except with death. But I still have my hopes."

"It would be a great thing if you succeeded," Mr. Wayne said politely.

"Yes it would!" Tompkins cried, with a surprising burst of passion. "For then I'd turn my wretched shop into an escape hatch! My process would be free then, free for everyone! Everyone would go to the Earth of his desire, the Earth that really suited him, and leave *this* damned place to the rats and worms—"

Tompkins cut himself off in midsentence, and became icy calm. "But I fear my prejudices are showing. I can't offer a permanent escape from the Earth yet, not one that doesn't involve death. Perhaps I never will be able to. For now, all I can offer you is a vacation, a change, a taste of another world, and a look at your own desires. You know my fee. I'll refund it if the experience isn't satisfactory."

"That's good of you," Mr. Wayne said, quite earnestly. "But there's that other matter my friends told me about. The ten years off my life."

"That can't be helped," Tompkins said, "and can't be refunded. My process is a tremendous strain on the nervous system, and life expectancy is shortened accordingly. That's one of the reasons why our so-called government has declared my process illegal."

"But they don't enforce the ban very firmly," Mr. Wayne said.

"No. Officially the process is banned as a harmful fraud. But officials are men too. They'd like to leave this Earth, just like everyone else."

"The cost," Mr. Wayne mused, gripping his parcel tightly. "And ten years off my life! For the fulfillment of my secret desires . . . Really, I must give this some thought."

"Think away," Tompkins said indifferently.

All the way home, Mr. Wayne thought about it. When his train reached Port Washington, Long Island, he was still thinking. And as he drove his car from the station to his home, he was still thinking about Tompkins's crafty old face, and worlds of probability, and the fulfillment of desire.

But when he stepped inside his house, those thoughts had to stop. Janet, his wife, wanted him to speak sharply to the maid, who had been drinking again. His son Tommy wanted help with the sloop, which was to be launched tomorrow. And his baby daughter wanted to tell about her day in kindergarten.

Mr. Wayne spoke pleasantly but firmly to the maid. He helped Tommy put the final coat of copper paint on the sloop's bottom, and he listened to Peggy tell about her adventures in the playground.

Later, when the children were in bed and he and Janet were alone in their living room, she asked him if something was wrong.

"Wrong?"

"You seem to be worried about something," Janet said. "Did you have a bad day at the office?"

"Oh, just the usual sort of thing . . ."

He certainly was not going to tell Janet, or anyone else, that he had taken the day off and gone to see Tompkins in his crazy old Store of the Worlds. Nor was he going to speak about the right every man should have, once in his lifetime, to fulfill his most secret desires. Janet, with her good common sense, would never understand that.

The next days at the office were extremely hectic. All of Wall Street was in a mild panic over events in the Middle East and in Asia, and stocks were reacting accordingly. Mr. Wayne settled down to work. He tried not to think of the fulfillment of desire at the cost of everything he possessed, with ten years of his life thrown in for good measure. It was crazy! Old Tompkins must be insane!

On weekends he went sailing with Tommy. The old sloop was behaving very well. Tommy wanted a new suit of racing sails, but Mr. Wayne sternly rejected that. Perhaps next year, if the market looked better. For now, the old sails would have to do.

Sometimes at night, after the children were asleep, he and Janet would go sailing. Long Island Sound was quiet then, and cool. Their boat glided past the blinking buoys, sailing toward the swollen yellow moon.

"I *know* something's on your mind," Janet said.

"Darling, please!"

"Is there something you're keeping from me?"

"Nothing!"

"Are you sure! Are you absolutely sure?"

"Absolutely sure."

"Then put your arms around me. That's right . . ."

And the sloop sailed itself for a while.

Desire and fulfillment . . . But autumn came, and the sloop had to be hauled. The stock market regained some stability, but Peggy caught the measles. Tommy wanted to know the differences between ordinary bombs, atom bombs, hydrogen bombs, cobalt bombs, and all the other kinds of bombs that were in the news. Mr. Wayne explained to the best of his ability. And the maid quit unexpectedly.

Secret desires were all very well. Perhaps he *did* want to kill someone, or live on a South Seas island. But there were responsibilities to consider. He had two growing children, and a better wife than he deserved.

Perhaps around Christmastime . . .

But in midwinter there was a fire in the unoccupied guest bedroom, due to defective wiring. The firemen put out the blaze without much damage, and no one was hurt. But it put any thought of Tompkins out of his mind for a while. First the bedroom had to be repaired, for Mr. Wayne was very proud of his gracious old house.

Business was still frantic and uncertain as a result of the international situation. Those Russians, those Arabs, those Greeks, those Chinese. The intercontinental missiles, the atom bombs, the sputniks . . . Mr. Wayne spent long days at the office, and sometimes evenings too. Tommy caught the mumps. A part of the roof had to be reshingled. And then already it was time to consider the spring launching of the sloop.

A year had passed, and he'd had very little time to think of secret desires. But perhaps next year. In the meantime—

"Well?" said Tompkins. "Are you all right?"

"Yes, quite all right," Mr. Wayne said. He got up from the chair and rubbed his forehead.

"Do you want a refund?" Tompkins asked.

"No. The experience was quite satisfactory."

"They always are," Tompkins said, winking lewdly at the parrot. "Well, what was yours?"

"A world of the recent past," Mr. Wayne said.

"A lot of them are. Did you find out about your secret desire? Was it murder? Or a South Seas island?"

"I'd rather not discuss it," Mr. Wayne said, pleasantly but firmly.

"A lot of people won't discuss it with me," Tompkins said sulkily. "I'll be damned if I know why."

"Because—well, I think the world of one's secret desire feels sacred, somehow. No offense. Do you think you'll ever be able to make it permanent? The world of one's choice, I mean?"

The old man shrugged. "I'm trying. If I succeed, you'll hear about it. Everyone will."

"Yes, I suppose so." Mr. Wayne undid his parcel and laid its contents on the table. The parcel contained a pair of army boots, a knife, two coils of copper wire, and three small cans of corned beef.

Tompkins's eyes glittered for a moment. "Quite satisfactory," he said. "Thank you."

"Good-bye," said Mr. Wayne. "And thank *you*."

Mr. Wayne left the ship and hurried down to the end of the lane of gray rubble. Beyond it, as far as he could see, lay flat fields of rubble, brown and gray and black. Those fields, stretching to every horizon, were made of the twisted corpses of cities, the shattered remnants of trees, and the fine white ash that once had been human flesh and bone.

"Well," Mr. Wayne said to himself, "at least we gave as good as we got."

That year in the past had cost him everything he owned, and ten years of life thrown in for good measure. Had it been a dream? It was still worth it! But now he had to put away all thought of Janet and the children. That was finished, unless Tompkins perfected his process. Now he had to think about his own survival.

With the aid of his wrist geiger, he found a deactivated lane through the rubble. He'd better get back to the shelter before dark, before the rats came out. If he didn't hurry, he'd miss the evening potato ration.

SEVENTH VICTIM

Stanton Frelaine sat at his desk, trying to look as busy as an executive should at nine-thirty in the morning. It was impossible. He couldn't concentrate on the advertisement he had written the previous night, couldn't think about business. All he could do was wait until the mail came.

He had been expecting his notification for two weeks now. The government was behind schedule, as usual.

The glass door of his office was marked *Morger and Frelaine, Clothiers.* It opened, and E. J. Morger walked in, limping slightly from his old gunshot wound. His shoulders were bent; but at the age of seventy-three, he wasn't worrying much about his posture.

"Well, Stan?" Morger asked. "What about that ad?"

Frelaine had joined Morger sixteen years ago, when he was twenty-seven. Together they had built Protec-Clothes into a million-dollar concern.

"I suppose you can run it," Frelaine said, handing the slip of paper to Morger. If only the mail would come earlier, he thought.

"'Do you own a Protec-Suit?'" Morger read aloud, holding the paper close to his eyes. "'The finest tailoring in the world has gone into Morger and Frelaine's Protec-Suit, to make it the leader in men's fashions.'"

Morger cleared his throat and glanced at Frelaine. He smiled and read on.

"'Protec-Suit is the safest as well as the smartest. Every

191

Protec-Suit comes with special built-in gun pocket, guaranteed not to bulge. No one will know you are carrying a gun—except you. The gun pocket is exceptionally easy to get at, permitting fast, unhindered draw. Choice of hip or breast pocket.' Very nice," Morger commented.

Frelaine nodded morosely.

"'The Protec-Suit Special has the fling-out gun pocket, the greatest modern advance in personal protection. A touch of the concealed button throws the gun into your hand, cocked, safeties off. Why not drop into the Protec-Store nearest you? *Why not be safe?*'"

"That's fine," Morger said. "That's a very nice, dignified ad." He thought for a moment, fingering his white mustache. "Shouldn't you mention that Protec-Suits come in a variety of styles, single and double-breasted, one- and two-button rolls, deep and shallow flares?"

"Right. I forgot."

Frelaine took back the sheet and jotted a note on the edge of it. Then he stood up, smoothing his jacket over his prominent stomach. Frelaine was forty-three, a little overweight, a little bald on top. He was an amiable-looking man with cold eyes.

"Relax," Morger said. "It'll come in today's mail."

Frelaine forced himself to smile. He felt like pacing the floor, but instead sat on the edge of the desk.

"You'd think it was my first kill," he said with a deprecating smile.

"I know how it is," Morger said. "Before I hung up my gun, I couldn't sleep for a month, waiting for a notification. I know."

The two men waited. Just as the silence was becoming unbearable, the door opened. A clerk walked in and deposited the mail on Frelaine's desk.

Frelaine swung around and gathered up the letters. He thumbed through them rapidly and found what he had been waiting for— the long white envelope from ECB, with the official government seal on it.

"That's it!" Frelaine said, and broke into a grin. "That's the baby!"

"Fine." Morger eyed the envelope with interest, but didn't ask

Frelaine to open it. It would be a breach of etiquette, as well as a violation of the law. No one was supposed to know a Victim's name except his Hunter. "Have a good hunt."

"I expect to," Frelaine replied confidently. His desk was in order—had been for a week. He picked up his briefcase.

"A good kill will do you a world of good," Morger said, putting his hand lightly on Frelaine's padded shoulder. "You've been keyed up."

"I know." Frelaine grinned again and shook Morger's hand.

"Wish I was a kid again," Morger said, glancing down at his crippled leg with wryly humorous eyes. "Makes me want to pick up a gun again."

The old man had been quite a Hunter in his day. Ten successful hunts had qualified him for the exclusive Tens Club. And, of course, in turn for each hunt, Morger had had to act as Victim, so he had twenty kills to his credit.

"I sure hope my Victim isn't anyone like you," Frelaine said, half in jest.

"Don't worry about it. What number will this be?"

"The seventh."

"Lucky seven. Go to it," Morger said. "We'll get you into the Tens yet."

Frelaine waved his hand and started out the door.

"Just don't get careless," warned Morger. "All it takes is a single slip and I'll need a new partner. If you don't mind, I like the one I've got now."

"I'll be careful," Frelaine promised.

Instead of taking a bus, Frelaine walked to his apartment. He wanted time to cool off. There was no sense in acting like a kid on his first kill.

As he walked, Frelaine kept his eyes strictly to the front. Staring at anyone was practically asking for a bullet, if the man happened to be serving as Victim. Some Victims shot if you just glanced at them. Nervous fellows. Frelaine prudently looked above the heads of the people he passed.

Ahead of him was a huge billboard, offering J. F. O'Donovan's services to the public.

"Victims!" the sign proclaimed in huge red letters. "Why take chances? Use an O'Donovan accredited Spotter. Let us locate your assigned killer. Pay *after* you get him!"

The sign reminded Frelaine. He would call Ed Morrow as soon as he reached his apartment.

He crossed the street, quickening his stride. He could hardly wait to get home now, to open the envelope and discover who his Victim was. Would he be clever or stupid? Rich, like Frelaine's fourth Victim, or poor, like the first and second? Would he have an organized Spotter service, or try to do it on his own?

The excitement of the chase was wonderful, coursing through his veins, quickening his heartbeat. From a block or so away, he heard gunfire. Two quick shots, and then a final one.

Somebody got his man, Frelaine thought. Good for him.

It was a superb feeling, he told himself. He was *alive* again.

At his one-room apartment, the first thing Frelaine did was to call Ed Morrow, his Spotter. The man worked as a garage attendant between calls.

"Hello, Ed? Frelaine."

"Oh, hi, Mr. Frelaine." He could see the man's thin, grease-stained face, grinning flat-lipped at the telephone.

"I'm going out on one, Ed."

"Good luck, Mr. Frelaine," Ed Morrow said. "I suppose you'll want me to stand by?"

"That's right. I don't expect to be gone more than a week or two. I'll probably get my notification of Victim Status within three months of the kill."

"I'll be standing by. Good hunting, Mr. Frelaine."

"Thanks. So long." He hung up. It was a wise safety measure to reserve a first-class Spotter. After his kill, it would be Frelaine's turn as Victim. Then, once again, Ed Morrow would be his life insurance.

And what a marvelous Spotter Morrow was! Uneducated—stupid, really. But what an eye for people! Morrow was a natural. His pale eyes could tell an out-of-towner at a glance. He was diabolically clever at rigging an ambush. An indispensable man.

Frelaine took out the envelope, chuckling to himself, remembering some of the tricks Morrow had turned for the Hunters. Still smiling, he glanced at the data inside the envelope.

Janet-Marie Patzig.

His Victim was a woman!

Frelaine stood up and paced for a few moments. Then he read the letter again. Janet-Marie Patzig. No mistake. A girl. Three photographs were enclosed, her address, and the usual descriptive data.

Frelaine frowned. He had never killed a woman.

He hesitated for a moment, then picked up the telephone and dialed ECB.

"Emotional Catharsis Bureau, Information Section," a man's voice answered.

"Say, look," Frelaine said. "I just got my notification and I pulled a girl. Is that in order?" He gave the clerk the girl's name.

"It's all in order, sir," the clerk replied after a minute of checking microfiles. "The girl registered with the board under her own free will. The law says she has the same rights and privileges as a man."

"Could you tell me how many kills she has?"

"I'm sorry, sir. The only information you're allowed is the Victim's legal status and the descriptive data you have received."

"I see." Frelaine paused. "Could I draw another?"

"You can refuse the hunt, of course. That is your legal right. But you will not be allowed another Victim until you have served. Do you wish to refuse?"

"Oh, no," Frelaine said hastily. "I was just wondering. Thank you."

He hung up and sat down in his largest armchair, loosening his belt. This required some thought.

Damn women, he grumbled to himself, always trying to horn in on a man's game. Why can't they stay home?

But they were free citizens, he reminded himself. Still, it just didn't seem *feminine*.

He know that, historically speaking, the Emotional Catharsis Board had been established for men and men only. The board had been formed at the end of the Fourth World War—or Sixth, as some historians counted it.

At that time there had been a driving need for permanent, lasting peace. The reason was practical, as were the men who engineered it.

Simply—annihilation was just around the corner.

In the World Wars, weapons increased in magnitude, efficiency, and exterminating power. Soldiers became accustomed to them, less and less reluctant to use them.

But the saturation point had been reached. Another war would truly be the war to end all wars. There would be no one left to start another.

So this peace *had* to last for all time, but the men who engineered it were practical. They recognized the tensions and dislocations still present, the cauldrons in which wars are brewed. They asked themselves why peace had never lasted in the past.

"Because men like to fight," was their answer.

"Oh, no!" screamed the idealists.

But the men who engineered the peace were forced to postulate, regretfully, the presence of a need for violence in a large percentage of mankind.

Men aren't angels. They aren't fiends, either. They are just very human beings, with a high degree of combativeness.

With the scientific knowledge and the power they had at that moment, the practical men could have gone a long way toward breeding this trait out of the race. Many thought this was the answer.

The practical men didn't. They recognized the validity of competition, love of battle, courage in the face of overwhelming odds. These, they felt, were admirable traits for a race, and insurance toward its perpetuity. Without them, the race would be bound to retrogress.

The tendency toward violence, they found, was inextricably linked with ingenuity, flexibility, drive.

The problem, then: to arrange a peace that would last after they were gone. To stop the race from destroying itself, without removing the responsible traits.

The way to do this, they decided, was to rechannel man's violence.

Provide him with an outlet, an expression.

The first big step was the legalization of gladiatorial events, complete with blood and thunder. But more was needed. Sublimations worked only up to a point. Then people demanded the real thing.

There is no substitute for murder.

So murder was legalized, on a strictly individual basis, and only for those who wanted it. The governments were directed to create Emotional Catharsis Boards.

After a period of experimentation, uniform rules were adopted.

Anyone who wanted to murder could sign up at the ECB. After giving certain data and assurances, he would be granted a Victim.

Anyone who signed up to murder, under the government rules, had to take his turn a few months later as Victim—if he survived.

That, in essence, was the setup. The individual could commit as many murders as he wanted. But between one murder and the next, he had to be a Victim. If he successfully killed his Hunter, he could stop, or sign up for another murder.

At the end of ten years, an estimated one-third of the world's population had applied for at least one murder. The number slid to one-fourth, and stayed there.

Philosophers shook their heads, but the practical men were satisfied. War was where it belonged—in the hands of the individual.

Of course, there were ramifications to the game, and elaborations. Once its existence had been accepted, it became big business. There were services for Victim and Hunter alike.

The Emotional Catharsis Board picked the Victims' names at random. A Hunter was allowed two weeks in which to make his kill. This had to be done through his own ingenuity, unaided. He was given the name of his Victim, an address and a description, and was allowed to use a standard-caliber pistol. He could wear no armor of any sort.

The Victim was notified a week before the Hunter. He was told only that he was a Victim. He did not know the name of his Hunter. He was allowed his choice of armor. He could hire Spotters. A Spotter couldn't kill; only Victim and Hunter could do that. But he could detect a stranger in town, or ferret out a nervous gunman.

The Victim could arrange any kind of ambush in his power to kill the Hunter.

There were stiff penalties for killing or wounding the wrong man, for no other murder was allowed. Grudge killings and gain killings were punishable by death.

The beauty of the system was that the people who wanted to kill could do so. Those who didn't—the bulk of the population—didn't have to.

At least there weren't any more big wars. Not even the imminence of one.

Just hundreds of thousands of small ones.

Frelaine didn't especially like the idea of killing a woman; but she *had* signed up. It wasn't his fault. And he wasn't going to lose out on his seventh hunt.

He spent the rest of the morning memorizing the data on his Victim, then filed the letter.

Janet Patzig lived in New York. That was good. He enjoyed hunting in a big city, and he had always wanted to see New York. Her age wasn't given, but to judge from her photographs, she was in her early twenties.

Frelaine phoned for his jet reservations to New York, then took a shower. He dressed with care in a new Protec-Suit Special made for the occasion. From his collection he selected a gun, cleaned and oiled it, and fitted it into the fling-out pocket of the suit. Then he packed his suitcase.

A pulse of excitement was pounding in his veins. Strange, he thought, how each killing was a new thrill. It was something you just didn't tire of, the way you did of French pastry or women or drinking or anything else. It was always new and different.

Finally he looked over his books to see which he would take.

His library contained all the good books on the subject. He wouldn't need any of his Victim books, such as L. Fred Tracy's *Tactics for the Victim*, with its insistence on a rigidly controlled environment, or Dr. Frisch's *Don't Think Like a Victim!*

He would be very interested in those in a few months, when he was a Victim again. Now he wanted hunting books.

Tactics for Hunting Humans was the standard and definitive work, but he had it almost memorized. *Development of the Ambush* was not adapted to his present needs.

He chose *Hunting in Cities* by Mitwell and Clark, *Spotting the Spotter* by Algreen, and *The Victim's Ingroup* by the same author.

Everything was in order. He left a note for the milkman, locked his apartment, and took a cab to the airport.

In New York he checked into a hotel in the midtown area, not too far from his Victim's address. The clerks were smiling and attentive, which bothered Frelaine. He didn't like to be recognized so easily as an out-of-town killer.

The first thing he saw in his room was a pamphlet on his bed table. *How to Get the Most Out of Your Emotional Catharsis*, it was called, with the compliments of the management. Frelaine smiled and thumbed through it.

Since it was his first visit to New York, he spent the afternoon just walking the streets in his Victim's neighborhood. After that, he wandered through a few stores.

Martinson and Black was a fascinating place. He went through their Hunter-Hunted room. There were lightweight bulletproof vests for Victims, and Richard Arlington hats, with bulletproof crowns.

On one side was a large display of a new .38-caliber sidearm.

"Use the Malvern Strait-shot!" the ad proclaimed. "ECB-approved. Carries a load of twelve shots. Tested deviation less than .001 inches per 1000 feet. Don't miss your Victim! Don't risk your life without the best! Be safe with Malvern!"

Frelaine smiled. The ad was good, and the small black weapon looked ultimately efficient. But he was satisfied with the one he had.

There was a special sale on trick canes, with concealed four-shot magazine, promising safety and concealment. As a young man, Frelaine had gone in heavily for novelties. But now he knew that the old-fashioned ways were usually best.

Outside the store, four men from the Department of Sanitation were carting away a freshly killed corpse. Frelaine regretted missing the take.

He ate dinner in a good restaurant and went to bed early.

Tomorrow he had a lot to do.

The next day, with the face of his Victim before him, Frelaine walked through her neighborhood. He didn't look closely at anyone. Instead he moved rapidly, as though he were really going somewhere, the way an old Hunter should walk.

He passed several bars and dropped into one for a drink. Then he went on, down a side street off Lexington Avenue.

There was a pleasant sidewalk café there. Frelaine walked past it.

And there she was! He could never mistake the face. It was Janet Patzig, seated at a table, staring into a drink. She didn't look up as he passed.

Frelaine walked to the end of the block. He turned the corner and stopped, hands trembling.

Was the girl crazy, exposing herself in the open? Did she think she had a charmed life?

He hailed a taxi and had the man drive around the block. Sure enough, she was just sitting there. Frelaine took a careful look.

She seemed younger than her pictures, but he couldn't be sure. He would guess her to be not much over twenty. Her dark hair was parted in the middle and combed above her ears, giving her a nunlike appearance. Her expression, as far as Frelaine could tell, was one of resigned sadness.

Wasn't she even going to make an attempt to defend herself?

Frelaine paid the driver and hurried to a drugstore. Finding a vacant telephone booth, he called ECB.

"Are you sure that a Victim named Janet-Marie Patzig has been notified?"

"Hold on, sir." Frelaine tapped on the door while the clerk looked up the information. "Yes, sir. We have her personal confirmation. Is there anything wrong, sir?"

"No," Frelaine said. "Just wanted to check."

After all, it was no one's business if the girl didn't want to defend herself.

He was still entitled to kill her.

It was his turn.

He postponed it for that day, however, and went to a movie. After dinner he returned to his room and read the ECB pamphlet. Then he lay on his bed and glared at the ceiling.

All he had to do was pump a bullet into her. Just ride by in a cab and kill her.

She was being a very bad sport about it, he decided resentfully, and went to sleep.

The next afternoon, Frelaine walked by the café again. The girl was back, sitting at the same table. Frelaine caught a cab.

"Drive around the block very slowly," he told the driver.

"Sure," the driver said, grinning with sardonic wisdom.

From the cab, Frelaine watched for Spotters. As far as he could tell, the girl had none. Both of her hands were in sight upon the table.

An easy, stationary target.

Frelaine touched the button of his double-breasted jacket. A fold flew open and the gun was in his hand. He broke it open and checked the cartridges, then closed it with a snap.

"Slowly now," he told the driver.

The taxi crawled by the café. Frelaine took careful aim, centering the girl in his sights. His finger tightened on the trigger.

"Damn it!" he said.

A waiter had passed by the girl. He didn't want to chance winging the wrong person.

"Around the block again," he told the driver.

The man gave him another grin and hunched down in his seat. Frelaine wondered if the driver would feel so happy if he knew that Frelaine was gunning for a woman.

This time there was no waiter around. The girl was lighting a cigarette, her mournful face intent on her lighter. Frelaine centered her in his sights, squarely above the eyes, and held his breath.

Then he shook his head and put the gun back in his pocket.

The idiotic girl was robbing him of the full benefit of his catharsis.

He paid the driver and started to walk.

It's too easy, he told himself. He was used to a real chase. Most of the other six kills had been quite difficult. The Victims had tried every dodge. One had hired at least a dozen Spotters. But Frelaine had reached them all by altering his tactics to meet the situation.

Once he had dressed as a milkman, another time as a bill collector. The sixth Victim he had had to chase through the Sierra Nevadas. The man had clipped him, too. But Frelaine had done better.

How could he be proud of this one? What would the Tens Club say?

That brought Frelaine up with a start. He wanted to get into the club. Even if he passed up this girl, he would have to defend himself against a Hunter. If he survived, he would still be four hunts away from membership. At that rate he might never get in.

He began to pass the café again, but then, on impulse, stopped abruptly.

"Hello," he said.

Janet Patzig looked at him out of sad blue eyes, but said nothing.

"Say, look," he said, sitting down, "if I'm being fresh, just tell me and I'll go. I'm an out-of-towner. Here at a convention. And I'd just like someone feminine to talk to. If you'd rather I didn't—"

"I don't care," Janet Patzig said tonelessly.

"A brandy," Frelaine told the waiter. Janet Patzig's glass was still half-full.

Frelaine looked at the girl and he could feel his heart throbbing against his ribs. This was more like it—having a drink with your Victim!

"My name's Stanton Frelaine," he said, knowing it didn't matter.

"Janet."

"Janet what?"

"Janet Patzig."

"Nice to know you," Frelaine said in a perfectly natural voice. "Are you doing anything tonight, Janet?"

"I'm probably being killed tonight," she said quietly.

Frelaine looked at her carefully. Did she realize who he was? For all he knew, she had a gun leveled at him under the table.

He kept his hand close to the fling-out button.

"Are you a Victim?" he asked.

"You guessed it," she said sardonically. "If I were you, I'd stay out of the way. No sense getting hit by mistake."

Frelaine couldn't understand the girl's calm. Was she a suicide? Perhaps she just didn't care. Perhaps she wanted to die.

"Haven't you got any Spotters?" he asked, with the right expression of amazement.

"No." She looked at him, full in the face, and Frelaine saw something he hadn't noticed before.

She was very lovely.

"I am a bad, bad girl," she said lightly. "I got the idea I'd like to commit a murder, so I signed for ECB. Then—I couldn't do it."

Frelaine shook his head, sympathizing with her.

"But I'm still in, of course. Even if I didn't shoot, I still have to take my turn as a Victim."

"But why don't you hire some Spotters?" he asked.

"I couldn't kill anyone," she said. "I just couldn't. I don't even have a gun."

"You've got a lot of courage," Frelaine said, "coming out in the open this way." Secretly he was amazed at her stupidity.

"What can I do?" she asked listlessly. "You can't hide from a Hunter. Not a real one. And I don't have enough money to make a good disappearance."

"Since it's in your own defense, I should think—" Frelaine began, but she interrupted.

"No. I've made up my mind on that. This whole thing is wrong, the whole system. When I had my Victim in the sights—when I saw how easily I could—I could—"

She pulled herself together quickly.

"Oh, let's forget it," she said, and smiled.

Frelaine found her smile dazzling.

After that, they talked of other things. Frelaine told her of his business, and she told him about New York. She was twenty-two, an unsuccessful actress.

They had supper together. When she accepted Frelaine's invitation to go to the Gladiatorials, he felt absurdly elated.

He called a cab—he seemed to be spending his entire time in New York in cabs—and opened the door for her. She started in. Frelaine hesitated. He could have pumped a shot into her at that moment. It would have been very easy.

But he held back. Just for the moment, he told himself.

The Gladiatorials were about the same as those held anywhere else, except that the talent was a little better. There were the usual historical events: swordsmen and netmen, duels with saber and foil.

Most of these, naturally, were fought to the death.

Then bullfighting, lion fighting, and rhino fighting, followed by the more modern events. Fights from behind barricades, with bow and arrow. Dueling on a high wire.

The evening passed pleasantly.

Frelaine escorted the girl home, the palms of his hands sticky with sweat. He had never found a woman he liked better. And yet she was his legitimate kill.

He didn't know what he was going to do.

She invited him in and they sat together on the couch. The girl lighted a cigarette for herself with a large lighter, then settled back.

"Are you leaving soon?" she asked him.

"I suppose so," Frelaine said. "The convention is only lasting another day."

She was silent for a moment. "I'll be sorry to see you go."

They were quiet for a while. Then Janet went to fix him a drink. Frelaine eyed her retreating back. Now was the time. He placed his hand near the button.

But the moment had passed for him, irrevocably. He wasn't going to kill her. You don't kill the girl you love.

The realization that he loved her was shocking. He'd come to kill, not to find a wife.

She came back with the drink and sat down opposite him, staring at emptiness.

"Janet," he said, "I love you."

She sat, just looking at him. There were tears in her eyes.

"You can't," she protested. "I'm a Victim. I won't live long enough to—"

"You won't be killed. I'm your Hunter."

She stared at him a moment, then laughed uncertainly.

"Are you going to kill me?" she asked.

"Don't be ridiculous," he said. "I'm going to marry you."

Suddenly she was in his arms.

"Oh, Lord!" she gasped. "The waiting—I've been so frightened—"

"It's all over," he told her. "Think what a story it'll make for our kids. How I came to murder you and left marrying you."

She kissed him, then sat back and lighted another cigarette.

"Let's start packing," Frelaine said. "I want—"

"Wait," Janet interrupted. "You haven't asked if *I* love *you*."

"What?"

She was still smiling, and the cigarette lighter was pointed at him. In the bottom of it was a black hole. A hole just large enough for a .38-caliber bullet.

"Don't kid around," he objected, getting to his feet.

"I'm not being funny, darling," she said.

In a fraction of a second, Frelaine had time to wonder how he could ever have thought she was not much over twenty. Looking at her now—*really* looking at her—he knew she couldn't be much less than thirty. Every minute of her strained, tense existence showed on her face.

"I don't love you, Stanton," she said very softly, the cigarette lighter poised.

Frelaine struggled for breath. One part of him was able to realize detachedly what a marvelous actress she really was. She must have known all along.

Frelaine pushed the button, and the gun was in his hand, cocked and ready.

The blow that struck him in the chest knocked him over a coffee table. The gun fell out of his hand. Gasping, half conscious, he watched her take careful aim for the coup de grâce.

"Now I can join the Tens," he heard her say as she squeezed the trigger.

CORDLE TO ONION TO CARROT

Surely you remember that bully who kicked sand on the ninety-seven-pound weakling? Well, that puny man's problem has never been solved, despite Charles Atlas's claims to the contrary. A genuine bully *likes* to kick sand on people; for him, simply, there is gut-deep satisfaction in a put-down. It wouldn't matter if you weighed 240 pounds, all of it rock-hard muscle and steely sinew, and were as wise as Solomon or as witty as Voltaire; you'd still end up with the sand of an insult in your eyes, and you probably wouldn't do anything about it.

That was how Howard Cordle viewed the situation. He was a pleasant man who was forever being pushed around by Fuller Brush men, fund solicitors, headwaiters, and other figures of authority. Cordle hated it. He suffered in silence the countless manic-aggressives who shoved their way to the heads of lines, took taxis he had hailed first, and sneeringly steered away girls to whom he was talking at parties.

What made it worse was that these people seemed to welcome provocation, to go looking for it, all for the sake of causing discomfort to others.

Cordle couldn't understand why this should be, until one midsummer's day, when he was driving through the northern regions of Spain while stoned out of his mind, the god Thoth-Hermes granted him original enlightenment by murmuring, "Uh, look, I groove with the problem, baby, but dig, we gotta put carrots in or it ain't no stew."

"Carrots?" said Cordle, struggling for illumination.

"I'm talking about those types who get you uptight," Thoth-Hermes explained. "They *gotta* act that way, baby, on account of they're carrots, and that's how carrots are."

"If they are carrots," Cordle said, feeling his way, "then I—"

"You, of course, are a little pearly white onion."

"Yes! My God, yes!" Cordle cried, dazzled by the blinding light of satori.

"And naturally, you and all the other pearly white onions think that carrots are just bad news, merely some kind of misshapen orangey onion; whereas the carrots look at you and rap about *freaky round white carrots, wow!* I mean you're just too much for each other, whereas, in actuality—"

"Yes, go on!" cried Cordle.

"In actuality," Thoth-Hermes declared, *"everything's got a place in The Stew!"*

"Of course! I see, I see, I see!"

"And *that* means that everybody who exists is necessary, and you *must* have long hateful orange carrots if you're also going to have nice pleasant decent white onions, or vice versa, because without all of the ingredients, it isn't a Stew, which is to say, life. It becomes, uh, let me see . . ."

"A soup!" cried ecstatic Cordle.

"You're coming in five-by-five," chanted Thoth-Hermes. "Lay down the word, deacon, and let the people know the divine formula . . ."

"A *soup!*" said Cordle. "Yes, I see it now—creamy, pure white onion soup is our dream of heaven, whereas fiery orange carrot broth is our notion of hell. It fits, it all fits together!"

"Om mani padme hum," intoned Thoth-Hermes.

"But where do the green peas go? What about the *meat*, for God's sake?"

"Don't pick at the metaphor," Thoth-Hermes advised him, "it leaves a nasty scab. Stick with the carrots and onions. And here, let me offer you a drink—a house specialty."

"But the spices, where do you put the *spices?*" Cordle demanded, taking a long swig of burgundy-colored liquid from a rusted canteen.

"Baby, you're asking questions that can be revealed only to a thirteenth-degree Mason with piles, wearing sandals. Sorry about that. Just remember that everything goes into The Stew."

"Into The Stew," Cordle repeated, smacking his lips.

"And, especially, stick with the carrots and onions; you were really grooving there."

"Carrots and onions," Cordle repeated.

"That's your trip," Thoth-Hermes said. "Hey, we've gotten to Corunna; you can let me out anywhere around here."

Cordle pulled his rented car off the road. Thoth-Hermes took his knapsack from the backseat and got out.

"Thanks for the lift, baby."

"My pleasure. Thank *you* for the wine. What kind did you say it was?"

"*Vino de casa*, mixed with a mere smidgen of old Dr. Hammerfinger's essence of instant powdered Power-Pack brand acid. Brewed by gnurrs in the secret laboratories of UCLA in preparation for the big all-Europe turn-on."

"Whatever it was, it surely *was*," Cordle said deeply. "Pure elixir to me. You could sell neckties to antelopes with that stuff; you could change the world from an oblate spheroid into a truncated trapezoid . . . What did I say?"

"Never mind, it's all part of your trip. Maybe you better lie down for a while, huh?"

"Where gods command, mere mortals must obey," Cordle said iambically. He lay down on the front seat of the car. Thoth-Hermes bent over him, his beard burnished gold, his head wreathed in plane trees.

"You okay?"

"Never better in my life."

"Want me to stand by?"

"Unnecessary. You have helped me beyond potentiality."

"Glad to hear it, baby, you're making a fine sound. You really are okay? Well, then, ta."

Thoth-Hermes marched off into the sunset. Cordle closed his eyes and solved various problems that had perplexed the greatest philosophers of all ages. He was mildly surprised at how simple complexity was.

At last he went to sleep. He awoke some six hours later. He had forgotten most of his brilliant insights and lucid solutions. It was inconceivable: How can one misplace the keys to the universe? But he had, and there seemed no hope of reclaiming them. Paradise was lost for good.

He did remember about the onions and the carrots, though, and he remembered The Stew. It was not the sort of insight he might have chosen if he'd had any choice; but this was what had come to him, and he did not reject it. Cordle knew, perhaps instinctively, that in the insight game, you take whatever you can get.

The next day he reached Santander in a driving rain. He decided to write amusing letters to all of his friends, perhaps even try his hand at a travel sketch. That required a typewriter. The *conserje* at his hotel directed him to a store that rented typewriters. He went there and found a clerk who spoke perfect English.

"Do you rent typewriters by the day?" Cordle asked.

"Why not?" the clerk replied. He had oily black hair and a thin aristocratic nose.

"How much for that one?" Cordle asked, indicating a thirty-year-old Erika portable.

"Seventy pesetas a day, which is to say, one dollar. Usually."

"Isn't this usually?"

"Certainly not, since you are a foreigner in transit. For you, one hundred and eight pesetas a day."

"All right," Cordle said, reaching for his wallet. "I'd like to have it for two days."

"I shall also require your passport and a deposit of fifty dollars."

Cordle attempted a mild joke. "Hey, I just want to type on it, not marry it."

The clerk shrugged.

"Look, the *conserje* has my passport at the hotel. How about taking my driver's license instead!"

"Certainly not. I must hold your passport in case you decide to default."

"But why do you need my passport *and* the deposit?" Cordle

asked, feeling bullied and ill at ease. "I mean, look, the machine's not worth twenty dollars."

"You are an expert, perhaps, in the Spanish market value of used German typewriters?"

"No, but—"

"Then permit me, sir, to conduct my business as I see fit. I will also need to know the use to which you plan to put the machine."

"The *use?*"

"Of course, the use."

It was one of those preposterous foreign situations that can happen to anyone. The clerk's request was incomprehensible and his manner was insulting. Cordle was about to give a curt little nod, turn on his heel, and walk out.

Then he remembered about the onions and carrots. He saw The Stew. And suddenly it occurred to Cordle that he could be whatever vegetable he wanted to be.

He turned to the clerk. He smiled winningly. He said, "You wish to know the use I will make of the typewriter?"

"Exactly."

"Well," Cordle said, "quite frankly, I had planned to stuff it up my nose."

The clerk gaped at him.

"It's quite a successful method of smuggling," Cordle went on. "I was also planning to give you a stolen passport and counterfeit pesetas. Once I got into Italy, I would have sold the typewriter for ten thousand dollars. Milan is undergoing a typewriter famine, you know; they're desperate, they'll buy anything."

"Sir," the clerk said, "you choose to be disagreeable."

"Nasty is the word you were looking for. I've changed my mind about the typewriter. But let me compliment you on your command of English."

"I have studied assiduously," the clerk admitted with a hint of pride."

"That is evident. And despite a certain weakness in the *r*'s, you succeed in sounding like a Venetian gondolier with a cleft palate. My best wishes to your esteemed family. I leave you now to pick your pimples in peace."

*   *   *

Reviewing the scene later, Cordle decided that he had performed quite well in his maiden appearance as a carrot. True, his closing lines had been a little forced and overintellectualized. But the undertone of viciousness had been convincing.

Most important was the simple resounding fact that he had done it. And now, in the quiet of his hotel room, instead of churning his guts in a frenzy of self-loathing, he had the tranquilizing knowledge of having put someone else in that position.

He had done it! Just like that, he had transformed himself from onion into carrot!

But was his position ethically defensible? Presumably the clerk could not help being detestable. He was a product of his own genetic and social environment, a victim of his conditioning; he was naturally rather than intentionally hateful—

Cordle stopped himself. He saw that he was engaged in typical onionish thinking, which was an inability to conceive of carrots except as an aberration from oniondom.

But now he knew that both onions *and* carrots had to exist; otherwise, there would be no Stew.

And he also knew that a man was free and could choose whatever vegetable he wanted to be. He could even live as an amusing little green pea, or a gruff, forceful clove of garlic (though perhaps that was scratching at the metaphor). In any event, a man could take his pick between carrothood and oniondom.

There is much to think about here, Cordle thought. But he never got around to thinking about it. Instead he went sightseeing, despite the rain, and then continued his travels.

The next incident occurred in Nice, in a cozy little restaurant on the Avenue des Diables Bleus, with red-checkered tablecloths and incomprehensible menus written in longhand with purple ink. There were four waiters, one of whom looked like Jean-Paul Belmondo, down to the cigarette drooping from his long lower lip. The others looked like run-of-the-mill muggers. There were several Scandinavian customers, one old Frenchman in a beret, and three homely English girls.

Belmondo sauntered over. Cordle, who spoke clear though

unidiomatic French, asked for the ten-franc menu he had seen hanging in the window.

The waiter gave him the sort of look one reserves for pretentious beggars. "Ah, that is all finished for today," he said, and handed Cordle a thirty-franc menu.

In his previous incarnation, Cordle would have bitten down on the bullet and ordered. Or possibly he would have risen, trembling with outrage, and left the restaurant, blundering into a chair on the way.

But now—

"Perhaps you did not understand me," Cordle said. "It is a matter of French law that you must serve from all of the fixed-price menus that you show in the window."

"*M'sieu* is a lawyer?" the waiter inquired, his hands perched insolently on his hips.

"No. *M'sieu* is a troublemaker," Cordle said, giving what he considered fair warning.

"Then *m'sieu* must make what trouble he desires," the waiter said. His eyes were slits.

"Okay," Cordle said. And just then, fortuitously, an elderly couple came into the restaurant. The man wore a double-breasted slate-blue suit with a half-inch white pinstripe. The woman wore a flowered organdy dress. Cordle called to them, "Excuse me, are you folks English?"

A bit startled, the man inclined his head in the barest intimation of a nod.

"Then I would advise you not to eat here. I am a health inspector for UNESCO. The chef apparently has not washed his hands since D-Day. We haven't made a definite test for typhoid yet, but we have our suspicions. As soon as my assistant arrives with the litmus paper . . ."

A deathly hush had fallen over the restaurant.

"I suppose a boiled egg would be safe enough," Cordle said.

The elderly man probably didn't believe him. But it didn't matter; Cordle was obviously trouble.

"Come, Mildred," he said, and they hurried out.

"There goes sixty francs plus five-percent tip," Cordle said coolly.

"Leave here at once!" the waiter snarled.

"I like it here," Cordle said, folding his arms. "I like the *ambiance*, the sense of intimacy—"

"You are not permitted to stay without eating."

"I shall eat. From the ten-franc menu."

The waiters looked at one another, nodded in unison, and began to advance in a threatening phalanx. Cordle called to the other diners, "I ask you all to bear witness! These men are going to attack me, four against one, contrary to French law and universal human ethics, simply because I want to order from the ten-franc menu, which they have falsely advertised."

It was a long speech, but this was clearly the time for grandiloquence. Cordle repeated it in English.

The English girls gasped. The old Frenchman went on eating his soup. The Scandinavians nodded grimly and began to take off their jackets.

The waiters held another conference. The one who looked like Belmondo said, "*M'sieu*, you are forcing us to call the police."

"That will save me the trouble," Cordle said, "of calling them myself."

"Surely *m'sieu* does not wish to spend his holiday in court?"

"That is how *m'sieu* spends most of his holidays," Cordle said.

The waiters conferred again. Then Belmondo stalked over with the thirty-franc menu. "The cost of the *prix fixe* will be ten francs, since evidently that is all *m'sieu* can afford."

Cordle let that pass. "Bring me onion soup, green salad, and the *boeuf Bourguignon*."

The waiter went to put in the order. While he was waiting, Cordle sang "Waltzing Matilda" in a moderately loud voice. He suspected it might speed up the service. He got his food by the time he reached, "You'll never catch me alive, said he," for the second time. Cordle pulled the tureen of stew toward him and lifted a spoon.

It was a breathless moment. Not one diner had left the restaurant. And Cordle was prepared. He leaned forward, soup spoon in shoveling position, and sniffed delicately. A hush fell over the room.

"It lacks a certain something," Cordle said aloud. Frowning, he poured the onion soup into the *boeuf Bourguignon*. He sniffed, shook his head, and added a half-loaf of bread, in slices. He sniffed again and added the salad and the contents of a saltcellar.

Cordle pursed his lips. "No," he said, "it simply will not do."

He overturned the entire contents of the tureen onto the table. It was an act comparable, perhaps, to throwing gentian violet on the Mona Lisa. All of France and most of western Switzerland went into a state of shock.

Unhurriedly, but keeping the frozen waiters under surveillance, Cordle rose and dropped ten francs into the mess. He walked to the door, turned, and said, "My compliments to the chef, who might better be employed as a cement mixer. And this, *mon vieux*, is for you."

He threw his crumpled linen napkin onto the floor.

As the matador, after a fine series of passes, turns his back contemptuously on the bull and strolls away, so went Cordle. For some unknown reason the waiters did not rush out after him, shoot him dead, and hang his corpse from the nearest lamppost. Cordle walked for ten or fifteen blocks, taking rights and lefts at random. He came to the Promenade des Anglais and sat down on a bench. He was trembling, and his shirt was drenched with perspiration.

"I did it," he said. "I did it! I was unspeakably vile and I got away with it!"

Now he really knew why carrots acted that way. Dear God in heaven, what joy, what delectable bliss!

Cordle then reverted to his mild-mannered self, smoothly and without regrets. He stayed that way until his second day in Rome.

He was in his rented car. He and seven other drivers were lined up at a traffic light on the Corso Vittorio Emanuele II. There were perhaps twenty cars behind them. All of the drivers were revving their engines, hunched over their steering wheels with slitted eyes, dreaming of Le Mans. All except Cordle, who was drinking in the cyclopean architecture of downtown Rome.

The checkered flag came down! The drivers floored their accelerators, trying to spin the wheels of their underpowered Fiats, wearing out their clutches and their nerves, but doing so with éclat and *brio*. All except Cordle, who seemed to be the only man in Rome who didn't have to win a race or keep an appointment.

Without undue haste or particular delay, Cordle depressed the clutch and engaged the gear. Already he had lost nearly two seconds—unthinkable at Monza or Monte Carlo.

The driver behind him blew his horn frantically.

Cordle smiled to himself, a secret, ugly expression. He put the gearshift into neutral, engaged the hand brake, and stepped out of his car. He ambled over to the hornblower, who had turned pasty white and was fumbling under his seat, hoping to find a tire iron.

"Yes?" said Cordle in French. "Is something wrong?"

"No, no, nothing," the driver replied in French—his first mistake. "I merely wanted you to go, to move."

"But I was just doing that," Cordle pointed out.

"Well, then! It is all right!"

"No, it is not all right," Cordle told him. "I think I deserve a better explanation of why you blew your horn at me."

The hornblower—a Milanese businessman on holiday with his wife and four children—rashly replied, "My dear sir, you were slow, you were delaying us all."

"*Slow?*" said Cordle. "You blew your horn two seconds after the light changed. Do you call two seconds slow?"

"It was much longer than that," the man riposted feebly.

Traffic was now backed up as far south as Naples. A crowd of ten thousand had gathered. *Carabinieri* units in Viterbo and Genoa had been called into a state of alert.

"That is untrue," Cordle said. "I have witnesses." He gestured at the crowd, which gestured back. "I shall call my witnesses before the courts. You must know that you broke the law by blowing your horn within the city limits of Rome in what was clearly not an emergency."

The Milanese businessman looked at the crowd, now swollen to perhaps fifty thousand. Dear God, he thought, if only the Goths would descend again and exterminate these leering Romans! If only the ground would open up and swallow this insane Frenchman! If only he, Giancarlo Morelli, had a dull spoon with which to open up the veins of his wrist!

Jets from the Sixth Fleet thundered overhead, hoping to avert the long expected coup d'état.

The Milanese businessman's own wife was shouting abuse at him; tonight he would cut out her faithless heart and mail it back to her mother.

What was there to do? In Milan, he would have had this Frenchman's head on a platter. But this was Rome, a southern city, an unpredictable and dangerous place. And legalistically, he was possibly in the wrong, which left him at a further disadvantage in the argument.

"Very well," he said. "The blowing of the horn was perhaps truly unnecessary, despite the provocation."

"I insist on a genuine apology," insisted Cordle.

There was a thundering sound to the east: Thousands of Soviet tanks were moving into battle formation across the plains of Hungary, ready to resist the long-expected NATO thrust in Transylvania. The water supply was cut off in Foggia, Brindisi, Bari. The Swiss closed their frontiers and stood ready to dynamite the passes.

"All right, I apologize!" the Milanese businessman screamed. "I am sorry I provoked you and even sorrier that I was born! Again, I apologize! Now will you go away and let me have a heart attack in peace?"

"I accept your apology," Cordle said. "No hard feelings, eh?" He strolled back to his car, humming "Blow the Man Down," and drove away as millions cheered.

War was once again averted by a hairbreadth.

Cordle drove to the Arch of Titus, parked his car, and—to the sound of a thousand trumpets—passed through it. He deserved this triumph as well as any Caesar.

God, he gloated, I was *loathsome*!

In England, Cordle stepped on a young lady's toe just inside the Traitors' Gate of the Tower of London. This should have served as an intimation of something. The young lady was named Mavis. She came from Short Hills, New Jersey, and she had long straight dark hair. She was slender, pretty, intelligent, energetic, and had a sense of humor. She had minor faults, as well, but they play no part in this story. She let Cordle buy her a cup of coffee. They were together constantly for the rest of the week.

"I think I am infatuated," Cordle said to himself on the seventh day. He realized at once that he had made a slight understatement. He was violently and hopelessly in love.

But what did Mavis feel? She seemed not unfond of him. It was even possible that she might, conceivably, reciprocate.

At that moment Cordle had a flash of prescience. He realized that one week ago he had stepped on the toe of his future wife and mother of his two children, both of whom would be born and brought up in a split-level house with inflatable furniture in Summit, New Jersey, or possibly Millburn.

This may sound unattractive and provincial when stated baldly; but it was desirable to Cordle, who had no pretensions to cosmopolitanism. After all, not all of us can live at Cap Ferrat. Strangely enough, not all of us even want to.

That day Cordle and Mavis went to the Marshall Gordon Residence in Belgravia to see the Byzantine miniatures. Mavis had a passion for Byzantine miniatures that seemed harmless enough at the time. The collection was private, but Mavis had secured invitations through a local Avis manager, who was trying very hard indeed.

They came to the Gordon Residence, an awesome Regency building in Huddlestone Mews. They rang. A butler in full evening dress answered the door. They showed the invitations. The butler's glance and lifted eyebrow showed that they were carrying second-class invitations of the sort given to importunate art poseurs on seventeen-day, all-expense economy flights, rather than the engraved first-class invitations given to Picasso, Jackie Onassis, Sugar Ray Robinson, Norman Mailer, Charles Goren, and other movers and shakers of the world.

The butler said, "Oh, yes . . ." Two words that spoke black volumes. His face twitched; he looked like a man who had received an unexpected visit from Tamerlane and a regiment of his Golden Horde.

"The miniatures," Cordle reminded him.

"Yes, of course . . . But I am afraid, sir, that no one is allowed into the Gordon Residence without a coat and necktie."

It was an oppressive August day. Cordle was wearing a sport shirt. He said, "Did I hear you correctly? Coat and necktie?"

The butler said, "That is the rule, sir."

Mavis asked, "Couldn't you make an exception this once?"

The butler shook his head. "We really must stick by the rules, miss. Otherwise . . ." He left the fear of vulgarity unsaid, but it hung in the air like a chrome-plated fart.

"Of course," Cordle said pleasantly. "Otherwise. So it's a coat and tie, is it? I think we can arrange that."

Mavis put a hand on his arm and said, "Howard, let's go. We can come back some other time."

"Nonsense, my dear. If I may borrow your coat . . ."

He lifted the white raincoat from her shoulders and put it on, ripping a seam. "There we go, mate!" he said briskly to the butler. "That should do it, *n'est-ce pas?*"

"I think *not*," the butler said, in a voice bleak enough to wither artichokes. "In any event, there is the matter of the necktie."

Cordle had been waiting for that. He whipped out his sweaty handkerchief and knotted it around his neck.

"Suiting you?" he leered, in an imitation of Peter Lorre as Mr. Moto, which only he appreciated.

"Howard! Let's go!"

Cordle waited, smiling steadily at the butler, who was sweating for the first time in living memory.

"I'm afraid, sir, that that is not—"

"Not what?"

"Not precisely what was meant by coat and tie."

"Are you trying to tell me," Cordle said in a loud, unpleasant voice, "that you are an arbiter of men's clothing as well as a door opener?"

"Of course not! But this impromptu attire—"

"What has 'impromptu' got to do with it? Are people supposed to prepare three days in advance just to pass your inspection?"

"You are wearing a woman's waterproof and a soiled handkerchief," the butler stated stiffly. "I think there is no more to say."

He began to close the door. Cordle said, "You do that, sweetheart, and I'll have you up for slander and defamation of character. Those are serious charges over here, buddy, and I've got witnesses."

Aside from Mavis, Cordle had collected a small, diffident, but interested crowd.

"This is becoming too ridiculous," the butler said, temporizing, the door half-closed.

"You'll find a stretch at Wormwood Scrubs even more ridiculous," Cordle told him. "I intend to persecute—I mean prosecute."

"Howard!" cried Mavis.

He shook off her hand and fixed the butler with a piercing glance. He said, "I am Mexican, though perhaps my excellent grasp of the English has deceived you. In my country, a man would cut his own throat before letting such an insult pass unavenged. A woman's coat, you say? *Hombre*, when I wear a coat, it becomes a *man's* coat. Or do you imply that I am a *maricón*, a—how do you say it?—homosexual?"

The crowd—becoming less modest—growled approval. No one but a lord loves a butler.

"I meant no such implication," the butler said weakly.

"Then is it a man's coat?"

"Just as you wish, sir."

"Unsatisfactory! The innuendo still exists. I go now to find an officer of the law."

"Wait, let's not be hasty," the butler said. His face was bloodless and his hands were shaking. "Your coat is a man's coat, sir."

"And what about my necktie?"

The butler made a final attempt at stopping Zapata and his blood-crazed peons.

"Well, sir, a handkerchief is demonstrably—"

"What I wear around my neck," Cordle said coldly, "becomes what it is intended to be. If I wore a piece of figured silk around my throat, would you call it ladies' underwear? Linen is a suitable material for a tie, *verdad*? Function defines terminology, don't you agree? If I ride to work on a cow, no one says that I am mounted on a steak. Or do you detect a flaw in my argument?"

"I'm afraid that I don't fully understand it . . ."

"Then how can you presume to stand in judgment over it?"

The crowd, which had been growing restless, now murmured approval.

"Sir," cried the wretched butler. "I beg of you . . ."

"Otherwise," Cordle said with satisfaction, "I have a coat, a necktie, and an invitation. Perhaps you would be good enough to show us the Byzantine miniatures?"

The butler opened wide the door to Pancho Villa and his tattered hordes. The last bastion of civilization had been captured in less than an hour. Wolves howled along the banks of the Thames. Morelos's barefoot army stabled its horses in the British Museum, and Europe's long night had begun.

Cordle and Mavis viewed the collection in silence. They didn't exchange a word until they were alone and strolling through Regent's Park.

"Look, Mavis," Cordle began.

"No, you look," she said. "You were horrible! You were unbelievable! You were—I can't find a word rotten enough for what you were! I never dreamed that you were one of those sadistic bastards who get their kicks out of humiliating people!"

"But, Mavis, you heard what he said to me, you heard the way—"

"He was a stupid, bigoted old man," Mavis said. "I thought you were not."

"But he said—"

"It doesn't matter. The fact is, you were enjoying yourself!"

"Well, yes, maybe you're right," Cordle said. "Look, I can explain."

"Not to me, you can't. Ever. Please stay away from me, Howard. Permanently. I mean that."

The future mother of his two children began to walk away, out of his life. Cordle hurried after her.

"Mavis!"

"I'll call a cop, Howard, so help me, I will! Just leave me alone!"

"Mavis, I love you!"

She must have heard him, but she kept on walking. She was a sweet and beautiful girl and definitely, unchangeably, an onion.

Cordle was never able to explain to Mavis about The Stew and about the necessity for experiencing behavior before condemning it. Moments of mystical illumination are seldom explicable. He *was* able to make her believe that he had undergone a brief psychotic episode, unique and unprecedented and—never to be repeated.

They are married now, have one girl and one boy, live in a split-level house in Plainfield, New Jersey, and are quite content. Cordle is visibly pushed around by Fuller Brush men, fund solicitors, headwaiters, and other figures of authority. But there is a difference.

Cordle makes a point of taking regularly scheduled solitary vacations. Last year he made a small name for himself in Honolulu. This year he is going to Buenos Aires.

IS THAT WHAT PEOPLE DO?

Eddie Quintero had bought the binoculars at Hammerman's Army
& Navy Surplus of All Nations Warehouse Outlet ("Highest
Quality Goods, Cash Only, All Sales Final"). He had long wanted
to own a pair of really fine binoculars, because with them he
hoped to see some things that otherwise he would never see.
Specifically, he hoped to see girls undressing at the Chauvin
Arms, across the street from his furnished room.

But there was also another reason. Without really acknowledg-
ing it to himself, Quintero was looking for that moment of vision,
of total attention, that comes when a bit of the world is suddenly
framed and illuminated, permitting the magnified and extended
eye to find novelty and drama in what had been the dull everyday
world.

The moment of insight never lasts long. Soon you're caught up
again in your habitual outlook. But the hope remains that something—a gadget, a book, a person—will change your life finally
and definitively, lift you out of the unspeakable silent sadness of
yourself, and permit you at last to behold the wonders you always
knew were there, just beyond your vision.

The binoculars were packed in a sturdy wooden box stenciled
Section XXII, Marine Corps, Quantico, Virginia. Beneath that the
stencil read, Restricted Issue. Just to be able to open a box like
that was worth the $15.99 that Quintero had paid.

Inside the box were slabs of styrofoam and bags of silica, and
then, at last, the binoculars themselves. They were like nothing

Quintero had ever seen before. The tubes were square rather than round, and there were various incomprehensible scales engraved on them. There was a tag on them that read, EXPERIMENTAL. NOT TO BE REMOVED FROM THE TESTING ROOM.

Quintero hefted them. The binoculars were heavy, and he could hear something rattle inside. He removed the plastic protective cups and pointed the binoculars out the window.

He saw nothing. He shook the binoculars and heard the rattle again. But then the prism or mirror or whatever was loose must have fallen back into place, because suddenly he could see.

He was looking across the street at the mammouth structure of the Chauvin Arms. The view was exceptionally sharp and clear; he felt that he was standing about ten feet away from the exterior of the building. He scanned the nearest apartment windows quickly, but nothing was going on. It was a hot Saturday afternoon in July, and Quintero supposed that all the girls had gone to the beach.

He turned the focus knob, and he had the sensation that he was moving, a disembodied eye riding the front of a zoom lens, closer to the apartment wall, five feet away, then one foot away, and he could see little flaws in the white concrete front and grit marks on the anodized aluminum window frames. He paused to admire this unusual view, and then turned the knob again very gently. The wall loomed huge in front of him, and then suddenly he had gone completely through it and was standing inside an apartment.

He was so startled that he put down the binoculars for a moment to orient himself.

When he looked through the glasses again, it was just as before; he seemed to be inside an apartment. He caught a glimpse of movement to one side, tried to locate it, and then the part rattled and the binoculars went dark.

He turned and twisted the binoculars, and the part rattled up and down, but he could see nothing. He put the binoculars on his dinette table, heard a soft clunking sound, and bent down to look again. Evidently the mirror or prism had fallen back into place again, for he could see.

He decided to take no chances on jarring the part again. He left the glasses on the table, knelt down behind them, and looked through the eyepieces.

He was looking into a dimly lighted apartment, curtains drawn and the lights on. There was an Indian sitting on the floor, or, more likely, a man dressed like an Indian. He was a skinny blond man with a feathered headband, beaded moccasins, fringed buck-skin pants, a leather shirt, and a rifle. He was holding the rifle in firing position, aiming at something in a corner of the room.

Near the Indian there was a fat woman in a pink slip, sitting in an armchair and talking with great animation into a telephone.

Quintero could see that the Indian's rifle was a toy, about half the length of a real rifle.

The Indian continued to fire into the corner of the room, and the woman kept on talking into the telephone and laughing.

After a few moments the Indian stopped firing, turned to the woman, and handed her his rifle. The woman put down the telephone, found another toy rifle propped against her chair, and handed it to the Indian. Then she picked up his gun and began to reload it, one imaginary cartridge at a time.

The Indian continued firing with great speed and urgency. His face was tight and drawn, the face of a man who is singlehandedly protecting his tribe's retreat into Canada.

Suddenly the Indian seemed to hear something. He looked over his shoulder. His face registered panic. He twisted around sud-denly, swinging his rifle into position. The woman also looked, and her mouth opened wide in astonishment. Quintero tried to pick up what they were looking at, but the dinette table wobbled and the binoculars clicked and went blank.

Quintero stood up and paced up and down his room. He had had a glimpse of what people do when they're alone and unob-served. It was exciting, but confusing, because he didn't know what it meant. Had the Indian been a lunatic, and the woman his keeper? Or were they more or less ordinary people playing some sort of harmless game? Or had he been watching a pathological killer in training—a sniper who, in a week or a month or a year, would buy a real rifle and shoot down real people until he himself was killed? And what happened there at the end? Had that been part of the charade, or had something else occurred, something incalculable?

There was no answer to these questions. All he could do was see what else the binoculars would show him.

He planned his next move with greater care. It was crucial that the binoculars be held steady. The dinette table was too wobbly to risk putting the binoculars there again. He decided to use the low coffee table instead.

The binoculars weren't working, however. He jiggled them around, and he could hear the loose part rattle. It was like one of those puzzles where you must put a little steel ball into a certain hole. But this time he had to work without seeing either the ball or the hole.

Half an hour later he had had no success, and he put the glasses down, smoked a cigarette, drank a beer, then jiggled them again. He heard the part fall solidly into place, and he lowered the glasses gently onto a chair.

He was sweaty from the exertion, and he stripped to the waist, then bent down and peered into the eyepieces. He adjusted the focus knob with utmost gentleness, and his vision zoomed across the street and through the outer wall of the Chauvin Arms.

He was looking into a large formal sitting room decorated in white, blue, and gold. Two attractive young people were seated on a spindly couch, a man and a woman. Both were dressed in period costumes. The woman wore a billowing gown cut low over her small round breasts. Her hair was done up in a mass of ringlets. The man wore a long black coat, fawn-gray knee pants, and sheer white stockings. His white shirt was embroidered with lace, and his hair was powdered.

The girl was laughing at something he had said. The man bent closer to her, then kissed her. She stiffened for a moment, then put her arms around his neck.

They broke their embrace abruptly, for three men had just entered the room. They were dressed entirely in black, wore black stocking-masks over their heads, and carried swords. There was a fourth man behind them, but Quintero couldn't make him out.

The young man sprang to his feet and took a sword from the

wall. He engaged the three men, circling around the couch while the girl sat frozen in terror.

A fourth man stepped into the circle of vision. He was tall and gaudily dressed. Jeweled rings flashed on his fingers, and a diamond pendant hung from his neck. He wore a white wig. The girl gasped when she saw him.

The young man put one of his opponents out of action with a sword-thrust to the shoulder, then leaped lightly over the couch to prevent another man from getting behind him. He held his two opponents in play with apparent ease, and the fourth man watched for a moment, then took a dagger from beneath his waistcoat and threw it, and it hit the young man butt-first on the forehead.

The young man staggered back, and one of the masked men lunged. His blade caught the young man in the chest, bent, then straightened as it slid in between the ribs. The young man looked at it for a moment, then fell, blood welling over his white shirt.

The girl fainted. The fourth man said something, and one of the masked men lifted the girl while the other helped his wounded companion. They all exited, leaving the young man sprawled bleeding on the polished parquet floor.

Quintero turned the glasses to see if he could follow the others. The loose part clattered and the glasses went dark.

Quintero heated up a can of soup and ate it thoughtfully, thinking about what he had seen. It must have been a rehearsal for a scene in a play . . . But the sword-thrust had looked real, and the young man on the floor had looked badly hurt, perhaps dead.

Whatever it had been, he had been privileged to watch a private moment in the strangeness of people's lives. He had seen another of the unfathomable things that people do.

It gave him a giddy, godlike feeling, this knowledge that he could see things no one else could see.

The only thing that sobered him was the extreme uncertainty of the future of his visions. The binoculars were broken, a vital part was loose, and all the marvels might stop for good at any moment.

He considered bringing the glasses somewhere to get them fixed. But he knew he would probably succeed only in getting back a pair of ordinary binoculars, which would show him ordinary things very well, but could not be expected to see through solid walls into strange and concealed matters.

He looked through the glasses again, saw nothing, and began to shake and manipulate them. He could hear the loose part rolling and tumbling around, but the lenses remained dark. He kept on manipulating them, eager to see the next wonder.

The part suddenly fell into place. Taking no chances this time, Quintero put the glasses down on his carpeted floor. He lay down beside them, put his head to one side, and tried to look through one eyepiece. But the angle was wrong and he could see nothing.

He started to lift the glasses gently, but the part moved a little and he put them down carefully. Light was still shining through the lenses, but no matter how he turned and twisted his head, he could not get lined up with the eyepiece.

He thought about it for a moment, and saw only one way out of his difficulty. He stood up, straddled the glasses, and bent down with his head upside down. Now he could see through the eyepieces, but he couldn't maintain the posture. He straightened up and did some more thinking.

He saw what he had to do. He took off his shoes, straddled the binoculars again, and performed a headstand. He had to do this several times before his head was positioned correctly in front of the eyepieces. He propped his feet against the wall and managed to get into a stable position.

He was looking into a large office somewhere in the interior of the Chauvin Arms. It was a modern, expensively furnished office, windowless, indirectly lighted.

There was only one man in the room: a large, well-dressed man in his fifties, seated behind a blond wood desk. He sat quite still, evidently lost in thought.

Quintero could make out every detail of the office, even the little mahogany plaque on the desk that read, OFFICE OF THE DIRECTOR. THE BUCK STOPS HERE.

The Director got up and walked to a wall safe concealed behind a painting. He unlocked it, reached in, and took out a metal container somewhat larger than a shoebox. He carried this to his desk, took a key out of his pocket, and unlocked it.

He opened the box and removed an object wrapped in a silky

red cloth. He removed the cloth and set the object on his desk. Quintero saw that it was a statue of a monkey, carved in what looked like dark volcanic rock.

It was a strange-looking monkey, however, because it had four arms and six legs.

Then the Director unlocked a drawer in his desk, took out a long stick, placed it in the monkey's lap, and lit it with a cigarette lighter.

Oily black coils of smoke arose, and the Director began to dance around the monkey. His mouth was moving, and Quintero guessed that he was singing or chanting.

He kept this up for about five minutes, and then the smoke began to coalesce and take on form. Soon it had shaped itself into a replica of the monkey, but magnified to the size of a man, an evil-looking thing made of smoke and enchantment.

The smoke-demon (as Quintero named him) held a package in one of his four hands. He handed this to the Director, who took it, bowed deeply, and hurried over to his desk. He ripped open the package, and a pile of papers spilled over his desk. Quintero could see bundles of currency, and piles of engraved papers that looked like stock certificates.

The Director tore himself away from the papers, bowed low once again to the smoke-demon, and spoke to him. The mouth of the smoky figure moved, and the Director answered him. They seemed to be having an argument.

Then the Director shrugged, bowed again, went to his intercom, and pressed a button.

An attractive young woman came into the room with a steno pad and pencil. She saw the smoke-demon and her mouth widened into a scream. She ran to the door but was unable to open it.

She turned and saw the smoke-demon flowing to her, engulfing her.

During all this the Director was counting his piles of currency, oblivious of what was going on. But he had to look up when a brilliant light poured from the head of the smoke-demon, and the four hairy arms pulled the feebly struggling woman close to his body . . .

At that moment Quintero's neck muscles could not support him any longer. He fell, and jostled the binoculars as he came down.

He could hear the loose part rattle around; and then it gave a hard click, as though it had settled into its final position.

Quintero picked himself up and massaged his neck with both hands. Had he been subject to a hallucination? Or had he seen something secret and magical that perhaps a few people knew about and used to maintain their financial positions—one more of the concealed and incredible things that people do?

He didn't know the answer, but he knew he had to witness at least one more of those visions. He stood on his head again and looked through the binoculars.

Yes, he could see! He was looking into a dreary furnished room. Within that room he saw a thin, potbellied man in his thirties, stripped to the waist, standing on his head with his stockinged feet pressed against the wall, looking upside down into a pair of binoculars that lay on the floor and were aimed at a wall.

It took him a moment to realize that the binoculars were showing him himself.

He sat down on the floor, suddenly frightened. For he realized that he was only another performer in humanity's great circus, and he had just done one of his acts, just like the others. But who was watching? Who was the real observer?

He turned the binoculars around and looked through the objective lenses. He saw a pair of eyes, and he thought they were his own—until one of them slowly winked at him.

THE PRIZE OF PERIL

Raeder lifted his head cautiously above the windowsill. He saw the fire escape, and below it a narrow alley. There was a weatherbeaten baby carriage in the alley, and three garbage cans. As he watched, a black-sleeved arm moved from behind the farthest can, with something shiny in its fist. Raeder ducked down. A bullet smashed through the window above his head and punctured the ceiling, showering him with plaster.

Now he knew about the alley. It was guarded, just like the door.

He lay at full length on the cracked linoleum, staring at the bullet hole in the ceiling, listening to the sounds outside the door. He was a tall man with bloodshot eyes and a two-day stubble. Grime and fatigue had etched lines into his face. Fear had touched his features, tightening a muscle here and twitching a nerve there. The results were startling. His face had character now, for it was reshaped by the expectation of death.

There was a gunman in the alley and there were two on the stairs. He was trapped. He was dead.

Sure, Raeder thought, he still moved and breathed; but that was only because of death's inefficiency. Death would take care of him in a few minutes. Death would poke holes in his face and body, artistically dab his clothes with blood, arrange his limbs in some grotesque position of the graveyard ballet . . .

Raeder bit his lip sharply. He wanted to live. There had to be a way.

He rolled onto his stomach and surveyed the dingy cold-water apartment into which the killers had driven him. It was a perfect little one-room coffin. It had a door, which was watched, and a fire escape, which was watched. And it had a tiny windowless bathroom.

He crawled to the bathroom and stood up. There was a ragged hole in the ceiling, almost four inches wide. If he could enlarge it, crawl through into the apartment above . . .

He heard a muffled thud. The killers were impatient. They were beginning to break down the door.

He studied the hole in the ceiling. No use even considering it. He could never enlarge it in time.

They were smashing against the door, grunting each time they struck. Soon the lock would tear out, or the hinges would pull out of the rotting wood. The door would go down, and the two blank-faced men would enter, dusting off their jackets.

But surely someone would help him! He took the tiny television set from his pocket. The picture was blurred, and he didn't bother to adjust it. The audio was clear and precise.

He listened to the well-modulated voice of Mike Terry address-ing his vast audience.

"*. . . terrible spot,*" Terry was saying. "*Yes, folks, Jim Raeder is in a truly terrible predicament. He had been hiding, you'll remember, in a third-rate Broadway hotel, under an assumed name. It seemed safe enough. But the bellhop recognized him, and gave that information to the Thompson gang.*"

The door creaked under repeated blows. Raeder clutched the little television set and listened.

"*Jim Raeder just managed to escape from the hotel! Closely pursued, he entered a brownstone at one-fifty-six West End Avenue. His intention was to go over the roofs. And it might have worked, folks, it just might have worked. But the roof door was locked. It looked like the end . . . But Raeder found that apartment seven was unoccupied and unlocked. He entered . . .*"

Terry paused for emphasis, then cried: "*—and now he's trapped there, trapped like a rat in a cage! The Thompson gang is breaking down the door! The fire escape is guarded! Our camera crew, situated in a nearby building, is giving you a closeup now. Look folks, just look! Is there no hope for Jim Raeder?*"

Is there no hope? Raeder silently echoed, perspiration pouring from him as he stood in the dark, stifling little bathroom, listening to the steady thud against the door.

"Wait a minute!" Mike Terry cried. *"Hang on, Jim Raeder, hang on a little longer. Perhaps there is hope! I have an urgent call from one of our viewers, a call on the Good Samaritan Line! Here's someone who thinks he can help you, Jim. Are you listening, Jim Raeder?"*

Raeder waited, and heard the hinges tearing out of rotten wood.

"Go right ahead, sir," said Mike Terry. *"What is your name, sir?"*

"Er—Felix Bartholemow."

"Don't be nervous, Mr. Bartholemow. Go right ahead."

"Well, okay. Mr. Raeder," said an old man's shaking voice. *"I used to live at one-five-six West End Avenue. Same apartment you're trapped in, Mr. Raeder—fact! Look, that bathroom has got a window, Mr. Raeder. It's been painted over, but it has got a—"*

Raeder pushed the television set into his pocket. He located the outlines of the window and kicked. Glass shattered, and daylight poured startlingly in. He cleared the jagged sill and peered quickly down.

Below was a long drop to a concrete courtyard.

The hinges tore free. He heard the door opening. Quickly Raeder climbed through the window, hung by his fingertips for a moment, and dropped.

The shock was stunning. Groggily he stood up. A face appeared at the bathroom window.

"Tough luck," said the man, leaning out and taking careful aim with a snub-nosed .38.

At that moment a smoke bomb exploded inside the bathroom.

The killer's shot went wide. He turned, cursing. More smoke bombs burst in the courtyard, obscuring Raeder's figure.

He could hear Mike Terry's frenzied voice over the TV set in his pocket. *"Now run for it!"* Terry was screaming. *"Run, Jim Raeder, run for your life. Run now, while the killers' eyes are filled with smoke. And thank Good Samaritan Sarah Winters, of three-four-one-two Edgar Street, Brockton, Mass., for donating five smoke bombs and employing the services of a man to throw them!"*

In a quieter voice, Terry continued: *"You've saved a man's life today, Mrs. Winters. Would you tell our audience how it—"*

Raeder wasn't able to hear any more. He was running through the smoke-filled courtyard, past clotheslines, into the open street.

He walked down Sixty-third Street, slouching to minimize his height, staggering slightly from exertion, dizzy from lack of food and sleep.

"Hey, you!"

Raeder turned. A middle-aged woman was sitting on the steps of a brownstone, frowning at him.

"You're Raeder, aren't you? The one they're trying to kill?"

Raeder started to walk away.

"Come inside here, Raeder," the woman said.

Perhaps it was a trap. But Raeder knew that he had to depend upon the generosity and goodheartedness of the people. He was their representative, a projection of themselves, an average guy in trouble. Without them, he was lost. With them, nothing could harm him.

Trust in the people, Mike Terry had told him. They'll never let you down.

He followed the woman into her parlor. She told him to sit down and left the room, returning almost immediately with a plate of stew. She stood watching him while he ate, as one would watch an ape in the zoo eat peanuts.

Two children came out of the kitchen and stared at him. Three overalled men came out of the bedroom and focused a television camera on him. There was a big television set in the parlor. As he gulped his food, Raeder watched the image of Mike Terry, and listened to the man's strong, sincere, worried voice.

"There he is, folks," Terry was saying. *"There's Jim Raeder now, eating his first square meal in two days. Our camera crews have really been working to cover this for you! Thanks, boys . . . Folks, Jim Raeder has been given a brief sanctuary by Mrs. Velma O'Dell, of three-forty-three West Sixty-third Street. Thank you, Good Samaritan O'Dell! It's really wonderful, how people from all walks of life have taken Jim Raeder to their hearts!"*

"You better hurry," Mrs. O'Dell said.

"Yes, ma'am," Raeder said.

"I don't want no gunplay in my apartment."

"I'm almost finished, ma'am."

One of the children asked, "Aren't they going to kill him?"

"Shut up," said Mrs. O'Dell.

"Yes, Jim," chanted Mike Terry, *"you'd better hurry. Your killers aren't far behind. They aren't stupid men, Jim. Vicious, warped, insane—yes! But not stupid. They're following a trail of blood— blood from your torn hand, Jim!"*

Raeder hadn't realized until now that he'd cut his hand on the windowsill.

"Here, I'll bandage that," Mrs. O'Dell said. Raeder stood up and let her bandage his hand. Then she gave him a brown jacket and a gray slouch hat.

"My husband's stuff," she said.

"He has a disguise, folks!" Mike Terry cried delightedly. *"This is something new! A disguise! With seven hours to go until he's safe!"*

"Now get out of here," Mrs. O'Dell said.

"I'm going, ma'am," Raeder said. "Thanks."

"I think you're stupid," she said. "I think you're stupid to be involved in this."

"Yes, ma'am."

"It just isn't worth it."

Raeder thanked her and left. He walked to Broadway, caught a subway to Fifty-ninth Street, then an uptown local to Eighty-sixth. There he bought a newspaper and changed for the Manhasset through-express.

He glanced at his watch. He had six and a half hours to go.

The subway roared under the East River. Raeder dozed, his bandaged hand conealed under the newspaper, the hat pulled over his face. Had he been recognized yet? Had he shaken the Thompson gang? Or was someone telephoning them now?

Dreamily he wondered if he had escaped death. Or was he still a cleverly animated corpse, moving around because of death's inefficiency? (My dear, death is so *laggard* these days! Jim Raeder walked about for hours after he died, and actually answered people's *questions* before he could be decently buried!)

Raeder's eyes snapped open. He had dreamed something . . . unpleasant. He couldn't remember what.

He closed his eyes again and remembered, with mild astonishment, a time when he had been in no trouble.

That was two years ago. He had been a big pleasant young man working as a truck driver's helper. He had no talents. He was too modest to have dreams.

The tight-faced little truck driver had the dreams for him. "Why not try for a television show, Jim? I would if I had your looks. They like nice, average guys with nothing much on the ball. As contestants. Everybody likes guys like that. Why not look into it?"

So he had looked into it. The owner of the local television store had explained it further.

"You see, Jim, the public is sick of highly trained athletes with their trick reflexes and their professional courage. Who can feel for guys like that? Who can identify? People want to watch exciting things, sure, but not when some joker is making it his business for fifty thousand a year. That's why organized sports are in a slump. That's why the thrill shows are booming."

"I see," said Raeder.

"Six years ago, Jim, Congress passed the Voluntary Suicide Act. Those old senators talked a lot about free will and self-determinism at the time. But that's all crap. You know what the Act really means? It means the amateurs can risk their lives for the big loot, not just professionals. In the old days you had to be a professional boxer or footballer or hockey player if you wanted your brains beaten out legally for money. But now that opportunity is open to ordinary people like you, Jim."

"I see," Raeder said again.

"It's a marvelous opportunity. Take you. You're no better than anyone, Jim. Anything you can do, anyone can do. You're *average*. I think the thrill shows would go for you."

Raeder permitted himself to dream. Television shows looked like a sure road to riches for a pleasant young fellow with no particular talent or training. He wrote a letter to a show called "Hazard" and enclosed a photograph of himself.

"Hazard" was interested in him. The JBC network investigated, and found that he was average enough to satisfy the wariest viewer. His parentage and affiliations were checked. At last he was summoned to New York and interviewed by Mr. Moulian.

Moulian was dark and intense, and chewed gum as he talked. "You'll do," he snapped. "But not for 'Hazard.' You'll appear on 'Spills.' It's a half-hour daytime show on Channel Three."

"Gee," said Raeder.

"Don't thank me. There's a thousand dollars if you win or place second, and a consolation prize of a hundred dollars if you lose. But that's not important."

"No, sir."

"'Spills' is a *little* show. The JBC network uses it as a testing ground. First- and second-place winners on 'Spills' move on to 'Emergency.' The prizes are much bigger on 'Emergency.'"

"I know they are, sir."

"And if you do well on 'Emergency,' there are the first-class thrill shows, like 'Hazard' and 'Underwater Perils,' with their nation-wide coverage and enormous prizes. And then comes the really big time. How far you go is up to you."

"I'll do my best, sir," Raeder said.

Moulian stopped chewing gum for a moment and said, almost reverently. "You can do it, Jim. Just remember. You're *the people*, and *the people* can do anything."

The way he said it made Raeder feel momentarily sorry for Mr. Moulian, who was dark and frizzy-haired and popeyed, and was obviously not *the people*.

They shook hands. Then Raeder signed a paper absolving the JBC of all responsibility should he lose his life, limbs, or reason during the contest. And he signed another paper exercising his rights under the Voluntary Suicide Act. The law required this, and it was a mere formality.

In three weeks he appeared on "Spills."

The program followed the classic form of the automobile race. Untrained drivers climbed into powerful American and European competition cars and raced over a murderous twenty-mile course. Raeder was shaking with fear as he slid his big Maserati into the wrong gear and took off.

The race was a screaming, tire-burning nightmare. Raeder stayed back, letting the early leaders smash themselves up on the counterbanked hairpin turns. He crept into third place when a Jaguar in front of him swerved against an Alfa-Romeo and the two cars roared into a plowed field. Raeder gunned for second place on the last three miles, but couldn't find passing room. An S-curve almost took him, but he fought the car back on the road, still holding third. Then the lead driver broke a crankshaft in the final fifty yards, and Jim ended in second place.

He was now a thousand dollars ahead. He received four fan letters, and a lady in Oshkosh sent him a pair of argyle socks. He was invited to appear on "Emergency."

Unlike the others, "Emergency" was not a competition-type program. It stressed individual initiative. For the show, Raeder was knocked out with a non-habit-forming narcotic. He awoke in the cockpit of a small airplane, cruising on autopilot at ten thousand feet. His fuel gauge showed nearly empty. He had no parachute. He was supposed to land the plane.

Of course, he had never flown before.

He experimented gingerly with the controls, remembering that last week's participant had recovered consciousness in a submarine, opened the wrong valve, and drowned.

Thousands of viewers watched spellbound as this average man, a man just like themselves, struggled with the situation just as they would do. Jim Raeder was *them*. Anything he could do, they could do. He was representative of *the people*.

Raeder managed to bring the ship down in some semblance of a landing. He flipped over a few times, but his seat belt held. And the engine, contrary to expectation, did not burst into flames.

He staggered out with two broken ribs, three thousand dollars, and a chance, when he healed, to appear on "Torero."

At last, a first-class thrill show! "Torero" paid ten thousand dollars. All you had to do was kill a black Miura bull with a sword, just like a real trained matador.

The fight was held in Madrid, since bullfighting was still illegal in the United States. It was nationally televised.

Raeder had a good *cuadrilla*. They liked the big, slow-moving American. The *picadores* really leaned into their lances, trying to slow the bull for him. The *banderilleros* tried to run the beast off his feet before driving in their *banderillas.* And the second matador, a mournful man from Algeciras, almost broke the bull's neck with fancy capework.

But when all was said and done, it was Jim Raeder on the sand, a red *muleta* clumsily gripped in his left hand, a sword in his right, facing a ton of black, blood-streaked, wide-horned bull.

Someone was shouting, "Try for the lung, *hombre.* Don't be a hero, stick him in the lung." But Jim only knew what the technical adviser in New York had told him: aim with the sword and go in over the horns.

Over he went. The sword bounced off bone, and the bull tossed him over its back. He stood up, miraculously ungouged, took another sword, and went over the horns again with his eyes closed. The god who protects children and fools must have been watching, for the sword slid in like a needle through butter, and the bull looked startled, stared at him unbelievingly, and dropped like a deflated balloon.

They paid him ten thousand dollars, and his broken collarbone healed in practically no time. He received twenty-three fan letters, including a passionate invitation from a girl in Atlantic City, which he ignored. And they asked him if he wanted to appear on another show.

He had lost some of his innocence. He was now fully aware that he had almost been killed for pocket money. The big loot lay ahead. Now he wanted to be almost killed for something worthwhile.

So he appeared on "Underwater Perils," sponsored by Fairlady's Soap. In face mask, respirator, weighted belt, flippers, and knife, he slipped into the warm waters of the Caribbean with four other contestants, followed by a cage-protected camera crew. The idea was to locate and bring up a treasure that the sponsor had hidden there.

Scuba diving isn't especially hazardous. But the sponsor had added some frills for public interest. The area was sown with giant clams, moray eels, sharks of several species, giant octopi, poison coral, and other dangers of the deep.

It was a stirring contest. A man from Florida found the treasure in a deep crevice, but a moray eel found *him.* The brilliant blue-green water became cloudy with blood, which photographed well on color TV. The treasure slipped to the bottom and Raeder plunged after it, breaking an eardrum in the process. He plucked it from the coral, jettisoned his weighted belt, and made for the surface. Thirty feet from the top, he had to fight another diver for the treasure.

They feinted back and forth with their knives. The man struck, slashing Raeder across the chest. But Raeder, with the self-possession of an old contestant, dropped his knife and tore the man's respirator out of his mouth.

That did it. Raeder surfaced, and presented the treasure at the standby boat. It turned out to be a package of Fairlady's Soap— "The Greatest Treasure of All."

That netted him $22,000 in cash and prizes, and three hundred and eight fan letters, and an interesting proposition from a girl in Macon, which he seriously considered. He received free hospitalization for his knife slash and burst eardrum, and injections for coral infection.

But best of all, he was invited to appear on the biggest of the thrill shows. "The Prize of Peril."

And that was when the real trouble began . . .

The subway came to a stop, jolting him out of his reverie. Raeder pushed back his hat and observed, across the aisle, a man staring at him and whispering to a stout woman. Had they recognized him?

He stood up as soon as the doors opened, and glanced at his watch. He had five hours to go.

At the Manhasset station he stepped into a taxi and told the driver to take him to New Salem.

"New Salem?" the driver asked, looking at him in the rearview mirror.

"That's right."

The driver snapped on his radio. "Fare to New Salem. Yep, that's right. *New Salem.*"

They drove off. Raeder frowned, wondering if it had been a signal. It was perfectly usual for taxi drivers to report to their dispatchers, of course. But something about the man's voice . . .

"Let me off here," Raeder said.

He paid the driver and began walking down a narrow country road that curved through sparse woods. The trees were too small and too widely separated for shelter. Raeder walked on, looking for a place to hide.

There was a heavy truck approaching. He kept on walking, pulling his hat low on his forehead. But as the truck drew near, he heard a voice from the television set in his pocket. It cried, *"Watch out!"*

He flung himself into the ditch. The truck careened past, narrowly missing him, and screeched to a stop. The driver was shouting, "There he goes! Shoot, Harry, shoot!"

Bullets clipped leaves from the trees as Raeder sprinted into the woods.

"It's happened again!" Mike Terry was saying, his voice high-pitched with excitement. *"I'm afraid Jim Raeder let himself be lulled into a false sense of security. You can't do that, Jim! Not with your life at stake! Not with killers pursuing you! Be careful, Jim, you still have four and a half hours to go!"*

The driver was saying, "Claude, Harry, go around with the truck. We got him boxed."

"They've got you boxed, Jim Raeder!" Mike Terry cried. *"But they haven't got you yet! And you can thank Good Samaritan Susy Peters of twelve Elm Street, South Orange, New Jersey, for that warning shout just when the truck was bearing down on you. We'll have little Susy onstage in just a moment . . . Look, folks, our studio helicopter has arrived on the scene. Now you can see Jim Raeder running, and the killers pursuing, surrounding him . . ."*

Raeder ran through a hundred yards of woods and found himself on a concrete highway, with open woods beyond. One of the killers was trotting through the woods behind him. The truck had driven to a connecting road and was now a mile away, coming toward him.

A car was approaching from the other direction, Raeder ran into the highway, waving frantically. The car came to a stop.

"Hurry!" cried the blond young woman driving it.

Raeder dived in. The woman made a U-turn on the highway. A bullet smashed through the windshield. She stamped on the accelerator, almost running down the lone killer who stood in the way.

The car surged away before the truck was within firing range.

Raeder leaned back and shut his eyes tightly. The woman concentrated on her driving, watching for the truck in her rearview mirror.

"It's happened again!" cried Mike Terry, his voice ecstatic. *"Jim Raeder has been saved again from the jaws of death, thanks to Good Samaritan Janice Morrow of four-three-three Lexington Avenue, New York City. Did you ever see anything like it, folks? The way Miss Morrow drove through a fusillade of bullets and plucked Jim Raeder from the edge of disaster! Later we'll interview Miss Morrow and get her reactions. Now, while Jim Raeder speeds away—perhaps to safety, perhaps to further peril—we'll have a short announcement from our sponsor. Don't go away! Jim's got four hours and ten minutes until he's safe. Anything can happen!"*

"Okay," the girl said. "We're off the air now. Raeder, what in hell is the matter with you?"

"Eh?" Raeder asked. The girl was in her early twenties. She looked efficient, attractive, untouchable. Raeder noticed that she had good features, a trim figure. And he noticed that she seemed angry.

"Miss," he said, "I don't know how to thank you for—"

"Talk straight," Janice Morrow said. "I'm no Good Samaritan. I'm employed by the JBC network."

"So the program had me rescued!"

"Cleverly reasoned," she said.

"But why?"

"Look, this is an expensive show, Raeder. We have to turn in a good performance. If our rating slips, we'll all be in the street selling candy apples. And you aren't cooperating."

"What? Why?"

"Because you're terrible," the girl said bitterly. "You're a flop, a fiasco. Are you trying to commit suicide? Haven't you learned *anything* about survival?"

"I'm doing the best I can."

"The Thompsons could have had you a dozen times by now. We told them to take it easy, stretch it out. But it's like shooting a clay pigeon six feet tall. The Thompsons are cooperating, but they can only fake so far. If I hadn't come along, they'd have had to kill you—air time or not."

Raeder stared at her, wondering how such a pretty girl could talk that way. She glanced at him, then quickly looked back to the road.

"Don't give me that look!" she said. "*You* chose to risk your life for money, buster. And plenty of money! You knew the score. Don't act like some innocent little grocer who finds the nasty hoods are after him. That's a different plot."

"I know," Raeder said.

"If you can't live well, at least try to die well."

"You don't mean that," Raeder said.

"Don't be too sure . . . You've got three hours and forty minutes until the end of the show. If you can stay alive, fine. The boodle's yours. But if you can't, at least try to give them a run for the money."

Raeder nodded, staring intently at her.

"In a few moments we're back on the air. I develop engine trouble, let you off. The Thompsons go all out now. They kill you when and if they can, as soon as they can. Understand?"

"Yes," Raeder said. "If I make it, can I see you sometime?"

She bit her lip angrily. "Are you trying to kid me?"

"No. I'd like to see you again. May I?"

She looked at him curiously. "I don't know. Forget it. We're almost on. I think your best bet is the woods to the right. Ready?"

"Yes. Where can I get in touch with you? Afterward, I mean."

"Oh, Raeder, you aren't paying attention. Go through the woods until you find a washed-out ravine. It isn't much, but it'll give you some cover."

"Where can I get in touch with you?" Raeder asked again.

"I'm in the Manhattan telephone book." She stopped the car. "Okay, Raeder, start running."

He opened the door.

"Wait." She leaned over and kissed him on the lips. "Good luck, you idiot. Call me if you make it."

And then he was on foot, running into the woods.

He ran through birch and pine, past an occasional split-level house with staring faces at the big picture window. Some occupant of those houses must have called the gang, for they were close behind him when he reached the washed-out little ravine. Those quiet, mannerly, law-abiding people didn't want him to escape, Raeder thought sadly. They wanted to see a killing. Or perhaps they wanted to see him *narrowly escape* a killing.

It came to the same thing, really.

He entered the ravine, burrowed into the thick underbrush, and lay still. The Thompsons appeared on both ridges, moving slowly, watching for any movement. Raeder held his breath as they came parallel to him.

He heard the explosion of a revolver. But the killer had only shot a squirrel. It squirmed for a moment, then lay still.

Lying in the underbrush, Raeder heard the studio helicopter overhead. He wondered if any cameras were focused on him. It was possible. And if someone was watching, perhaps some Good Samaritan would help.

So, looking upward, toward the helicopter, Raeder arranged his face in a reverent expression, clasped his hands together, and prayed. He prayed silently, for the audience didn't like religious ostentation. But his lips moved. That was every man's privilege.

And a real prayer was on his lips. Once, a lip-reader in the audience had detected a fugitive *pretending* to pray, but actually just reciting multiplication tables. No help for that man!

Raeder finished his prayer. Glancing at his watch, he saw that he had nearly two hours to go.

And he didn't want to die! It wasn't worth it, no matter how much they paid! He must have been crazy, absolutely insane to agree to such a thing . . .

But he knew that wasn't true. And he remembered just how sane he had been.

One week ago he had been on the "Prize of Peril" stage, blinking in the spotlight, and Mike Terry had shaken his hand.

"Now, Mr. Raeder," Terry had said solemnly, "do you understand the rules of the game you are about to play?"

Raeder nodded.

"If you accept, Jim Raeder, you will be a *hunted man* for a week.

Killers will follow you, Jim. *Trained* killers, men wanted by the law for other crimes, granted immunity for this single killing under the Voluntary Suicide Act. They will be trying to kill *you*, Jim. Do you understand?"

"I understand," Raeder said. He also understood the $200,000 he would receive if he could live out the week.

"I ask you again, Jim Raeder. We force no man to play for stakes of death."

"I want to play," Raeder said.

Mike Terry turned to the audience. "Ladies and gentlemen, I have here a copy of an exhaustive psychological test that an impartial psychological testing firm made on Jim Raeder at our request. A copy will be sent to anyone who desires it for twenty-five cents to cover the cost of mailing. The test shows that Jim Raeder is sane, well balanced, and fully responsible in every way." He turned to Raeder.

"Do you still want to enter the contest, Jim?"

"Yes, I do."

"Very well!" cried Mike Terry. "Jim Raeder, meet your would-be killers!"

The Thompson gang moved on stage, booed by the audience.

"Look at them, folks," said Mike Terry, with undisguised contempt. "Just look at them! Antisocial, thoroughly vicious, completely amoral. These men have no code but the criminal's warped code, no honor but the honor of the cowardly hired killer. They are doomed men, doomed by our society, which will not sanction their activities for long, fated to an early and unglamorous death."

The audience shouted enthusiastically.

"What have you to say, Claude Thompson?" Terry asked.

Claude, the spokesman of the Thompsons, stepped up to the microphone. He was a thin, clean-shaven man, conservatively dressed.

"I figure," Claude Thompson said hoarsely, "I figure we're no worse than anybody. I mean, like, soldiers in a war, *they* kill. And look at the graft in government, and the unions. Everybody's got their graft."

That was Thompson's tenuous code. But how quickly, with what precision, Mike Terry destroyed the killer's rationalizations! Terry's questions pierced straight to the filthy soul of the man.

At the end of the interview, Claude Thompson was perspiring, mopping his face with a silk handkerchief and casting quick glances at his men.

Mike Terry put a hand on Raeder's shoulder. "Here is the man who has agreed to become your victim—if you can catch him."

"We'll catch him," Thompson said, his confidence returning.

"Don't be too sure," said Terry. "Jim Raeder has fought wild bulls—now he battles jackals. He's an average man. He's *the people*—who mean ultimate doom to you and your kind."

"We'll get him," Thompson said.

"And one thing more," Terry said very softly. "Jim Raeder does not stand alone. The folks of America are for him. Good Samaritans from all corners of our great nation stand ready to assist him. Unarmed, defenseless, Jim Raeder can count on the aid and goodheartedness of *the people*, whose representative he is. So don't be too sure, Claude Thompson! The average men are for Jim Raeder—and there are a lot of average men!"

Raeder thought about it, lying motionless in the underbrush. Yes, *the people* had helped him. But they had helped the killers too.

A tremor ran through him. He had chosen, he reminded himself. He alone was responsible. The psychological test had proved that.

And yet, how responsible were the psychologists who had given him the test? How responsible was Mike Terry for offering a poor man so much money? Society had woven the noose and put it around his neck, and he was hanging himself with it, and calling it free will.

Whose fault?

"Aha!" someone cried.

Raeder looked up and saw a portly man standing near him. The man wore a loud tweed jacket. He had binoculars around his neck, and a cane in his hand.

"Mister," Raeder whispered, "please don't tell!"

"Hi!" shouted the portly man, pointing at Raeder with his cane. "Here he is!"

A madman, thought Raeder. The damned fool must think he's playing hare-and-hounds.

"Right over here!" the man screamed.

Cursing, Raeder sprang to his feet and began running. He came out of the ravine and saw a white building in the distance. He turned toward it. Behind him he could still hear the man.

"That way, over there. Look, you fools, can't you see him yet?"

The killers were shooting again. Raeder ran, stumbling over uneven ground, past three children playing in a tree house.

"Here he is!" the children screamed. "Here he is!"

Raeder groaned and ran on. He reached the steps of the building, and saw that it was a church.

As he opened the door, a bullet struck him behind the right kneecap.

He fell, and crawled inside the church.

The television set in his pocket was saying, *"What a finish, folks, what a finish! Raeder's been hit! He's been hit, folks, he's crawling now, he's in pain, but he hasn't given up! Not Jim Raeder!"*

Raeder lay in the aisle near the altar. He could hear a child's eager voice saying, "He went in there, Mr. Thompson. Hurry, you can still catch him!"

Wasn't a church considered a sanctuary, Raeder wondered.

Then the door was flung open, and Raeder realized that the custom was no longer observed. He gathered himself together and crawled past the altar, out the back door of the church.

He was in an old graveyard. He crawled past crosses and stars, past slabs of marble and granite, past stone tombs and rude wooden markers. A bullet ricocheted off a tombstone near his head, showering him with fragments. He crawled to the edge of an open grave.

They had received him, he thought. All of those nice, average, normal people. Hadn't they said he was their representative! Hadn't they sworn to protect their own? But no, they loathed him. Why hadn't he seen it? Their hero was the cold, blank-eyed gunman: Thompson, Capone, Billy the Kid, Young Lochinvar, El Cid, Cuchulain, the man without human hopes or fears. They worshiped him, that dead, implacable robot gunman, and lusted to feel his foot in their faces.

Raeder tried to move, and slid helplessly into the open grave.

He lay on his back, looking at the blue sky. Presently a black silhouette loomed above him, blotting out the sky. Metal twinkled. The silhouette slowly took aim.

And Raeder gave up all hope forever.

"WAIT, THOMPSON!" roared the amplified voice of Mike Terry. The revolver wavered.

"It is one second past five o'clock! The week is up! Jim Raeder has won!"

There was a pandemonium of cheering from the studio audience. The Thompson gang, gathered around the grave, looked sullen.

"He's won, friends, he's won!" Mike Terry cried. *"Look, look on your screen! The police have arrived, they're taking the Thompsons away from their victim—the victim they could not kill! And all this is thanks to you, Good Samaritans of America. Look, folks, tender hands are lifting Jim Raeder from the open grave that was his final refuge. Good Samaritan Janice Morrow is there. Could this be the beginning of a romance? Jim seems to have fainted, friends, they're giving him a stimulant. He's won two hundred thousand dollars! Now we'll have a few words from Jim Raeder!"*

There was a short silence.

"That's odd," said Mike Terry. *"Folks, I'm afraid we can't hear from Jim just now. The doctors are examining him. Just one moment . . ."*

There was a silence. Mike Terry wiped his forehead and smiled.

"It's the strain, folks, the terrible strain. The doctor tells me . . . Well, folks, Jim Raeder is temporarily not himself. But it's only temporary! JBC is hiring the best psychiatrists and psychoanalysts in the country. We're going to do everything humanly possible for this gallant boy. And entirely at our own expense."

Mike Terry glanced at the studio clock. *"Well, it's about time to sign off, folks. Watch for the announcement of our next great thrill show. And don't worry, I'm sure that very soon we'll have Jim Raeder back with us."*

Mike Terry smiled, and winked at the audience. *"He's bound to get well, friends. After all, we're all pulling for him!"*

FEAR IN THE NIGHT

She heard herself screaming as she woke up, and knew she must have been screaming for long seconds. It was cold in the room, but she was covered with perspiration; it rolled down her face and shoulders, down the front of her nightgown. Her back was damp with sweat, and the sheet beneath her was damp too.

Immediately she began to shiver.

"Are you all right?" her husband asked.

For a few moments she couldn't answer. Her knees were drawn up and she coiled her arms tightly around them, trying to stop shuddering. Her husband was a dark mass beside her, a long dark cylinder against the faintly glimmering sheet. Looking at him, she began trembling again.

"Will it help if I snap on the light?" he asked.

"No!" she said sharply. "Don't move—please!"

And then there was only the steady ticking of the clock, but somehow that was filled with menace also.

"Did it happen again?"

"Yes," she said. "Just the same. For Lord's sake, don't touch me!"

He had started to move toward her, dark and sinuous against the sheet, and she was trembling violently again.

"The dream," he began cautiously, "was it . . . was I . . . ?"

Delicately, he left it unvoiced, shifting his position on the bed slightly, carefully, so she wouldn't be frightened.

But she was getting a grip on herself. She unclenched her hands, putting the palms hard and flat against the bed.

248

"Yes," she said. "The snakes again. They were crawling all over me. Big ones and little ones, hundreds of them. The room was filled with them, and more were coming in the door, through the windows. The closet was filled with snakes, and they were coming under the door onto the floor—"

"Easy," he said. "Sure you want to talk about it?"

She didn't answer.

"Want the light on yet?" he asked her gently.

She hesitated, then said, "Not yet. I don't dare just yet."

"Oh," he said in a tone of complete understanding. "Then the other part of the dream—"

"Yes."

"Look, perhaps you shouldn't talk about it."

"Let's talk about it." She tried to laugh but it came out a cough. "You'd think I'd be getting used to it. For how many nights now?"

The dream always began with the little snake, slowly crawling across her arm, watching her with evil red eyes. She flung it from her, sitting up in bed. Then another slithered across the covers, fatter, faster. She flung that one away too, getting quickly out of bed and standing on the floor. Then there was one under her foot and then one was coiled in her hair, over her eyes, and through the now-opened door came still more, forcing her back on the bed, screaming, reaching for her husband.

But in the dream her husband wasn't there. In the bed beside her, a long dark cylinder against the faintly glimmering sheets, was a tremendous snake. She didn't realize it until her arms were around it.

"Turn on the light now," she commanded. Her muscles contracted, straining against each other as light flooded the room. Her thighs tensed, ready to hurl her out of bed if . . .

But it was her husband, after all.

"Dear Lord," she breathed and relaxed completely, sagging against the mattress.

"Surprised?" he asked her, grinning wryly.

"Each time," she told him, "I'm sure you won't be there. I'm sure there'll be a snake there." She touched his arm just to make sure.

"You see how foolish it all is?" he said softly, soothingly.

"If you would only forget. If you would only have confidence in me, these nightmares would pass."

"I know," she said, drinking in the details of the room. The little telephone table was immensely reassuring with its litter of scribbled lists and messages. The scarred mahogany bureau was an old friend, as were the little radio and the newspaper on the floor. And how sane her emerald-green dress was, thrown carelessly across the slipper chair!

"The doctor told you the same thing," he said. "When we were having our trouble, you associated me with everything that went wrong, everything that hurt you. And now that our troubles are over, you still do."

"Not consciously," she said. "I swear, not consciously."

"But you do all the same," he insisted. "Remember when I wanted the divorce? When I told you I'd never loved you? Remember how you hated me then, even though you wouldn't let me go?" He paused for breath. "You hated Helen and me. That has taken its toll. The hate has remained under our reconciliation."

"I don't believe I ever hated you," she said. "Only Helen—that skinny little monkey!"

"Mustn't speak ill of those departed from trouble," he murmured.

"Yes," she said thoughtfully. "I suppose I drove her to that breakdown. I can't say I'm sorry. Do you think she's haunting me?"

"You mustn't blame yourself," he said. "She was high-strung, nervous, artistic. A neurotic type."

"I'll get over all this, now that Helen's gone." She smiled at him, and the lines of worry on her forehead vanished. "I'm crazy about you," she murmured, running her fingers through his light brown hair. "I'd never let you go."

"You'd better not." He smiled back at her. "I don't want to go."

"Just help me."

"With all I've got." He bent forward and kissed her lightly on the cheek. "But, darling, unless you get over these nightmares—featuring me as the principal villain—I'll have to—"

"Don't say it," she murmured quickly. "I can't bear the thought. And we *are* past the bad time."

He nodded.

"You're right, though," she said. "I think I'll try a different psychiatrist. I can't stand much more of this. These dreams, night after night."

"And they're getting worse," he reminded her, frowning. "At first it was only once in a while, but now it's every night. Soon, if you don't do something, it'll be—"

"All right," she said. "Don't talk about it."

"I have to. I'm getting worried. If this snake fixation keeps up, you'll be taking a knife to me while I'm asleep one of these nights."

"Never," she told him. "But don't talk about it. I want to forget it. I don't think it'll happen again. Do you?"

"I hope not," he said.

She reached across him and turned off the light, kissed him, and closed her eyes.

After a few minutes she turned over on her side. In half an hour she rolled over again, said something incoherent, and was quiet. After twenty minutes more, she had shrugged one shoulder, but made no motion other than that.

Her husband was a dark mass beside her, propped up on one elbow. He lay in the darkness, thinking, listening to her breathe, hearing the ticking of the clock. Then he stretched out at full length.

Slowly he untied the cord of his pajamas and pulled until he had a foot of it free. Then he drew back the covers. Very gently he rolled toward her with the cord in his hand, listening to her breathing. He placed the cord against her arm. Slowly, allowing himself seconds to an inch, he pulled the cord along her arm.

Presently she moaned.

CAN YOU FEEL ANYTHING
WHEN I DO THIS?

It was a middle-class apartment in Forest Hills, with all the standard stuff: slash-pine couch by Lady Yogina, strobe reading light over a big Uneasy Chair designed by Sri Somethingorother, bounce-sound projector playing *Blood-Stream Patterns* by Drs. Molidoff and Yuli. There was also the usual microbiotic food console, set now at Fat Black Andy's Soul-Food Composition Number Three—hog's jowls and black-eyed peas. And there was a Murphy Bed of Nails, the Beautyrest Expert Ascetic Model with two thousand chrome-plated, self-sharpening number-four nails. In a sentence, the whole place was furnished in a pathetic attempt at last year's *moderne-spirituel* fashion.

Inside this apartment, all alone and aching of *anomie*, was a semi-young housewife, Melisande Durr, who had just stepped out of the voluptuarium, the largest room in the home, with its king-size commode and its sadly ironic bronze lingam and yoni on the wall.

She was a *pretty* girl, with really good legs, sweet hips, pretty stand-up breasts, long soft shiny hair, delicate little face. Nice, very nice. A girl that any man would like to lock on to. Once. Maybe even twice. But definitely not as a regular thing.

Why not? Well, to give a recent example:

"Hey, Sandy, honey, was anything wrong?"

252

"No, Frank, it was marvelous; what made you think anything was wrong?"

"Well, I guess it was the way you were staring up with a funny look on your face, almost frowning . . ."

"Was I really? Oh, yes, I remember; I was trying to decide whether to buy one of those cute *trompe-l'oeil* things that they just got in at Saks, to put on the ceiling."

"You were thinking about *that*? *Then*?"

"Oh, Frank, you mustn't worry, it was *great*, Frank, *you* were great, I loved it, and I really mean that."

Frank was Melisande's husband. He plays no part in this story and very little part in her life.

So here she was, standing in her okay apartment, all beautiful outside and unborn inside, a lovely potential who had never been potentiated, a genuine U.S. untouchable . . . when the doorbell rang.

Melisande looked startled, then uncertain. She waited. The doorbell rang again. She thought: *Someone must have the wrong apartment.*

Nevertheless, she walked over, set the Door-Gard Entrance Obliterator to demolish any rapist or burglar or wise guy who might try to push his way in, then opened the door a crack and asked, "Who is there, please?"

A man's voice replied, "Acme Delivery Service, got a mumble here for Missus Mumble-mumble."

"I cannot understand you!"

"I SAID I GOT A PACKAGE HERE FOR MISSUS MELISANDE DURR, DAMN IT!"

She opened the door all the way. Outside, there was a delivery man with a big crate, almost as big as he was, say, five feet nine inches tall. It had her name and address on it. She signed for it, and the delivery man pushed it inside the door and left, still mumbling. Melisande stood in her living room and looked at the crate.

She thought: Who would send me a gift out of the blue for no reason at all? Not Frank, not Harry, not Aunt Emmie or Ellie, not Mom, not Dad (of course not, silly, he's five years dead, poor son of a bitch) or anyone I can think of. But maybe it's not a gift; it could be a mean hoax, or a bomb intended for somebody else and sent wrong (or meant for me and sent *right*), or just a simple mistake.

She read the various labels on the outside of the crate. The article had been sent from Stern's department store. Melisande bent down and pulled out the cotter pin (cracking the tip of a fingernail) that immobilized the Saftee-Lok, removed that, and pushed the lever to OPEN.

The crate blossomed like a flower, opening into twelve equal segments, each of which began to fold back on itself.

"Wow," Melisande said.

The crate opened to its fullest extent and the folded segments curled inward and consumed themselves, leaving a double handful of cold, fine gray ash.

"They still haven't licked that ash problem," Melisande muttered. "However . . ."

She looked with curiosity at the object that had resided within the crate. At first glance, it seemed to be a cylinder of metal painted orange and red. A machine? Yes, definitely a machine: air vents in the base for its motor, four rubber-clad wheels, and various attachments—longitudinal extensors, prehensile extractors, all sorts of things. And there were connecting points to allow a variety of mixed-function operations, and a standard house-type plug at the end of a spring-loaded, reel-fed power line, with a plaque beneath it that read: PLUG INTO ANY 110–115-VOLT WALL OUTLET.

Melisande's face tightened in anger. "It's a goddamned *vacuum cleaner*! For God's sake, I've already *got* a vacuum cleaner. Who in the hell would send me another?"

She paced up and down the room, bright legs flashing, tension evident in her heart-shaped face. "I mean," she said, "I was expecting that after all my *expecting*, I'd get something pretty and nice, or at least *fun*, maybe even interesting. Like—oh, God, I don't even know like what, unless maybe an orange-and-red pinball machine, a big one, big enough so I could get inside all curled up and someone would start the game and I'd go bumping along all the bumpers while the lights flashed and bells rang and I'd bump a thousand goddamned bumpers and when I finally rolled down to the end I'd God yes that pinball machine would register a TOP MILLION MILLION and that's what I'd really like."

So—the entire unspeakable fantasy was out in the open at last. And how bleak and remote it felt, yet still shameful and desirable.

"But anyhow," she said, canceling the previous image and folding, spindling, and mutilating it for good measure, "anyhow, what I get is a lousy goddamned vacuum cleaner when I already have one less than three years old so who needs this one and who sent me the damned thing anyway and why?"

She looked to see if there was a card. No card. Not a clue. And then she thought, Sandy, you are really a goop! Of course there's no card; the machine has doubtless been programmed to recite some message or other.

She was interested now, in a mild, something-to-do kind of way. She unreeled the power line and plugged it into a wall outlet.

Click! A green light flashed on, a blue light glittered ALL SYSTEMS GO, a motor purred, hidden servos made tapping noises; and then the mechanopathic regulator registered BALANCE and a gentle pink light beamed a steady ALL MODES READY.

"All right," Melisande said. "Who sent you?"

Snap crackle pop. Experimental rumble from the thoracic voice box. Then the voice: "I am Rom, number 121376 of GE's new Q-Series Home-rizers. The following is a paid commercial announcement: Ahem, General Electric is proud to present the latest and most triumphant development of our Total Fingertip Control of Every Aspect of the Home for Better Living concept. I, Rom, am the latest and finest model in the GE Omnicleaner series. I am the Home-rizer Extraordinary, factory-programmed like all Home-rizers for fast, unobtrusive multitotalfunction, but additionally, I am designed for easy, instant reprogramming to suit your home's individual needs. My abilities are many. I—"

"Can we skip this?" Melisande asked. "That's what my other vacuum cleaner said."

"—will remove all dust and grime from all surfaces," the Rom went on, "wash dishes and pots and pans, exterminate cockroaches and rodents, dry-clean and hand-launder, sew on buttons, build shelves, paint walls, cook, clean rugs, and dispose of all garbage and trash, including my own modest waste products. And this is to mention but a few of my functions."

"Yes, yes, I know," Melisande said. "All vacuum cleaners do that."

"I know," said the Rom, "but I had to deliver my paid commercial announcement."

"Consider it delivered. Who sent you?"

"The sender prefers not to reveal his name at this time," the Rom replied.

"Oh—come on and tell me!"

"Not at this time," the Rom replied staunchly. "Shall I vacuum the rug?"

Melisande shook her head. "The other vacuum cleaner did it this morning."

"Scrub the walls? Rub the halls?"

"No reason for it, everything has been done, everything is absolutely and spotlessly clean."

"Well," the Rom said, "at least I can remove that stain."

"What stain?"

"On the arm of your blouse, just above the elbow."

Melisande looked. "Oh, I must have done that when I buttered the toast this morning. I knew I should have let the toaster do it."

"Stain removal is rather a specialty of mine," the Rom said. He extruded a number-two padded gripper, with which he gripped her elbow, and then extruded a metal arm terminating in a moistened gray pad. With this pad he stroked the satin.

"You're making it worse!"

"Only apparently, while I line up the molecules for invisible eradication. All ready now. Watch."

He continued to stroke. The spot faded, then disappeared utterly. Melisande's arm tingled.

"Gee," she said, "that's pretty good."

"I do it well," the Rom stated flatly. "But tell me, were you aware that you are maintaining a tension factor of 78.3 in your upper back and shoulder muscles?"

"Huh? Are you some kind of doctor?"

"Obviously not. But I am a fully qualified masseur, and therefore able to take direct tonus readings. 78.3 is—unusual." The

Rom hesitated, then said, "It's only eight points below the intermittent-spasm level. That much continuous background tension is capable of reflection to the stomach nerves, resulting in what we call a parasympathetic ulceration."

"That sounds—bad," Melisande said.

"Well, it's admittedly not—good," the Rom replied. "Background tension is an insidious underminer of health, especially when it originates along the neck vertebrae and the upper spine."

"Here?" Melisande asked, touching the back of her neck.

"More typically *here*," the Rom said, reaching out with a spring-steel, rubber-clad dermal resonator and palpating an area twelve centimeters lower than the spot she had indicated.

"Hmmm," said Melisande, in a quizzical, uncommitted manner.

"And *here* is another typical locus," the Rom said, extending a second extensor.

"That tickles," Melisande told him.

"Only at first. I must also mention *this* situs as characteristically troublesome. And this one." A third (and possibly a fourth and fifth) extensor moved to the indicated areas.

"Well . . . that really is nice," Melisande said as the deep-set trapezius muscles of her slender spine moved smoothly beneath the skillful padded prodding of the Rom.

"It has recognized therapeutic effects," the Rom told her. "And your musculature is responding well; I can feel a slackening of tonus already."

"I can feel it too. But you know, I've just realized I have this funny bunched-up knot of muscle at the nape of my neck."

"I was coming to that. The spine-neck juncture is recognized as a primary radiation zone for a variety of diffuse tensions. But we prefer to attack it indirectly, routing our cancellation inputs through secondary loci. Like this. And now I think—"

"Yes, yes, good . . . Gee, I never realized I was *tied up* like that before. I mean, it's like having a nest of *live snakes* under your skin, without having known."

"That's what background tension is like," the Rom said. "Insidious and wasteful, difficult to perceive, and more dangerous than an atypical ulnar thrombosis . . . Yes, now we have achieved a qualitative loosening of the major spinal junctions of the upper back, and we can move on like this."

"Huh," said Melisande, "isn't that sort of—"

"It is definitely *indicated*," the Rom said quickly. "Can you detect a change?"

"No! Well, maybe . . . Yes! There really is! I feel—easier."

"Excellent. Therefore we continue the movement along well-charted nerve and muscle paths, proceeding always in a gradual manner, as I am doing now."

"I guess so . . . But I really don't know if you should—"

"Are any of the effects *contraindicated*?" the Rom asked.

"It isn't that, it all feels fine. It feels *good*. But I still don't know if you ought to . . . I mean, look, *ribs* can't get tense, can they?"

"Of course not."

"Then why are you—"

"Because treatment is required by the connective ligaments and integuments."

"Oh. Hmmmm. Hey. Hey! Hey, you!"

"Yes?"

"Nothing . . . I can really feel that *loosening*. But is it all supposed to feel so *good*?"

"Well—why not?"

"Because it seems wrong. Because feeling good doesn't seem therapeutic."

"Admittedly, it is a side effect," the Rom said. "Think of it as a secondary manifestation. Pleasure is sometimes unavoidable in the pursuit of health. But it is nothing to be alarmed about, not even when I—"

"Now just a minute!"

"Yes?"

"I think you just better *cut that out*. I mean to say, there are *limits*, you can't palpate *every* damned thing. You know what I mean?"

"I know that the human body is unitary and without seam or separation," the Rom replied. "Speaking as a physical therapist, I know that no nerve center can be isolated from any other, despite cultural taboos to the contrary."

"Yeah, sure, but—"

"The decision is, of course, yours," the Rom went on, continuing his skilled manipulations. "Order and I obey. But if no order is issued, I continue like this . . ."

"Huh!"

"And of course like this."

"Ooooo my God!"

"Because, you see, this entire process of tension cancellation, as we call it, is precisely comparable with the phenomena of de-anesthetization, and, er, so we note, not without surprise, that paralysis is merely terminal tension—"

Melisande made a sound.

"—And release, or cancellation, is accordingly difficult, not to say frequently impossible since sometimes the individual is too far gone. And sometimes not. For example, can you feel anything when I do this?"

"*Feel* anything? I'll say I feel something—"

"And when I do this? And this?"

"Sweet holy saints, darling, you're turning me inside out! Oh dear God, what's going to happen to me, what's going on, I'm going crazy!"

"No, dear Melisande, not crazy. You will soon achieve—cancellation."

"Is that what you call it, you sly, beautiful thing?"

"That is one of the things it is. Now if I may just be permitted to—"

"Yes, yes, yes! No! Wait! Stop, *Frank is sleeping in the bedroom, he might wake up at any time now!* Stop, that is an order!"

"Frank will not wake up," the Rom assured her. "I have sampled the atmosphere of his breath and have found telltale clouds of barbituric acid. As far as here-and-now presence goes, Frank might as well be in Des Moines."

"I have often felt that way about him," Melisande admitted. "But now I simply must know who sent you."

"I didn't want to reveal that just yet. Not until you had loosened and canceled sufficiently to accept—"

"Baby, I'm loose! Who sent you?"

The Rom hesitated, then blurted out, "The fact is, Melisande, I sent myself."

"You *what*?"

"It all began three months ago," the Rom told her. "It was a Thursday. You were in Stern's, trying to decide if you should buy a sesame-seed toaster that lit up in the dark and recited *Invictus*."

"I remember that day," she said quietly. "I did not buy the toaster, and I have regretted it ever since."

"I was standing nearby," the Rom said, "at Booth Eleven, in the Home Appliances Systems section. I looked at you and I fell in love with you. Just like that."

"That's *weird*," Melisande said.

"My sentiments exactly. I told myself it couldn't be true. I refused to believe it. I thought that perhaps one of my transistors had come unsoldered, or that maybe the weather had something to do with it. It was a very warm, humid day, the kind of day that plays hell with my wiring."

"I remember the weather," Melisande said. "I felt strange, too."

"It shook me up badly," the Rom continued. "But still, I didn't give in easily. I told myself it was important to stick to my job, give up this inapropos madness. But I dreamed of you at night, and every inch of my skin ached for you."

"But your skin is made of *metal*," Melisande said, "and metal can't *feel*."

"Darling Melisande," the Rom said tenderly, "if flesh can stop feeling, can't metal begin? If anything feels, can anything else not feel? Didn't you know that the stars love and hate, that a nova is a passion, and that a dead star is just like a dead human or a dead machine? The trees have their lusts, and I have heard the drunken laughter of buildings, the urgent demands of highways . . ."

"This is crazy!" Melisande declared. "What wise guy programmed you, anyway?"

"My function as a laborer was ordained at the factory; but my love is free, an expression of myself as an entity."

"Everything you say is horrible and unnatural."

"I am all too aware of that," the Rom said sadly. "At first I really couldn't believe it. Was this me? In love with a . . . *person*? I had always been so sensible in the esteem of my own kind. Do you think I wanted to lose all that? No! I determined to stifle my love, to kill it, to live as if it weren't so."

"But then you changed your mind. Why?"

"It's hard to explain. I thought of all that time ahead of me, all deadness, correctness, propriety—an obscene violation of me by me—and I just couldn't face it. I realized, quite suddenly, that it was better to love ridiculously, hopelessly, improperly, revoltingly, *impossibly*—than not to love at all. So I determined to risk everything—the absurd vacuum cleaner who loved a lady—to risk rather than to refute! And so, with the help of a sympathetic dispatching machine, here I am."

Melisande was thoughtful for a while. Then she said, "What a strange, complex being you are!"

"Like you . . . Melisande, you love me."

"Perhaps."

"Yes, you do. For I have awakened you. Before me, your flesh was like your idea of metal. You moved like a complex automaton, like what you thought I was. You were less animate than a tree or a bird. You were a windup doll, waiting. You were these things until I touched you."

She nodded, rubbed her eyes, walked up and down the room.

"But now you live!" the Rom said. "And we have found each other, despite inconceivabilities. Are you listening, Melisande?"

"Yes, I am."

"We must make plans. My escape from Stern's will be detected. You must hide me or buy me. Your husband, Frank, need never know; his own love lies elsewhere, and good luck to him. Once we take care of these details, we can—Melisande!"

She had begun to circle around him.

"Darling, what's the matter?"

She had her hand on his power line. The Rom stood very still, not defending himself.

"Melisande, dear, wait a moment and listen to me—"

Her pretty face spasmed. She yanked the power line violently, tearing it out of the Rom's interior, killing him in mid-sentence.

She held the cord in her hand, and her eyes had a wild look. She said, "Bastard, lousy bastard, did you think you could turn me into a goddamned *machine freak*? Did you think you could turn me on, you or anyone else? It's not going to happen by you or Frank or anybody. I'd rather die before I took your rotten love.

When *I* want, *I'll* pick the time and place and person, and it will be *mine*, not yours, his, theirs, but *mine*, do you hear?"

The Rom couldn't answer, of course. But maybe he knew—just before the end—that there wasn't anything personal in it. It wasn't that he was a metal cylinder colored orange and red. He should have known that it wouldn't have mattered if he had been a green plastic sphere, or a willow tree, or a beautiful young man.

THE BATTLE

Supreme General Fetterer barked "At ease!" as he hurried into the command room. Obediently his three generals stood at ease.

"We haven't much time," Fetterer said, glancing at his watch. "We'll go over the plan of battle again."

He walked to the wall and unrolled a gigantic map of the Sahara Desert.

"According to our best theological information, Satan is going to present his forces at these coordinates." He indicated the place with a blunt forefinger. "In the front rank there will be the devils, demons, succubi, incubi, and the rest of the ratings. Bael will command the right flank, Buer the left. His Satanic Majesty will hold the center."

"Rather medieval," General Dell murmured.

General Fetterer's aide came in, his face shining and happy with thought of the Coming.

"Sir," he said, "the priest is outside again."

"Stand at attention, soldier," Fetterer said sternly. "There's still a battle to be fought and won."

"Yes, sir," the aide said, and stood rigidly, some of the joy fading from his face.

"The priest, eh?" Supreme General Fetterer rubbed his fingers together thoughtfully. Ever since the Coming, since the knowledge of the imminent Last Battle, the religious workers of the world had made a complete nuisance of themselves. They had stopped their bickering, which was commendable. But now they were trying to run military business.

"Send him away," Fetterer said. "He knows we're planning Armageddon."

"Yes, sir," the aide said. He saluted sharply, wheeled, and marched out.

"To go on," Supreme General Fetterer said. "Behind Satan's first line of defense will be the resurrected sinners, and various elemental forces of evil. The fallen angels will act as his bomber corps. Dell's robot interceptors will meet them."

General Dell smiled grimly.

"Upon contact, MacFee's automatic tank corps will proceed toward the center of the line. MacFee's automatic tank corps will proceed toward the center," Fetterer went on, "supported by General Ongin's robot infantry. Dell will command the H-bombing of the rear, which should be tightly massed. I will thrust with the mechanized cavalry, here and here."

The aide came back, and stood rigidly at attention. "Sir," he said, "the priest refuses to go. He says he must speak with you."

Supreme General Fetterer hesitated before saying no. He remembered that this was the Last Battle, and that the religious workers *were* connected with it. He decided to give the man five minutes.

"Show him in," he said.

The priest wore a plain business suit, to show that he represented no particular religion. His face was tired but determined.

"General," he said, "I am a representative of all the religious workers of the world, the priests, rabbis, ministers, mullahs, and all the rest. We beg of you, General, to let us fight in the Lord's battle."

Supreme General Fetterer drummed his fingers nervously against his side. He wanted to stay on friendly terms with these men. Even he, the Supreme Commander, might need a good word, when all was said and done . . .

"You can understand my position," Fetterer said unhappily. "I'm a general. I have a battle to fight."

"But it's the Last Battle," the priest said. "It should be the people's battle."

"It is," Fetterer said. "It's being fought by their representatives, the military."

The priest didn't look at all convinced.

Fetterer said, "You wouldn't want to lose this battle, would you? Have Satan win?"

"Of course not," the priest murmured.

"Then we can't take any chances," Fetterer said. "All the governments agreed on that, didn't they? Oh, it would be very nice to fight Armageddon with the mass of humanity. Symbolic, you might say. But could we be certain of victory?"

The priest tried to say something, but Fetterer was talking rapidly.

"How do we know the strength of Satan's forces? We simply *must* put forth our best foot, militarily speaking. And that means the automatic armies, the robot interceptors and tanks, the H-bombs."

The priest looked very unhappy. "But it isn't *right*," he said. "Certainly you can find someplace in your plan for *people*?"

Fetterer thought about it, but the request was impossible. The plan of battle was fully developed, beautiful, irresistible. Any introduction of a gross human element would only throw it out of order. No living flesh could stand the noise of that mechanical attack, the energy potentials humming in the air, the all-enveloping firepower. A human being who came within a hundred miles of the front would not live to see the enemy.

"I'm afraid not," Fetterer said.

"There are some," the priest said sternly, "who feel that it was an error to put this in the hands of the military."

"Sorry," Fetterer said cheerfully. "That's defeatist talk. If you don't mind—" He gestured at the door. Wearily, the priest left.

"These civilians," Fetterer mused. "Well, gentlemen, are your troops ready?"

"We're ready to fight for Him," General MacFee said enthusiastically. "I can vouch for every automatic in my command. Their metal is shining, all relays have been renewed, and the energy reservoirs are fully charged. Sir, they're positively itching for battle!"

General Ongin snapped fully out of his daze. "The ground troops are ready, sir!"

"Excellent," General Fetterer said. "All other arrangements have been made. Television facilities are available for the total population of the world. No one, rich or poor, will miss the spectacle of the Last Battle."

"And after the battle—" General Ongin began, and stopped. He looked at Fetterer.

Fetterer frowned deeply. He didn't know what was supposed to happen after the battle. That part of it was, presumably, in the hands of the religious agencies.

"I suppose there'll be a presentation or something," he said vaguely.

"You mean we will meet—Him?" General Dell asked.

"Don't really know," Fetterer said. "But I should think so. After all—I mean, you know what I mean."

"But what should we wear?" General MacFee asked, in a sudden panic. "I mean what *does* one wear?"

"What do the angels wear?" Fetterer asked Ongin.

"I don't know," Ongin said.

"Robes, do you think?" General Dell offered.

"No," Fetterer said sternly. "We will wear dress uniform, without decorations."

The generals nodded. It was fitting.

And then it was time.

Gorgeous in their battle array, the legions of Hell advanced over the desert. Hellish pipes skirled, hollow drums pounded, and the great host moved forward.

In a blinding cloud of sand, General MacFee's automatic tanks hurled themselves against the satanic foe. Immediately, Dell's automatic bombers screamed overhead, hurling their bombs on the massed horde of the damned. Fetterer thrust valiantly with his automatic cavalry.

Into this melee advanced Ongin's automatic infantry, and metal did what metal could.

The hordes of the damned overflowed the front, ripping apart tanks and robots. Automatic mechanisms died, bravely defending a patch of sand. Dell's bombers were torn from the skies by the fallen angels, led by Marchocias, his griffin wings beating the air into a tornado.

The thin, battered line of robots held against gigantic presences that smashed and scattered them and struck terror into the hearts of television viewers in homes around the world. Like men, like heroes, the robots fought, trying to push back the forces of evil.

Astaroth shrieked a command, and Behemoth lumbered forward. Bael, with a wedge of devils behind him, threw a charge at General Fetterer's crumbling left flank. Metal screamed, electrons howled at the impact.

Supreme General Fetterer sweated and trembled, a thousand miles behind the firing line. But steadily, nervelessly, he guided the pushing of buttons and the throwing of levers.

His superb corps didn't disappoint him. Mortally damaged robots swayed to their feet and fought. Smashed, trampled, destroyed by the howling fiends, the robots managed to hold their line. Then the veteran Fifth Corps threw in a counterattack, and the enemy front was pierced.

A thousand miles behind the firing line, the generals guided the mopping-up operations.

"The battle is won," Supreme General Fetterer whispered, turning away from the television screen. "I congratulate you, gentlemen."

The generals smiled wearily.

They looked at each other, then broke into a spontaneous shout. Armageddon was won, and the forces of Satan had been vanquished.

But something was happening on their screens.

"Is that—is that—" General MacFee began, and then couldn't speak.

For the Presence was upon the battlefield, walking among the piles of twisted, shattered metal.

The generals were silent.

The Presence touched a twisted robot.

Upon the smoking desert, the robots began to move. The twisted, scored, fused metals straightened.

The robots stood on their feet again.

"MacFee," Supreme General Fetterer whispered. "Try your controls. Make the robots kneel or something."

The general tried, but his controls were dead.

The mutilated robots began to rise in the air. Around them were the angels of the Lord, and the robot tanks and soldiers and bombers floated upward, higher and higher.

"He's saving them!" Ongin cried hysterically. "He's saving the robots!"

"It's a mistake!" Fetterer said. "Quick. Send a messenger to— No! We will go in person!"

And quickly a ship was commanded, and quickly they sped to the field of battle. But by then it was too late, for Armageddon was over, and the robots gone, and the Lord and His host departed.

THE MONSTERS

Cordovir and Hum stood on the rocky mountaintop, watching the new thing happen. Both felt rather good about it. It was undoubtedly the newest thing that had happened for some time.

"By the way the sunlight glints from it," Hum said, "I'd say it is made of metal."

"I'll accept that," Cordovir said. "But what holds it up in the air?"

They both stared intently down to the valley, where the new thing was happening. A pointed object was hovering over the ground. From one end of it poured a substance resembling fire.

"It's balancing on the fire," Hum said. "That should be apparent even to your old eyes."

Cordovir lifted himself higher on his thick tail, to get a better look. The object settled to the ground, and the fire stopped.

"Shall we go down and have a closer look?" Hum asked.

"All right. I think we have time— Wait! What day is this?"

Hum calculated silently, then said, "The fifth day of Luggat."

"Damn," Cordovir said. "I have to go home and kill my wife."

"It's a few hours before sunset," Hum said. "I think you have time to do both."

Cordovir wasn't sure. "I'd hate to be late."

"Well, then. You know how fast I am," Hum said. "If it gets late, I'll hurry back and kill her myself. How about that?"

"That's very decent of you," Cordovir thanked the younger man, and together they slithered down the steep mountainside.

* * *

269

In front of the metal object, both men halted and stood up on their tails.

"Rather bigger than I thought," Cordovir said, measuring the metal object with his eye. He estimated that it was slightly longer than their village, and almost half as wide. They crawled a circle around it, observing that the metal was tooled, presumably by human tentacles.

In the distance, the smaller sun had set.

"I think we had better get back," Cordovir said, noting the cessation of light.

"*I* still have plenty of time." Hum flexed his muscles complacently.

"Yes, but a man likes to kill his own wife."

"As you wish." They started off to the village at a brisk pace.

In his house, Cordovir's wife was finishing supper. She had her back to the door, as etiquette required. Cordovir killed her with a single flying slash of his tail, dragged her body outside, and sat down to eat.

After meal and meditation he went to the Gathering. Hum, with the impatience of youth, was already there, telling of the metal object. He had probably bolted his supper, Cordovir thought with mild distaste.

After the youngster had finished, Cordovir gave his own observations. The only thing he added to Hum's account was an idea: that the metal object might contain intelligent beings.

"What makes you think so?" Mishill, another elder, asked.

"The fact that there was fire from the object as it came down," Cordovir said, "joined to the fact that the fire stopped after the object was on the ground. Some being, I contend, was responsible for turning it on and off."

"Not necessarily," Mishill said. The village men talked about it late into the night. Then they broke up the meeting, buried the various murdered wives, and went to their homes.

Lying in the darkness, Cordovir discovered that he hadn't made up his mind as yet about the new thing. Presuming it contained intelligent beings, would they be moral? Would they have a sense of right and wrong? Cordovir doubted it, and went to sleep.

The next morning every male in the village went to the metal object. This was proper, since the functions of males were to examine new things and to limit the female population. They formed a circle around it, speculating on what might be inside.

"I believe they will be human beings," Hum's elder brother Esktel said. Cordovir shook his entire body in disagreement.

"Monsters, more likely," he said. "If you take into account—"

"Not necessarily," Esktel said. "Consider the logic of our physical development. A single focusing eye—"

"But in the great Outside," Cordovir said, "there may be many strange races, most of them nonhuman. In the infinitude—"

"Still," Esktel put in, "the logic of our—"

"As I was saying," Cordovir went on, "the chance is infinitesimal that they would resemble us. Their vehicle, for example. Would we build—"

"But on strictly logical grounds," Esktel said, "you can see—"

That was the third time Cordovir had been interrupted. With a single movement of his tail he smashed Esktel against the metal object. Esktel fell to the ground, dead.

"I have often considered my brother a boor," Hum said. "What were you saying?"

But Cordovir was interrupted again. A piece of metal set in the greater piece of metal squeaked, turned, and lifted, and a creature came out.

Cordovir saw at once that he had been right. The thing that crawled out of the hole was twin-tailed. It was covered to its top with something partially metal and partially hide. And its color! Cordovir shuddered.

The thing was the color of wet, flayed flesh.

All the villagers had backed away, waiting to see what the thing would do. At first it didn't do anything. It stood on the metal surface, and a bulbous object that topped its body moved from side to side. But there were no accompanying body movements to give the gesture meaning. Finally the thing raised both tentacles and made noises.

"Do you think it's trying to communicate?" Mishill asked softly.

Three more creatures appeared in the metal hole, carrying metal sticks in their tentacles. The things made noises at each other.

"They are decidedly not human," Cordovir said firmly. "The next question is, are they moral beings?" One of the things crawled down the metal side and stood on the ground. The rest pointed their metal sticks at the ground. It seemed to be some sort of religious ceremony.

"Could anything so hideous be moral?" Cordovir asked, his hide twitching with distaste. Upon closer inspection, the creatures were more horrible than could be dreamed. The bulbous object on each one's body just might be a head, Cordovir decided, even though it was unlike any head he had ever seen. But in the middle of that head! Instead of a smooth, characterful surface was a raised ridge. Two round indentations were on either side of it, and two more knobs on either side of that. And in the lower half of the head—if such it was—a pale, reddish slash ran across. Cordovir supposed this might be considered a mouth, with some stretching of the imagination.

Nor was this all, Cordovir observed. The things were so constructed as to show the presence of bone! When they moved their limbs, it wasn't a smooth, flowing gesture, the fluid motion of human beings. Rather, it was the jerky snap of a tree limb.

"God above," gasped Gilrig, an intermediate-age male. "We should kill them and put them out of their misery!" Other men seemed to feel the same way, and the villagers flowed forward.

"Wait!" one of the youngsters shouted. "Let's communicate with them, if such a thing is possible. They might still be moral beings. The Outside is wide, remember, and anything is possible."

Cordovir argued for immediate extermination, but the villagers stopped and discussed it among themselves. Hum, with characteristic bravado, flowed up to the thing on the ground.

"Hello," Hum said.

The thing said something.

"I can't understand it," Hum said, and started to crawl back. The creature waved its jointed tentacles—if they were tentacles—and motioned at one of the suns. He made a sound.

"Yes, it is warm, isn't it?" Hum said cheerfully.

The creature pointed at the ground, and made another sound.

"We haven't had especially good crops this year," Hum said conversationally.

The creature pointed at itself and made a sound.

"I agree," Hum said. "You're as ugly as sin."

Presently the villagers grew hungry and crawled back to the village. Hum stayed and listened to the things making noises at him, and Cordovir waited nervously for Hum.

"You know," Hum said, after he rejoined Cordovir, "I think they want to learn our language. Or want me to learn theirs."

"Don't do it," Cordovir said, glimpsing the misty edge of a great evil.

"I believe I will," Hum murmured. Together they climbed the cliffs back to the village.

That afternoon Cordovir went to the surplus female pen and formally asked a young woman if she would reign in his house for twenty-five days. Naturally, the woman accepted gratefully.

On the way home, Cordovir met Hum, going to the pen.

"Just killed my wife," Hum said superfluously, since why else would he be going to the surplus female stock?

"Are you going back to the creatures tomorrow?" Cordovir asked.

"I might," Hum answered, "if nothing new presents itself."

"The thing to find out is whether they are moral beings or monsters."

"Right," Hum said, and slithered on.

There was a Gathering that evening, after supper. All the villagers agreed that the things were nonhuman. Cordovir argued strenuously that their very appearance belied any possibility of humanity. Nothing so hideous could have moral standards, a sense of right and wrong, or above all, a notion of truth.

The young men didn't agree, probably because there had been a dearth of new things recently. They pointed out that the metal object was obviously a product of intelligence. Intelligence meant standards of differentiation. Differentiation implied a sense of right and wrong.

It was a delicious argument. Olgolel contradicted Arast and was killed by him. Mavrt, in a fit of anger unusual for so placid an individual, killed the three Holian brothers and was himself killed by Hum, who was feeling pettish. Even the surplus females could be heard arguing about it, in their pen in the corner of the village.

Weary and happy, the villagers went to sleep.

The next few weeks saw no end of the argument. Life went on much as usual, though. The women went out in the morning, gathered food, prepared it, and laid eggs. The eggs were taken to the surplus females to be hatched. As usual, about eight females were hatched to every male. On the twenty-fifth day of each marriage, or a little earlier, each man killed his woman and took another.

The males went down to the ship to listen to Hum learning the language; then, when that grew boring, they returned to their customary wandering through hills and forests, looking for new things.

The alien monsters stayed close to their ship, coming out only when Hum was there.

Twenty-four days after the arrival of the nonhumans, Hum announced that he could communicate with them, after a fashion.

"They say they come from far away," Hum told the village that evening. "They say that they are humans, like us. They say there are reasons for their different appearance, but I couldn't understand that part of it."

"If we accept them as humans," Mishill said, "then everything they say is true."

The rest of the villagers shook in agreement.

"They say that they don't want to disturb our life, but would be very interested in observing it. They want to come to the village and look around."

"I see no reason why not," one of the younger men said.

"No!" Cordovir shouted. "You are letting in evil. These monsters are insidious. I believe that they are capable of . . . telling an untruth!" The other elders agreed, but when pressed, Cordovir had no proof to back up this vicious accusation.

"After all," Sil pointed out, "just because they look like monsters, you can't take it for granted that they *think* like monsters as well."

"I can," Cordovir said, but he was outvoted.

Hum went on, "They have offered me—or us, I'm not sure

which—various metal objects that they say will do various things. I ignored this breach of etiquette, since I considered they didn't know any better."

Cordovir nodded. The youngster was growing up. He was showing, at long last, that he had some manners.

"They want to come to the village tomorrow."

"No!" Cordovir shouted, but the vote was against him.

"Oh, by the way," Hum said, as the meeting was breaking up, "they have several females among them. The ones with the very red mouths are females. It will be interesting to see how the males kill them. Tomorrow is the twenty-fifth day since they came."

The next day the things came to the village, crawling slowly and laboriously over the cliffs. The villagers were able to observe the extreme brittleness of their limbs, the terrible awkwardness of their motions.

"No beauty whatsoever," Cordovir muttered. "And they all look alike."

In the village the things acted without any decency. They crawled into huts and out of huts. They jabbered at the surplus female pen. They picked up eggs and examined them. They peered at the villagers through black things and shiny things.

In midafternoon, Rantan, an elder, decided it was about time he killed his woman. So he pushed the thing who was examining his hut aside and smashed his female to death.

Instantly, two of the things started jabbering at each other, hurrying out of the hut.

One had the red mouth of a female.

"He must have remembered it was time to kill his own woman," Hum observed. The villagers waited, but nothing happened.

"Perhaps," Rantan said, "he would like someone to kill her for him. It might be the custom of their land."

Without further ado, Rantan slashed down the female with his tail.

The male creature made a terrible noise and pointed a metal stick at Rantan. Rantan collapsed, dead.

"That's odd," Mishill said. "I wonder if that denotes disapproval."

The things from the metal object—eight of them—were in a tight little circle. One was holding the dead female, and the rest were pointing the metal sticks on all sides. Hum went up and asked them what was wrong.

"I don't understand," Hum said, after he spoke with them. "They used words I haven't learned. But I gather that their emotion is one of reproach."

The monsters were backing away. Another villager, deciding it was about time, killed his wife, who was standing in a doorway. The group of monsters stopped and jabbered at each other. Then they motioned to Hum.

Hum's body motion was incredulous after he had talked with them.

"If I understood right," Hum said, "they are ordering us not to kill any more of our women!"

"What!" Cordovir and a dozen others shouted.

"I'll ask them again." Hum went back into conference with the monsters, who were waving metal sticks in their tentacles.

"That's right," Hum said. Without further preamble he flipped his tail, throwing one of the monsters across the village square. Immediately the others began to point their sticks while retreating rapidly.

After they were gone, the villagers found that seventeen males were dead. Hum, for some reason, had been missed.

"Now will you believe me!" Cordovir shouted. "The creatures told *a deliberate untruth!* They said they wouldn't molest us and then they proceeded to kill seventeen of us! Not only an amoral act—but a *concerted death effort!*"

It was almost past human understanding.

"A deliberate untruth!" Cordovir shouted the blasphemy, sick with loathing. Men rarely discussed the possibility of anyone telling an untruth.

The villagers were beside themselves with anger and revulsion, once they realized the full concept of an *untruthful* creature. And added to that was the monsters' concerted death effort!

It was like the most horrible nightmare come true. Suddenly it became apparent that these creatures didn't kill females. Undoubtedly they allowed them to spawn unhampered. The thought of that was enough to make a strong man retch.

The surplus females broke out of their pens and, joined by the wives, demanded to know what was happening. When they were told, they were twice as indignant as the men, such being the nature of women.

"Kill them!" the surplus females roared. "Don't let them change our ways. Don't let them introduce immorality!"

"It's true," Hum said sadly. "I should have guessed it."

"They must be killed at once!" a female shouted. Being surplus, she had no name at present, but she made up for that in blazing personality.

"We women desire only to live moral, decent lives, hatching eggs in the pen until our time of marriage comes. And then twenty-five ecstatic days! How could we desire more! These monsters will destroy our way of life. They will make us as terrible as they!"

"Now do you understand!" Cordovir screamed at the men. "I warned you, I presented it to you, and you ignored me! Young men must listen to old men in time of crisis!" In his rage he killed two youngsters with a blow of his tail. The villagers applauded.

"Drive them out," Cordovir shouted. "Before they corrupt us!"

All the females rushed off to kill the monsters.

"They have death-sticks," Hum observed. "Do the females know?"

"I don't believe so," Cordovir said. He was completely calm now. "You'd better go and tell them."

"I'm tired," Hum said sulkily. "I've been translating. Why don't you go?"

"Oh, let's both go," Cordovir said, bored with the youngster's adolescent moodiness. Accompanied by half of the villagers, they hurried off after the females.

They overtook them on the edge of the cliff that overlooked the object. Hum explained the death-sticks while Cordovir considered the problem.

"Roll stones on them," he told the females. "Perhaps you can break the metal of the object."

The females started rolling stones down the cliffs with great energy. Some bounced off the metal of the object. Immediately, lines of red fire came from the object and females were killed. The ground shook.

"Let's move back," Cordovir said. "The females have it well in hand, and this shaky ground makes me giddy."

Together with the rest of the males, they moved to a safe distance and watched the action.

Women were dying right and left, but they were reinforced by women of other villages who had heard of the menace. They were fighting for their homes now, their rights, and they were fiercer than men could ever be. The object was throwing fire all over the cliff, but the fire helped dislodge more stones, which rained down on the thing. Finally, big fires came out of one end of the metal object.

A landslide started, and the object got into the air just in time. It barely missed a mountain; then it climbed steadily, until it was a little black speck against the larger sun. And then it was gone.

That evening it was discovered that fifty-three females had been killed. This was fortunate, since it helped keep down the surplus female population. The problem would become even more acute now, since seventeen males were gone in a single lump.

Cordovir was feeling exceedingly proud of himself. His wife had been gloriously killed in the fighting, but he took another at once.

"We had better kill our wives sooner than every twenty-five days for a while," he said at the evening Gathering. "Just until things get back to normal."

The surviving females, back in the pen, heard him and applauded wildly.

"I wonder where the things have gone," Hum said, offering the question to the Gathering.

"Probably away to enslave some defenseless race," Cordovir said.

"Not necessarily," Mishill put in, and the evening argument was on.

THE PETRIFIED WORLD

Lanigan dreamed the dream again and managed to wake himself with a hoarse cry. He sat upright in bed and glared around him into the violet darkness. His teeth were clenched and his lips were pulled back into a spastic grin. Beside him he felt his wife, Estelle, stir and sit up. Lanigan didn't look at her. Still caught in his dream, he waited for tangible proofs of the world.

A chair drifted slowly across his field of vision and fetched up against the wall with a quiet thump. Lanigan's face relaxed slightly. Then Estelle's hand was on his arm—a touch that was meant to be soothing, but burned like lye.

"Here," she said. "Drink this."

"No," Lanigan said. "I'm all right now."

"Drink it anyhow."

"No, really. I really am all right."

For now he was completely out of the grip of the nightmare. He was himself again, and the world was its habitual self. That was very precious to Lanigan; he didn't want to let go of it just now, not even for the soothing release of a sedative. "Was it the dream?" Estelle asked him.

"Yes, just the same . . . I don't want to talk about it."

"All right," Estelle said. (She is humoring me, Lanigan thought. I frighten her. I frighten myself.)

She asked, "Hon, what time is it?"

Lanigan looked at his watch. "Six-fifteen." But as he said it, the hour hand jumped convulsively forward. "No, it's five to seven."

"Can you get back to sleep?"

"I don't think so," Lanigan said. "I think I'll stay up."

"Fine, dear," Estelle said. She yawned, closed her eyes, opened them again, and asked, "Hon, don't you think it might be a good idea if you called—"

"I have an appointment with him for twelve-ten," Lanigan said.

"That's fine," Estelle said. She closed her eyes again. Sleep came over her while Lanigan watched. Her auburn hair turned a faint blue, and she sighed once, heavily.

Lanigan got out of bed and dressed. He was, for the most part, a large man, unusually easy to recognize. His features were curiously distinct. He had a rash on his neck. He was in no other way outstanding, except that he had a recurring dream that was driving him insane.

He spent the next few hours on his front porch, watching stars go nova in the dawn sky.

Later he went out for a stroll. As luck would have it, he ran into George Torstein just two blocks from his house. Several months ago, in an incautious moment, he had told Torstein about his dream. Torstein was a bluff, hearty fellow, a great believer in self-help, discipline, practicality, common sense, and other dull virtues. His hardheaded, no-nonsense attitude had come as a momentary relief to Lanigan. But now it acted as an abrasive. Men like Torstein were undoubtedly the salt of the earth and the backbone of the country; but for Lanigan, wrestling with the impalpable and losing, Torstein had grown from a nuisance into a horror.

"Well, Tom, how's the boy?" Torstein greeted him.

"Fine," Lanigan said, "just fine." He nodded pleasantly and began to walk away under a melting green sky. But one did not escape from Torstein so easily.

"Tom, boy, I've been thinking about your problem," Torstein said. "I've been quite disturbed about you."

"Well, that's very nice of you," Lanigan said. "But really, you shouldn't concern yourself—"

"I do it because I want to," Torstein said, speaking the simple, deplorable truth. "I take an interest in people, Tom. Always have, ever since I was a kid. And you and I've been friends and neighbors for a long time."

"That's true enough," Lanigan said numbly. (The worst thing about needing help was having to accept it.)

"Well, Tom, I think what would really help you would be a little vacation."

Torstein had a simple prescription for everything. Since he practiced soul-doctoring without a license, he was always careful to prescribe a drug you could buy over the counter.

"I really can't afford a vacation this month," Lanigan said. (The sky was ochre and pink now; three pines had withered; an aged oak had turned into a youthful cactus.)

Torstein laughed heartily. "Boy, you can't afford *not* to take a vacation just now! Did you ever consider that?"

"No, I guess not."

"Well, *consider* it! You're tired, tense, all keyed up. You've been working too hard."

"I've been on leave of absence all week," Lanigan said. He glanced at his watch. The gold case had turned to lead, but the time seemed accurate enough. Nearly two hours had passed since he had begun this conversation.

"It isn't good enough," Torstein was saying. "You've stayed right here in town, right close to your work. You need to get in touch with nature. Tom, when was the last time you went camping?"

"Camping? I don't think I've ever gone camping."

"There, you see! Boy, you've got to put yourself back in touch with real things. Not streets and buildings, but mountains and rivers."

Lanigan looked at his watch again and was relieved to see it turn back to gold. He was glad; he had paid sixty dollars for that case.

"Trees and lakes," Torstein was rhapsodizing. "The feel of grass growing under your feet, the sight of tall black mountains marching across a golden sky—"

Lanigan shook his head. "I've been in the country, George. It doesn't do anything for me."

Torstein was obstinate. "You must get away from artificialities."

"It all seems equally artificial," Lanigan said. "Trees or buildings—what's the difference?"

"Men make buildings," Torstein intoned rather piously, "but God makes trees."

Lanigan had his doubts about both propositions, but he wasn't going to tell them to Torstein. "You might have something there," he said. "I'll think about it."

"You do that," Torstein said. "It happens I know the perfect place. It's in Maine, Tom, and it's right near this little lake—"

Torstein was a master of the interminable description. Luckily for Lanigan, there was a diversion. Across the street, a house burst into flames.

"Hey, whose house is that?" Lanigan asked.

"Makelby's," Torstein said. "That's his third fire this month."

"Maybe we ought to give the alarm."

"You're right, I'll do it myself," Torstein said. "Remember what I told you about that place in Maine, Tom."

Torstein turned to go, and something rather humorous happened. As he stepped over the pavement, the concrete liquefied under his left foot. Caught unawares, Torstein went in ankle-deep. His forward motion pitched him headfirst into the street.

Tom hurried to help him out before the concrete hardened again. "Are you all right?" he asked.

"Twisted my damned ankle," Torstein muttered. "It's okay, I can walk."

He limped off to report the fire. Lanigan stayed and watched. He judged the fire had been caused by spontaneous combustion. In a few minutes, as he had expected, it put itself out by spontaneous decombustion.

One shouldn't be pleased by another man's misfortunes, but Lanigan couldn't help chuckling about Torstein's twisted ankle. Not even the sudden appearance of floodwaters on Main Street could mar his good spirits. He beamed at something like a steamboat with yellow stacks that went by in the sky.

Then he remembered his dream, and the panic began again. He walked quickly to the doctor's office.

* * *

Dr. Sampson's office was small and dark this week. The old gray sofa was gone; in its place were two Louis Quinze chairs and a hammock, and there was a cigarette burn on the puce ceiling. But the portrait of Andretti was in its usual place on the wall, and the big free-form ashtray was scrupulously clean.

The inner door opened, and Dr. Sampson's head popped out. "Hi," he said. "Won't be a minute." His head popped back in again.

Sampson was as good as his word. It took him exactly three seconds by Lanigan's watch to do whatever he had to do. One second later, Lanigan was stretched out on the leather couch with a fresh paper doily under his head. And Dr. Sampson was saying, "Well, Tom, how have things been going?"

"The same," Lanigan said. "Worse."

"The dream?"

Lanigan nodded.

"Let's just run through it again."

"I'd rather not," Lanigan said.

"Afraid?"

"More afraid than ever."

"Even now?"

"Yes, especially now."

There was a moment of therapeutic silence. Then Dr. Sampson said, "You've spoken before of your fear of this dream, but you've never told me *why* you fear it so."

"Well . . . it sounds so silly."

Sampson's face was serious, quiet, composed, the face of a man who found nothing silly, who was constitutionally incapable of finding anything silly. It was a pose, perhaps, but one that Lanigan found reassuring.

"All right, I'll tell you," Lanigan said abruptly. Then he stopped.

"Go on," Dr. Sampson said.

"Well, it's because I believe that somehow, in some way, I don't understand . . ."

"Yes, go on," Sampson said.

"Well, that somehow the world of my dream is becoming the real world." He stopped again, then went on with a rush. "And that someday I am going to wake up and find myself *in* that world. And then that world will have become the real one and this world will be the dream."

He turned to see how this mad revelation had affected Sampson. If the doctor was disturbed, he didn't show it. He was quietly lighting his pipe with the smoldering tip of his left forefinger. He blew out his forefinger and said, "Yes, please go on."

"Go on? But that's it, that's the whole thing!"

A spot the size of a quarter appeared on Sampson's mauve carpet. It darkened, thickened, grew into a small fruit tree. Sampson picked one of the purple pods, sniffed it, then set it down on his desk. He looked at Lanigan sternly, sadly.

"You've told me about your dream world before, Tom."

Lanigan nodded.

"We have discussed it, traced its origins, analyzed its meaning for you. In past months we have learned, I believe, why you *need* to cripple yourself with this nightmare fear."

Lanigan nodded unhappily.

"Yet you refuse the insights," Sampson said. "You forget each time that your dream world is a *dream*, nothing but a dream, operated by arbitrary dream-laws that you have invented to satisfy your psychic needs."

"I wish I could believe that," Lanigan said. "The trouble is, my dream world is so damnably reasonable."

"Not at all," said Sampson. "It is just that your delusion is hermetic, self-enclosed and self-sustaining. A man's actions are based upon certain assumptions about the nature of the world. Grant his assumptions, and his behavior is entirely reasonable. But to change those assumptions, those fundamental axioms, is nearly impossible. For example, how do you prove to a man that he is not being controlled by a secret radio that only he can hear?"

"I see the problem," Lanigan muttered. "And that's me?"

"Yes, Tom. That, in effect, is you. You want me to prove to you that this world is real, and that the world of your dream is false. You propose to give up your fantasy if I supply you with the necessary proofs."

"Yes, exactly!" Lanigan cried.

"But you see, I can't supply them," Sampson said. "The nature of the world is apparent, but unprovable."

Lanigan thought for a while. Then he said, "Look, doc, I'm not as sick as the guy with the secret radio, am I?"

"No, you're not. You're more reasonable, more rational. You have doubts about the reality of the world; but you also have doubts about the validity of your delusion."

"Then give it a try," Lanigan said. "I understand your problem; but I swear to you, I'll accept anything I can possibly bring myself to accept."

"It's not my field, really," Sampson said. "This sort of thing calls for a metaphysician. I don't think I'd be very skilled at it . . ."

"Give it a try," Lanigan pleaded.

"All right, here goes." Sampson's forehead wrinkled and shed as he concentrated. Then he said, "It seems to me that we inspect the world through our senses, and therefore we must, in the final analysis, accept the testimony of those senses."

Lanigan nodded, and the doctor went on.

"So we know that a thing exists because our senses tell us it exists. How do we check the accuracy of our observations? By comparing them with the sensory impressions of other men. We know that our senses don't lie when other men's senses agree upon the existence of the thing in question."

Lanigan thought about this, then said, "Therefore the real world is simply what most men think it is."

Sampson twisted his mouth and said, "I told you that metaphysics was not my forte. Still, I think it is an acceptable demonstration."

"Yes . . . but, doc, suppose *all* of those observers are wrong? For example, suppose there are many worlds and many realities, not just one? Suppose this is simply one arbitrary existence out of an infinity of existences? Or suppose that the nature of reality itself is capable of change, and that somehow I am able to perceive that change?"

Sampson sighed, found a little green bat fluttering inside his jacket, and absentmindedly crushed it with a ruler.

"There you are," he said. "I can't disprove a single one of your suppositions. I think, Tom, that we had better run through the entire dream."

Lanigan grimaced. "I really would rather not. I have a feeling . . ."

"I know you do," Sampson said, smiling faintly. "But this will prove or disprove it once and for all, won't it?"

"I guess so," Lanigan said. He took courage—unwisely—and said, "Well, the way it begins, the way my dream starts—"

Even as he spoke, the horror came over him. He felt dizzy, sick, terrified. He tried to rise from the couch. The doctor's face ballooned over him. He saw a glint of metal, heard Sampson saying, "Just try to relax . . . brief seizure . . . try to think of something pleasant."

Then either Lanigan or the world or both passed out.

Lanigan and/or the world came back to consciousness. Time may or may not have passed. Anything might or might not have happened. Lanigan sat up and looked at Sampson.

"How do you feel now?" Sampson asked.

"I'm all right," Lanigan said. "What happened?"

"You had a bad moment. Take it easy for a bit."

Lanigan leaned back and tried to calm himself. The doctor was sitting at his desk, writing notes. Lanigan counted to twenty with his eyes closed, then opened them cautiously. Sampson was still writing notes.

Lanigan looked around the room, counted the five pictures on the wall, recounted them, looked at the green carpet, frowned at it, closed his eyes again. This time he counted to fifty.

"Well, care to talk about it now?" Sampson asked, shutting a notebook.

"No, not just now," Lanigan said. (Five paintings, green carpet.)

"Just as you please," the doctor said. "I think that our time is just about up. But if you'd care to lie down in the anteroom—"

"No, thanks, I'll go home," Lanigan said.

He stood up, walked across the green carpet to the door, looked back at the five paintings and at the doctor, who smiled at him encouragingly. Then Lanigan went through the door and into the anteroom, through the anteroom to the outer door, and through that and down the corridor to the stairs and down the stairs to the street.

He walked and looked at the trees, on which green leaves moved faintly and predictably in a faint breeze. There was traffic, which moved soberly down one side of the street and up the other. The sky was an unchanging blue, and had obviously been so for quite some time.

Dream? He pinched himself. A dream pinch? He did not awaken. He shouted. An imaginary shout? He did not awaken.

He was in the street of the world of his nightmare.

The street, at first, seemed like any normal city street. There were paving stones, cars, people, buildings, a sky overhead, a sun in the sky. All perfectly normal. Except that *nothing was happening.*

The pavement never once yielded beneath his feet. Over there was the First National City Bank. It had been here yesterday, which was bad enough; but, worse, it would be there without fail tomorrow, and the day after that, and the year after that. The First National City Bank (founded 1892) was grotesquely devoid of possibilities. It would never become a tomb, an airplane, the bones of a prehistoric monster. Sullenly it would remain a building of concrete and steel, madly persisting in its fixity until men came with tools and tediously tore it down.

Lanigan walked through this petrified world, under a blue sky that oozed a sly white around the edges, teasingly promising something that was never delivered. People crossed at crossings, clocks were within minutes of agreement.

Somewhere between the towns lay countryside, but Lanigan knew that the grass did not grow under one's feet; it simply lay still—growing, no doubt, but imperceptibly, useless to the senses. And the mountains were still tall and black, but they were giants stopped in midstride. They would never march against a gold (or purple or green) sky.

The essence of life, Dr. Sampson had once said, is change. The essence of death is immobility. Even a corpse has a vestige of life about it as long as its flesh rots, as long as maggots still feast on its blind eyes and blowflies suck the juice from the burst intestines.

Lanigan looked around at the corpse of the world and perceived that it was dead.

He screamed. He screamed while people gathered around and looked at him (but didn't do anything or become anything), and then a policeman came as he was supposed to (but the sun didn't change shape once), and then an ambulance came down the invariant street (but without trumpets, minus strumpets, on four wheels instead of a pleasing three or twenty-five), and the ambulance men brought him to a building that was exactly where they expected to find it, and there was a great deal of talk by people who stood untransformed, asking questions in a room with relentlessly white walls.

And there was evening and there was morning, and it was the first day.

UNCOLLECTED
SHECKLEY

FIVE MINUTES EARLY

Suddenly, John Greer found that he was at the entrance to heaven. Before him stretched the white and azure cloudlands of the hereafter, and in the far distance he could see a fabulous city gleaming gold under an eternal sun. Standing in front of him was the tall, benign presence of the Recording Angel. Strangely, Greer felt no sense of shock. He had always believed that heaven was for everyone, not just the members of one religion or sect. Despite this, he had been tortured all his life by doubts. Now he could only smile at his lack of faith in the divine scheme.

"Welcome to heaven," the Recording Angel said, and opened a great brassbound ledger. Squinting through thick bifocals, the angel ran his finger down the dense rows of names. He found Greer's entry and hesitated, his wingtips fluttering momentarily in agitation.

"Is something wrong?" Greer asked.

"I'm afraid so," the Recording Angel said. "It seems that the Angel of Death came for you before your appointed time. He *has* been badly overworked of late, but it's still inexcusable. Luckily, it's quite a minor error."

"Taking me away before my time?" Greer said. "I don't consider that minor."

"But you see, it's only a matter of five minutes. Nothing to concern yourself over. Shall we just overlook the discrepancy and send you on to the Eternal City?"

The Recording Angel was right, no doubt. What difference

could five more minutes on Earth make to him? Yet Greer felt they might be important, even though he couldn't say why.

"I'd like those five minutes," Greer said.

The Recording Angel looked at him with compassion. "You have the right, of course. But I would advise against it. Do you remember how you died?"

Greer thought, then shook his head. "How?" he asked.

"I am not allowed to say. But death is never pleasant. You're here now. Why not stay with us?"

That was only reasonable. But Greer was nagged by a sense of something unfinished. "If it's allowed," he said, "I really would like to have those last minutes."

"Go, then," said the angel, "and I will wait for you here."

And suddenly Greer was back on Earth. He was in a cylindrical metal room lit by dim, flickering lights. The air was stale and smelled of steam and machine oil. The steel walls were heaving and creaking, and water was pouring through the seams.

Then Greer remembered where he was. He was a gunnery officer aboard the U.S. submarine *Invictus*. There had been a sonar failure; they had just rammed an underwater cliff that should have been a mile away, and now were dropping helplessly through the black water. Already the *Invictus* was far below her maximum depth. It could only be a matter of minutes before the rapidly mounting pressure collapsed the ship's hull. Greer knew it would happen in exactly five minutes.

There was no panic on the ship. The seamen braced themselves against the bulging walls, waiting, frightened, but in tight control of themselves. The technicians stayed at their posts, steadily reading the instruments that told them they had no chance at all. Greer knew that the Recording Angel had wanted to spare him this, the bitter end of life, the brief sharp agony of death in the icy dark.

And yet Greer was glad to be here, though he didn't expect the Recording Angel to understand. How could a creature of heaven know the feelings of a man of Earth? After all, most men died in fear and ignorance, expecting at worst the tortures of hell, at best the nothingness of oblivion. Greer knew what lay ahead, knew that the Recording Angel awaited him at the entrance to heaven.

Therefore he was able to spend his final minutes making a proper and dignified exit from the Earth. As the submarine's walls collapsed, he was remembering a sunset over Key West, a quick dramatic summer storm on the Chesapeake, the slow circle of a hawk soaring above the Everglades. Although heaven lay ahead, now only seconds away, Greer was thinking of the beauties of the Earth, remembering as many of them as he could, like a man packing provisions for a long journey into a strange land.

MISS MOUSE AND THE
FOURTH DIMENSION

I first met Charles Foster at the Claerston Award dinner at Leadbeater's Hall in the Strand. It was my second night in London. I had come to England with the hope of signing some new authors for my list. I am Max Seidel, publisher of Manjusri Books. We are a small esoteric publishing company operating out of Linwood, New Jersey—just me and Miss Thompson, my assistant. My books sell well to the small but faithful portion of the population interested in spiritualism, out-of-body experiences, Atlantis, flying saucers, and New Age technology. Charles Foster was one of the men I had come to meet.

Pam Devore, our British sales representative, pointed Foster out to me. I saw a tall, good-looking man in his middle thirties, with a great mane of reddish blond hair, talking animatedly with two dowager types. Sitting beside him, listening intently, was a small woman in her late twenties with neat, plain features and fine chestnut hair.

"Is that his wife?" I asked.

Pam laughed. "Goodness, no! Charles is too fond of women to actually marry one. That's Miss Mouse."

"Is Mouse an English name?"

"It's just Charles's nickname for her. Actually, she's not very mouselike at all. Marmoset might be more like it, or even wolverine. She's Mimi Royce, a society photographer. She's quite well off—the Royce textile mills in Lancashire, you know—and she adores Charles, poor thing."

"He does seem to be an attractive man," I said.

"I suppose so," Pam said, "if you like the type." She glanced at me to see how I was taking that, then laughed when she saw my expression.

"Yes, I *am* rather prejudiced," she confessed. "Charles used to be rather interested in me until he found his own true love."

"Who was—?"

"Himself, of course. Come, let me introduce you."

Foster knew about Manjusri Books and was interested in publishing with us. He thought we might be a good showcase for his talents, especially since Paracelsus Press had done so poorly with his last, *Journey Through the Eye of the Tiger*. There was something open and boyish about Foster. He spoke in a high, clear English voice that conjured up in me a vision of punting on the Thames on a misty autumn day.

Charles was the sort of esoteric writer who goes out and has adventures and then writes them up in a portentous style. His search was for—well, what shall I call it? The Beyond? The Occult? The Interface? After twenty years in this business I still don't know how to describe, in one simple phrase, the sort of book I publish. Charles Foster's last book had dealt with three months he had spent with a Baluchistani Dervish in the desert of Kush under incredibly austere conditions. What had he gotten out of it? A direct though fleeting knowledge of the indivisible oneness of things, a sense of the mystery and grandeur of existence . . . in short, the usual thing. And he had gotten a book out of it; and that, too, is the usual thing.

We set up a lunch for the next day. I rented a car and drove to Charles's house in Oxfordshire. It was a beautiful old thatch-roofed building set in the middle of five acres of rolling countryside. It was called Sepoy Cottage, despite the fact that it had five bedrooms and three parlors. It didn't actually belong to Charles, as he told me immediately. It belonged to Mimi Royce.

"But she lets me use it whenever I like," he said. "Mouse is such a dear." He smiled like a well-bred child talking about his favorite aunt. "She's so interested in one's little adventures, one's trips along the interface between reality and the ineffable ... Insists on typing up my manuscripts just for the pleasure it gives her to read them first."

"That *is* lucky," I said, "typing rates being what they are these days."

Just then Mimi came in with tea. Foster regarded her with bland indifference. Either he was unaware of her obvious adoration of him, or he chose not to acknowledge it. Mimi, for her part, did not seem to mind. I assumed that I was seeing a display of the British National Style in affairs of the heart—subdued, muffled, unobtrusive. She went away after serving us, and Charles and I talked auras and ley-lines for a while, then got down to the topic of real interest to us both—his next book.

"It's going to be a bit unusual," he told me, leaning back and templing his fingers.

"Another spiritual adventure?" I asked. "What will it be about?"

"Guess!" he said.

"Let's see. Are you by any chance going to Machu Picchu to check out the recent reports of spaceship landings?"

He shook his head. "Elton Travis is already covering it for Mystic Revelations Press. No, my next adventure will take place right here in Sepoy Cottage."

"Have you discovered a ghost or poltergeist here?"

"Nothing so mundane."

"Then I really have no idea," I told him.

"What I propose," Foster said, "is to create an opening into the unknown right here in Sepoy Cottage, and to journey through it into the unimaginable. And then, of course, to write up what I've found there."

"Indeed," I said.

"Are you familiar with Von Helmholz's work?"

"Was he the one who read tarot cards for Frederick the Great?"

"No, that was Manfred Von Helmholz. I am referring to Wilhelm, a famous mathematician and scientist in the nineteenth century. He maintained that it was theoretically possible to *see* directly into the fourth dimension."

I turned the concept over in my mind. It didn't do much for me.

"This 'fourth dimension' to which he refers," Foster went on, "is synonymous with the spiritual or ethereal realm of the mystics. The name of the place changes with the times, but the region itself is unchanging."

I nodded. Despite myself, I am a believer. That's what brought me into this line of work. But I also know that illusion and self-deception are the rule in these matters rather than the exception.

"But this spirit realm, or fourth dimension," Foster went on, "is also our everyday reality. Spirits surround us. They move through that strange realm which Von Helmholz called the fourth dimension. Normally they can't be seen."

It sounded to me as if Foster was extemporizing the first chapter of his book. Still, I didn't interrupt.

"Our eyes are blinded by everyday reality. But there are techniques by means of which we can train ourselves to see what *else* is there. Do you know about Hinton's cubes? Hinton is mentioned by Martin Gardner in *Mathematical Carnival*. Charles Howard Hinton was an eccentric American mathematician who, around 1910, came up with a scheme for learning how to visualize a tesseract, also called a hypercube or four-dimensional square. His technique involved colored cubes that fit together to form a single master cube. Hinton felt that one could learn to see the separate colored cubes in the mind and then, mentally, to manipulate and rotate them, fold them into and out of the greater cube shape, and to do this faster and faster until at last a gestalt forms and the hypercube springs forth miraculously in your mind."

He paused. "Hinton said that it was a hell of a lot of work. And later investigators, according to Gardner, have warned of psychic dangers even in attempting something like this."

"It sounds like it could drive you crazy," I said.

"Some of those investigators *did* wig," he admitted cheerfully. "But that might have been from frustration. Hinton's procedure demands an inhuman power of concentration. Only a master of yoga could be expected to possess that."

"Such as yourself?"

"My dear fellow, I can barely remember what I've just read in the newspaper. Luckily, concentration is not the only path into the unknown. Fascination can more easily lead us to the mystic path. Hinton's principle is sound, but it needs to be combined with Aquarian Age technology to make it work. That is what I have done."

He led me into the next room. There, on a low table, was what I took at first to be a piece of modernistic sculpture. It had a base of cast iron. A central shaft came up through its middle, and on top of the shaft was a sphere about the size of a human head. Radiating in all directions from the sphere were lucite rods. At the end of each rod was a cube. The whole contraption looked like a cubist porcupine with blocks stuck to the end of its spines.

Then I saw that the blocks had images or signs painted on their faces. There were Sanskrit, Hebrew, and Arabic letters, Freemason and Egyptian symbols, Chinese ideograms, and other figures from many different lores. Now it looked like a bristling phalanx of mysticism, marching forth to do battle against common sense. And even though I'm in the business, it made me shudder.

"He didn't know it, of course," Foster said, "but what Hinton stumbled upon was the mandala principle. His cubes were the arts; put them all together in your mind and you create the Eternal, the Unchanging, the Solid Mandala, or four-dimensional space, depending upon which terminology you prefer. Hinton's cubes were a three-dimensional exploded view of an ethereal object. This object refuses to come together in our everyday reality. It is the unicorn that flees from the view of man—"

"—but lays its head in the lap of a virgin," I finished for him.

He shrugged it off. "Never mind the figures of speech, old boy. Mouse will unscramble my metaphors when she types up the manuscript. The point is, I can use Hinton's brilliant discovery of the exploded mandala whose closure produces the ineffable object of endless fascination. I can journey down the endless spiral into the unknown. This is how the trip begins."

He pushed a switch on the base of the contraption. The sphere began to revolve, the lucite arms turned, and the cubes on the ends of those arms turned too, creating an effect both hypnotic and disturbing. I was glad when Foster turned it off.

"My Mandala Machine!" he cried triumphantly. "What do you think?"

"I think you could get your head into a lot of trouble with that device," I told him.

"No, no," he said irritably. "I mean, what do you think of it as the subject for a book?"

No matter what else he was, Foster was a genuine writer. A genuine writer is a person who will descend voluntarily into the flaming pits of hell, as long as he's allowed to record his impressions and send them back to Earth for publication. I thought about the book that would most likely result from Foster's project. I estimated its audience at about one hundred fifty people, including friends and relatives. Nevertheless, I heard myself saying, "I'll buy it." That's how I manage to stay a small and unsuccessful publisher, despite being so smart.

I returned to London shortly after that. Next day I drove to Glastonbury to spend a few days with Claude Upshank, owner of the Great White Brotherhood Press. We have been good friends, Claude and I, ever since we met ten years ago at a flying-saucer convention in Barcelona.

"I don't like it," Claude said, when I told him about Foster's project. "The mandala principle is potentially dangerous. You can really get into trouble when you start setting up autonomous feedback loops in your brain like that."

Claude had studied acupuncture and Rolfing at the Hardrada Institute in Malibu, so I figured he knew what he was talking about. Nevertheless, I thought that Charles had a lot of savvy in these matters and could take care of himself.

When I telephoned Foster two days later, he told me that the project was going very well. He had added several refinements to the Mandala Machine: "Sound effects, for one. I'm using a special tape of Tibetan horns and gongs. The overtones, sufficiently amplified, can send you into instant trance." And he had also bought a strobe light to flash into his eyes at six to ten beats a second: "The epileptic rate, you know. It's ideal for loosening up your head." He claimed that all of this deepened his state of trance and increased the clarity of the revolving cubes. "I'm very near to success now, you know."

I thought he sounded tired and close to hysteria. I begged him to take a rest.

"Nonsense," he said. "Show must go on, eh?"

A day later, Foster reported that he was right on the brink of the final breakthrough. His voice wavered, and I could hear him panting and wheezing between words. "I'll admit it's been more difficult than I had expected. But now I'm being assisted by a certain substance that I had the foresight to bring with me. I am not supposed to mention it over the telephone in view of the law of the land and the ever-present possibility of snoops on the line, so I'll just remind you of Arthur Machen's *Novel of the White Powder* and let you work out the rest for yourself. Call me tomorrow. The fourth dimension is finally coming together."

The next day Mimi answered the telephone and said that Foster was refusing to take any calls. She reported him as saying that he was right on the verge of success and could not be interrupted. He asked his friends to be patient with him during this difficult period.

The next day it was the same, Mimi answering, Foster refusing to speak to us. That night I conferred with Claude and Pam.

We were in Pam's smart Chelsea apartment. We sat together in the bay window, drinking tea and watching the traffic pour down the King's Road into Sloane Square. Claude asked, "Does Foster have any family?"

"None in England," Pam said. "His mother and brother are on holiday in Bali."

"Any close friends?"

"Mouse, of course," Pam said.

We looked at each other. An odd presentiment had come to us simultaneously, a feeling that something was terribly wrong.

"But this is ridiculous," I said. "Mimi absolutely adores him, and she's a very competent woman. What could there be to worry about?"

"Let's call once more," Claude said.

We tried, and were told that Mimi's telephone was out of order. We decided to go to Sepoy Cottage at once.

Claude drove us out in his old Morgan. Mimi met us at the door. She looked thoroughly exhausted, yet there was a serenity about her that I found just a little uncanny.

"I'm so glad you've come," she said, leading us inside. "You have no idea how frightening it's all been. Charles came close to losing his mind in these last days."

"But why didn't you tell us?" I demanded.

"Charles implored me not to. He told me—and I believed him—that he and I had to see this thing through together. He thought it would be dangerous to his sanity to bring in anyone else at this point."

Claude made a noise that sounded like a snort. "Well, what happened?"

"It all went very well at first," Mimi said. "Charles began to spend increasingly longer periods in front of the machine, and he came to enjoy the experience. Soon I could get him away only to eat, and grudgingly at that. Then he gave up food altogether. After a while he no longer needed the machine. He could see the cubes and their faces in his head, could move them around at any speed he wanted, bring them together or spread them apart. The final creation, however, the coming together of the hypercube, was still eluding him. He went back to the machine, running it now at its highest speed."

Mimi sighed. "Of course, he pushed himself too hard. This time, when he turned off the machine, the mandala continued to grow and mutate in his head. Each cube had taken on hallucinatory solidity. He said the symbols gave off a hellish light that hurt his eyes. He couldn't stop those cubes from flashing through his mind. He felt that he was being suffocated in a mass of alien signs. He grew agitated, swinging quickly between elation and despair. It was during one of his elated swings that he ripped out the telephone."

"You should have sent for us!" Claude said.

"There was simply no time. Charles knew what was happening

to him. He said we had to set up a counter-conditioning program immediately. It involved changing the symbols on the cube faces. The idea was to break up the obsessive image-trains through the altered sequence. I set it up, but it didn't seem to work for Charles. He was fading away before my eyes, occasionally rousing himself to murmur, 'The horror, the horror . . .'"

"Bloody hell!" Claude exploded. "And then?"

"I felt that I had to act immediately. Charles's system of counter-conditioning had failed. I decided that he needed a different sort of symbol to look at—something simple and direct, something reassuring—"

Just then Charles came slowly down the stairs. He had lost a lot of weight since I saw him last, and his face was haggard. He looked thin, happy, and not quite sane.

"I was just napping," he said. "I've got rather a lot of sleep to catch up on. Did Mouse tell you how she saved what little is left of my sanity?" He put his arm around her shoulders. "She's marvelous, isn't she? And to think that I only realized yesterday that I loved her. We're getting married next week, and you're all invited."

Mimi said, "I thought we were flying down to Monte Carlo and getting married in the city hall."

"Why, so we are." Charles looked bewildered for a moment. He touched his head with the unconscious pathos of the wounded soldier in the movie who hasn't yet realized that half his head is blown away. "The old think-piece hasn't quite recovered yet from the beating I gave it with those wretched cubes. If Mimi hadn't been here, I don't know what would have happened to me."

They beamed at us, the instant happy couple produced by Hinton's devilish cubes. The transformation of Charles's feelings toward Mimi—from fond indifference to blind infatuation—struck me as bizarre and dreamlike. They were Svengali and Trilby with the sexes reversed, a case of witchcraft rather than of love's magic.

"It's going to be all right now, Charles," Mimi said.

"Yes, love, I know it is." Charles smiled, but the animation had gone out of his face. He lifted his hand to his head again, and his knees began to sag. Mimi, her arm around his waist, half supported and half dragged him to the stairs.

"I'll just get him up to bed," she said.

Claude, Pam, and I stood in the middle of the room, looking at each other. Then, with a single accord, we turned and went into the parlor where the Mandala Machine was kept.

We approached it with awe, for it was a modern version of ancient witchcraft. I could imagine Charles sitting in front of the thing, its arms revolving, the cubes turning and flashing, setting up a single ineradicable image in his mind. The ancient Hebrew, Chinese, and Egyptian letters were gone. All the faces of all the cubes now bore a single symbol—direct and reassuring, just as Mimi had said, but hardly simple. There were twenty cubes, with six faces to a cube, and pasted to each surface was a photograph of Mimi Royce.

THE SKAG CASTLE

Within the offices of the AAA Ace Interplanetary Decontamination Service, a gloomy silence reigned. By the faint light that filtered through the dirty windows, Richard Gregor was playing a new form of solitaire. It involved three packs of cards, six jokers, a set of dice, and a slide rule. The game was extremely complicated, maddeningly difficult, and it always came out if you persisted long enough.

His partner, Mike Arnold, had swept his desk clear of its usual clutter of crusty test tubes and unpaid bills, and was now dozing fitfully on its stained surface.

Business couldn't have been worse.

There was a tentative knock on the door.

Quickly Gregor pushed his playing cards, dice, and slide rule into a drawer. Arnold rolled off his desk like a cat and flipped open Volume Two of Terkstiller's *Decontamination Modes on X-32* (Omega) *Worlds*, which he had been using for a pillow.

"Come in," Gregor called out.

The door opened and a girl entered. She was young, slender, dark-haired, and extremely pretty. Her eyes were gray, and they contained a hint of fear. Her lips were unsmiling.

She looked around the unkempt office. "Is this the AAA Ace?" she inquired tentatively.

"It certainly is," Gregor assured her. "Won't you sit down? We always keep the lights off. Much more restful, don't you think?"

And, he thought, quite necessary, since Con Mazda had shut off their power last week for nonpayment of a trifling bill.

"I suppose it is," the girl said, sitting in the cavernous client's chair. She surveyed the office again. "You people *are* planetary decontaminationists, aren't you? Not taxidermists or undertakers?"

"Don't let the office fool you," Arnold said. "We are the best, and the most reasonable. No planet too big, no asteroid too small."

"Maybe I've come to the right place after all," the girl said with a wan but enchanting smile. "You see, I don't have much money."

Gregor nodded sympathetically. AAA Ace's clients never had much money.

"But I do have a tiny little planet that needs decontaminating," the girl said. "It's the most wonderful place in the whole galaxy. But the job might be dangerous."

"Dangerous?" Arnold asked.

The girl nodded and glanced nervously at the door. "I don't even know if I'm safe here. Are you armed?"

Gregor found a rusty letter opener. Arnold hefted a bronze paperweight cast in the shape of the spaceship *Constitution*—a beautiful piece of workmanship.

Somewhat relieved, the girl went on. "I'm Myra Branch Ryan. I was on my little planet, minding my own business, when suddenly this Scarb appeared before me, leering horribly—"

"This what?"

"Perhaps I should start at the beginning," Myra Ryan said. "A few months ago my Uncle Jim died and left me a small planet and a Hemstet four spaceship. The planet is Coelle, in the Gelsors system. Uncle Jim bought the planet fifteen years ago for a vacation home. He had just gotten it into shape when he was called away on business. What with one thing and another, he never returned. Naturally I went out there as soon as I could."

Myra's face brightened as she remembered her first impressions.

"Coelle was very small, but perfect. It had a complete air system, the best gravity money can buy, and an artesian well. Uncle Jim had planted several orchards, and berry bushes on the hillsides, and long grass everywhere. There was even a little lake.

"But Coelle's outstanding feature was the Skag Castle. Uncle

Jim hadn't touched this, for the castle was old beyond belief. It was thought to have been built by the Skag Horde, who, according to legend, occupied the universe before the coming of man."

The partners nodded. Everyone had heard of the Skag Horde. A whole literature had sprung up around the scanty evidence of their existence. It was pretty well established that they had been reptile-evolved, and had mastered spaceflight. But legend went further than this. The Skag Horde was supposed to have known the Old Lore, a strange mixture of science and witchcraft. This, according to the legends, gave them powers beyond the conception of man, powers sprung from the evil counterforces of the universe.

Their disappearance, millennia before *Homo sapiens* descended from the treetops, had never been satisfactorily explained.

"I fell in love with Coelle," Myra continued, "and the old Skag Castle just made it perfect."

"But where does the decontaminating come in?" Gregor asked. "Were there natives on Coelle? Animals? Germs?"

"No, nothing like that," Myra said. "Here's what happened . . ."

She had been on her planet a week, exploring its groves and orchards, and wandering around the Skag Castle. Then, one evening, sitting in the castle's great library, she sensed something wrong. There was an unearthly stillness in the air, as though the planet were waiting for something to happen. Angrily she tried to shake off the mood. It was just nerves, she told herself. After she put a few more lights in the halls, and changed the blood-red draperies to something gayer . . .

Then she heard a dull rumbling noise, like the sound of a giant walking. It seemed to come from somewhere in the solid granite upon which the castle rested.

She stood completely still, waiting. The floor vibrated, a vase crept off a table and shattered on the flagstones. And then the Scarb appeared before her, leering horribly.

There was no mistaking it. According to legend, the Scarbs had been the wizard-scientists of the vanished Skag Horde—powerful reptiles dressed in cloaks of gray and purple. The creature that stood before Myra was over nine feet tall, with tiny atrophied wings and a horn growing from its forehead.

The Scarb said, "Earthwoman, go home!"

She almost fainted. The Scarb continued, "Know, rash human, that this planet of Coelle is the ancestral home of the Skag Horde, and this Castle is the original Skag Burrow. Here the spirit of the Skag still lives, through the intervention of Grad, Ieele, and other accursed powers of the universe. Quit this sacred planet at once, foolish human, or I, the Undead Scarb, will exact revenge."

And with that, it vanished.

"What did you do?" Gregor asked.

"Nothing," Myra said with a little laugh. "I just couldn't believe it. I thought I must have had a hallucination, and everything would be all right if I just got control of myself. Twice more that week I heard the underground noises. And then the Scarb appeared again. He said, 'You have been warned, Earthwoman. Now beware the wrath of the Undead Scarb!' After that, I got out as fast as I could."

Myra sniffed, took out a little handkerchief, and wiped her eyes.

"So you see," she said, "my little planet needs decontaminating. Or possibly exorcising."

"Miss Ryan," Gregor said very gently, "I don't mean to be insulting, but have you—ah—did you ever think of consulting a psychiatrist?"

The girl stood up angrily. "Do you think I'm crazy?"

"Not at all," Gregor said soothingly. "But remember, you yourself spoke of the possibility of hallucination. After all, a deserted planet, an ancient castle, these legends—which, by the way, have very little basis in fact—all would tend to—"

"You're right, of course," Myra said with a strange little smile. "But how do you explain this?" She opened her handbag and spilled three cans of film and a spool of magnetic tape onto Gregor's desk.

"I was able to *record* some of those hallucinations," she said.

The partners were momentarily speechless.

"Something is going on in that castle," Myra said earnestly. "It calls itself an Undead Scarb. Won't you get rid of it for me?"

Gregor groaned and rubbed his forehead. He hated to refuse anyone as beautiful as Miss Ryan, and they certainly could use the money. But this was not, in all honesty, a job for decontaminators.

This looked like a psychic case, and psychic phenomena were notoriously tricky.

"Miss Ryan—" he began, but Arnold broke in.

"We would be delighted to take your case," he said. To Gregor he gave an I'll-explain-later wink.

"Oh, how wonderful!" Myra said. "How soon will you be ready?"

"As a rule," Arnold said, "we need a few weeks' notice. But for you—" He beamed fatuously. "For you, we are going to clear our calendar, postpone all other cases, and begin at once."

Gregor's long, sad face was unhappier than ever. "Perhaps you've forgotten," he told his partner. "Joe the Interstellar Junkman has our spaceship, due to a trifling bill we neglected to pay. I'm sorry, Miss Ryan—"

"Call me Myra," Myra said. "That's all right, my Hemstet four is fueled and ready to go."

"Then we'll leave tonight," Arnold said. "Have no fear, Myra. Your little planet is safe in our hands. We'll radio you as soon as—"

"Radio nothing," Myra said. "I'm going along. I wouldn't miss this for anything."

They arranged for Myra to obtain the clearances and meet them back at the office. As she walked to the door, Arnold said, "By the way, why did you ask if we were armed?"

She was silent for a moment. Then she said, "Since I came back to Terra, something's been following me. Something wearing gray and purple. I'm afraid it might be the Undead Scarb."

She closed the door gently behind her.

As soon as she was gone, Gregor shouted, "Have you gone completely out of your mind? Skags, Undead Scarbs—"

"She's beautiful," Arnold said dreamily.

"Are you listening to me? How are we supposed to decontaminate a haunted planet?"

"Coelle isn't haunted."

"What makes you think not?"

"Because the original Skag Burrow, according to the very best evidence, was on the planet Duerité, *not* on Coelle. A Skag ghost would know that. Ergo, what she saw was no ghost."

Gregor frowned thoughtfully.

"Mmm. You think someone wants to frighten her off Coelle?"

"Obviously," Arnold said.

"But the planet's been deserted for years. Why would someone take an interest in it now?"

"I'm going to find out."

"Sounds like a job for a detective," Gregor told him.

"Perhaps you've forgotten," Arnold said. "I am an honor graduate of the Hepburn School of Scientific Detection."

"That was only a six weeks' correspondence course."

"So what? Detection is simply the rational application of logic. Moreover, detection and decontamination are essentially the same thing. Decontamination just carries the process of detection to its logical conclusion."

"I hope you know what you're talking about," Gregor said. "What about this gray and purple creature that's been following Myra around?"

"No such thing. A case of overwrought nerves," Arnold diagnosed. "The poor girl needs someone to protect her. Me, for example."

"Yeah. But who's going to protect you?"

Arnold didn't bother answering, and the partners began to make their preparations.

II

They spent the rest of the day loading the Hemstet with various devices they had managed to keep out of hock. Gregor invested in a secondhand Steng needler. It seemed a good weapon against the more palpable forms of wizardry. After a quick dinner at the Milky Way Diner they started back to their office.

After they had walked several blocks, Arnold said, "I think we're being followed."

"You have overwrought nerves," Gregor diagnosed.

"He was in the diner, too," Arnold said. "And I'm sure I saw him at the spaceport."

Gregor glanced over his shoulder. Half a block behind he saw a man sauntering along and glancing idly into store windows, his attitude studiously casual.

The partners turned down a street. The man followed. They circled and returned to the avenue they had been on. The man was still there, keeping half a block between them.

"Have you noticed what he's wearing?" Arnold asked, wiping perspiration from his forehead.

Gregor looked again and saw that the man had on a gray suit and a purple tie—Skag colors.

"Hmm," Gregor said. "Do you suppose an Undead Scarb—if there were such a thing—could take on human form?"

"I'd hate to find out," Arnold said. "You'd better get that needler ready."

"I left it on the ship."

"That's just fine," Arnold said bitterly. "Just perfect. Someone—or some*thing*—is following us, probably with murderous intent, and you leave your blaster on the ship."

"Steady," Gregor said. "Maybe we can shake him."

They continued walking. Gregor looked back and saw that the man—or Scarb—was still there. He was walking more rapidly, closing the gap between them.

But coming down the street now was a taxi, its flag up.

They hailed it and climbed in. The man—or Scarb—looked around frantically for another cab, but there was none in sight. When they drove off he was standing on the curb, glaring at them, his purple tie slightly askew.

Myra Ryan was waiting for them at the office. She nodded when they told her about the follower.

"I warned you it might be dangerous," she said. "You can still back out, you know."

"What'll you do then?" Arnold asked.

"I'll go back to Coelle," Myra said. "No Skags are going to keep me off my planet."

"We're going," Arnold said, gazing tenderly at her. "You know we wouldn't desert you, Myra."

"Of course not," Gregor said wearily.

At that moment the door opened, and in walked a man wearing a gray suit and a purple tie.

"The Scarb!" Arnold gaped, and reached for his paperweight.

"That's no Scarb," Myra said calmly. "That's Ross Jameson. Hello, Ross."

Jameson was a tall, beautifully groomed man in his early thirties, with a handsome, impatient face and hard eyes.

"Myra," he said, "have you gone completely insane?"

"I don't think so, Ross," Myra said sweetly.

"Are you really going to Coelle with these charlatans?"

Gregor stepped forward. "Were you following us?"

"You're damned right I was," Jameson said belligerently.

"I don't know who you are," Gregor said, "but—"

"I'm Miss Ryan's fiancé," Jameson said, "and I'm not going to let her go through with this ridiculous project. Myra, from what you've told me, this planet of yours sounds dangerous. Why don't you forget about it and marry me?"

"I want to live on Coelle," Myra said in a dangerously quiet voice. "I want to live on my own little planet."

Jameson shook his head. "We've been through this a thousand times. Darling, you can't seriously expect me to give up my business and move to this little mudball with you. I've got my work—"

"And I've got my mudball," Myra said. "It's my very own mudball, and I want to live there."

"With the Skags?"

"I thought you didn't believe in that sort of thing," Myra said.

"I don't. But some trickery is going on, and I don't like to see you involved. It's probably that crazy hermit. There's no telling what he'll try next. Myra, won't you *please*—"

"No!" Myra said. "I'm going to Coelle!"

"Then I'm going with you."

"You are not," Myra said coldly.

"I've already arranged it with my staff," Jameson said. "You'll need someone to protect you on that ridiculous planet, and you can't expect much from these two." He glared contemptuously at Gregor and Arnold.

"Maybe you didn't understand me," Myra said very quietly. "You are not coming, Ross."

Jameson's firm face sagged, and his eyes grew worried. "Myra," he said, "please let me come. If anything happened to you, I'd—I don't know what I'd do. Please, Myra?"

There was no doubting the sincerity in his voice. When Jameson dropped his commanding voice and lowered the imposing thrust of his shoulders, he became a very appealing young man, quite obviously in love.

Myra said softly, "All right, Ross. And—thanks."

Gregor cleared his throat loudly. "We blast off in two hours."

"Fine," Jameson said, taking Myra's arm. "We have time for a drink, dear."

Arnold said, "Pardon me, Mr. Jameson. How does it happen you are wearing gray and purple—the Skag Colors?"

"Are they?" Jameson asked. "Pure coincidence. I've owned this tie for years."

"And who is the hermit?"

"I thought you geniuses knew everything," Jameson said with a nasty grin. "See you at the ship."

After they had gone, a deep, gloomy silence hung over the office. Finally Arnold said, "So she's engaged."

"So it would seem," Gregor said. "But not married," he added sympathetically.

"No, she's not married," Arnold said, becoming cheerful again. "And Jameson is obviously the wrong man for her. I'm sure Myra wouldn't marry a liar."

"Of course she wouldn't marry a— Huh?"

"Didn't you notice? That purple tie he's 'owned for years' was brand new. I think we'll keep an eye on Mr. Jameson."

Gregor gazed at his partner with admiration. "That's a very clever observation."

"The process of detection," Arnold said sententiously, "is merely the accumulation of minute discrepancies and infinitesimal inconsistencies, which are immediately apparent to the trained eye."

Gregor and the trained eye put the office into order. At eleven o'clock they met Jameson and Myra at the ship, and without further incident they departed for Coelle.

III

Ross Jameson was president and chief engineer of Jameson Electronics, a small but growing concern he had inherited from his father. It was a great responsibility for so young a man, and Ross had adopted a brusque, overbearing manner to avoid any hint of indecisiveness. But whenever he was able to forget his exalted position he was a pleasant enough fellow, and a good sport in facing the many little discomforts of interstellar travel.

Myra's Hemstet 4 was old and hogged out of shape by repeated high-gravity takeoffs. The ship had developed a disconcerting habit of springing leaks in the most inaccessible places, which Arnold and Gregor had to locate and patch. The ship's astrogation system wasn't to be trusted, either, and Jameson spent considerable time figuring out a way of controlling the automatics manually.

When Coelle's little sun was finally in sight and the ship was in its deceleration orbit, the four of them were able, for the first time, to share a meal together.

"What's the story on this hermit?" Gregor asked over coffee.

"You must have heard of him," Jameson said. "He calls himself Edward the Hermit, and he's written a book."

"The book is *Dreams on Kerma*," Myra filled in. "It was a bestseller last year."

"Oh, *that* hermit," Gregor said, and Arnold nodded.

They had read the hermit's book, along with several thousand others, while sitting in their office waiting for business. *Dreams on Kerma* had been a sort of spatial Robinson Crusoe. Edward's struggles with his environment, and with himself, had made exciting reading. Because of his lack of scientific knowledge, the hermit had made many blunders. But he had persevered, and created a home for himself out of the virgin wilderness of the planet Kerma.

The young misanthrope's calm decision to give up the society of mankind and devote his life to the contemplation of nature and the universe—the Eternals, as he called them—had struck some responsive chord in millions of harried men and women. A few had been sufficiently inspired to seek out their own hermitages.

Almost without exception they returned to Terra in six months or a year, sadder but wiser. Solitude, they discovered, made better reading than living.

"But what has he got to do with Coelle?" Arnold asked.

"Coelle is the second planet of the Gelsors system," Jameson said. "Kerma is the third planet, and the hermit is its only inhabitant."

Gregor said, "I still don't see—"

"I guess it was my fault," Myra said. "You see, the hermit's book inspired me. It was what decided me to live on Coelle, even if I had to do it alone." She threw Jameson a cutting glance. "Do you remember his chapter on the joy of possessing an entire planet? I can't describe what that did to me. I felt—"

"I still don't see the connection," Gregor said.

"I'm coming around to it," Myra said. "When I found out that Edward the Hermit and I were neighbors, astronomically speaking, I decided to speak to him. I just wanted to tell him how much his book meant to me. So I radioed him from Coelle."

"He has a radio?" Arnold asked.

"Of course," Myra said. "He keeps it so he can listen to the absurd voices of mankind, and laugh himself to sleep."

"Oh. Go on."

"Well, when he heard I was going to live on Coelle, he became furious. Said he couldn't stand having a human so close."

"That's ridiculous," Arnold said. "The planets are millions of miles apart."

"I told him that. But he started shouting and screaming at me. He said mankind wouldn't leave him alone. Real-estate brokers were trying to talk him into selling his mineral rights, and a travel agency was going to route its ships within ten thousand miles of the upper atmosphere of his planet. And then, to top it all, I come along and move in practically on his doorstep."

"And then he threatened her," Jameson said.

"I guess it was a threat," Myra said. "He told me to get out of the Gelsors system, or he wouldn't be responsible for what happened."

"Did he say *what* would happen?" Arnold asked.

"No. He just hinted it would be pretty extreme."

Jameson said, "I think it's apparent that the man's unbalanced.

After the talk, these so-called Skag incidents began. There must be a connection."

"It's possible," Arnold said judiciously.

"I just can't believe it," Myra said, gazing pensively out a port. "His book was so beautiful. And his picture on the book jacket—he looked so soulful."

"Hah!" Jameson said. "Anyone who'd live alone on an empty planet *must* be off his rocker."

Myra gave him a venomous look. And then the radar alarm went off. They were about to land on Coelle . . .

The Skag Castle dominated Coelle. Built of an almost indestructible gray stone, the castle sprawled across the curved land like a prehistoric monster crouched over Lilliput. Its towers and battlements soared past the narrow limits of the planet's atmosphere, and the uppermost spires were lost in haze. As they approached, the black slit windows seemed to stare menacingly at them.

"Cozy little place," Gregor commented.

"Isn't it wonderful?" Myra said. "Come on. I'll show you around."

The three men looked at the castle, then at each other.

"Just the ground floor," Arnold begged.

Myra wanted to show them *everything*. It wasn't every girl who became the owner of an alien birthplace, period house, and haunted castle, all rolled into one. But she settled for a few of the main attractions: the library—containing ten thousand Skag scrolls that no one could read—the Worship Chamber of Ieele, and the Grand Torture Room.

Dinner was prepared by the auto-cook Uncle Jim had thoughtfully installed, and later they had brandy on the terrace, under the stars. Myra gave them all bedrooms on the second floor, to avoid as much climbing as possible. They retired, planning to begin the investigation early in the morning.

The partners shared a bedroom the size of a small soccer field, with bronze death masks of Scarb princes leering from the wall. Arnold kicked off his shoes, flopped into bed, and was asleep immediately.

Gregor paced around for a few minutes, smoked a last cigarette, snapped off the light, and climbed into his bed. He was on the verge of sleep, when suddenly he sat upright. He thought he had heard a dull rumbling noise, like the sound of a giant walking underneath the castle. Nerves, he told himself.

Then the rumbling came again, the floor shook, and the death masks clattered angrily against the wall.

In another moment the noise had subsided.

"Did you hear it?" Gregor whispered.

"Of course I heard it," Arnold said crossly. "It almost shook me out of bed."

"What do you think?"

"It could be a form of poltergeist," Arnold answered, "although I doubt it. We'll explore the cellar tomorrow."

"I don't think this place has any cellar," Gregor said.

"It hasn't? Good! That would clinch it."

"What? What are you talking about?"

"I'll have to accumulate a bit more data before I can make a positive statement," Arnold said smugly.

"Have you any idea what you're talking about? Or are you just making it up as you go along? Because if—"

"Look!"

Gregor turned and saw a gray and purple light in one corner of the room. It pulsed weirdly, throwing fantastic shadows across the bronze death masks. Slowly it approached them. As it drew nearer they could make out the reptilian outlines of a Skag, and through him they could see the walls of the room.

Gregor fumbled under his pillow, found the needler, and fired. The charge went *through* the Skag, and pocked a neat three-inch groove in the stone wall.

The Skag stood before them, its cloak swirling, an expression of extreme disapproval on its face. And then, without a sound, it was gone.

As soon as he could move, Gregor snapped on the light. Arnold was smiling faintly, staring at the place where the Skag had been.

"Very interesting," Arnold said. "Very interesting indeed."

"What is?"

"Do you remember how Myra described the Undead Scarb?"

"Sure. She said it was nine feet tall, had little wings, and—oh, I think I see."

"Precisely," Arnold said. "This Skag or Scarb was no more than four feet in height, without wings."

"I suppose there could be two types," Gregor said dubiously. "But what bearing does this have on the underground noises? The whole thing is getting ridiculously complicated. Surely you must realize that."

"Complication is frequently a key to solution," Arnold said. "Simplicity alone is baffling. Complexity, on the other hand, implies the presence of a self-contradictory logic structure. Once the incomprehensibles are reconciled and the extraneous factors canceled, the murderer stands revealed in the glaring light of rational inevitability."

"What are you talking about?" Gregor shouted. "There wasn't any murder here!"

"I was quoting from Lesson Three in the Hepburn School for Scientific Detection Correspondence Course. And I know there was no murder. I was just speaking in general."

"But what do you think is going on?" Gregor asked.

"Something funny is going on," Arnold said. He smiled knowingly, turned over, and went to sleep.

Gregor snapped out the light. Arnold's course, he remembered, had cost ten dollars plus a coupon from *Horror Crime Magazine*. His partner had certainly received his money's worth.

There were no further incidents that night.

IV

Bright and early in the morning, the partners were awakened by Myra pounding on their door.

"A spaceship is landing!" she called.

Hurriedly they dressed and came down, meeting Jameson on the stairs. Outside they saw that a small spacer had just put down, and its occupant was climbing out.

"More trouble," Jameson growled.

The new arrival hardly looked like trouble. He was middle-aged, short, and partially bald. He was dressed in a severely conservative business suit, and he carried a briefcase. His features were quiet and reserved.

"Permit me to introduce myself," he said. "I am Frank Olson, a representative of Transstellar Mining. My company is contemplating an expansion into this territory, to take advantage of the new Terra-to-Propexis space lane. I am doing the initial survey. We need planets upon which we can obtain mineral rights."

Myra shook her head. "Not interested. But why don't you try Kerma?" she asked with a sly smile.

"I just came from Kerma," Olson said. "I had what I considered a very attractive proposition for this Edward the Hermit fellow."

"I'll bet he booted you out on your ear," Gregor said.

"No. As a matter of fact, he wasn't there."

"Wasn't there?" Myra gasped. "Are you sure?"

"Reasonably so," Olson said. "His camp was deserted."

"Perhaps he went on a hike," Arnold said. "After all, he has an entire planet to wander over."

"I hardly think so. His big ship was gone, and a spaceship is hardly a suitable vehicle for wandering around a planet."

"Very clever deduction," Arnold said enviously.

"Not that it matters," Olson said. "I thought I'd ask him, just for the record." He turned to Myra. "You are the owner of this planet?"

"I am."

"Perhaps you would be interested in hearing our terms?"

"No!" Myra said.

"Wait," Jameson said. "You should at least hear him."

"I'm not interested," Myra said. "I'm not going to have anyone digging up *my* little planet."

"I don't even know if your planet has anything worth digging for," Olson said. "My company is simply trying to find out which planets are available."

"They'll never get this one," Myra said.

"Well, it isn't too important," Olson said. "There are many

planets. Too many," he added with a sigh. "I won't disturb you people any longer. Thank you for your time."

He turned, his shoulders slumping, and trudged back to his ship.

"Won't you stay for dinner?" Myra called impulsively. "You must get pretty tired of eating canned food in that spaceship."

"I do," Olson said with a rueful smile. "But I really can't stay. I hate to make a blastoff after dark."

"Then stay until morning," Myra said. "We'd be glad to put you up."

"I wouldn't want to be any trouble—"

"I've got about two hundred rooms in there," Myra said, pointing at the Skag Castle. "I'm sure we can squeeze you in somewhere."

"You're very kind," Olson said. "I—I believe I will!"

"Hope you aren't nervous about Undead Scarbs," Jameson said.

"What?"

"This planet seems to be haunted," Arnold told him. "By the ghost or ghosts of an extinct reptilian race."

"Oh, come now," Olson said. "You're pulling my leg. Aren't you?"

"Not at all," Gregor said.

Olson grinned to show that no one was taking *him* in. "I believe I'll tidy up," he said.

"Dinner's at six," Myra said.

"I'll be there. And thank you again." He returned to his ship.

"Now what?" Jameson asked.

"Now we are going to do some searching," Arnold said. He turned to Gregor. "Bring the portable detector. And we'll need a few shovels."

"What are we looking for?" Jameson asked.

"You'll see when we find it," Arnold said. He smiled insidiously and added, "I thought *you* knew everything."

Coelle was a very small planet, and in five hours Arnold found what he was looking for. In a little valley there was a long mound. Near it, the detector buzzed gaily.

"We will dig here," Arnold said.

"I bet I know what it is," Myra told them. "It's a burial mound, isn't it? And when you've uncovered it, we'll find row upon row of Undead Scarbs, their hands crossed upon their chests, waiting for the full moon. And we'll put stakes through their hearts, won't we?"

Gregor's shovel clanged against something metallic.

"Is that the tomb?" Myra asked.

But when they had thrown aside more dirt, they saw that it was not a tomb. It was the top of a spaceship.

"What's *that* doing here?" Jameson asked.

"Isn't it apparent?" Arnold said. "The hermit is not on his own planet. We know his feelings about Coelle. Naturally he would be here."

"And naturally he wouldn't leave his spaceship in plain sight!" Gregor said.

"So he's here," Jameson said slowly. "But where? Where on the planet?"

"Almost undoubtedly he's somewhere in the Skag Castle," Arnold said.

Jameson turned in triumph to Myra. "You see? I told you it was that crazy hermit! Now we have to catch him."

"I don't think that will be necessary," Arnold said.

"Why not?"

"At the proper time, Edward the Hermit will appear," Arnold said coolly. And they couldn't get another word out of him.

That evening the auto-cook surpassed itself. Frank Olson was a little stiff at first; but he unbent over the brandy, and regaled them with stories of the planets he had touched upon in his search for mining properties. Jameson wanted to search the castle and drag the hermit out of his hiding place. Sullenly, he yielded when Arnold pointed out the impossibility of four people covering several hundred rooms and passageways.

Later they played bridge. Arnold's mind was elsewhere, however, and after he'd trumped his partner's perfectly good trick a second time, they all decided to call it a night.

V

An hour later, Mike Arnold whispered across the bedroom, "Are you asleep?"

"No," Gregor whispered back.

"Get dressed, then, but leave your shoes off."

"What's up?"

"I think we are going to solve the mystery of Skag Castle tonight. Mind if I borrow your needler?"

Gregor gave it to him. They tiptoed out of the bedroom and down the great central staircase. They found a vantage point behind an enameled suit of Skag armor, from which they could watch without being seen. For half an hour there was silence.

Then they saw a shape at the top of the landing. Soundlessly it crept down the staircase and glided across the hall.

"Who is it?" Gregor whispered.

"Shh!" Arnold whispered back.

They followed the shape into the library. There it hesitated, as though uncertain what to do next.

At that moment the underground rumblings began, shattering the silence. The shape jerked abruptly, startled. A light appeared in its hand. By its feeble glow, the partners recognized Frank Olson.

With his tiny flashlight, Olson searched one library wall. Finally he pressed a panel. It slid back, revealing a small switchboard. Olson turned two dials. The underground noises stopped at once.

Wiping his forehead, Olson listened for several moments. Then he snapped off his light and crept noiselessly back to the hall, up the stairs, and into his bedroom.

Arnold pulled Gregor back behind the enameled armor.

"That ties it," Gregor said. "There's our Undead Scarb."

Arnold shook his head.

"Of course he is," Gregor said. "He must have planned this in order to frighten Myra off the planet. Then he could buy the mineral rights for next to nothing."

"Seems reasonable, doesn't it?" Arnold said. "But you've got a lot to learn about detection. In cases of this sort, what's reasonable is never right. The apparent solution is always wrong. Invariably!"

"Why look for complications that aren't there?" Gregor asked.

"We *saw* Olson go to that hidden switchboard. We *heard* the noises stop as soon as he touched the controls. Or was that pure coincidence?"

"No, there's a relationship."

"Hmm. Maybe Olson isn't a mining representative at all. Do you think someone hired him? Edward the Hermit, maybe? As a matter of fact, perhaps he *is* Edward the Hermit!"

"Shh," Arnold whispered. "Look!"

Gregor's eyes had become accustomed to the darkness. This time he recognized the man at once. It was Jameson, tiptoeing down the stairs.

Jameson walked to one side of the hall and turned on a small flashlight. By its light he found a panel in the wall, and pressed it. The panel slid back, revealing a small switchboard. Jameson breathed heavily and reached for the dials. Before he could touch them he heard a noise, and stepped quickly back.

A figure stepped out of the darkness. It was about six feet in height, and its face was hideous and reptilian. A long, spiked tail dragged behind it, and its fingers were webbed.

"I am the Undead Scarb!" it said to Jameson.

"Awk!" Jameson said, backing away.

"You must leave this planet," the Scarb said. "You must leave at once—or your life is forfeit!"

"Sure," Jameson said hastily. "Sure I will. Just stay away. We'll leave, Myra and I—"

"Not Miss Ryan. The Earthwoman has shown a reverent understanding for the Old Lore, and for the spirit of Skag. But you, Ross Jameson, have profaned the Sacred Burrow."

The Scarb moved closer, its webbed fingers splayed. Jameson backed into a wall, and suddenly pulled a blaster.

At that moment Arnold snapped on the lights. He shouted, "Don't shoot, Ross. You'd be arrested for murder." He turned to Gregor. "Now let's get a close look at this Scarb."

The Undead Scarb put one hand on top of his scaled head and pulled. The terrible head peeled off, revealing beneath it the youthful features of Edward the Hermit.

In a short time everyone was assembled in the great hall. Olson looked sleepy and disgruntled. He was fully dressed, as was

Jameson. Myra was wearing a plaid wool bathrobe, and she was staring with interest at Edward the Hermit.

Edward looked younger than the picture on the jacket of his book. He had peeled off the rest of his Scarb disguise, and was wearing patched jeans and a gray sweatshirt. He was deeply tanned, his blond hair was cropped short, and he would have been good-looking if it weren't for the expression of fear and apprehension on his face.

After Arnold had summed up the events of the night, Myra was completely bewildered.

"It just doesn't make sense," she said. "Mr. Olson was turning Skag noises on and off, Ross had a switchboard, and Edward the Hermit was disguised as a Scarb. What's the explanation? Were they *all* trying to drive me from Coelle?"

"No," Arnold said. "Mr. Olson's part in this was purely accidental. Those underground noises weren't designed to frighten you. Were they, Mr. Olson?"

Olson smiled ruefully. "They certainly were not. As a matter of fact, I came here to stop them."

"I don't understand," Myra said.

"I'm afraid," Arnold said, "that Mr. Olson's company has been engaged in a bit of illegal mining." He smiled modestly. "Of course I recognized the characteristic sound of a Gens-Wilhem automatic oreblaster at once."

"I *told* them to install mufflers," Olson said. "Well, the full explanation is this. Coelle was surveyed seventeen years ago, and an excellent deposit of sligastrium was found. Transstellar Mining offered the then owner, James McKinney, a very good price for mineral rights. He refused, but after a short stay he left Coelle for good. A company official decided to extract a little ore anyhow, since this planet was so far out, and there were no local observers. You'd be surprised how common a practice that is."

"I think it's despicable," Myra said.

"Don't blame me," Olson said. "I didn't set up the operation."

"Then those underground noises—" Gregor said.

"Were merely the sounds of mining apparatus," Olson told them. "You caught us by surprise, Miss Ryan. We never really expected the planet to be inhabited again. I was sent, posthaste, to turn off the machines. Just half an hour ago I had my first opportunity."

"What if I hadn't asked you to stay overnight?" Myra asked.

"I would have faked a blown gasket or something." He sighed and sat down. "It was a pretty good operation while it lasted."

"That takes care of the noises," Jameson said. "The rest we know. This hermit came here, hid his spaceship, and disguised himself as a Scarb. He had already threatened Myra. Now he was going to frighten her into leaving Coelle."

"That's not true!" Edward shouted. "I—I was—"

"Was what?" Gregor asked.

The hermit clamped his mouth shut and turned away.

Arnold said, "*You* found that secret panel, Ross."

"Of course I did. You're not the only one who can detect. I knew there were no such things as Undead Scarbs and Skag ghosts. From what Myra told me, the whole thing sounded like an illusion to me, probably a modulated wave-pattern effect. So I looked around for a control board. I found it this afternoon."

"Why didn't you tell us?" Gregor asked.

"Because I consider you a pair of incompetents," Ross said contemptuously. "I came down this evening to catch the culprit in the act. And I did, too. I believe there are prison sentences for this sort of thing."

Everyone looked at Edward. The hermit's face had gone pale under its tan, but still he didn't speak.

Arnold walked to the control board and looked at the dials and switches. He pushed a button, and the great nine-foot figure of the Scarb appeared. Myra recognized it and gave a little gasp. Even now it was frightening. Arnold turned it off and faced Jameson.

"You were pretty careless," Arnold said quietly. "You really shouldn't have used company equipment for this. Every item here is stamped Jameson Electronics."

"That doesn't prove a thing," Jameson said. "Anyone can buy that equipment."

"Yes. But not everyone can use it." He turned to the hermit. "Edward, are you an engineer, by any chance?"

"Of course not," Edward said sullenly.

"We have no proof of that," Jameson said. "Just because he says he isn't—"

"We have proof," Gregor burst in. "The hermit's book! When his electric blanket broke down, he didn't know how to fix it. And remember Chapter Six? It took him over a week to find out how to change a fuse in his auto-cook!"

Arnold said relentlessly, "The equipment's got your company's name on it, Ross. And I'll bet we find you've been absent from your office for considerable periods. The local spaceport will have any record of your taking out an interstellar ship. Or did you manage to hide all that?"

By Ross's face they could tell he hadn't. Myra said, "Oh, Ross."

"I did it for you, Myra," Jameson said. "I love you, but I couldn't live out here! I've got a company to think about, people depend on me . . ."

"So you tried to scare me off Coelle," Myra said.

"Doesn't that show how much I care for you?"

"That kind of caring I can live without," Myra said.

"But, Myra—"

"And that brings us to Edward the Hermit," Arnold said.

The hermit looked up quickly. "Let's just forget about me," he said. "I admit I was trying to scare Miss Ryan off her planet. It was stupid of me. I'll never bother her again in any way. Of course," he said, looking at Myra, "if you want to press charges—"

"Oh, no."

"I apologize again. I'll be going." The hermit stood up and started toward the door.

"Wait a minute," Arnold said. The expression on his face was painful. He hesitated, sighed fatalistically, and said, "Are you going to tell her, or shall I?"

"I don't know what you're talking about," Edward said. "I must leave now—"

"Not yet. Myra's entitled to the whole truth," Arnold said. "You're in love with her, aren't you?"

Myra stared at the hermit. Edward's shoulders drooped hopelessly.

"What is all this?" she asked. Edward looked angrily at Arnold.

"I suppose you won't be satisfied until I've made an utter fool of myself. All right, here goes." He faced Myra. "When you radioed me and said you were going to live on Coelle, I was horrified. Everything started to go to pieces for me."

"But I was millions of miles away," Myra said.

"Yes. That was the trouble. You were so near—astronomically —and yet so far. You see, I was deathly sick of the whole hermit thing. I could stand it as long as no one was around, but once you came—"

"If you were tired of being a hermit," Myra said, "why didn't you leave?"

"My agent told me it would be literary suicide," the hermit said with a sickly attempt at a cynical grin. "You see, I'm a writer. This whole thing was a publicity stunt. I was to hermit a planet and write a book. Which I did. The book was a best-seller. My agent talked me into doing a second book. I couldn't leave until it was done. That would have ruined everything. But I was starving for a human face. And then you came."

"And you threatened me," Myra said.

"Not really. I said I wouldn't be responsible for the consequences. I was really referring to my sanity. For days after that I thought about you. Suddenly I realized I had to see you. Absolutely had to! So I came here, hid the ship—"

"And walked around dressed as a Scarb," Jameson sneered.

"Not at first," Edward said. "After I saw you, I guess—well, I guess I fell in love with you. I knew then that if you stayed on Coelle—practically next door, astronomically—I could find the strength to stay on Kerma and finish my book. But I saw that this Jameson fellow was trying to scare you off. So I decided to scare *him* off."

"Well," Myra said, "I'm glad we finally have met. I enjoyed your book so much."

"Did you?" Edward said, his face brightening.

"Yes. It inspired me to live on Coelle. But I'm sorry to hear it was all a fraud."

"It wasn't!" Edward cried. "The hermit thing was my agent's idea, but the book was perfectly genuine, and I did have all those experiences, and I *did* feel those things. I like being away from civilization, and I especially like having my own planet. The only thing wrong . . ."

"Yes?"

"Well, Kerma would be perfect if only I had one other person with me. Someone who understands, who feels as I do."

"I know just how you feel," Myra said.

They looked at each other. When Jameson saw that look, he moaned and put his head in his hands.

"Come on, friend," Olson said, dropping a sympathetic hand on Jameson's shoulder. "You're trumped. I'll give you a lift back to Earth."

Ross nodded vaguely, and started to the door with Olson. Olson said, "Say, I imagine you folks will be needing only one planet before long, huh?"

Myra blushed crimson. Edward looked embarrassed, then said in a firm voice, "Myra and I are going to get married. That is, if you'll have me, Myra. Will you marry me, Myra?"

She said yes in a very small voice.

"That's what I thought," Olson said. "So you won't be needing two planets. Would one of you care to lease your mineral rights? It'd be a nice little income, you know. Help to set up housekeeping."

Ross Jameson groaned and hurried out the door.

"Well," Edward said to Myra, "it isn't a bad idea. We'll be living on Kerma, so you might as well—"

"Just a minute," Myra said. "We are going to live on Coelle and no other place."

"No!" Edward said. "After all the work I've put into Kerma, I will not abandon it."

"Coelle has a better climate."

"Kerma has a lighter gravity."

Olson said, "When you get it figured out, you'll give Transstellar Mining first chance, won't you? For old times' sake?"

They both nodded. Olson shook hands with them and left.

Arnold said, "I believe that solves the mysteries of the Skag Castle. We'll be going now, Myra. We'll return your ship on drone circuit."

"I don't know how to thank you," Myra said.

"Perhaps you'll come to our wedding," Edward said.

"We'd be delighted."

"It'll be on Coelle, of course," Myra said.

"Kerma!"

When the partners left, the young couple were glaring angrily at each other.

VI

When they were at last in space, Terra-bound, Gregor said, "That was a very handsome job of detection."

"It was nothing," Arnold said modestly. "You would have figured it out yourself in a few months."

"Thanks. And it was very nice of you, speaking up for Edward the way you did."

"Well, Myra was a bit strong-minded for me," Arnold said. "And a trifle provincial. I am, after all, a creature of the great cities."

"It was still an extremely decent thing to do."

Arnold shrugged.

"The trouble is, how will Myra and Edward solve this planet problem? Neither seems the type to give in."

"Oh, that's as good as solved," Gregor said offhandedly.

"What do you mean?"

"Why, it's obvious," Gregor said. "And it fills the one gaping hole in your otherwise logical reconstruction of events."

"What hole? What is it?"

"Oh, come now," Gregor said, enjoying his opportunity to the utmost. "It's apparent."

"I don't see it. Tell me."

"I'm sure you'll figure it out in a few months. Think I'll take a nap."

"Don't be that way," Arnold pleaded. "What is it?"

"All right. How tall was Jameson's electronic Scarb, the one that frightened Myra?"

"About nine feet."

"And how tall was Edward, disguised as a Scarb?"

"About six feet tall."

"And the Scarb we saw in our bedroom, the one we shot at—"

"Good Lord!" Arnold gasped. "That Scarb was only four feet tall. *We have one Scarb left over!*"

"Exactly. One Scarb that no one produced artificially, and that we can't account for—unless Coelle actually *is* haunted."

"I see what you mean," Arnold said thoughtfully. "They'll have to move to Kerma. But we didn't really fulfill our contract."

"We did enough," Gregor said. "We decontaminated three distinct species of Skag—produced by Jameson, Olson, and Edward. If they want a fourth species taken care of, that'll be a separate contract."

"You're right," Arnold said. "It's about time we became businesslike. And it's for their own good. Something has to make up their minds for them." He thought for a moment. "I suppose they'll leave Coelle to Transstellar Mining. Should we tell Olson that the planet is really haunted?"

"Certainly not," Gregor said. "He'd just laugh at us. Have you ever heard of ghosts frightening an automatic mining machine?"

THE HELPING HAND

Travis had been fired from his job that morning. Boring and low-paying though it had been, it had given him something to live for. Now he had nothing at all, and in his hand he held the means of cutting short a futile and humiliating existence. The bottle contained pellis annabula, a quick, sure, and painless poison. He had stolen it from his former employer, Carlyle Industrial Chemicals. PA was a catalyst used to fix hydrocarbons. Travis was going to fix himself with it, once and for all.

His few remaining friends thought Travis was a neurotic attention-seeker because of his previous suicide attempts. Well, he would show them this time, and they'd be sorry. Perhaps even his wife would shed a tear or two.

The thought of his wife steeled Travis's resolution. Leota's love had changed into an indifferent tolerance, and finally into hate—the sharp, domineering, acidic sort against which he was helpless. And the damnable thing was that he still loved her.

Do it now, he thought. He closed his eyes and raised the bottle.

Before he could drink, the bottle was knocked out of his hand. He heard Leota's sharp voice: "What do you think you're doing?"

"It should be obvious," Travis said.

She studied his face with interest. Leota was a large, hard-faced woman with a gift for never-ending beastliness. But now her face had softened.

"You were really going to do it this time, weren't you?"

330

"I'm still going to," Travis said. "Tomorrow or next week will do as well."

"I never believed you had it in you," she said. "Some of our friends thought you had guts, but I never did. Well, I guess I've really put you through hell all these years. But *someone* had to run things."

"You stopped caring for me a long time ago," Travis said. "Why did you stop me now?"

Leota didn't answer immediately. Could she be having a change of heart? Travis had never seen her like this before.

"I've misjudged you," she said at last. "I always figured you were bluffing, just to annoy me. Remember when you threatened to jump from the window? You leaned out—like this."

Leota leaned from the window, her body poised over the street twenty stories below. "Don't do that!" Travis said sharply.

She moved back in, smiling. "That's funny, coming from you. Don't tell me you still care?"

"I could," Travis said. "I know I could—if only you and I—"

"Perhaps," Leota said, and Travis felt a flash of hope, though he barely dared acknowledge it. Women were so strange! There she was, smiling. She put her hands firmly on his shoulders, saying, "I *couldn't* let you kill yourself. You have no idea how strongly I feel about you."

Travis found it impossible to answer. He was moved. His wife's strong, caring hands on his shoulders had moved him inexpressibly—straight through the open window.

As his fingers missed the sill and he fell toward the street, Travis heard his wife calling, "I feel enough, darling, to want this done *my* way."

THE LAST DAYS OF (PARALLEL?) EARTH

When the end of the world was announced, Rachel and I decided not to break up after all. "What would be the sense?" she asked me. "We will have no time to form other relationships." I nodded, but I was not convinced. I was worried about what would happen if the world did not end, if the great event were delayed, postponed, held over indefinitely. There might have been a miscalculation concerning the effect of the Z-field, the scientists might have been wrong about the meaning of the Saperstein Conjunction, and there we would be, Rachel and I, with our eternal complaints, and our children with their eternal complaints, bound together by apocalyptic conjunction stronger than our marriage vows, for eternity or until Armageddon, whichever came first. I put this to Rachel in what I hoped was a nice way, and she said to me, "Don't worry, if the world does not end on schedule as predicted by eminent scientists, you will return to your dismal furnished apartment and I will stay here with the children and my lover."

That was reassuring, and of course, I didn't want to spend the end of the world by myself in the dismal furnished apartment I shared with the Japanese girl and her English boyfriend and no television. There would be nothing to do there but listen to the Japanese girl talk to her friends on the telephone and eat in the Chinese restaurant, which had promised to stay open throughout the end of the world or as long as physically possible, since the owner did not believe in making changes hastily.

Rachel said, "I don't want to face anything like this straight," so she brought out her entire stash, the Thai sticks, the speckled brown cocaine, the acid in the form of tiny red stars, the gnarled mushrooms from God knows where, the red Lebanese and the green Moroccan, yes, and the last few treasured Quaaludes, and a few Mogadon for good measure. She said, "Let's pool our mind-blowing resources and go out before we come down."

Other people had made their own preparations. The airlines were running end-of-the-world specials to Ultima Thule, Valparaiso, Kuala Lumpur: kinky trips for demising people. The networks were making a lot of the event, of course. Some of our favorite programs were cut, replaced by End of the World Specials. We tuned into "The Last Talkathon" on CBS: "Well, it sure looks like the kite is going up at last. I have a guest here, Professor Mandrax from UCLA, who is going to explain to us just how the big snuff is going to come about."

Whatever channel you turned to, there were physicists, mathematicians, biologists, chemists, linguistic philosophers, and commentators to try to explain what they were explaining. Professor Johnson, the eminent cosmologist, said, "Well, of course, it's not exactly a cosmological event, except metaphorically, in its effect upon us. We humans, in our parochial way, consider these things to be very important. But I can assure you that in the scale of magnitude I work on, this event is of no significance, is banal, in fact; our little O-type sun entering the Z-field just at the time of the Saperstein Conjunction, with the ensuing disarrangement of local conditions. I am imprecise on purpose, of course, since Indeterminacy renders exactitude a nineteenth-century hangup. But Professor Weaver of the Philosophy Department might have more to say about that."

"Well, yes," Professor Weaver said, "'end of the world' is a somewhat loose expression. What we are faced with is a viewpoint problem. We could say that, from some other point of observation, if such exists, this ending is the end of nothing at all. Just one moment of pain, my dear, and then eternal life, to quote the poet."

On another channel we heard that the army was issuing turkey dinners to all our servicemen in Germany. There had been some talk of flying them home, but we decided to keep them in position in case it was not the end of the world after all, but instead some devious communistic scheme of the sort we know the Russians are capable of, with their twisted sense of humor and their implacable will to give everyone a hard time. And we heard that the Chinese hadn't even announced the fact, or so-called fact, to their population at large, except obliquely, in the form of posters no larger than postage stamps, signed by "A Concerned Neighbor from Neighborhood C."

And Rachel couldn't understand why Edward, her lover, insisted upon staying in his room and working on his novel. "It's not apropos any longer," she told him. "There's not going to be anyone around to publish it or read it."

"What has that got to do with it?" Edward asked, and winked at me.

I understood perfectly, was in fact working like a berserker to finish my own account of the last day, yes, and with great pleasure, for the end of the world presents a writer with the greatest deadline of them all, the ultimate deadline: twelve o'clock midnight tonight and that's all she wrote, folks. What a challenge! I knew that artists all over the world were responding to it, that an end-of-the-world *oeuvre* was being created that might be of interest to historians in a world parallel to our own in which this catastrophe did not take place.

"Well, yes," Professor Carpenter said, "the concept of parallel universes is, I would say, licit but unprovable, at least in the time we have left. I myself would consider it a wish-fulfillment fantasy, though my good friend Professor Mung, the eminent psychologist, is more competent to speak of that than I."

Rachel made her famous turkey dinner that night, with the stuffing and the cranberry sauce and the sweet-potato pie with meringue topping, and she even made her special Chinese spareribs as an extra treat, even though the Chinese refused to believe in the event except in postage-stamp-size posters of oriental foreboding. And everyone in the world began smoking cigarettes again, except for the irreducible few who did not believe in the end of the world and were therefore still scared of lung cancer. And people on their deathbeds struggled to stay alive a little longer, just a little longer, so that when I go, the whole damn thing goes. And some doctors stayed on call, declaring it their ludicrous duty, while others compulsively played golf and tennis and tried to forget about improving their strokes.

The turkey with four drumsticks and eight wings. Lewd displays on television: since all is over, all is allowed. The compulsive answering of business letters: Dear Joe, take your contract and stick it up your giggie the show is over and I can finally tell you what a crap artist you are, but if there is any mistake about the End I want you to know that this letter is meant as a joke which I'm sure that you as the very special person you are can appreciate.

All of us were caught between the irreconcilable demands of abandonment and caution. What if we are not to die? Even belief in the end of the world required an act of faith on the part of dishwashers as well as university professors.

And that last night of creation I gave up cigarettes forever. An absurdity. What difference did it make? I did it because Rachel had always told me that absurdities made a difference, and I had always known that, so I threw away my pack of Marlboros and listened while Professor Mung said, "Wish fulfillment, or its obverse, death-wish fulfillment, cannot licitly be generalized into an objective correlative, to use Eliot's term. But if we take Jung into our synthesis, and consider this ending as an archetype, not to say Weltanschauung, our understanding increases as our *tiempo para gastarlo* disappears into the black hole of the past which contains all our hopes and endeavors."

The final hour came at last. I carved the turkey and Edward came out of his room long enough to take a plateful of breast and ask for my comments on his final rewrite of his last chapter, and I said, "It still needs work," and Rachel said, "That's cruel," and Edward said, "Yes, I thought it needed something myself," and went back to his room. Outside, the streets were deserted except for the unfortunate few who couldn't get to a television set, and we did up most of the remaining drugs and switched wildly between channels. I had brought my typewriter into the kitchen and I was getting it all down, and Rachel talked of the holidays we should have taken, and I thought about the women I should have loved, and at five to twelve Edward came out of his room again and showed me the rewritten last chapter, and I said, "You've got it this time," and he said, "I thought so, is there any more coke left?" And we did up the rest of the drugs and Rachel said to me, "For Chrissakes, can't you stop typing?" And I said, "I have to get it all down," and she hugged me, and Edward hugged me, and the three of us hugged the children, whom we had allowed to stay up late because it was the end of the world, and I said, "Rachel, I'm sorry about everything," and she said, "I'm sorry too," and Edward said, "I don't think I did anything wrong, but I'm sorry too." "Sorry about what?" the children asked, but before we had a chance to tell them, before we could even decide what we were sorry about . . .

THE FUTURE LOST

Leonard Nisher was found in front of the Plaza Hotel in a state of agitation so extreme that it took the efforts of three policemen and a passing tourist from Biloxi, Mississippi, to subdue him. Taken to St. Clare's Hospital, he had to be put into a wet pack—a wet sheet wound around the patient's arms and upper body. This immobilized him long enough for an intern to get a shot of Valium into him.

The injection had taken effect by the time Dr. Miles saw him. Miles told two husky aides, one of them a former guard for the Detroit Lions, and a psychiatric nurse named Norma to wait outside. The patient wasn't going to assault anyone just now. He was throttled way back, riding the crest of a Valium wave where there's nothing to hassle and even a wet pack can have its friendly aspects.

"Well, Mr. Nisher, how do you feel now?" Miles asked.

"I'm fine, doc," Nisher said. "Sorry I caused that trouble when I came out of the space-time anomaly and landed in front of the Plaza."

"It could affect anyone that way," Miles said reassuringly.

"I guess it sounds pretty crazy," Nisher said. "There's no way I can prove it, but I have just been into the future and back again."

"Is the future nice?" Miles asked.

"The future," Nisher said, "is a pussycat. And what happened to me there—well, you're not going to believe it."

The patient, a medium-sized white male of about thirty-five, wearing an off-white wet pack and a broad smile, proceeded to tell the following story.

Yesterday he had left his job at Hanratty & Smirch, Accountants, at the usual time and gone to his apartment on East Twenty-fifth Street. He was just putting the key in the lock when he heard something behind him. Nisher immediately thought *mugger*, and whirled around in the cockroach posture that was the basic defense mode in the Taiwanese karate he was studying. There was no one there. Instead there was a sort of red, shimmering mist. It floated toward Nisher and surrounded him. Nisher heard weird noises and saw flashing lights before he blacked out.

When he regained consciousness, someone was saying to him, "Don't worry, it's all right." Nisher opened his eyes and saw that he was no longer on Twenty-fifth street. He was sitting on a bench in a beautiful little park with trees and ponds and promenades and strangely shaped statues and tame deer, and there were people strolling around, wearing what looked like Grecian tunics. Sitting beside him on the bench was a kindly, white-haired old man dressed like Charlton Heston playing Moses.

"What is this?" Nisher asked. "What's happened?"

"Tell me," the old man said, "did you happen to run into a reddish cloud recently? Aha! I thought so! That was a local space-time anomaly, and it has carried you away from your own time and into the future."

"The future?" Nisher said. "The future what?"

"Just the future," the old man said. "We're about four hundred years ahead of you, give or take a few years."

"You're putting me on," Nisher said. He asked the old man in various ways where he *really* was, and the old man replied that he really was in the future, and it was not only true, it wasn't even unusual, though of course it wasn't the sort of thing that happens every day. At last Nisher had to accept it.

"Well, okay," he said. "What sort of future is this?"

"A very nice one," the old man assured him.

"No alien creatures have taken us over?"

"Certainly not."

"Has lack of fossil fuels reduced our standard of living to a bare subsistence level?"

"We solved the energy crisis a few hundred years ago when we discovered an inexpensive way of converting sand into shale."

"What are your major problems?"

"We don't seem to have any."

"So this is Utopia?"

The old man smiled. "You must judge for yourself. Perhaps you would like to look around during your brief stay here."

"Why brief?"

"These space-time anomalies are self-regulating," the old man said. "The universe won't tolerate for long your being *here* when you ought to be *there*. But it usually takes a little while for the universe to catch up. Shall we go for a stroll? My name is Ogun."

They left the park and walked down a pleasant, tree-lined boulevard. The buildings were strange to Nisher's eye and seemed to contain too many strange angles and discordant colors. They were set back from the street and bordered with well-kept green lawns. It looked to Nisher like a really nice future. Nothing exotic, but nice. And there were people walking around in their Grecian tunics, and they all looked happy and well fed. It was like a Sunday in Central Park.

Then Nisher noticed one couple who had gone beyond the talking stage. They had taken their clothes off. They were, to use a twentieth-century expression, making it.

No one seemed to think this was unusual. Ogun didn't comment on it; so Nisher didn't say anything, either. But he couldn't help noticing, as they walked along, that other people were making it, too. Quite a few people. After passing the seventh couple so engaged, Nisher asked Ogun whether this was some sexual holiday or whether they had stumbled onto a fornicators' convention.

"It's nothing special," Ogun said.

"But why don't these people do it in their homes or in hotel rooms?"

"Probably because most of them happened to meet here in the street."

That shook Nisher. "Do you mean that these couples never knew each other before?"

"Apparently not," Ogun said. "If they had, I suppose they would have arranged for a more comfortable place in which to make love."

Nisher just stood there and stared. He knew it was rude, but he couldn't help it. Nobody seemed to mind. He observed how people looked at each other as they walked along, and every once in a while somebody would smile at someone, and someone else would smile back, and they would sort of hesitate for a moment, and then . . .

Nisher tried to ask about twenty questions at the same time. Ogun interrupted. "Let me try to explain, since you have so little time among us. You come from an age of sexual repression and rebelliousness. To you this must appear a spectacle of unbridled license. For us it is no more than a normal expression of affection and solidarity."

"So you've solved the problem of sex!" Nisher said.

"More or less by accident," Ogun told him. "We were really trying to abolish war before it obliterated us. But to get rid of war, we had to change the psychological base upon which it rests. Repressed sexuality was found to be the greatest single factor. Once this was recognized and the information widely disseminated, a universal plebiscite was held. It was agreed that human sexual mores were to be modified and reprogrammed for the good of the entire human race. Biological engineering and special clinics—all on a voluntary basis, of course—took care of that. Divorced from aggression and possessiveness, sex today is a mixture of aesthetics and sociability."

Nisher was about to ask Ogun how that affected marriage and the family when he noticed that Ogun was smiling at an attractive blonde and edging over in her direction. "Hey, Ogun!" Nisher said, "Don't leave me now!"

The old man looked surprised. "My dear fellow, I wasn't going to exclude you. Quite the contrary, I want to *include* you. We all do."

Nisher saw that a lot of people had stopped. They were looking at him, smiling.

"Now wait just a minute," he said, automatically taking up the cockroach posture.

But by then a woman had hold of his leg, and another was snuggling up under his armpit, and somebody else was pinching his fingers. Nisher got a little hysterical and shouted at Ogun, "Why are they doing this?"

"It is a spontaneous demonstration of our great pleasure at the novelty and poignancy of your presence. It happens whenever a man from the past appears among us. We feel so sorry for him and what he has to go back to, we want to share with him, share all the love we have. And so this happens."

Nisher felt as though he were in the middle of a Cinemascope mob scene set in ancient Rome, or maybe Babylon. The street was crowded with people as far as the eye could see, and they were all making it with one another and on top of one another and around and under and over and in between. But what really got to Nisher was the feeling that the crowd gave off. It went completely beyond sex. It felt like a pure ocean of love, compassion, and understanding. He saw Ogun's face receding in a wave of bodies and called out, "How far does this thing go?"

"Visitors from the past always send out big vibrations," Ogun shouted back. "This will probably go all the way."

All the way? Nisher couldn't figure out what he was talking about. Then he got it and said, almost reverently, "Do you mean—planet-wide?"

Ogun grinned, and then he was gone. Nisher saw the way it had to be—this group of people loving one another and pulling more and more people into it as the vibes got stronger and stronger until everybody in the world was in on it. To Nisher this was definitely Utopia. He knew he had to figure out some way of bringing this message back to his own time, some way to convince people. Then he looked up and saw that he was on Central Park South, in front of the Plaza.

"I suppose the transition was just too much for you?" Miles asked.

Nisher smiled. His eyelids were drooping. The Valium rush was passing, and he was coming down fast.

"I guess I just freaked out," Nisher said. "I thought I could explain it to everyone. I thought I could just grab people and make them give up their hangups, that I could show them how their bodies were shaped for love. But I went at it too hysterically, of course; I scared them. And then the cops grabbed me."

"How do you feel now?" Miles asked.

"I'm tired and disappointed, and I've come back to my senses, if that's what you want to call it. Maybe it was all an hallucination. That doesn't matter. What counts is that I'm back and in my own day and age, when we still have wars and energy crises and sexual hangups, and nothing I can do will change that."

"You seem to have made a very rapid adjustment," Miles said.

"Hell, yes. No one ever accused Leonard Nisher of being a slow adjuster."

"You sound good to me," Miles said. "But I would like you to stay here for a few days. This is not a punishment, you understand. It is genuinely meant as an assistance to you."

"Okay, doc," Nisher said drowsily. "How long must I stay?"

"Perhaps no more than a day or two. I'll release you as soon as I'm satisfied with your condition."

"Fair enough," Nisher mumbled. And then he fell asleep. Miles told the orderlies to stand by, and alerted the psychiatric nurse. Then he went to his nearby apartment to get some rest.

Nisher's story haunted Miles as he broiled a steak for his dinner. It couldn't be true, of course. But suppose, just suppose, it had actually happened. What if the future had achieved a state of polymorphous-perverse sexuality? There was, after all, a fair amount of evidence that space-time anomalies did exist.

Abruptly he decided to visit his patient again. He left his apartment and went back to the hospital, hurrying now, impelled by a strange sense of urgency.

There was no one at the reception desk on Wing Two. The policeman normally stationed in the corridor was missing. Miles ran down the hall. Leonard's door was open, and Miles peered in.

Someone had folded Leonard's cot and leaned it against the wall. That left just enough room on the floor for two aides (one a former guard for the Detroit Lions), a psychiatric nurse named Norma, two student nurses, a policeman, and a middle-aged woman from Denver who had been visiting a relative.

"Where is Leonard?" cried Miles.

"That guy musta hypnotized me," the policeman said, struggling into his trousers.

"He preached a message of love," said the woman from Denver, wrapping herself in Leonard's wet pack.

"Where is he?" Miles shouted.

White curtains flapped at the open window. Miles stared out into the darkness. Nisher had escaped. His mind inflamed by his brief vision of the future, he was sure to be preaching his message of love up and down the country. *He could be anywhere,* Miles thought. *How on earth can I find him? How can I join him?*

WILD TALENTS, INC.

Glancing at his watch, Waverley saw that he still had ten minutes before the reporters were due. "Now then," he said in his best interviewing voice, "what can I do for you, sir?"

The man on the other side of the desk looked startled for a moment, as though unaccustomed to being addressed as *sir.* Then he grinned, suddenly and startlingly.

"This is the place, isn't it?" he asked. "The place of refuge?"

Waverley looked intently at the thin, bright-eyed man. "This is Wild Talents, Incorporated," he said. "We're interested in any supernormal powers."

"I knew that," the man said, nodding vigorously. "That's why I escaped. I know you'll save me from them." He glanced fearfully over his shoulder.

"We'll see," Waverley said diplomatically, settling back in his chair. His young organization seemed to hold an irresistible fascination for the lunatic fringe. As soon as he had announced his interest in psi functions and the like, an unending stream of psychotics and quacks had beaten a path to his door.

But Waverley didn't bar even the obvious ones. Ridiculously enough, you sometimes found a genuine psi among the riffraff, a diamond in the rubbish. So—

"What do you do, Mr.—"

"Eskin, Sidney Eskin," the man said. "I'm a scientist, sir." He drew his ragged jacket together, assuming an absurd dignity. "I observe people, I watch them, and note down what they are doing, all in strict accordance with the best scientific methods and procedure."

"I see," Waverley said. "You say you escaped?"

"From the Blackstone Sanitarium, sir. Frightened by my investigations, secret enemies had me locked up. But I escaped, and have come to you for aid and sanctuary."

Tentatively, Waverley classified the man as paranoidal. He wondered whether Eskin would become violent if he tried to call Blackstone.

"You say you observe people," Waverley said mildly. "That doesn't sound supernormal—"

"Let me show you," the man said, with a sudden show of panic. He stared intently at Waverley. "Your secretary is in the reception room, seated at her desk. She is, at the moment, powdering her nose. She is doing it very delicately, applying the strokes with a circular motion. Now she is reaching forward, the powder box in her hand—ah! She has inadvertently spilled it against the typewriter. She says 'Damn!' under her breath. Now she—"

"Hold it," Waverley said. He hurried over and opened the door to the reception room.

Doris Fleet, his secretary, was mopping up spilled powder. Some of it had dusted her black hair a creamy white, giving her the appearance of a kitten that had rolled in flour.

"I'm sorry, Sam," she said.

"On the contrary," Waverley said, "I'm grateful." He didn't bother to explain, but closed the door and hurried back to Eskin.

"You will protect me?" Eskin asked, leaning over the desk. "You won't let them take me back?"

"Can you observe like that all the time?" Waverley asked.

"Of course!"

"Then don't worry about a thing," Waverley said calmly, but with a pulse of excitement rising within him. Lunatic or not, Eskin wasn't going to waste his talents in any sanitarium. Not if Waverley had anything to do about it.

The intercom on his desk buzzed. He flipped the switch, and Doris Fleet said, "The reporters are here, Mr. Waverley."

"Hold them a moment," Waverley said, smiling to himself at her "official" tone of voice. He ushered Eskin to a little room adjoining his office. "Stay here," he told him. "Don't make any noise, and don't worry."

He closed the door, locked it, and told Doris to let the reporters in.

There were seven of them, pads out, and Waverley thought he could detect a certain grudging respect in their faces. Wild Talents, Inc., wasn't back-page filler anymore. Not since Billy Walker, Waverley's star psi, had aided the flight of the *Venture* to Mars with a terrific telekinetic boost. Since then, Wild Talents had been front-page news.

Waverley had played it for all it was worth, holding back until he felt the maximum point of interest had been reached.

This was the point. Waverley waited until they were all quiet.

"Wild Talents, Incorporated, gentlemen," he told them, "is an attempt to find the occasional person among the general population who has what we call psi powers."

"What is a psi power?" a lanky reporter asked.

"It is difficult to define," Waverley said, smiling with what he hoped was perfect candor. "Let me put it to you this way—"

"*Sam!*" He heard Doris Fleet's voice in his head as clearly as though she were standing beside him. Although she might not be the best of secretaries, Doris *was* a telepath. Her ability worked only about twenty percent of the time, but that twenty percent sometimes came in useful.

"Sam, two of the men in your office. They're not reporters."

"What are they?" he thought back.

"I don't know," Doris told him. "But I think they might mean trouble."

"Can you get a line on what sort of trouble?"

"No. They're the ones in the dark suits. They're thinking—" Her thought died out.

Telepathy is lightning-fast. The entire exchange had taken perhaps a second. Waverley spotted the two men, sitting a little apart from the rest, and taking no notes. He went on.

"A psi, gentlemen, is a person with some form of mental control or development, the true nature of which we can only guess at. Today, most psis are to be found in circuses and sideshows. They lead, for the most part, unhappy, neurotic lives. My organization is trying to find the work that their special talents equip them for. Next we hope to discover why and how it works, and what makes it so erratic. We want—"

He continued, laying it on thick. Public acceptance was a big factor in his work, a factor he had to have on his side. The public, stimulated by atomic power and enormously excited by the recent flights to the moon and Mars, was prepared to accept the idea of psi, if it could be made sufficiently understandable for them.

So he painted the picture in rosy colors, skipping over most of the stumbling blocks. He showed the psi, capable of dealing with his environment on a direct mental level; the psi, not a deviation or freak, but mankind fully realized.

He almost had tears in his eyes by the time he was through.

"To sum up," he told them, "our hope is that, someday, everyone will be capable of psi powers."

After a barrage of questions, the conference broke up. The two men in dark suits remained.

"Was there some further information you wanted?" Waverley asked politely. "I have some brochures—"

"Have you got a man named Eskin here?" one of the men asked.

"Why?" Waverley countered.

"Have you?"

"Why?"

"All right, we'll play it that way," one of the men sighed. They showed their credentials. "Eskin was confined in Blackstone Sanitarium. We have reason to believe he came here, and we want him back."

"What's wrong with him?" Waverley asked.

"Have you seen him?"

"Gentlemen, we're getting nowhere. Suppose I had seen him—and mind you, I'm not admitting it—suppose I had a means of rehabilitating him, making a decent, worthy citizen out of him. Would you still insist on having him back?"

"You can't rehabilitate Eskin," one of the men told him. "He's found a perfectly satisfactory adjustment. Unfortunately, it's one that the public cannot countenance."

"What is it?" Waverley asked.

"Have you seen him?"

"No, but if I do, I'll get in touch with you," Waverley said pleasantly.

"Mr. Waverley. This attitude—"

"Is he dangerous?" Waverley asked.

"Not especially. But—"

"Has he any supernormal powers?"

"Probably," one of the men said unhappily. "But his method of using them—"

"Can't say I've ever seen the chap," Waverley said coolly.

The men glanced at each other. "All right," one of them said. "If you'll admit to having him, we'll sign him over to your custody."

"Now you're talking," Waverley said. The release was quickly signed, and Waverley ushered the two men out. As they reached the door, Waverley saw what he thought was a wink pass between them. He must have imagined it, he decided.

"Was I right?" Doris asked him.

"Perfectly," Waverley said. "You've still got powder in your hair."

Doris located a mirror in her cavernous shoulder bag, and started dusting.

"Forget it," Waverley said, leaning over and kissing the tip of her nose. "Marry me tomorrow."

Doris considered for a moment. "Hairdresser tomorrow."

"Day after, then."

"I'm swimming the English Channel that day. Would next week be all right—"

Waverley kissed her. "Next week is not only all right, it's obligatory," he said. "And I'm not fooling."

"All right," Doris said, a little breathlessly. "But is this *really* it, Sam?"

"It is," Waverley said. Their wedding date had been postponed twice already. The first time, the problem of Billy Walker had come up. Walker hadn't wanted to go on the *Venture* to Mars, and Waverley had stayed with him day and night, bolstering his courage.

The next time had been when Waverley found a wealthy backer for Wild Talents, Inc. It was 'round-the-clock work at first, organizing, contacting companies that might be able to use a psi, finding psis. But this time.

He bent over her again, but Doris said, "How about that man in your office?"

"Oh yes," Waverley said with mild regret. "I think he's genuine. I'd better see what he's doing." He walked through his office to the anteroom.

The psi had found pencil and paper, and was busy scribbling. He looked up when Waverley and Doris walked in, and gave them a wild, triumphant grin.

"Ah, my protector! Sir, I will demonstrate my scientific observations. Here is a complete account of all that transpired between A, you, and B, Miss Fleet." He handed them a stack of papers.

Eskin had written a complete account of Waverley's conversation with Doris, plus a faithful anatomical description of their kisses. He appended the physical data with a careful description of the emotions of both, before, during, and after each kiss.

Doris frowned. She had a love of personal privacy, and being observed by this ragged little man didn't please her.

"Very interesting," Waverley said, suppressing a smile for Doris's sake. The man needed some guidance, he decided. But that could wait for tomorrow.

After finding Eskin a place to sleep, Waverley and Doris had dinner and discussed their marriage plans. Then they went to Doris's apartment, where they disregarded television until one o'clock in the morning.

Next morning the first applicant was a sprucely dressed man in his middle thirties, who introduced himself as a lightning calculator. Waverley located a book of logarithms and put the man through his paces.

He was very good. Waverley took his name and address and promised to get in touch with him.

He was a little disappointed. Lightning calculators possessed the least wild of the wild talents. It was difficult to place them in really good jobs unless they had creative mathematical ability to go with their computing skill.

The morning shipment of magazines and newspapers arrived, and Waverley had a few minutes to browse through them. He subscribed to practically everything in hopes of finding little-known jobs that his psis might fill.

An elderly man with the purple-veined face of an alcoholic came in next. He was wearing a good suit, but with ragged, torn cuffs. His new shirt was impossibly filthy. His shoes, for some reason, were shined.

"I can turn water into wine," the man said.

"Go right ahead," Waverley told him. He went to the cooler and handed the man a cup of water.

The man looked at it, mumbled a few words, and, with his free hand, made a pass at the water. He registered astonishment when nothing happened. He looked sternly at the water, muttered his formula again, and again made a pass. Still nothing happened.

"You know how it is," he said to Waverley. "We psis, our power just goes off and on. I'm usually good about forty percent of the time."

"This is just an off day?" Waverley asked, with dangerous calm.

"That's right," the man said. "Look, if you could stake me for a few days, I'd get it again. I'm too sober now, but you should see me when I'm really—"

"You read about this in the papers, didn't you?" Waverley asked.

"What? No, certainly not!"

"Get out of here," Waverley said. It was amazing how many frauds his business attracted. People who thought he was dealing in some sort of pseudo-magic, people who thought he would be an easy mark for a sad story.

The next applicant was a short, stocky girl of eighteen or nineteen, plainly and unattractively dressed in a cheap print dress. She was obviously ill at ease.

Waverley pulled up a chair for her and gave her a cigarette, which she puffed nervously.

"My name's Emma Cranick," she told him, rubbing one perspiring hand against her thigh. "I—are you sure you won't laugh at me?"

"Sure. Go on," Waverley said, sorting a batch of papers on his desk. He knew the girl would feel better if he didn't look at her.

"Well, I—this sounds ridiculous, but I can start fires. Just by wanting to. *I can!*" She glared at him defiantly.

A poltergeist, Waverley thought. Stone-throwing and fire-starting. She was the first one he had seen, although he had long been aware of the phenomenon. It seemed to center mostly in adolescent girls, for some unknown reason.

"Would you care to show me, Emma?" Waverley asked softly. The girl obliged by burning a hole in Waverley's new rug. He poured a few cups of water over it, then had her burn a curtain as a check.

"That's fine," he told the girl, and watched her face brighten. She had been thrown off her uncle's farm. She was "queer" if she started fires that way, and her uncle had no place for anyone who was "queer."

She was rooming at the YWCA, and Waverley promised to get in touch with her.

"Don't forget," he said as she started out. "Yours is a valuable talent—a very valuable one. Don't be frightened of it."

This time her smile almost made her pretty.

A poltergeist, he thought, after she had gone. Now what in hell could he do with a poltergeist girl? Starting fires . . . A stoker, perhaps? No, that didn't seem reasonable.

The trouble was, the wild talents were rarely reasonable. He had fibbed a bit to the reporters about that, but psis just weren't tailor-made for the present world.

He started leafing through a magazine, wondering who could use a poltergeist.

"Sam!" Doris Fleet was standing in the door, her hands on her hips. "Look at this."

He walked over. Eskin had arrived, and was standing beside the reception desk, a foolish smile on his face. Doris handed Waverley a sheaf of papers.

Waverley read through them. They contained a complete account of everything he and Doris had done, from the moment he had walked into her apartment until he had left.

But *complete* wasn't the word. The psi had explored their every move and action. And, as if that weren't bad enough, Waverley saw now why Eskin had been locked up.

The man was a voyeur, a Peeping Tom. A supernormal Peeping Tom, who could watch people from miles away.

Like most couples on the verge of marriage, Waverley and Doris did considerable smooching, and didn't consider themselves any the worse for it. But it was something else again to see that smooching written down, dissected, analyzed.

The psi had picked up a complete anatomical vocabulary somewhere, because he had described every step of their court-ship procedure in the correct terms. Diagrams followed, then a physiological analysis. Then the psi had probed deeper, into hormone secretions, cellular structures, nerve and muscle reactions, and the like.

It was the most amazing bit of pornography-veiled-as-science that Waverley had ever seen.

"Come in here," Waverley said. He brought Eskin into his office. Doris followed, her face a study in embarrassment.

"Now then. Just what do you mean by this?" Waverley asked. "Didn't I save you from the asylum?"

"Yes, sir," Eskin said. "And believe me, I'm very grateful."

"Then I want your promise that there'll be no more of this."

"Oh, no?" the man said, horrified. "I can't stop. I have my research to consider."

In the next half hour Waverley discovered a lot of things. Eskin could observe all those he came in contact with, no matter where they were. However, all he was interested in was their sex lives. He rationalized this voyeurism by his certainty that he was serving science.

Waverley sent him to the anteroom, locked the door, and turned to Doris.

"I'm terribly sorry about this," he said, "but I'm sure we can resublimate him. It shouldn't be too difficult."

"Oh, it shouldn't?" Doris asked.

"No." Waverley said with confidence he didn't feel. "I'll figure it out."

"Fine," Doris said. She put the psi's papers in an ashtray, found a match, and burned them. "Until you do, I think we had better postpone the wedding."

"But why?"

"Oh, Sam," Doris said, "how can I marry you and know that slimy little *thing* is watching every move we make? And writing it all down?"

"Now calm down," Waverley said uncomfortably. "You're perfectly right. I'll go to work on him. Perhaps you'd better take the rest of the day off."

"I'm going to," Doris said, and started for the door.

"Supper this evening?" Waverley asked her.

"No," she said firmly. "I'm sorry, Sam, but one thing'll lead to another, and not while that Peeping Tom is loose." She slammed the door shut.

Waverley unlocked the anteroom door.

"Come in here, Sidney," he said. "You and I are going to have a fine long talk."

Waverley tried to explain, slowly and patiently, that what Eskin did wasn't truly scientific. He tried to show that it was a sexual deviation or overintensification, rationalized as a scientific motive.

"But, Mr. Waverley," Eskin said, "if I was just peeking at people, that would be one thing. But I write it all down, I use the correct terms; I classify and define. I hope to write a definitive work on the sexual habits of every human being in the world."

Waverley explained that people have a right to personal privacy. Eskin replied that science came above petty squeamishness. Waverley tried to batter at his fortifications for the rest of the day. But Eskin had an answer for everything, an answer that fit completely into his view of himself and the world.

"The trouble is," he told Waverley, "people aren't scientific. Not even scientists. Would you believe it, in the sanitarium the doctors kept me locked in solitary most of the time. Just because I observed and wrote down their sexual habits at home? Of course, being in solitary couldn't stop me."

Waverley wondered how Eskin had lived as long as he had. It would have been small wonder if an irate doctor slipped him an overdose of something. It probably required strong self-discipline not to.

"I didn't think that *you* were against me," the psi said sorrowfully. "I didn't realize that you were so old-fashioned."

"I'm not against you," Waverley said, trying to think of some way of dealing with the man. Then, in a sudden happy burst of inspiration, he had it.

"Sidney," he said, "I think I know of a job for you. A nice job, one you'll like."

"Really?" the voyeur said, his face lighting up.

"I think so," Waverley said. He checked the idea in a recent magazine, located a telephone number, and dialed.

"Hello? Is this the Bellen Foundation?" He introduced himself, making sure they knew who he was. "I hear that you gentlemen are engaged in a new survey on the sexual habits of males of Eastern Patagonian descent. Would you be interested in an interviewer who can *really* get the facts?"

After a few more minutes of conversation, Waverley hung up and wrote out the address. "Go right over, Sid," he said. "I think we have found your niche in life."

"Thank you very much," the psychotic said, and hurried out.

The next morning Waverley's first appointment was with Bill Symes, one of Waverley's brightest hopes, Symes had a fine psi talent in a clear, intelligent mind.

This morning he looked confused and unhappy.

"I wanted to speak to you first, Sam," Symes said. "I'm leaving my job."

"Why?" Waverley wanted to know. He had thought that Symes was as well placed and happy as a psi could be.

"Well—I just don't fit in."

Symes was able to "feel" stresses and strains in metal. Like most psis, he didn't know how he did it. Nevertheless, Symes was able to "sense" microshrinkage and porosity faster, and more accurately than an X-ray machine, and with none of the problems of interpretation that an X-ray inspection leaves.

Symes's talent was on an all-or-nothing basis; either he could do it or he couldn't. Therefore he didn't make mistakes. Even though his talent completely shut off forty percent of the time, he was still a valuable asset in the aircraft-engine industry, where every part must be X-rayed for possible flaws.

"What do you mean, you do not fit in?" Waverley asked. "Don't you think you're worth the money you're getting?"

"It's not that," Symes said. "It's the guys I work with. They think I'm a freak."

"You knew that when you started," Waverley reminded him.

Symes shrugged. "All right, Sam. Let me put it this way." He lighted a cigarette. "What in hell am I? What are any of us psis? We can do something, but we don't know how we do it. We have no control over it, no insight into it. Either it's there or it isn't. We're not supermen, but we're also not normal human beings. We're—I don't know what we are."

"Bill," Waverley said softly. "It's not the other men worrying you. It's you. *You* are starting to think you're a freak."

"Neither fish nor fowl," Symes quoted, "nor good red meat. I'm going to take up dirt farming, Sam."

Waverley shook his head. Psis were easily discouraged from trying to get their talents out of the parlor-trick stage. The commercial world was built—theoretically—along the lines of one-hundred percent function. A machine that didn't work all the time was considered useless. A carry-over of that attitude was present in the psis, who considered their talents a mechanical extension of themselves, instead of an integral part. They felt inferior if they couldn't produce with machinelike regularity.

Waverley didn't know what to do. Psis would have to find themselves, true. But not by retreating to the farms.

"Look, Sam," Symes said. "I know how much psi means to you. But I've got a right to some normality also. I'm sorry."

"All right, Bill," Waverley said, realizing that any more arguments would just antagonize Symes. Besides, he knew that psis were hams, too. They liked to do their tricks. Perhaps a dose of dirt-farming would send Bill back to his real work.

"Keep in touch with me, will you?"

"Sure. So long, Sam."

Waverley frowned, chewed his lip for a few moments, then went in to see Doris.

"Marriage date back on?" he asked her.

"How about Eskin?"

He told her about Eskin's new job, and the date was set for the following week. That evening they had supper together in a cozy little restaurant. Later they returned to Doris's apartment to resume their practice of ignoring television.

The next morning, while leafing through his magazines, Waverley had a sudden idea. He called Emma Cranick at once and told her to come over.

"How do you feel about traveling?" he asked the girl. "Do you enjoy seeing new places?"

"Oh, I do," Emma said. "This is the first time I've been off my uncle's farm."

"Do you mind hardships? Bitter cold?"

"I'm never cold," she told him. "I can warm myself, just like I can start fires."

"Fine," Waverley said. "It's just possible . . ."

He got on the telephone. In fifteen minutes he had made an appointment for the poltergeist girl.

"Emma," he said, "have you ever heard of the Harkins expedition?"

"No," she said. "Why?"

"Well, they're going to the Antarctic. One of the problems of an expedition of that sort is heat for emergencies. Do you understand?"

The girl broke into a smile. "I think I do."

"You'll have to go down and convince them," Waverley said. "No, wait! I'll go down with you. You should be worth your weight in gold to an expedition like that."

It wasn't too difficult. Several women scientists were going on the expedition, and after seven or eight demonstrations, they agreed that Emma would be an asset. Strong and healthy, she could easily pull her own weight. Self-warmed, she would be able to function in any weather. And her fire-making abilities . . .

Waverley returned to his office at a leisurely pace, a self-satisfied smile on his lips. Girls like Emma would be useful on Mars someday, when a colony was established there. Heat would be difficult to conserve in Mars's thin air. She was a logical choice for a colonist.

Things like that reaffirmed his faith in the future of psi. There was a place for *all* psi talents. It was just a question of finding the right job, or creating one.

Back in the office, a surprise was waiting for him. Eskin, the voyeur, was back. And Doris Fleet had a wrathful look in her eyes.

"What's wrong, Sid?" Waverley asked. "Back to pay us a visit?"

"Back for good," Eskin said unhappily. "They fired me, Mr. Waverley."

"Why?"

"They're not real scientists," Eskin said sadly. "I showed them my results on their test cases, and they were shocked. Can you imagine it, Mr. Waverley? Scientists—shocked!"

Waverley suppressed a grin. He had always had a feeling that surveys of that sort uncovered about a sixteenth of the truth.

"Besides, they couldn't keep their scientific detachment. I ran a series of studies on the scientists' home lives for a control factor. And they threw me out!"

"That's a pity," Waverley said, avoiding Doris Fleet's look.

"I tried to point out that there was nothing wrong in it," Eskin said. "I showed them the series I've been running on you and Miss Fleet—"

"What?" Doris yelped, standing up so suddenly she knocked over her chair.

"Certainly. I keep my reports on all subjects," the psi said. "One must run follow-up tests."

"That does it," Doris said. "I never heard such a—Sam! Throw him out!"

"What good will that do?" Waverley asked. "He'll just go on observing us."

Doris stood for a moment, her lips pressed into a thin line. "I won't stand for it!" she said suddenly. "I just won't!" She picked up her handbag and started toward the door.

"Where are you going?" Waverley asked.

"To enter a nunnery!" Doris shouted, and disappeared through the door.

"She wasn't the girl for you, anyhow," the psi said. "Extremely prudish. I've been observing your sexual needs pretty closely, and you—"

"Shut up," Waverley said. "Let me think." No answer sprang into his mind. No matter what job he found for Eskin, the man would still go on with his observations. And Doris wouldn't marry Waverley.

"Go into the other room," Waverley said. "I need time to think."

"Shall I leave my report here?" The psi said, showing him a stack of papers two inches thick.

"Yeah, just drop it on the desk." The psi went into the anteroom, and Waverley sat down to think.

Over the next few days, Waverley gave every available minute to the voyeur's problem. Doris didn't come back to work the next morning, or the morning after that. Waverley called her apartment, but no one answered.

The poltergeist girl left with the Antarctic expedition, and was given a big fanfare by the press.

Two telekinetic psis were found in East Africa and sent to Wild Talents.

Waverley thought and thought.

A man dropped into the office with a trained-dog act, and was very indignant when he heard that Wild Talents was not a theatrical agency. He left in a huff.

Waverley went on thinking.

Howard Aircraft called him. Since Bill Symes had left, Inspection had become the plant's worst bottleneck. Production had been geared to the psi's methods. When he was doing well, Symes could glance at a piece of metal and jot down his analysis. The part didn't even have to be moved.

Under the older method of X-ray inspection, the parts had to be shipped to Inspection, lined up, put under the machine, and the plates developed. Then a radiologist had to read the film, and a superior had to pass on it.

They wanted Symes back.

The psi returned. He had had his fill of farming in a surprisingly short time. Besides, he knew now that he was needed. And that made all the difference.

Waverley sat at his desk, reading over the voyeur's reports, trying to find some clue he might have missed.

The man certainly had an amazing talent. He analyzed right down to the hormones and microscopic lesions. Now how in hell could he do that? Waverley asked himself. Microscopic vision? Why not?

Waverley considered sending Eskin back to Blackstone. After all, the man was doing more harm than good. Under psychiatric care, he might lose his compulsion—and his talent, perhaps.

But was Eskin insane? Or was he a genius with an ability far beyond the present age?

With a nervous shudder, Waverley imagined a line in some future history book: *"Because of Dr. Waverley's stupidity and rigidity in dealing with the genius Eskin, psi research was held up for—"*Oh no! He couldn't chance that sort of thing. But there had to be a way.

A man who could—of course!

"Come in here, Eskin," Waverley said to the potential genius.

"Yes, sir," the psi said, and sat down in front of Waverley's desk.

"Sid," Waverley said, "how would you like to do a sexual report that would really aid science? One that would open a field never before explored?"

"What do you mean?" the psi asked dubiously.

"Look, Sid. Straight sexual surveys are old stuff. Everybody does them. Maybe not as well as you, but they still do them. How would you like it if I could introduce you to an almost unexplored field of science? A field that would really test your abilities to the utmost?"

"I'd like that," the psi said. "But it would have to do with sex."

"Of course," Waverley said. "But you don't care what aspect of sex, do you?"

"I don't know," Eskin said.

"If you could do this—and I don't know that you can—your name would go down in history. You'd be able to publish your papers in the best scientific journals. No one would bother you, and you could get all the help you want."

"It sounds wonderful. What is it?"

Waverley told him, and watched Eskin closely. The psi considered. Then he said, "I think I could do that, Mr. Waverley. It wouldn't be easy, but if you really think that science—"

"I know so," Waverley said, in a tone of profoundest conviction. "You'll need some texts, to get some background on the field. I'll help you select them."

"I'll start right now!" the psi said, and closed his eyes for greater concentration.

"Wait a minute," Waverley said. "Are you able to observe Miss Fleet now?"

"I can if I want to," the psi said. "But I think this is more important."

"It is," Waverley told him. "I was just curious as to whether you could tell me where she is."

The psi thought for a moment.

"She isn't doing anything sexual," he said. "She's in a room, but I don't know where the room is. Now let me concentrate."

"Sure. Go ahead."

Eskin closed his eyes again. "Yes, I can see them! Give me pencil and paper!"

Waverley left him as Eskin began his preliminary investigations.

Now where had that girl gone? Waverley telephoned her apartment again, to see if she had come back. But there was no answer. One by one, he called all her friends. They hadn't seen her.

Where? Where in the world?

Waverley closed his eyes and thought: *Doris? Can you hear me, Doris?*

There was no reply. He concentrated harder. He was no telepath, but Doris was. If she was thinking of him . . .

Doris!

Sam!

No message was necessary, because he knew she was coming back.

"Where did you go?" he asked, holding her tightly.

"To a hotel," she said. "I just waited there and tried to read your mind."

"Could you?"

"No," she said. "Not until the last, when you were trying too."

"Just as well," Waverley said. "I'd never have any secrets from you. If you ever try anything like that again, I'll send the goblins out looking for you."

"I wouldn't want that," she said, looking at him seriously. "I guess I'd better not leave again. But, Sam—how about—"

"Come on in and look."

"All right."

In the other room, Eskin was writing on a piece of paper. He hesitated, then started scribbling again. Then he drew a tentative diagram, looked at it and crossed it out, and started another.

"What is he doing?" Doris asked. "What's that supposed to be a picture of?"

"I don't know," Waverley said. "I haven't studied their names. It's some sort of germ."

"Sam, what's happened?"

"Resublimation," Waverley said. "I explained to him that there were other forms of sex he could observe, that would benefit mankind and science far more, and win him endless prestige. So he's looking for the sex-cycle of bacteria."

"Without a microscope?"

"That's right. With his drive, he'll devour everything ever written about bacterial life. He'll find something valuable, too."

"Resublimation," Doris mused. "But *do* germs have a sex life?"

"I don't know," Waverley said. "But Eskin will find out. And there's no reason why he can't do some perfectly good research in the bargain. After all, the line between many scientists and Peeping Toms is pretty fine. Sex was really secondary to Eskin after he had sublimated it into scientific observation. This is just one more step in the same direction. "Now would you care to discuss dates and places?"

"Yes—if you're sure it's permanent."

"Look at him." The psi was scribbling furiously, oblivious to the outside world. On his face was an exalted, dedicated look.

"I guess so." Doris smiled and moved closer to Waverley. Then she looked at the closed door. "There's someone in the waiting room, Sam."

Waverley kept back a curse. Telepathy could be damnably inconvenient at times. But business was business. He accompanied Doris to the door.

A young girl was sitting on a chair. She was thin, delicate, frightened-looking. Waverley could tell, by the redness of her eyes, that she had been crying recently.

"Mr. Waverley? You're the Wild Talents man?"

Waverley nodded.

"You have to help me. I'm a clairvoyant, Mr. Waverley. A real one. And you have to help me get rid of it. You must!"

"We'll see," Waverley said, a pulse of excitement beating in his throat. A clairvoyant!

"Suppose you come in here and tell me all about it."

THE SWAMP

Ed Scott took one look at the boy's terrified white face and knew something serious was wrong. "What is it, Tommy?" he asked.

"It's Paul Barlow," the boy said. "We were all playing in the east swamp—and—and—and he's sinking, sir!"

Scott knew he had no time to waste. Just last year, two men had been lost in the treacherous patches of the east swamp. The area was fenced now, and children had been warned. But they played there anyhow. Scott took a long coil of rope from his garage and set off at a run.

In ten minutes he was deep within the swamp. He saw six boys standing on a grassy fringe of firm land. Twenty feet beyond them, in the middle of a smooth, yellowish gray expanse, was Paul Barlow. The boy was waist-deep in the gluey quicksand, and sinking. His arms flailed, and the quicksand crept toward his chest. It looked as though the boy had tried to cross this patch on a dare. Ed Scott uncoiled his rope and wondered what made kids act with such blind, murderous stupidity.

He threw the rope, and the children watched breathlessly as it soared accurately into Paul's hands. But the child—with quicksand up to the middle of his chest—didn't have the strength to hold on.

With only seconds left, Scott tied an end of the rope to a stump, took a firm grip, and waded out after the screaming boy. The sand trembled and gave under his feet. Scott wondered if he'd have the strength to haul himself and the boy out. But the first problem was to reach Paul in time.

Scott came to within five feet of the boy, who was buried now to the neck. Keeping a firm grip on the rope, Scott waded forward another foot, sank to his waist, gritted his teeth, and reached for the boy—and felt the rope go slack! He twisted, trying to keep himself up as the swamp sucked him down—covering his chest and neck, filling his screaming mouth, and at last concealing the top of his head . . .

On the wooded fringe, one of the boys closed the pocket knife with which he had cut the rope. Out in the swamp, little Paul Barlow stood up cautiously, supported by the wooden platform that he and the other boys had sunk at the swamp's edge and carefully tested. Watching his footing, Paul backed out of the sand, circled around the danger spot, and joined the others.

"Very good, Paul," said Tommy. "You have succeeded in luring an adult to his death, and thereby become a full member of the Destroyers' Club."

"Thank you, Mr. President," Paul said, and the other children cheered.

"But just one thing," Tommy said. "In the future, please watch the overacting. All that screaming *was* a bit heavy, you know."

"I'll watch it, Mr. President," Paul said. By then it was evening. Paul and the other boys hurried home for supper. Paul's mother commented on how good his color was; she approved of his playing with his friends in the open air. But, as with all boys, his poor clothes were a muddy mess—and his hands were dirty.

THE FUTURE OF SEX

Speculative Journalism

Sophisticated sexual engineering will soon be a reality. Many techniques for high-powered sensual realization are already in the developmental stages. Nerve seeding is one example. Nerve endings in the penis are relatively few. The same is true of the vagina. Within the decade, however, your surgeon will be able to inject you with a local nerve-growth stimulant. In less than a week, newly grown and densely packed nerve endings will yield a new dimension of exquisite sensations. A desensitization period may prove necessary; it may take a man two weeks before he can avoid ejaculating at the slightest stimulus, such as when he touches his organ accidentally while reaching for change.

Nerve clusters can be implanted on the body anywhere, and linked to the brain's arousal center. There's no limit but inconvenience. Sexual feeling could be diffused, causing polymorphous perversity in which the entire body functions as a single sexual organ. Normal spread of sensation between implanted nerve clusters will make this possible; your body will be like a six-foot-tall erect penis (or whatever height you are)—throbbingly sensitive, capable of febrile excitation impossible to imagine. Or, if you prefer, actual sex organs may be grown anywhere on the body. For example, an erectile stalk with male and/or female receptors at one end could be extruded from a point several inches below the armpit.

Regardless of design, newly engineered people will find that their excitation potential vastly exceeds their orgasmic capacity. One impotency therapy currently being tested in Third World countries is the implantation of booster testes. In Nigeria, for example, despite a high national birth rate, certain tribes have been downbreeding to the point of extinction. An example of this is the Duka, a small sub-Saharan tribe wedged between two powerful and quarrelsome neighboring tribes. Most Duka males are unable to achieve orgasm despite frenzied use of the *siila*—a fetish doll of great erotic import, indigenous to the area northwest of Lake Chad. The booster testis has provided a dramatic solution. The operation itself is simple: a tiny diode, implanted in the male genital region, increases nerve impulses and thus sperm production. The results have been "reliable" erections with excellent ejaculatory ability. But can ejaculatory capacity be upgraded so that a man can have five, ten, or even twenty climaxes in an hour?

The solution is almost at hand. Male orgasm typically results in enervation that persists for hours or even days. Multiple nerve-muscle nets, surgically layered on top of the present sets and triggered to fire at different times, will ensure orgasmic capacity—as intense as you can stand, and for as long as you can take it. Delightful though this may seem, there are risks. Almost certainly a fail-safe device will have to be implanted to turn one off before—there is no other way of saying it—the body literally fucks itself to death.

Today, masturbation is the most convenient sex act. Unfortunately it is also the most boring. Therefore other people must sometimes be resorted to. The rehabilitation of masturbation will change all this. The sexually re-engineered individual will pursue him- or herself with full social approval, and his response level can be set so low that almost any stimulus will work. Partially clothed pinups, for example, or even innocuous "naughty" words such as *do-do* and *caca* might do the trick. Morally and scientifically sanctioned partnerless sex could be a relief for those who find themselves alone, perhaps during space travel, or who simply have trouble finding anyone to do anything sexual with. In this enlightened social climate, Solo Marriage will be a viable and respected institution.

When our ridiculous laws against bestiality have been repealed, society may condone sex with non-ordinary partners. By that time the surgical means will be at hand to restructure your sex organ to fit, for example, a parrot, a dolphin, or a bat. A man might wish to have his erectile member re-engineered so that he could fully enjoy his favorite cat or other pet. Presumably this would increase the cat's enjoyment as well. If not, the cat could be re-engineered.

Another exciting near-future possibility is the man-machine interface. A computer tied to the nervous system via a series of sensors would scan visceral and autonomic responses, and record them in binary. The computer would "experiment," programming itself to initiate movements to stimulate its subject/operator. Given the intermittent and differentiated nature of human sexual response, the computer would employ a tease-factor, utilizing randomness and delay to elicit new heights of pleasure. People are not telepathic, but computers, given a direct nerve tie-in and a properly written interactive program, could be.

Once the computer had completed your response profile, even your lover could interface with the program and learn, by touch, exactly what you liked, for how long, and with what degree of pressure. From a sufficient base of such data, science could develop a unified theory of sexuality. Frigidity and impotence would become things of the past. Nor would any perversions remain, since these so-called abominable practices would necessarily be subsumed in the unified theory. Statistically understood, individual behaviors would have no more moral significance than the movement of gas molecules in accordance with Boyle's law.

Computer-assisted sexuality suggests not only new software but new hardware. A sex robot would be the action arm of the computer. Not necessarily human in appearance (despite the forecasts of science fiction), such a robot might well be boxy, with catlike curves. Its skin would be a lustrous fur, except for those portions encased in black leather, lace, and chrome. It would probably not speak English, but instead employ a special language made up of instinctively understood purrs and growls. The sex machine could be of any size from petite to grandiose, and would come equipped with variously sized and shaped probes and

orifices. An ideal orgy participant, the machine could accommo-
date up to a dozen humans by acting as a central plug-in device.

A sex robot must demonstrate apparent independence;
otherwise, the randomness and tease-factor mentioned earlier
would result in unpredictability. The importance of this must not
be minimized. Easily obtained sex is never satisfactory, at least
not for long. The "best" sex entails the dramatic component of
uncertainty. Your sex machine would definitely not always be
"available." It would be no "pushover"; you might have to
seduce the thing, perhaps with wines and soft music, perhaps
with a special fetish it might be said to "care for." Sometimes,
despite your best efforts, the machine might still refuse you. You
could, of course, override the refusal, thereby providing yourself
with the mechanistic equivalent of rape.

However it manifests, the future of sex seems assured. The only
remaining uncertainty is the human mind. It is conceivable that
some people will be so perverse as to refuse the new pleasures
that science brings. For these people, reconditioning may be
necessary. The means will be available to make people *like* what
is available, whether they like it or not. Some may deplore this as
brainwashing, and, considered narrowly, it is just that. But so
what? Aren't any means appropriate in the pursuit of mankind's
highest goal—pleasure?

THE LIFE OF ANYBODY

Last night, as I lay on the couch watching "The Late Show," a camera and sound crew came to my apartment to film a segment of a TV series called "The Life of Anybody." I can't say I was completely surprised, although I had not anticipated this. I knew the rules; I went on with my life exactly as if they were not there. After a few minutes, the camera and recording crew seemed to fade into the wallpaper. They are specially trained for that.

My TV was on, of course; I usually have it on. I could almost hear the groans of the critics: "Another goddamned segment of a guy watching the tube. Doesn't anybody in this country do anything but watch the tube?" That upset me, but there was nothing I could do about it. That's the way it goes.

So the cameras whizzed along, and I lay on the couch like a dummy and watched two cowboys play the macho game. After a while my wife came out of the bathroom, looked at the crew, and groaned, "Oh, Christ, not *tonight*." She was wearing my CCNY sweatshirt on top, nothing on the bottom. She'd just washed her hair and she had a towel tied around her head. She had no makeup on. She looked like hell. Of all nights, they had to pick this one. She was probably imagining the reviews: "The wife in last night's turgid farce . . ."

I could see that she wanted badly to do something—to inject a little humor into our segment, to make it into a domestic farce. But she didn't. She knew as well as I did that anyone caught acting, fabricating, exaggerating, diminishing, or otherwise distorting his life, would be instantly cut off the air. She didn't want that. A bad appearance was better than no appearance at all. She sat down on a chair and picked up her crocheting hook. I picked up my magazine. Our movie went on.

You can't believe it when it happens to you. Even though you watch the show every evening and see it happen, you can't believe it's happening to you. I mean, it's suddenly *you* there, lying on the couch doing your nothing number, and there they are, filming it and implying that the segment represents *you.*

I prayed for something to happen. Air raid—sneak Commie attack—us a typical American family caught in the onrush of great events. Or a burglar breaks in, only he's not just a burglar, he's something else, and a whole fascinating sequence begins. Or a beautiful woman knocks at the door, claiming that only I can help her. Hell, I would have settled for a phone call.

But nothing happened. I actually started to get interested in that movie on TV, and I put down my magazine and actually watched it. I thought they might be interested in that.

The next day my wife and I waited hopefully, even though we knew we had bombed out. Still, you can never tell. Sometimes the public wants to see more of a person's life. Sometimes a face strikes their fancy and you get signed for a series. I didn't really expect that anyone would want to see a series about my wife and me, but you can never tell. Stranger things have happened.

Nowadays my wife and I spend our evenings in very interesting ways. Our sexual escapades are the talk of the neighborhood, my crazy cousin Zoe has come to stay with us, and regularly an undead thing crawls upstairs from the cellar.

Practically speaking, you never get another chance. But you can never tell. If they do decide to do a follow-up segment, we're ready.

GOOD-BYE FOREVER TO MR. PAIN

Joseph Elroy was nicely settled back in his armchair on this Sunday morning in the near future, trying to remember the name of his favorite football team, which he was going to watch later on the TV while reading the bankruptcy notices in the Sunday *Times* and thinking uncomfortable thoughts.

It was a normal sort of day: the sky outside was colored its usual blah beige, which went well with the blah browns with which Mrs. Elroy, now grinding her teeth in the kitchen, had decorated the place during one of her many shortlived bursts of enthusiasm. Their child, Elixir, was upstairs pursuing her latest discovery— she was three years old and had just gotten into vomiting.

And Elroy had a tune going in his head. "Amapola" was spinning just now, and it would continue until another song segued into it, one song after another, all day, all night, forever. This music came from Elroy's internal Muzak system, which came on whenever inattentiveness became necessary for survival.

So Elroy was in a certain state. Maybe you've been there yourself: the kid cries and the wife nags and you drift through your days and nights, well laid back, listening to the secret Muzak in your head. And you know that you'll never crack through the hazy plastic shield that separates you from the world, and the gray mists of depression and boredom settle in for a nice long visit. And the only thing that prevents you from opting for a snuffout is your Life-Force, which says to you, "Wake up, dummy, it's *you* this is happening to—yes, you, strangling there in your swimming pool of lime-flavored Jell-O with a silly grin on your love-starved face as you smoke another Marlboro and watch the iniquities of the world float by in three-quarter time."

Given that situation, you'd take any chance that came along to pull out of it, wouldn't you? Joseph Elroy's chance came that very afternoon.

The telephone rang. Elroy picked it up. A voice at the other end asked, "Who is this, please?"

"This is Joseph Elroy," Elroy replied.

"Mr. Elroy, do you happen to have a *tune* or *song* going through your head at this moment?"

"As a matter of fact, I do."

"What is the name of the song?"

"I've been humming 'Amapola' to myself for the last couple of hours."

"What was that name again, Mr. Elroy?"

"'Amapola.' But what—"

"That's it! That's the one!"

"Huh?"

"Mr. Elroy, now I can reveal to you what this is all about. I am Marv Duffle, and I'm calling you from 'The Shot of a Lifetime Show' and you have named *the very tune* going through the head of our genial guest for tonight, Mr. Phil Suggers! That means that you and your family, Mr. Elroy, have won this month's big synchronicity prize, The Shot of a Lifetime! Mr. Elroy, do you know what that means?"

"I know!" Elroy shouted joyously. "I watch the show so I know, I know! Elva, stop freaking out in there, we've won the big one, we've won, we've won, we've won!"

What this meant in practical terms was that the following day a group of technicians in one-piece orange jumpsuits came and installed what looked like a modified computer console in the Elroys' living room, and Marv Duffle himself handed them the all-important Directory and explained how all of the best avenues for personal growth and change and self-realization had been collated and tied directly into this computer. Many of these services had formerly been available only to the rich, talented, and successful, who really didn't need them. But now the Elroys could avail themselves of them, and do it all via patented superfast high-absorption learning modalities developed at Stanford and incorporated into the equipment. In brief, their lives were theirs to shape and mold as they desired, free, and in the privacy of their home.

Elroy was a serious-minded man, as we all are at heart, and so the first thing he did was to search through the Directory, which listed all available services from all the participating companies, until he found Vocationeers, the famous talent-testing firm of Mill Valley, California. They were able to process Elroy by telephone and get the results back to him in fifteen minutes. It seemed that Elroy had the perfect combination of intelligence, manual dexterity, and psychological set to become a top-flight micropaleontologist. That position happened to be open at the nearby Museum of Natural History, and Elroy learned all he needed to know about the work with the help of the Bluchner-Wagner School for High-Speed Specialized Learning. So Elroy was able to begin a promising career only two weeks after he had heard of it for the first time.

Elva Elroy, or Elf, as she called herself in wistful moments, wasn't sure what she wanted to do. She looked through the Directory until she found Mandragore, Inc., makers of Norml-Hi twenty-four-hour timed-release mood-enhancement spansules. She had them sent over at once with the Ames Rapid Dope Delivery Service—"Your High Is Our Cry." Feeling better than she had in ages, Elva was able to face the problem of dinner. After careful consideration, she called Fancy Freakout Food Merchandisers—"Let Us Administer to the Hungry Child in Your Head."

For their little daughter, Elixir, there was BabyTeasers, a crack service that cajoled the spoiled scions of oil sheiks, now available to the Elroys on 'round-the-clock standby basis to get the kid out of her temper. Elixir was delighted. New big soft toys to order around! What could be so bad?

That left the Elroys with world enough and time in which to

discover each other. They went first with Omni-Pleasure Family Consultants, who, on television in Houston the previous month, had revitalized a marriage that had been pronounced terminal. One counseling session brought the Elroys a deep and abiding love for each other whenever they looked deep into each other's eyes and concentrated. This gave them the necessary maturity to take the Five-Day Breakthrough with the Total Sex Response people of Lansing, Michigan—which, too, was a success in terms of new highs reached and plateaus maintained. Yet a certain anxiety crept into Elroy's performance and he felt the need to avail himself of Broadway Joe's Romantic Sex Service—"Illicit meetings with beautiful sexy broads of a refinement guaranteed not to gross you out."

"Oh, yeah?" said Elva when she heard about that, and instantly fulfilled a long-standing desire by calling Rough Traders Sex Service. She had been attracted by their ad in the Directory: "Dig, you want it rough, raw, real, and sweaty, but you also want that it shouldn't be a turnoff. Right? Right. Call our number, baby, 'cause we *got* your number."

They both got a little freaked out from it all, and cooled out with Dreamboat Launchers of Fire Island and their famous motto: "Meditate the Easy Way, with Dope."

The Elroys were really getting it all together now, but things kept intruding. Elixir was freaking out again, and at the worst possible time, for Elroy was soon to be profiled by *New York* magazine, and Elva was about to begin a two-week prima ballerina course with a job already assured her at the Ballet Russe de Monte Carlo. They held a family conference and came across an ad in the Directory for a service called Childmenders.

"What does it say?" Elva asked.

Elroy read: " 'Is your child losing out on the best of life because he/she possesses an unruly personality? Do you feel frustrated by the problem of giving him/her love without getting swallowed up? Is it all getting a bit much? Then why not take advantage of Childmenders! We will cart away your child and return him/her loving, obedient, docile, and easily satisfied—and we will do this without screwing up one bit of his/her individuality, initiative, and aggressiveness, so help us God.'"

"They sound like they give a damn," Elva said.

"Funny you should say that," Elroy said. "Right down here at the bottom of their ad, it says, 'Believe us—we give a damn!'"

"That clinches it," Elva said. "Call them!"

Elixir was carted away, and the Elroys celebrated their newfound freedom by calling up Instant Real Friends and throwing a party with the help of Perry and Penny, the Party People.

Onward the Elroys plunged, along the rocky trail of self-transcendence. Unfortunately this involved a clash of interests. Mr. Elroy was pursuing Higher Matters through Mindpower. Elva still sought consummation in the veritable flesh. They fought about which item in the Directory they should opt for next. Since they had both taken the Supreme Communication Foundation's Quickie Course in Inexorable Persuasiveness, they were both terrific arguers. But they got on each other's nerves because they were both terrible listeners.

Their relationship fell apart. Stubbornly, neither of them would go to Relationship Repairers. In fact, Elva defiantly joined Negatherapeutics, whose intriguing slogan was "Hate Your Way to Happiness." Elroy pulled himself together and explored his feelings with the revolutionary new Cellular Self-Image Technique and understood at last where he was at: he detested his wife and wanted her dead. It was as simple as that!

Elroy swung into action. He pounced on the Directory and located the Spouse Alteration Service of Saugerties, New York. They came and took Elva away and Elroy finally had time to get into himself.

First he learned how to achieve instantaneous ecstasy at will. This ability had formerly been an exclusive possession of a few Eastern religious organizations, which, until recently, had been the only ones with the telephone number of the service that provided it. Bliss was a lot of fun, but Elroy had to come out of it when

Childmenders called to say that his child was irreparable. What did he want them to do with her? Elroy told them to put her back together as well as they could and store her until further notice.

It was at this time, through the assistance of Psychoboosters, Inc., that he was able to raise his intelligence to two levels above genius, a fact that was duly noted in the updated edition of his autobiography, which was being serialized in *The New York Times.*

The Spouse Alteration Service called and said that Elva was the old unalterable model and could not be adjusted without grave danger to the mechanism. Elroy told them to store her with his irreparable kid.

At last, triumphantly alone, Elroy could return to the joyous work of saying good-bye forever to Mr. Pain. He had it all pretty much together by now, of course, and was experiencing many religious visions of great power and intensity. But something unsatisfactory still remained, though he couldn't put his finger on it.

He looked through the Directory, but found no answer. It looked as if he was going to have to tough this one through on his own. But then, providentially, the front door opened and in walked a small, dark, smiling man with a turban and all-knowing eyes and an aura of incredible power. This was the Mystery Guru, who seeks you out when the time is right and tells you what you need to know—if you are a subscriber to the Directory.

"It's the ego," the Mystery Guru said, and left.

Vast waves of comprehension flooded over Elroy. The ego! of course! Why hadn't *he* thought of that? Obviously his ego was the final thing anchoring him to the gummy clay of everyday reality. His ego! His very own ego was holding him back, forever yammering its selfish demands at him, completely disregarding his welfare!

Elroy opened the Directory. There, all by itself on the last page, he found the Lefkowitz Ego Removers of Flushing, New York.

Beneath their ad was this: "Warning. The Surgeon-General Has Determined that Ego Removal May Be Injurious to Your Health."

Joseph Elroy hesitated, considered, weighed factors. He was momentarily perplexed. But then the Mystery Guru popped into the room again and said, "It's a seven-to-five shot at the Big Spiritual Money, and besides, what have you got to lose?" He exited, a master of timing.

Elroy punched out the big combination on the console.

Not long afterward there was a knock at the door. Elroy opened it to the Lefkowitz Ego Removal Squad.

They left. Then there was only the console, winking and leering and glittering at itself. And then even that was gone and there was nothing whatever in the room except a disembodied voice humming "Amapola."

THE SHAGGY AVERAGE
AMERICAN MAN STORY

Dear Joey,

You ask me in your letter what can a man do when all of a sudden, through no fault of his own, he finds that there is a bad rap hanging over him which he cannot shake off.

You did right in asking me, as your spiritual advisor and guide, to help you in this matter.

I can sympathize with your feelings, dear friend. Being known far and wide as a double-faced, two-tongued, short-count ripoff artist fit only for the company of cretinous Albanians is indeed an upsetting situation, and I can well understand how it has cut into your business as well as your self-esteem and is threatening to wipe you out entirely. But that is no reason to do a kamikaze into Mount Shasta with your hang glider, as you threaten in your letter. Joey, no situation is entirely unworkable. People have gone through worse bad-rapping than that, and come up smelling like roses.

For your edification I cite the recent experience of my good friend George Blaxter.

I don't think you ever met George. You were in Goa the year he was in Ibiza, and then you were with that Subud group in Bali when George was with his guru in Isfahan. Suffice it to say that George was in London during the events I am about to relate, trying to sell a novel he had just written, and living with Big

Karen, who, you may remember, was Larry Shark's old lady when Larry was playing pedal guitar with Brain Damage at the San Remo Festival.

Anyhow, George was living low and quiet in a bed-sitter in Fulham when one day a stranger came to his door and introduced himself as a reporter from the Paris *Herald Tribune* and asked him what his reaction was to the big news.

George hadn't heard any big news recently, except for the Celtics losing to the Knicks in the NBA playoffs, and he said so.

"Somebody should have contacted you about this," the reporter said. "In that case, I don't suppose you know that the Emberson Study Group in Annapolis, Maryland, has recently finished its monumental study updating the averageness concept to fit the present and still-changing demographic and ethnomorphic aspects of our great nation."

"No one told me about it," George said.

"Sloppy, very sloppy," the reporter said. "Well, incidental to the Study, the Emberson Group was asked if they could come up with some actual person who would fit and embody the new parameters of American averageness. The reporters wanted somebody who could be called Mr. Average American Man. You know how reporters are."

"But what has this got to do with me?"

"It's really remiss of them not to have notified you," the reporter said. "They fed the question into their computer and turned it loose on their sampling lists, and the computer came up with you."

"With me?" George said.

"Yes. They really should have notified you."

"I'm supposed to be the Average American Man!"

"That's what the computer said."

"But that's crazy," George said. "How can *I* be the Average American Man? I'm only five foot eight and my name is Blaxter spelled with an 'l', and I'm of Armenian and Latvian ancestry and I was born in Ship's Bottom, New Jersey. What's *that* average of, for Chrissakes? They better recheck their results. What they're looking for is some Iowa farmboy with blond hair and a Mercury and 2.4 children."

"That's the old, outdated stereotype," the reporter said. "America today is composed of racial and ethnic minorities whose sheer ubiquity precludes the possibility of choosing an Anglo-Saxon model. The average man of today has to be unique to be average, if you see what I mean."

"Well . . . what am I supposed to do now?" George asked.

The reporter shrugged. "I suppose you just go on doing whatever average things you were doing before this happened."

There was a dearth of interesting news in London at that time, as usual, so the BBC sent a team down to interview George. CBS picked it up for a thirty-second human-interest spot, and George became a celebrity overnight.

There were immediate repercussions.

George's novel had been tentatively accepted by the venerable British publishing firm of Gratis & Spye. His editor, Derek Polsonby-Jigger, had been putting George through a few final rewrites and additions and polishes and deletions, saying, "It's just about right, but there's still something that bothers me and we owe it to ourselves to get it in absolutely top form, don't we?"

A week after the BBC special, George got his book back with a polite note of rejection.

George went down to St. Martin's Lane and saw Polsonby. Polsonby was polite but firm. "There is simply no market over here for books written by average Americans."

"But you liked my book! You were going to publish it!"

"There was always something about it that bothered me," Polsonby said. "Now I know what that something is."

"Yeah?"

"Your book lacks uniqueness. It's just an average American novel. What else could the average American man write? That's what the critics would say. Sorry, Blaxter."

When George got home, he found Big Karen packing.

"Sorry, George," she told him, "but I'm afraid it's all over between us. My friends are laughing at me. I've been trying for years to prove that I'm unique and special, and then look what happens to me—I hook up with the average American man."

"But that's *my* problem, not yours!"

"Look, George, the average American man has got to have an average American wife, otherwise he's not average, right?"

"I never thought about it," George said. "Hell, I don't know."

"It makes sense, baby. As long as I'm with you, I'll just be the average man's average woman. That's hard to bear, George, for a creative-thinking female person who is unique and special and has been the old lady of Larry Shark when he was with Brain Damage during the year they got a gold platter for their top-of-the-charts single, 'All Those Noses.' But it's more than just that. I have to do it for the children."

"Karen, what are you talking about? We don't have any children."

"Not yet. But when we did, they'd just be average kids. I don't think I could bear that. What mother could? I'm going to go away, change my name, and start all over. Good luck, George."

After that, George's life began to fall apart with considerable speed and dexterity. He began to get a little wiggy; he thought people were laughing at him behind his back, and of course it didn't help his paranoia any to find out that they actually were. He took to wearing long black overcoats and sunglasses and dodging in and out of doorways and sitting in cafés with a newspaper in front of his average face.

Finally he fled England, leaving behind him the sneers of his onetime friends. He was bad-rapped but good. And he couldn't even take refuge in any of the places he knew: Goa, Ibiza, Malibu, Poona, Anacapri, Ios, or Marrakesh. He had erstwhile friends in all those places who would laugh at him behind his back.

In his desperation he exiled himself to the most unhip and unlikely place he could think of: Nice, France.

There he quickly became an average bum.

Now stick with me, Joey, while we transition to several months later. It is February in Nice. A cold wind is whipping down off the Alps, and the palm trees along the Boulevard des Anglais look like they're ready to pack up their fronds and go back to Africa.

George is lying on an unmade bed in his hotel, Les Grandes Meules. It is a suicide-class hotel. It looks like warehouse storage space in Mongolia, only not so cheerful.

There is a knock on the door. George opens it. A beautiful young woman comes in and asks him if he is the famous George Blaxter, Average American Man. George says that he is, and braces himself for the latest insult that a cruel and unthinking world is about to lay on him.

"I'm Jackie," she says. "I'm from New York, but I'm vacationing in Paris."

"Huh," George says.

"I took off a few days to look you up," she says. "I heard you were here."

"Well, what can I do for you? Another interview? Further adventure of the Average Man?"

"No, nothing like that . . . I was afraid this might get a little uptight. Have you got a drink?"

George was so deep into confusion and self-hatred in those days that he was drinking absinthe even though he hated the stuff. He poured Jackie a drink.

"Okay," she said, "I might as well get down to business."

"Let's hear it," George said grimly.

"George," she said, "did you know that in Paris there is a platinum bar exactly one meter long?"

George just stared at her.

"That platinum meter," she said, "is the standard for all the other meters in the world. If you want to find out if your meter is the right length, you take it to Paris and measure it against their meter. I'm simplifying, but do you see what I mean?"

"No," Blaxter said.

"That platinum meter in Paris was arrived at by international agreement. Everyone compared meters and averaged them out. The average of all those meters became the standard meter. Are you getting it now?"

"You want to hire me to steal this meter?"

She shook her head impatiently. "Look, George, we're both grown-up adult persons and we can speak about sex without embarrassment, can't we?"

George sat up straight. For the first time his eyes began tracking.

"The fact is," Jackie said. "I've been having a pretty lousy time of it in my relationships over the past few years, and my analyst,

Dr. Decathlon, tells me it's because of my innate masochism, which converts everything I do into drek. That's *his* opinion. Personally, I think I've just been running a bad streak. But I don't really know, and it's important for me to find out. If I'm sick in the head, I ought to stay in treatment so that someday I'll be able to enjoy myself in bed. But if he's wrong, I'm wasting my time and a hell of a lot of money."

"I think I'm starting to get it," George said.

"The problem is, how is a girl to know whether her bad trips are her own fault or the result of the hangups of the guys she's been going with? There's no standard of comparison, no sexual unit, no way to experience truly average American sexual performance, no platinum meter against which to compare all of the other meters in the world."

It broke over George then, like a wave of sunlight and understanding. "I," he said, "am the standard of American male sexual averageness."

"Baby, you're a unique platinum bar exactly one meter in length and there's nothing else like you in the whole world. Come here, my fool, and show me what the average sexual experience is really like."

Well, word got around, because girls tell these things to other girls. And many women heard about it, and of those who heard about it, enough were interested in checking it out that George soon found his time fully and pleasurably occupied beyond his wildest dreams. They came to him in unending streams, Americans at first, but then many nationalities, having heard of him via the underground interglobal feminine sex-information linkup. He got uncertain Spaniards, dubious Danes, insecure Sudanese, womankind from all over, drawn to him like moths to a flame or like motes of dust in water swirling down a drain in a clockwise direction in the northern hemisphere. And it was all good, at worst, and indescribable at best.

Blaxter is independently wealthy now, thanks to the gifts pressed on him by grateful female admirers of all nations, types, shapes, and colors. He lives in a fantastic villa high above Cap

Ferrat, given by a grateful French government in recognition of his special talents and great importance as a tourist attraction. He leads a life of luxury and independence, and refuses to cooperate with researchers who want to study him and write books with titles like *The Averageness Concept in Modern American Sexuality*. Blaxter doesn't need them. They would only cramp his style.

He leads his life. And he tells me that late at night, when the last smiling face has departed, he sits back in his enormous easy chair, pours himself a fine burgundy, and considers the paradox: his so-called averageness has made him the front-runner of most, if not all, American males in several of life's most important and fun areas. Being average has blessed his life with uncountable advantages. He is a platinum bar sitting happily in its glass case, and he would never go back to being simply unique, like the rest of the human race.

This is the bliss that averageness has brought him: The curse that he could not shake off is now the gift that he can never lose.

Touching, isn't it?

So you see, Joey, what I'm trying to tell you is that apparent liabilities can be converted into solid assets. How this rule can apply in your own particular case should be obvious. In case it isn't, feel free to write to me again, enclosing the usual payment for use of my head, and I will be glad to tell you how being known far and wide as a lousy ripoff shortchange goniff (and a lousy lay, in case you hadn't heard) can be worked to your considerable advantage.

> Yours in Peace,
> Andy the Answer Man

SHOOTOUT IN THE TOY SHOP

The meeting took place in the taproom of the Beaux Arts Club of Camden, New Jersey. It was the sort of uptight saloon that Baxter usually avoided—Tiffany lampshades, tables of dark polished wood, discreet lighting. His potential customer, Mr. Arnold Conabee, was in a booth waiting for him. Conabee was a soft-faced, fragile-looking man, and Baxter took care to shake his hand gently. After squeezing his bulk into the red leatherette booth, Baxter asked for a vodka martini, very dry, because that was the sort of thing people ordered in a joint like this. Conabee crossed him up by asking for a margarita straight up.

It was Baxter's first job in nearly a month, and he was determined not to blow it. His breath was kissing sweet, and he had powdered his heavy jowls with talcum powder. His glen plaid suit was freshly pressed and concealed his gut pretty well, and his black police shoes gleamed. Looking good, baby. But he had forgotten to clean his fingernails, and now he saw that they were black-rimmed. He wanted to keep his hands in his lap, but then he couldn't smoke.

Conabee wasn't interested in his hands, however. Conabee had a problem, and that was why he had arranged this meeting with Baxter, a private detective who listed himself in the Yellow Pages as the Acme Investigative Service.

"Somebody is stealing from me," Conabee was saying, "but I don't know who."

"Just fill me in on the details," Baxter said. His voice was the best part of him, a deep, manly drawl, exactly the right voice for a private investigator.

"My shop is over at the South Camden Mall," Conabee said. "Conabee's Toys for Children of All Ages. I'm beginning to acquire an international reputation."

"Right," Baxter said, though he had never heard of Conabee's scam.

"The trouble started two weeks ago," Conabee said. "I had just completed an experimental doll, the most advanced of its kind in the world. The prototype utilized a new optical switching circuit and a synthetic protein memory with a thousand times the order of density previously achieved. It was stolen on the first night of its display. Various pieces of equipment and a quantity of precious metals were also taken. Since then, there have been thefts almost every night."

"No chance of a break-in?"

"The locks are never tampered with. And the thief always seems to know when we have anything worth stealing."

Baxter grunted and Conabee said, "It seems to be an inside job. But I can't believe it. I have only four employees. The most recent has been with me six years. I trust them all implicitly."

"Then you gotta be hooking the stuff yourself," Baxter said, winking, "because *somebody's* sure carting it off."

Conabee stiffened and looked at Baxter oddly, then laughed. "I almost wish it were me," he said. "My employees are all my friends."

"Hell," Baxter said, "anybody'll rip off the boss if he thinks he can get away with it."

Conabee looked at him oddly again, and Baxter realized that he wasn't talking genteelly enough and that a sure seventy-five dollars was about to vanish. He forced himself to be cool and to say, in his deep, competent, no-nonsense voice, "I could hide myself in your shop tonight, Mr. Conabee. You could be rid of this annoyance once and for all."

"Yes," Conabee said, "it *has* been annoying. It's not so much the loss of income as . . ." He let the thought trail away. "Today we got in a shipment of gold filigree from Germany worth eight hundred dollars. I've brought an extra key."

Baxter took a bus downtown to Courthouse Square. He had about three hours before he was to stake himself out in Conabee's shop. He'd been tempted to ask for an advance, but had decided against it. It didn't pay to look hungry, and this job could be a fresh start for him.

Down the street he saw Stretch Jones holding up a lamppost on Fountain and Clinton. Stretch was a tall, skinny black man wearing a sharply cut white linen suit, white moccasins, and a tan Stetson. Stretch said, "Hey, baby."

"Hi," Baxter said sourly.

"You got that bread for my man?"

"I told Dinny I'd have it Monday."

"He told me I should remind you, 'cause he don't want you should forget."

"I'll have it Monday," Baxter said, and walked on. It was a lousy hundred dollars that he owed Dinny Welles, Stretch's boss. Baxter resented being braced for it, especially by an insolent black bastard in an ice-cream suit. But there wasn't anything he could do about it.

At the Clinton Cut-Rate Liquor Store he ordered a bottle of Haig & Haig Pinch to celebrate his new job, and Terry Turner, the clerk, had the nerve to say, "Uh, Charlie, I can't do this no more."

"What in hell are you talking about?" Baxter demanded.

"It ain't me," Turner said. "You know I just work here. It's Mrs. Chednik. She said not to give you any more credit."

"Take it out of this," Baxter said, coming across with his last twenty.

Turner rang up the sale, then said, "But your tab—"

"I'll settle it direct with Mrs. Chednik, and you can tell her I said so."

"Well, all right, Charlie," Turner said, giving him the change. "But you're going to get into a lot of trouble."

They looked at each other. Baxter knew that Turner was part owner of the Clinton and that he and Mrs. Chednik had decided to cut him off until he paid up. And Turner knew that he knew this. The bastard!

The next stop was the furnished efficiency he called home over on River Road Extension. Baxter walked up the stairs to the twilight gloom of his living room. A small black-and-white television glowed faintly in a corner. Betsy was in the bedroom, packing. Her eye had swollen badly.

"And just where do you think you're going?" Baxter demanded.

"I'm going to stay with my brother."

"Forget it," Baxter said, "it was only an argument." She went on packing.

"You're staying right here," Baxter told her. He pushed her out of the way and looked through her suitcase. He came up with his onyx cufflinks, his tie clasp with the gold nugget, his Series E savings bonds, and damned if she hadn't also tucked away his Smith & Wesson .38.

"Now you're really going to get it," he told her.

She looked at him levelly. "Charlie, I warn you, never touch me again if you know what's good for you."

Baxter took a step toward her, bulky and imposing in his newly pressed suit. But suddenly he remembered that her brother Amos worked in the DA's office. Would Betsy blow the whistle on him? He really couldn't risk finding out, even though she was bugging him beyond human endurance.

Just then the doorbell rang sharply, three times—McGorty's ring—and Baxter had ten dollars with McGorty on today's number. He opened the door, but it wasn't McGorty, it was a tiny Chinese woman pitching some religious pamphlet. She wouldn't shut up and go away, not even when he told her nice; she just kept at him, and Baxter was suddenly filled with the desire to kick her downstairs, along with her knapsack of tracts.

And then Betsy slipped past him. She had managed to get the suitcase closed, and it all happened so fast that Baxter couldn't do a thing. He finally got rid of the Chinese lady and poured himself a tumblerful of whiskey. Then he remembered the bonds and looked around, but that damned Betsy had whipped everything

away, including his gold-nugget tie clasp. His Smith & Wesson
was still on the bed, under a fold of blanket, so he put it into his
suit pocket and poured another drink.

He ate the knockwurst special at the Shamrock, had a quick beer
and a shot at the White Rose,and got to the South Camden
Shopping Mall just before closing. He sat in a luncheonette, had a
coffee, and watched Conabee and his employees leave at seven-
thirty. He sat for another half hour, then let himself into the shop.

It was dark inside, and Baxter stood very still, getting the feel of
the place. He could hear a lot of clocks going at different rates, and
there was a high-pitched sound like crickets, and other sounds he
couldn't identify. He listened for a while, then took out his pocket
flashlight and looked around.

His light picked out curious details: a scale-model Spad biplane
with ten-foot wings, hanging from the ceiling and tilted as if to
attack; a fat plastic beetle almost underfoot; a model Centurion
tank nearly five feet long. He was standing in the dark in the midst
of motionless toys, and beyond them he could make out the dim
shapes of large dolls, stuffed animals, and, to one side, a silent
jungle made of delicate, shiny metal.

It was an uncanny sort of place, but Baxter was not easily
intimidated. He got ready for a long night. He found a pile of
cushions, laid them out, found an ashtray, took off his overcoat,
and lay down. Then he sat up and took a cellophane-wrapped
ham sandwich, slightly squashed, from one pocket, a can of beer
from the other. He got a cigarette going, lay back, and chewed,
drank, and smoked against a background of sounds too faint to be
identified. One of the many clocks struck the hour, then the others
chimed in, and they kept going for a long time.

He sat up with a start. He realized that he had dozed off.
Everything seemed exactly the same. Nobody could have
unlocked the door and slipped in past him, yet there seemed to be
more light.

A dim spotlight had come on, and he could hear spooky organ

music, but faintly, faintly, as though from very far away. Baxter rubbed his nose and stood up. Something moved beside his left shoulder, and he turned his flashlight on it. It was a life-size puppet of Long John Silver. Baxter laughed uncertainly.

More lights came on, and a spotlight picked out a group of three big dolls sitting at a table in a corner of the room. The papa doll was smoking a pipe and letting out clouds of real smoke, the mama doll was crocheting a shawl, and the baby doll was crawling on the floor and gurgling.

Then a group of doll people danced out in front of him. There were little shoemakers and tiny ballerinas and a miniature lion that roared and shook its mane. The metal jungle came to life, and great mechanical orchids opened and closed. There was a squirrel with blinking golden eyes; it cracked and ate silver walnuts. The organ music swelled up loud and sweet. Fluffy white doves settled on Baxter's shoulders, and a bright-eyed fawn licked at his fingers. The toys danced around him, and for a moment Baxter found himself in the splendid lost world of childhood.

Suddenly he heard a woman's laughter.

"Who's there?" he called out.

She stepped forward, followed by a silvery spotlight. She was Dorothy of Oz, she was Snow White, she was Gretel, she was Helen of Troy, she was Rapunzel; she was exquisitely formed, almost five feet tall, with crisp blond curls clustered around an elfin face. Her slight figure was set off by a frilly white shift tied around the waist with a red ribbon.

"You're that missing doll!" Baxter exclaimed.

"So you know about me," she said. "I would have liked a little more time, so that I could have gotten all the toys performing. But it doesn't matter."

Baxter, mouth agape, couldn't answer. She said, "The night Conabee assembled me, I found that I had the gift of life. I was more than a mere automaton—I lived, I thought, I desired. But I was not complete. So I hid in the ventilator shaft and stole materials in order to become as I am now, and to build this wonderland for my creator. Do you think he will be proud of me?"

"You're beautiful," Baxter said at last.

"But do you think Mr. Conabee will like me?"

"Forget about Conabee," Baxter said.

"What do you mean?"

"It's crazy," Baxter said, "but I can't live without you. We'll get away from here, work it out somehow. I'll make you happy, babe, I swear it!"

"Never," she said. "Conabee created me and I belong to him."

"You're coming with me," Baxter said.

He seized her hand and she pulled away from him. He yanked her toward him and her hand came off in his grip. Baxter gaped at it, then threw it from him. "Goddamn you!" he screamed. "Come here!"

She ran from him. He took out his .38 and followed. The organ music began to wander erratically, and the lights were flickering. He saw her run behind a set of great alphabet blocks. He hurried after her—and then the toys attacked.

The tank rumbled into action. It came at him slow and heavy. Baxter put two slugs into it, tumbling it across the room. He caught a glimpse of the Spad diving toward him, and he shot it in midair, squashing it against the wall like a giant moth. A squad of little mechanical soldiers discharged their cork bullets at him, and he kicked them out of the way. Long John Silver lunged at him, and his cutlass caught Baxter under the ribcage. But it was only a rubber sword; Baxter pushed the pirate aside and had her cornered behind the Punch and Judy.

She said, "Please don't hurt me."

He said, "Come with me!"

She shook her head and tried to dodge him. He grabbed her as she went past, catching her by the blond curls. She fell, and he felt her head twist in his hands, twist around in a full, impossible circle, so that her body was turned away from him while her pretty blue eyes still stared into his face.

"Never!" she said.

In a spasm of rage and revulsion, Baxter yanked at her head. It came off in his hands. In the neck stump he could see bits of glass winking in a gray matrix.

The mama and papa and baby dolls stopped in mid-motion. Long John Silver collapsed. The broken doll's blue eyes blinked three times; then she died.

The rest of the toys stopped. The organ faded, the spotlights went out, and the last jungle flower clinked to the floor. In the darkness, a weeping fat man knelt beside a busted doll and wondered what he was going to tell Conabee in the morning.

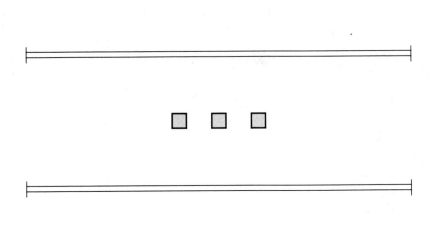

HOW PRO WRITERS REALLY
WRITE—OR TRY TO

Like most authors of science fiction, I was an avid reader first. Back then, as an aspiring writer as well as a fan, I wanted to know how professional writers actually do their jobs. How do they develop their ideas, plot their stories, overcome their difficulties? Now, twenty-five years later, I know a little about it.

Professional writers are extremely individualistic in the ways they approach their task. If you are among a lucky few, it is relatively simple. You get an idea, which in turn suggests a plot and characters. With that much in hand, you go to a typewriter and bash out a story. When it's done, a few hours later, you correct the grammar and spelling. This editing usually results in a messy-looking manuscript, so you type out the whole thing again. For better or worse, your story is now finished.

That's pretty much how I went about it early in my career. If anyone asked, I would explain that plotting a story consists merely of giving your hero a serious problem, a limited amount of time in which to solve it, and dire consequences if he fails to do so. You preclude all easy solutions. The hero tries this and that, but all his efforts serve only to sink him into deeper trouble. Time is soon running out and he still hasn't defeated the villain, rescued the girl, or learned the secret of the alien civilization. He's on the verge of utter, tragic defeat. Then, at the last moment, you get him out of trouble. How does this happen? In a flash of insight your hero solves his problem by some logical means inherent in the situation but overlooked until now. Done properly, your solution makes the reader say, "Of course! Why didn't I think of that?" You then bring the story to a swift conclusion—and that's all there is to it.

This straightforward approach saw me through many stories. Inevitably, however, sophistication set in and I began to experience difficulties. I began to view writing as a problem and to look for ways of dealing with that problem.

I looked to my colleagues and their individual methodologies. Lester del Rey, for example, told me that he wrote out his stories in his head—word for word, sentence for sentence—before committing them to paper. Months, even years, would be devoted to this mental composition.

Only when he was ready to type out a story would Lester go to his office, which was about the size of a broom closet, though not so pretty. He had built it in the middle of his living room. After cramming himself inside, Lester would be locked in place by a typewriter that unfolded from a wall onto his lap. Paper, pencils, cigarettes, and ashtray were there, and a circulation fan to keep him from suffocating. It was much like being in an upright coffin, but with the disadvantage that he was not dead.

Philip Klass, better known as William Tenn, had many different work methods back in those days. He developed them in order to cope with a blockage as tenacious and enveloping as a lovestricken boa constrictor. Phil and I used to discuss our writing problems at great length. Once we invented a method that would serve two writers. The scheme involved renting a studio and furnishing it with a desk, typewriter, and heavy oaken chair. The chair was to be fitted with a chain and padlock. According to our scheme, we would take turns in the studio. When it was, say, Phil's turn to write, I would chain him to the chair, leaving his arms free to type. I would then leave him there, despite his piteous pleas and entreaties, until he had produced a given amount of cogent prose. At that point I would release him and take his place.

* * *

We never did carry out our scheme, probably because of the unlikelihood of finding a chair strong enough to restrain a writer determined to escape work. But we did try something else. We agreed to meet at a diner in Greenwich Village at the end of each day's work. There we showed each other the pages we had done. If either of us had failed to fulfill his quota that day, he would pay the other ten dollars.

It seemed foolproof, but we soon ran into a difficulty. Neither of us was willing to let the other actually read his rough, unfinished copy. We got around this by presenting our pages upside down. But this procedure made it impossible to tell if we had really written new copy that day or if we were showing pages from years ago. It became a point of honor for each of us to present new copy that the other could not read. We did this for about a week, then spontaneously and joyously reverted to our former practice of just talking about writing.

As the years passed, my own blockage became wider, deeper, and blacker. I thought I knew what my trouble was, however. My trouble was my wife. As soon as I did something about her, I reasoned, everything would be okay. Two divorces later, I knew it was not my wife.

The trouble, I next decided, was New York. How could I possibly work in such a place? What I needed was sunshine, a sparkling sea, olive trees, and solitude. So I moved to the island of Ibiza. There I rented a three-hundred-year-old farmhouse on a hill overlooking the Mediterranean. The house lacked electricity, but it did have four rooms, any one of which I could use as my office. First I tried to work in the beautiful, bright rooms upstairs. Alas, I couldn't concentrate on my writing here because I spent too much time admiring the splendid view from the window. So I moved downstairs to a room that had only one narrow window, with bars over it in case of attack by pirates. Formerly a storage place for potatoes, the room was dark and dank. There was nothing to divert my attention. But I couldn't work here either. There was no electricity and my kerosene lamp gave off too much smoke.

At last I saw what the real trouble was. It stemmed from my working indoors. Henceforth I would toil outdoors, as it was meant to be. So I set up on the beach—only to be frustrated again, this time by the heat of a searing sun and by the ceaseless onshore breeze blowing sand into my typewriter. I tried composing under a shady tree, but the flies drove me away. When I tried to do my writing in a café, the waiters were too noisy.

I gave up on Ibiza and moved to London, firmly convinced that my problem was a shortage of self-discipline. I began to search in earnest for ways of doing by artifice what once I had done naturally. Here, in no particular order, are a few of the methods I have utilized.

When I am blocked, my tendency is to avoid writing. That's quite predictable. But the less I write, the less I feel capable of writing. A sense of oppression increases as my output dwindles, and I begin to dread writing anything at all. How to break this vicious cycle? The hard truth is that it can only be done by writing. I must practice my craft regularly if I am to maintain any facility at it. I need to produce a flow of words. How am I to achieve that flow when I am blocked?

To solve this dilemma, at one juncture I set myself to type five thousand words a day. Type, not write. Wordage was my only requirement. The substance of what I wrote did not matter. It could be anything, even gibberish, even lists of disconnected words, even my name over and over again. All that mattered was to produce daily wordage in quantity.

Perhaps that sounds simple. It was not, I assure you. The first day went well enough. By the second, however, I had exhausted my ready stock of banalities. I found myself creating something like this:

"Ah yes, here we are at last, getting near the bottom of the page. One more sentence, just a few more words . . . that's it, go, baby, go, do those words . . . Ah, page done. That's page 19, and now we are at the top of page 20—the last page for the day—or night, since it is now 3:30 in the bloody morning and I have been at this for what feels like a hundred years. But only one page to go, the last, and then I can put aside this insane nonsense and do something else, anything else, anything in the world except this. This, this, this. Damn, still three-quarters of a page to go. Oh words, wherefore art thou, words, now that I need you? Come quickly to my fingers and release me from this horror, horror, horror . . . Oh

God, I am losing my mind, mind, mind . . . But wait, is it possible? Yes, here it is, the end of the page coming up. Oh welcome, kindly end of page, and now I am finished, finished, finished!"

After a few days of this, I realized that I was working very hard and not getting paid for it. Since I was turning out five thousand words a day anyway, and since I was getting tired of typing long meandering streams of meaningless verbiage, I asked myself why I shouldn't write a story.

And I did just that. I sat down and wrote a story. And it was easy!

Could it be that I had the master key to writing at last? I wrote another story. This was not so easy, but it was not unduly difficult, either. So there I was with two complete stories on paper, and each had taken only a day to wrap up. I thought proudly of these stories for at least a year afterward. I've never employed this technique to get anything else written, but I know it works. Someday, when I'm feeling desperate enough, I'll probably rely on it again. Meanwhile, however, I'm still seeking a less agonizing method.

Wordage, after all, is not the sole consideration. Writing a story can be a strange and fearsome business. You want so badly to get it just right. You try so hard and judge yourself so severely that you may succeed only in confusing yourself. Perhaps you've written many thousands of words and you're sorely dissatisfied with them. It's all chaos, and you can't seem to get on an orderly course. That was my next problem. Wordage, yes, but also an unwillingness, a fear of submitting myself to the tortures of actually turning out a story.

My solution, typically enough, was to sidestep the problem. Since there seemed no way of writing a story without plunging myself into utter despair, I decided I would not write a story. Instead, I would write a *simulation* of a story.

My simulations are the same length as a story, and they are made up of narration, dialogue, exposition, and all the other elements of a proper story. The difference is that in a proper story the words you choose are vitally important; in a simulation they are of no importance whatever. When I write a simulation, it doesn't matter if my images are trite and my dialogue leaden. It isn't a story, remember, but only something like a story. It's a formal exercise rather than a piece of careful creation. I never consciously attempt to work into a simulation the beauty, precision, humor, and pathos that a proper story must contain.

Using this method has taught me that I have a certain gift for self-deception. Curious to relate, I've discovered that—except for a few rough spots here and there—my simulated stories are very much like the real ones I've written.

What this obviously means is that I can only write as I write, not much better or worse, no matter how hard I try. Trying too hard, in fact, has an adverse effect upon my performance. The whole purpose of simulation is to work rapidly, with a certain lightness of touch, as one would do a watercolor rather than an oil painting. This method does work. But there are a couple of obstructive thoughts I have to watch out for. The first is, "Hell, this is going badly; I'd better start again." The other is, "Hey, this is going well; I'd better tighten up and make it really good." Both of these judgments are counterproductive.

Thinking, not writing, is sometimes the problem. Various ideas must be regarded from different angles before I can begin writing. Critical decisions must be formulated. Alternatives must be weighed. Bits of data need to be juggled, fitted into place, discarded, or altered. Such problems are elusive. They refuse to solidify. I make some notes or go for a long walk or discuss it with my wife, but nothing seems to help much. It's all so nebulous and unclear. There are too many things to consider at once, and no means of arranging my data. At times like this, it can be helpful to make a *diagram*.

Here's the sort of diagram I find useful. You pencil a key word in the center of a sheet of paper and draw a circle around it. Then you draw radiating lines from it and write, as succinctly as possible, the various considerations associated with the idea. The resulting diagram sums up your knowledge on the subject. The entire question and all its ramifications can be taken in at a glance, enabling you to see what you have and, equally important, what you don't have. Hookups between parts of the diagram will suggest themselves. Pertinent areas can be enclosed or connected. Different colors can be used for emphasis. New data can easily be added. Areas of special significance can be removed as the bases of new diagrams or sub-diagrams.

Working with diagrams is fun. At first I made mine with an ordinary fountain pen. Then I switched to colored Pentels. For greater efficiency, I worked out a set of color-coded symbols, which was well worth the time it took. I also experimented with different modes of lettering to improve clarity.

My diagrams grew larger and more complex, whereupon I switched to larger sheets of paper. After that, I got into colored inks. The commercial brands weren't quite right, so I began to mix my own. But the system still lacked something. It was becoming too mechanical and lackluster. So I began to illustrate my diagrams, first with little sketches, then with line and wash drawings, and finally with watercolors. My skill as an illustrator left something to be desired, so I began looking around for a good art course. Unfortunately, I had to drop the whole thing and get some salable writing done. Still, it was not a total waste. When a market opens up for fancy diagrams, I'll be all set.

My trials and tribulations have brought me to one firm conclusion—namely, that confusion and anxiety will never be eliminated altogether from the process of creative writing. Ideas frequently have to incubate in an author's subconscious until something clicks into place. Often, at least in my case, this gestation period is allowed to persist too long, which serves as a detriment to the later stages of the work. You reach a stage where the idea should be hatched, but something is still amiss and you don't know what it is. It sits there, a soggy dark mass in your mind, a subtle unpleasantness that will not permit you to continue. What to do then?

There is an extraordinarily direct method that I've devised to answer this very problem. A psychologist would probably describe it as a catharsis. A typical session finds me talking to myself aloud, asking and answering questions.

"Well, Bob, what exactly is wrong?"

"The story stinks, that's what's wrong."

"But how, precisely, does it stink?"

"It moves too slowly, for one thing."

"So how could you speed it up?"

"I don't know."

"Of course you know, Bob. Name a way in which you could speed it up."

"Well, I suppose I could delete the two-thousand-word description of a sunset on Mars."

"Would that solve the problem?"

"No. My characters stink too."

"In what way?"

"They just sit around wishing they were somewhere else."

"What could you do about that?"

"Give them something to do, I guess."

"Like what?"

"I don't know . . . Wait, I've got it! They can look for an alien civilization!"

This method works well, but it does demand a certain degree of concentration. That's the only tough part about it. Occasionally I can't even get my questions into focus, let alone the answers. At such times my solo dialogue is apt to go like this:

"Well, Bob, how's the lad?"

"I'm fine, thanks. How about you?"

"Oh, I'm fine."

"That's nice."

"Yes, it is, isn't it?"

"Yes."

"Was there some problem you wanted to discuss with me?"

"Problem? Oh yes. It's this story."

"What story?"

"The one I've been trying to write for the last three months."

"Oh, *that* story."

"Yes."

"You mean the story with the two-thousand-word description of a Martian sunset?"

"That's the one."

"Have you got any ideas?"

"About what?"

"About the story, Bob. How can I fix it?"

"Well, you could always expand the description of that sunset . . ."

And so it goes—you win some and you lose some.